The

MILL
HOUSE

Also by Paul McCusker

Epiphany

The Faded Flower

The

MILL HOUSE

PAUL McCUSKER

ZONDERVAN™
GRAND RAPIDS, MICHIGAN 49530 USA

We want to hear from you. Please send your comments about this book to us in care of zreview@zondervan.com. Thank you.

ZONDERVAN™

The Mill House
Copyright © 2004 by Paul McCusker

Requests for information should be addressed to:
Zondervan, *Grand Rapids, Michigan 49530*

Library of Congress Cataloging-in-Publication Data

McCusker, Paul, 1958-
    The mill house / Paul McCusker.
      p. cm.
    ISBN 0-310-25354-3 (softcover)
    1. Grandparent and child—Fiction. 2. English Americans—Fiction.
3. Women immigrants—Fiction. 4. Grandmothers—Fiction.
5. Older women—Fiction. 6. Secrecy—Fiction. I. Title.
PS3563.C3533M55 2004
813'.54—dc22

                          2004010288

Interior design by Beth Shagene

Printed in the United States of America

05 06 07 08 09 10 /❖ DC/ 10 9 8 7 6 5 4 3 2

PROLOGUE

THURSDAY, 24TH OF JUNE

S HE SAT ON A LOG NEAR THE OLD CHAPEL AS THE RAIN FELL MERCILESSLY upon her. The trees offered little protection. It was as if someone had poked a hole in the canopy of green overhead.

It wasn't a cleansing rain. She knew it wouldn't renew her. Instead she expected it to wear her down, obliterate her features, and allow her to dissolve back into the earth like a cube of sugar.

Leaning forward, she crossed her arms on her lap and hung her head low as the fat drops turned her distinguished silver crown into a twisted gray mop. She wore a thick pink bathrobe, now drenched and clinging to her thin body like a wet rug. Her bare feet were white and pale against the mud—the brown splashes striping her naked flesh like wounds. She began to cry with heaving sobs.

In tightly balled fists she gripped the colored glass as if to cling to the past that had been so cruelly taken from her. It cut into her palms and drew blood like stigmata.

"Mrs. Arthur," a voice said. "What are you doing out here?"

She looked up at the young police constable. His expression betrayed his shock. She must look a fright. But he was so very young. How could he know or understand why she was there? How could she explain? "I had to find them. To finish it," was all she could say before the words welled up in her throat. She lowered her head again and wept.

He spoke to someone else in that formal way the police do. And a crackling voice came back to him; feminine, small, and thin like the voices she heard on the wireless when she was a child. For a moment she was in the front room with her parents, listening to the antics of the actors on *It's That Man Again*—her father laughing at things she was too young to appreciate, her mother sitting in the wingback chair, knitting needles moving like twitching rabbit ears.

Gently the young constable took her arm and asked gently, "Can you stand?"

Of course she could—and to prove it to him, she did. But she had no desire to move.

"Come on, Mrs. Arthur, I'll take you home," he said into her ear as he took off his jacket and wrapped it around her. Within a minute his own white uniform shirt was soaked against him. Then his arms were around her as if he intended to embrace her. It had been a long, long time since she'd felt anyone's embrace. "You'll hurt your feet if you walk, Mrs. Arthur. I'll carry you back."

Carry her back? Back to where? This was where she belonged. But she was too tired to protest. So very tired.

He picked her up, cradling her in his arms. His jacket was warm. She hadn't realized how cold the rain was until this moment. She lifted her face toward the sky and felt the rain against her eyelids. Was she melting? Perhaps she might become smaller and smaller in his arms until she was nothing at all, a small stain on his shirt. Oblivion. Now wouldn't that be lovely.

Closing her eyes, she felt the rocking and swaying of his movements and allowed them to lead her to rest. She fell into a deep sleep like a small child.

CHAPTER ONE

SATURDAY, THE 26TH OF JUNE

LAINEY BISHOP GROUND THE GEARS ON HER MINI-COOPER, MUTTERED recriminations to herself, then found first as she pulled away from the stoplight on the outskirts of Stonebridge. She was late. Worse, she was agitated by the cryptic message her mother had left on her answering machine, and every delay made her annoyance grow.

She never should have taken the unfamiliar shortcut through East Grinstead rather than her usual route on the motorway via Brighton. The earlier downpour of rain had snarled London traffic. The usual ninety-minute journey now hit the two-hour mark.

Normally the transition from the concrete and noise of Shepherd's Bush in London to the lush forests and rolling downs of Sussex helped to relax her. It was one of the reasons she came to visit every weekend. The green beauty touched her soul, renewed her to the core. Today, however, Lainey didn't feel renewed. She was late. And she was worried.

She guided her car through the one-way system that formed a triangle around Stonebridge's town center. She drove past the quaint shops that now sat alongside the national chains of grocery, book, and electronics stores. Just over the tops of the Georgian and Victorian buildings she could see the perpendicular tower of St. Mark's, the twelfth-century church that sat in the very heart of the town. The rain had stopped; the sun broke through the clouds, giving the tower's brown stones a golden glow. The clock in the tower—a much later addition to the building—came into view and showed ten past one. She was ten minutes late.

George Street led her around to High Street, which she crossed and found a parking spot in the large lot behind the Waitrose food store. She parked and raced toward the Great War Memorial that sat in the middle of the main shopping area. It was an obelisk with the names of fallen soldiers carved into the pedestal at the base. A wreath of white lilies—now fringed with a forlorn brown—leaned on a stand against the side. Puddles dotted the pavement around it.

Lainey saw her mother and stopped short. Margaret Bishop was sitting on one of the benches that faced the memorial. Her black-and-gray hair was pulled back in a tight bun and her hands clasped the handbag in her lap. Her brown overcoat was snug around her. She looked tightly wound, coiled like a spring. Her eyes were on a wreath that hung in front of her.

"Hello," Lainey said as she dropped down on the bench next to her mother and kissed her quickly on the cheek. Her mother's skin was milk white and soft as velvet. She smelled of sweet perfume.

"Was the traffic bad?" her mother asked, her eyes still on the wreath.

"Yes. Sorry I'm late."

Her mother tilted her head and said, "That wreath is crooked."

"Is it?"

Margaret frowned, deepening the lines around her eyes and highlighting the wrinkles around her lips. "People need to take more pride in their surroundings."

"I don't care about the wreath, Mother," Lainey said. "Now, please tell me what your message meant. I've been in a state the entire way down."

"Let's stroll over to the Mill House," her mother said. "I'd like a small glass of something before we talk."

"You need a drink first?" Dread ignited like a small burst of flame in the center of Lainey's stomach. "Tell me what's happened, Mother."

"Be patient."

THE MILL HOUSE WAS AN EASY WALK JUST OUTSIDE THE TOWN CENTER. Originally built as a flour mill sometime in the fifteenth century, it had been added to and renovated over the years and was now the most popular restaurant and pub in the area. Outside was a waterwheel that slowly turned in the man-made pond—the original river long since gone. Inside, the restaurant was a charming mixture of uneven doorways and ceilings, Tudor beams, and dark paneling. A new wing, built in the early twentieth century, had an entire wall of windows that allowed the early afternoon sun to shine in. Booths lined the remaining walls, and freestanding tables were scattered around the main floor.

Margaret insisted on a booth in a corner to insure maximum privacy. Lainey sat down, trying to control her anxiety, while her mother ordered a glass of house white wine from the waiter. Lainey indicated that she was happy with water. "It must be serious if you're drinking wine this early in the day," Lainey said in what she hoped was a carefree voice.

Margaret gazed at her daughter for a moment, then reached across the table and took her hand. To someone watching them, it might have appeared like a moment of tenderness between a mother and her daughter. Lainey knew better. Her mother was stalling for time until the waiter was out of earshot.

"Mum—"

"You favor her, you know," she said as she withdrew her hand.

"Who?"

"Your grandmother. I found a few photos of her when she was your age. Pull your hair back."

Lainey obeyed, pulling her long chestnut brown hair back behind her.

"You could be twins. You have that dainty Holmes nose and dark eyes, from Great-grandfather's side of the family. Dangerous eyes, people always said. And those thick pouty lips. Not thin, like mine or your father's."

Leaning forward, Lainey asked, "The bad news is about Gran?"

"She's not well at all."

Lainey had seen her grandmother only a week ago and she'd seemed as strong and robust as ever. "What's wrong?"

Margaret was still. The waiter returned with her glass of wine and placed it on the small round napkin in front of her. "Would you like to order?"

"Nothing right now," Lainey said impatiently. "Come back in a few minutes."

The waiter, a splotchy-faced man with steel gray hair, looked at her indignantly, then spun on his heel and strode away.

"There's no need to be rude," her mother said, sharing the waiter's disapproval.

"Tell me about Gran," Lainey insisted.

Her mother sighed. "We had an incident."

"What kind of incident?"

"Your grandmother was found in the woods."

"Was *found?* Had she been lost?"

"For a little while." Margaret sipped a little of her wine, then grimaced. "Too dry."

"Mother."

She patiently resumed. "Early Thursday morning, Serena took in a tray of tea, as she does every morning. But your grandmother was gone. The bed had been slept in, but she had vanished. She was nowhere in the house, nor in the garden, nor anywhere on the grounds—which didn't make sense because it was dropping buckets of rain."

"It isn't like her to take a walk in the rain."

"Well, Serena called the family right away and we tried to solve the mystery. She had no engagements that anyone knew about. Worse, she hadn't taken any clothes."

"She'd left the house *naked?*"

"Don't be silly. She was in her nightgown, robe, and slippers."

"Oh, well, that's so much better."

"I should think it is," her mother said firmly and took another drink of her wine. It was more than a sip. "We don't know what became of the slippers, come to think of it."

"I don't care about the slippers," Lainey said. "Tell me about *her.*"

"She was found two hours later, sitting alone in the pouring rain near the old chapel."

"What old chapel?"

"The one at the edge of the Boswell Farm. You've seen the top of it, I'm sure. From over the old wall. It's the one the Germans destroyed."

Lainey remembered it. During the Blitz, the Germans had a nasty habit of dumping their excess payload onto the south of England as they returned to their air bases in France. The bombings were indiscriminate. One of several casualties in the Stonebridge area included the small chapel. "What was she doing there?"

"We don't know. A constable found her and, thank God, had the presence of mind to get her home without a public fuss."

"We can't have *that*," Lainey teased.

"We certainly can't," her mother returned seriously. "As it is, the entire town is jabbering about it. I received no less than *six* calls, all from—"

"Mother, please."

Margaret gazed at her with strained patience. "She was taken home and is now in bed."

"So she wasn't hurt?"

"Not physically. She was soaked more than anything. I won't be a bit surprised if she winds up with a cold."

"What happened? Did she explain why she'd wandered out like that?"

"No. She won't say a word. She's completely withdrawn. We've all tried to speak to her and she simply won't respond. She sits and stares."

This was so unlike her grandmother that it took Lainey a minute to think through the possibilities. "Was it a stroke?"

"Dr. Gilthorpe doesn't think so. He made an unprecedented house visit and then insisted that we take her to the hospital in Southaven immediately. It was a waste of time. They couldn't find anything physically wrong with her."

"If it's not physical, what is it?"

"Emotional, Dr. Gilthorpe thinks. He believes she has *chosen* to withdraw. What else could it possibly be? Of course, he still wants her to go back to the hospital for tests, but I don't see the point, really. If he's sure there's nothing *physically* wrong, then why go to the trouble of—"

"Wait. Go back." Lainey was still trying to figure out whatever it was her mother was saying. "I don't understand what you mean by *chosen to withdraw*."

"I'm not certain I understand either. She sits in her bed and looks vacantly into space."

Lainey blinked, trying to take in this new information about her grandmother. None of it lined up with the woman Lainey had known her entire life. If ever there was a woman who refused to withdraw, it was her grandmother. She was the embodiment of a fierce strength—as if life was an unpredictable foe that had to be mastered. Lainey often thought that Elaine Arthur was like that character from the Bible—the one who wrestled the angel all night for a blessing and got it because he persisted. Whatever happened, whatever life threw her way, Elaine Arthur was going to overcome it and even get a blessing.

"What does Dad think?" Lainey asked.

"Your father says it's as if she's given up."

"Given up on what?"

Her mother lifted her eyebrows in a facial equivalent to a shrug.

"Did something happen this past week? Bad news we haven't heard? A death?"

"Your father and I have discussed it and can only assume it's somehow related to your uncle Gerard."

Gerard Sommersby wasn't really Lainey's uncle, but had been like an uncle for as long as she could remember. He was a childhood friend of her grandmother's and a member of the wealthy and powerful Haysham family. Lord Haysham and his clan owned much of the land surrounding Stonebridge and had been a reigning family in that area for at least three centuries. Gerard was recently diagnosed with lung cancer and, sadly, wasn't given very long to live. It was grievous to Elaine Arthur, there was no doubt about that, but she'd shown no symptoms of being depressed about it. On the contrary, she was her usual pillar of strength, visiting Uncle Gerard daily to chat, read, or play board games.

"Is Uncle Gerard getting worse?" Lainey asked.

"Yes. I saw him earlier in the week and he has *that look.*"

Lainey shook her head. "What look?"

"You know the one I mean. His face is a death mask." Her expression betrayed no particular sadness. Only the awkwardness of having to deal with an untidy illness. "He was the last person she saw before she took on this behavior."

"Has anyone talked to him?"

"No."

"I'll go and see him."

"You'll see your grandmother first."

"Of course."

"We've decided that if anyone can get through to her, you can. You were always her favorite."

"I'm her *only* granddaughter," Lainey said defensively.

"No, you were always her favorite of anyone alive—full stop."

"Now, Mum, *you*—"

Her mother held up her slender hand. "Oh, please, Lainey, it isn't a source of discomfort to me. Your grandmother was fond of me. Perhaps she even loves me in a particular way. She performed her motherly duties well. I have no complaints, nor any illusions about her affections. But she *loves* you as she loves no other. The entire family knows it. That's why you must go to see her the instant we've had our lunch."

With that, Margaret opened her menu. Lainey knew the conversation was finished.

ARTHUR HOUSE WAS A SPRAWLING GEORGIAN ASSEMBLAGE OF HIGH-ceilinged rooms, gold chandeliers, intricately carved wood, ornate wallpaper, exotic carpets, and hardwood floors. And though it had been a second home to her, Lainey never got over the awe of its beauty or the wonder of its opulence. It was vast and mysterious, a haunt of two centuries of Arthur family indulgences and secrets. One day she hoped to write a family history—and she had explored the many nooks and crannies. To her delight, she had even discovered a secret passageway behind a panel in the study. It eventually connected to a room that some believed Thomas Arthur, the builder of the house, used for his trysts with one—or several—of the servants.

Lainey walked down the hall towards her grandmother's ground-floor bedroom, the goose bumps rising on her arms and the back of her neck. She had no idea what to expect, or how she would be received. Her mother, in typical fashion, had abandoned her to the meeting alone.

"It will be better for you to speak privately," her mother had said when they left the Mill House. "She may feel more willing to talk than if I were present."

"Coward," Lainey growled at her.

"Serena will be there."

"Serena is *always* there," Lainey said. To those outside of the family, Serena was a live-in servant and paid companion for Elaine Arthur. The truth was far more complicated. Serena was a distant cousin who'd wrecked her life, her marriage, and her relationships with her children through drinking. Elaine Arthur had taken her in when no one else wanted anything to do with her. That act of compassion helped put Serena back on the path to sobriety. Serena's husband remarried and her children were grown, and Serena had become so much a part of the house that no one questioned why she was still living there. Lainey assumed Serena would remain at the Arthur House for the rest of her life.

Lainey's eyes were fixed on her grandmother's doorway at the end of the hall when Serena suddenly stepped out of a side room. Startled, both women let out sharp gasps.

"You gave me a fright," Serena half whispered, her hand on her heart.

"I let myself in," Lainey explained. "I'm sorry. I should have rung the bell."

"No, no—don't worry about it." Serena was a middle-aged woman with a dark complexion and jet-black hair that betrayed an Italian or Hispanic line in the family genetic code. No one could tell for certain. She had a youthful face and hourglass figure that was the envy of most women her age. Only the lines around her large round coffee-brown eyes betrayed the toll her life had taken on her. Those eyes spoke of longing; of the years she'd lost and would never get back. "I'm glad you're here," Serena said softly.

"Is she still in bed?"

"Yes. I've been playing her favorite music on the stereo, to soothe her. But she hasn't said anything. I take her trays of tea, which she drinks, but she hasn't eaten. Apart from trips to the toilet, she doesn't move."

Lainey looked anxiously down the hall. Her grandmother's bedroom door was open. She could see the corner of the four-poster bed and the thick comforter spilling off the mattress. But that was all. A clock tolled in another part of the house. "Should I be warned of anything?"

"Warned?" Serena looked at her, puzzled, and then seemed to understand. "No. I fixed her hair and put on a little bit of makeup, so she looks much like herself. There are bandages on her hands."

"Bandages? Why?"

"Didn't your mother tell you?"

"No," Lainey replied, annoyed at the omission.

"When the police constable found her she was holding onto two pieces of—" She stopped herself, then gestured for Lainey to follow her into the room from which she'd just come. "I'll show you."

The room was both a library and an office, with a large oak desk in the middle and full bookcases taking up all the available wall space. This had been James Arthur's home office until he died. Elaine Arthur then used it to conduct family business. More recently it had become Serena's center of operations for running the house. She picked up two shards of colored glass from the desk blotter and gave them to Lainey.

Lainey held them up. Blue, red, and green winked at her. "She was holding these?"

"So tightly that they cut into her palms. We very nearly had to fight with Mrs. Arthur to open her fists so we could treat the cuts."

"Do you have any idea where she got them?"

"We're pretty sure they're from the old chapel. I understand that if you dig around what's left of the walls, you'll find the pieces of the windows scattered on the ground."

"But why would she hold on to these?"

Serena held up her hands. "I have no idea. I think your grandmother said something to the officer about needing to find them."

"Find them? Did she mean the stained glass?"

Again, her hands went up in reply.

"But *why?*" Lainey asked, speaking more to herself than Serena.

"To finish something," Serena replied. "At least, that's what she said."

Lainey shook her head thoughtfully. "How odd."

"It's as if she was in a dream. Sleepwalking."

Lainey glanced down the hall again. "I'd better go in."

"I'll bring you some tea."

"Thank you."

Lainey stepped back into the hall but hesitated. Portraits of the various Arthurs gazed upon her from their gold frames. There was her grandfather, sitting casually on a stool, posing with his favorite pipe in his hand. He had died after a long and protracted battle with heart disease. Lainey remembered that Elaine Arthur had grieved over his death, but hadn't succumbed to depression or withdrawal. On the opposite wall was a portrait of Uncle David, a vibrant-looking young man in military uniform. He was Elaine Arthur's only son who had been shot while serving as an officer in the Ulster Constabulary—another bullet, another victim of the "troubles" in Northern Ireland. Elaine Arthur had remained steadfast even with that loss.

So surely, Lainey reasoned, Uncle Gerard's illness could not break her. Not after her other losses.

Or could it? Anything was possible. How could she really know how her grandmother was feeling? It was a characteristic of Arthur women, Lainey's own mother included, to gather up and lock away their emotions in whatever secret place they stored such things.

Lainey sighed. She had more questions than she had answers, and her only hope of finding out was at the end of the hall.

It was a long walk to the bedroom.

ELAINE ARTHUR LAY ON HER FOUR-POSTER BED WITH HER EYES CLOSED AND her hands clasped over her chest. Lainey's heart lurched. Her grandmother's face was so pale and fragile. She looked dead. The French doors leading to the patio and gardens were open and the white chiffon curtains blew gently inward, billowing like angel's wings as if some supernatural being was coming into the room for a landing. *To take her soul*, Lainey thought. It was like a vision—a room of pure dazzling white with a choral piece from Bach, something beautiful and majestic, playing in the background. Lainey thought, *This is heaven. She has died and this is heaven.*

Lainey put a hand to her mouth to hold back her fear. She never believed that death could have its way with someone as formidable as Elaine Arthur. Now it seemed possible. Pressing her hand against her heart, Lainey suddenly felt the reality of what it would be like to lose this woman from her life. She felt the absence of their conversations, her advice, her unspoken affection and pride, the knowing glances and secret exchanges that went on between them when they were around the other members of the family, the deep understanding they had of one another.

She is the reason I've done anything with my life, however small. Her determination, her belief in me, her insistence that I make something of myself . . .

Lainey had always wanted to be a writer, which seemed horribly inappropriate in a family where the men were successful businessmen and the women were homemakers. Only her grandmother had encouraged her to think beyond the boxes they'd created for her. "You want to be a writer? You must leave Stonebridge," she'd said to Lainey. "Move to London. Find out what you're capable of doing." Her grandmother then used her contacts to get Lainey a job at Carper & Hollings Publishing in Hammersmith. She'd said, "I can think of no better experience than to work for a publisher. You can earn a living while you read and learn from the best writers."

Lainey, in her own strength, could never have done it. But she believed it was possible because her grandmother had believed it was possible. Her spirit had quickened Lainey's own.

Now Lainey stared at the pale figure on the bed and knew for certain that if her grandmother died, something vital would die within Lainey, too. In that moment a desperate loneliness enveloped her, as if the angel's wings were really the arms of the angel of death, pulling her into a cold embrace.

Lainey felt weak-kneed and grabbed one of the bedposts for support.

Elaine opened her eyes. She didn't look at Lainey. Her gaze seemed fixed on something above her, perhaps something in the fabric of the canopy.

Relieved, Lainey moved to the side of the bed, slowly approaching the top. She sneaked a peek upward in case there really was something above the bed. Only the calico fabric. "Gran?"

Elaine's gaze drifted to her granddaughter's face. Lainey may have imagined it, but she thought that her grandmother's face registered recognition. For only a second. Then it seemed to change back to an expression of emptiness.

"Gran, it's Lainey." She took her grandmother's hand, giving it a gentle squeeze. Her skin was cool and soft, her fingers limp. "Where are you, Gran? What's happened to make you this way?"

Tears formed in her grandmother's eyes and slid down her temples to her hair and ears. Had Lainey not been looking directly at her, she wouldn't have known it was happening. She made no sound.

"Oh, Gran," Lainey said, clasping her hand and moving closer. "What's wrong? Please tell me."

Elaine shook her head back and forth, her mouth opening and closing as if she was trying to say something.

"What?" asked Lainey as she put her ear closer to her grandmother's lips.

"Go away," Elaine whispered.

Startled, Lainey lifted her head to look her in the eyes.

"There is nothing," her grandmother whispered. "Leave me alone."

"Why?" Lainey pleaded.

Elaine pressed her pale lips together. The tears stopped, their trails remaining on the sides of her face. But her eyes remained on Lainey.

"Gran, you must tell me," Lainey said firmly, then stopped. She looked into Elaine's eyes and felt something stir in her heart. It was a terribly dark feeling, unfamiliar and disturbing. *Help*, her eyes cried to Lainey. *Help me*.

"What do you need from me, Gran? What can I do?"

Help.

"Is it something to do with the old chapel? Why were you there?"

Help.

"Why were you holding the stained glass?"

Help.

"Please." Lainey felt exasperated by her own impotency. "Talk to me, Gran! Tell me what to do to help!"

Elaine Arthur turned her head away and closed her eyes.

Letting go of her hand, Lainey stepped away from the bed. She spoke softly but firmly. "All right, Gran. If you won't tell me, then I'm going to find out what's wrong with you myself. *You're going to come back to me.*" It was a promise—even a threat.

Her grandmother didn't move.

Lainey walked out of the room, down the long hall to the vestibule. The expressions of the dead Arthurs hanging on the walls seemed disapproving now. She felt their rebuke as she quickened her step. She took a right to another passageway that led to the large kitchen in the back. Serena was just lifting up a tray of tea. She looked surprised at Lainey and put it down on the counter again. "Well?"

Lainey shook her head and slid onto one of the cushioned stools surrounding the large chopping table.

"I knew she wouldn't tell you anything," Serena said.

"But she did. She told me to go away. She said there's nothing we can do for her."

"That's remarkable," she said. "It's not like her at all."

"No, it isn't," Lainey agreed, then looked directly at Serena. "I want you to tell me everything my grandmother has said and done over the past few days. *Everything.*"

GEORGE SANDERS, LAINEY THOUGHT. UNCLE GERARD REMINDED LAINEY of the actor George Sanders. Dapper and handsome with a knowing smile and easy charm. And though his hair was now reduced to mere wisps above his spotted scalp and his pale face had become a death mask because of his illness, Lainey could still see a resemblance. His blue eyes flickered with the jaded mirth of privilege. Life had always gone his way and, for that reason, was never to be taken too seriously. Even now, with the cancer ravaging his body, he placed a cigarette in a cigarette holder, lit it with shaky hands, and began to puff away with short, spasmodic breaths.

"My dear girl," he said in a low voice of broken glass. "How lovely to see you."

He sat in an easy chair with his feet up on an ottoman. He was dressed in worn silk pajamas and a robe that was loosely tied at his waist. His toes, white as any pair of stockings could be, poked through the holes in the tops of his favorite, worn-out slippers. He wiggled them with childlike amusement. Kissing her hand, he beckoned her to sit down.

She sat in the matching easy chair opposite him. The thick red velvet curtains were drawn over the four massive windows that lined the outside wall, each framed in gray lines by the daylight outside. A Tiffany lamp on the table next to him gave out a weak yellow light that reduced Uncle Gerard's enormous study to a small box of shadows. As he gestured with his hand, which he did often, the shadows moved forward and retreated like uneasy ghosts.

"How are you, Uncle Gerard?" she asked.

"I'm in tip-top condition for a man who is dying," he said jovially. "I have no complaints whatsoever."

He barely squeezed out the last word before he was seized with a coughing fit. Pressing a handkerchief against his mouth, he wheezed and hacked away for a moment, then stopped and continued as if nothing had happened.

"You should do something about that cough," Lainey said with a wry smile.

Gerard laughed and almost went into another coughing fit. "Indeed, my dear. But they don't make lozenges large enough to tackle it. How are you? Are you still reading those boring manuscripts for that awful publishing house?"

"Yes."

"And I suppose you're still living in that dreary flat?"

"It's a comfortable flat and close to work."

"But it's in *Shepherd's Bush*, my dear. There's no excuse for living in Shepherd's Bush and working in Hammersmith."

"It will do for now."

"Yes, yes, I know, suffering for your art and all that rubbish. You expect to be the next Jane Austen."

She smiled at him. "I could do a lot worse."

"How about your love life? Have you caught any eligible bachelors?"

"Not this week."

"What was his name? The one you brought last time?"

"Stephen. And that was almost a year ago," she corrected him. "I've been round to see you since then."

"Stephen. Yes. What happened to him? He seemed suitable enough."

"Unfortunately, he thought his suitability extended to a lot of other women. All at the same time," she replied, knowing that they'd had this very conversation several times before.

"A playboy!" he exclaimed. "I thought they were out of fashion for this generation."

"Apparently not."

"Ah. Well. There you are. You have to be careful with those London yobs. Stay down here and find yourself a local boy. Good stock. True as the day is long." He took another drag on his cigarette, coughing and sputtering as he did. "Your grandmother was supposed to drop round today. Is she not well?"

"Not very."

"What's wrong with her?"

"We don't know. She won't tell us. She's not saying much at all."

Uncle Gerard squinted at Lainey over a puff of smoke. "Eh? Say that again?"

"Something's wrong with her. She's upset or depressed. Hasn't anyone told you?"

"Nobody tells me anything anymore. They want to spare me any bad news, as if it could somehow add to the burden of dying. What's wrong with the old girl?"

"I had hoped you could tell me."

"What makes you think I'd know anything about it?"

"Because you were the last person she spoke to before . . ." Lainey was stuck for the right phrase. "Before her attitude changed."

He scrubbed his chin thoughtfully and repeated slowly, "Her attitude changed." Then he looked at Lainey as if suddenly realizing the answer and becoming annoyed by it. "Good heavens. I had no idea she'd be upset about *that*."

"Upset about what?"

"A little thing that happened years and years ago. We talked about it the other day . . ." His voice trailed off as he sank into his own thoughts. The furrows on his brow deepened. "Well, it would have been a disaster," he said as if concluding an internal argument.

"*What* would have been a disaster, Uncle Gerard?"

"That London boy. The one she became so fond of. Powell. Something-or-other Powell. It never would have worked. Everyone knew it."

Lainey leaned forward, trying to get her uncle's eye. "Uncle Gerard, I don't know what you're talking about."

"Of course you don't," he said, looking at her now with a stern expression. "Why would you? She never talked about it. She never even knew what had happened in the end. But it was for the best, I tell you."

Lainey held back her growing impatience. "*What* was?"

"I only brought it up the other day because I'm dying. Should have kept my mouth shut, I suppose. I thought she'd be grateful to know."

"Grateful about *what?*"

"I had saved her life, after all. Oh, the silly creature!" He was agitated now as he took another drag on his cigarette and this time the coughing fit came in full force. Through his wrenching barks and gasps he said, "She's a . . . fool . . . if she's . . . depressed about . . . that . . ."

Lainey was on her feet now. She didn't know what to do. Spying a pitcher of water and glasses on a sideboard, she poured it and took the glass to him. His face was beet red and his breathing more labored as he doubled over in the chair.

Like one of the shadows come to life, a nurse appeared from nowhere and now stood at his side. "Leave us, please."

"Will he be all right?" she asked, feeling responsible for the attack.

"Go, please," the nurse said firmly.

Lainey left the study with an image of the nurse trying to right her uncle Gerard, the lamp casting a nicotine-stained glow on both of them.

A GRANDFATHER CLOCK TICKED IN THE CORNER, MARKING THE SECONDS and minutes with maddening regularity as Lainey paced anxiously in the front sitting room. As the clock chimed the quarter hour the nurse passed the doorway.

"Pardon me—," Lainey called out.

The nurse reappeared and Lainey got a clearer look at her. She had a pudgy face that hung over her thin body like a balloon. "Yes?" She squinted at Lainey as if she'd forgotten her glasses, though they dangled from her neck on a chain.

"I was wondering about my uncle—"

The nurse didn't step into the room but stood in the doorway with her hands folded in front of her. "He's sleeping now."

"Will he be all right?"

"You know his condition, I assume?" she asked.

"Yes."

"Then I venture to say that he won't be all right. But he's sleeping peacefully for the moment."

"May I talk to him when he wakes up?"

"That depends on whether you're going to upset him again."

"It wasn't my intention to upset him. I only asked—"

"I suggest that you ring first. Then we'll determine whether he can have visitors or not."

"Yes. Of course." Lainey frowned, stung by the rebuke.

The nurse disappeared from the doorway, her white sneakers padding softly down the hall.

Lainey looked for a telephone, couldn't find one, so she pulled her mobile phone from her handbag. She punched in her mother's number and waited for the double chirp of the phone on the other end.

"Two three double-eight five," her mother answered. She never said hello. She always identified her phone number as her greeting. It was more efficient, she'd always said, just in case someone had dialed the wrong number. Lainey considered it impersonal.

"Hello, Mum."

"Lainey? Where are you? I rang your grandmother's, but Serena said—"

"Has Gran ever mentioned someone by the name of Powell?"

"Powell? Powell who?"

"Powell is the surname. It's an old boyfriend, I think."

"I wasn't aware that she had any boyfriends, apart from your grandfather."

Lainey sighed. "Never mind, then."

"Never mind!" her mother said indignantly. "Where are you? When can we expect you for supper?"

"Soon. I have an errand to run first."

THE BOSWELL FARM NESTLED AGAINST STONEBRIDGE ON THE NORTHEAST side. The high stone wall cut an east-to-west slice alongside Boswell Road. The road was rarely used, except by those who were purposefully going to visit the Boswells, which wouldn't have been very many people.

Most of the family now lived in other parts of England and the large, ugly rambling house was being managed by a caretaker and his family.

A sign at the very top of the road announced the development of the farm into a golf course and luxury hotel. They planned to call it Boswell Park.

Lainey drove slowly, keeping an eye on the road and the wall. On one of her many walks around Stonebridge, she remembered seeing what had looked like the side of an old chapel just beyond the top of the wall. She hadn't paid it much attention at the time, but now she had no doubt that it was the old chapel to which her grandmother had gone.

Overgrown trees and ivy nearly masked the chapel from Lainey's view. Lainey got out of her car and spied a break in the wall. It appeared as if it had been repaired and broken many times over the years. Lainey stepped through.

Looking through the wood, she could see more of the old chapel. From this vantage point inside the wall, it was clearly a mere shell of whatever had once stood there. Lainey made her way down a path toward a clearing. To the right, the woods opened up onto the rolling and unkempt green hills of the Boswell Estate. In the distance she could see the main house, splashed now by the late afternoon sunlight. At the rear of the house was a small cottage, probably the home of the caretaker. To the left the woods stretched out like cliffs on a coastline. Half of the chapel stood in the clearing while the other half was now part of the wood—as if some poor ship's captain had sailed it there by accident and couldn't pull it out again. Trees thrust through the gray walls, and ivy covered whole sections like green netting. The arched windows were dark, and Lainey assumed they were the sources of the stained glass.

Sitting on a log, Lainey was suddenly struck by the peaceful beauty of the spot. From here, the chapel seemed serene and comforting, rather than decrepit. Its thick stones and Gothic architecture conveyed a certain nobility, as if it was quietly defying its abandonment to the ravages of time and nature.

Lainey stood and walked along the log with the intention of going around to the other side of the chapel. But the sound of her feet on the ground changed suddenly from a gentle swish to an odd crunch. She looked down at the carpet of leaves, then knelt and pushed them away. Underneath she found pieces of stained glass.

She thought about her grandmother again. What was the connection between Elaine Arthur and the stained glass from the chapel? Why was this spot important enough for her to walk so far in the rain to reach? And did it have anything to do with her secret boyfriend, the mysterious Powell?

A branch snapped behind her and, startled, she swung around, lost her balance, and fell on her rear. A small white-haired old man with bushy eyebrows and winglike muttonchops stood at the edge of the wood facing her. He was dressed in a rough collarless shirt and brown breeches held up by suspenders. He wore worn knee-high green rubber boots.

"Oh dear," he said and came quickly forward to help her up. "I startled you."

"I'm so clumsy," she laughed and accepted his outstretched hands. His grip was firm and strong as he pulled her to her feet. "Thank you," she puffed. Brushing off the back of her jeans, she guessed that he was little more than five feet tall. He looked at her and his brown eyes came alight with something like surprise or recognition, Lainey couldn't tell which. "Is something wrong?" she asked.

"You're related to Mrs. Arthur, aren't you?" he asked with a soft country accent.

She nodded. "Do you know my grandmother?"

"Only as acquaintances," he said. "How is she? I know she hasn't been in good health."

"Word travels fast."

He pointed to the cottage in the distance. "I live there. I saw her. Here."

"You saw her sitting here from that far away?"

He chuckled, "Not with these eyes, I didn't. Binoculars. Though it was raining, you see, and I didn't realize it was her when I phoned the police. The constable told me later."

"*You* phoned them?"

"We've had occasional trouble with trespassers. Vagrants, mostly. We don't want them camping on our property. I'm the caretaker, you see. Trevor Mann."

"Lainey Bishop." She extended her hand and he took it in his. It was rough and dry.

"Ah," he said. "I've heard of you."

"Have you?"

"Don't be alarmed," he said with a reassuring smile. "I've heard only that you're Mrs. Arthur's granddaughter. No malicious gossip or scandalous news."

"I wish I had some malicious gossip or scandalous news. I'm not terribly interesting."

"But you are *interested*."

"Interested?"

"In something here. Otherwise, why would you be looking at the old chapel? Are you interested in churches?"

"In a manner of speaking. Have you been the caretaker here very long?"

"Most of my life."

Lainey tried to guess the math from the looks of him. Was he here before her grandmother was married? Did he know Powell? Might he know why her grandmother was attracted to this place? "You came to work here as a young man?" she asked.

"No. I was born here. My father was the caretaker before me. Just as his father was the caretaker before him."

"That's quite a legacy," she smiled.

"It may change when they build Boswell Park. We haven't negotiated our role with the developers yet. I'm leaving that to my son. You've heard of Mann Landscapers?"

She nodded. "I've seen signs for them."

"My son owns that business. So he's bidding to do the work on the golf course. It's appropriate, I think, considering our history with the place. I know no other work, actually."

"Does that mean you saw this chapel before it was bombed?"

"I was baptized in this chapel when I was but a week old and attended services ever after."

"When was it hit?"

He sat down on the log and indicated that she should do the same. She did. "Twenty-eighth of September, 1940," he said. "It was my tenth birthday. I remember that night like it was yesterday."

"Please tell me about it," she said, as if she needed to ask. It was clear he would anyway.

"We had built one of those Anderson shelters behind the cottage, just at the edge of the field. The ground's wet around here and it seemed as if the thing always had water on the floor. I remember my slippers getting soaked that night and I was cold. But I didn't tell my mother. I didn't want to worry her any more than she already was—what with the sounds of the planes flying overhead and our wondering if we'd get hit. You couldn't know what it was like, of course. Your generation couldn't."

"You must have been terribly frightened."

"That's the funny thing, really. You're never really as afraid as you imagine you'll be. My brothers and sisters were older and treated the whole thing as an annoyance. My father was indignant. 'We'll give it back to Jerry,' he used to say. Whenever the sirens started, he insisted on staying outside. He told my mother that he wanted to be ready if the big house was hit. I learned differently from him much later. After the war. He told me he was deeply afraid of being buried alive inside the shelter. So he stood outside and clung to a shovel, as if it would single-handedly make a difference. As a boy, I imagined that he could hit the bombs with it and knock them back up to the Germans."

"What happened to the chapel?"

"Well, there was a loud bang—the kind you feel go through your chest. And my oldest brother ran out of the shelter to see and yelled, 'They got the chapel.' So we all raced out, which was a stupid thing to do, and there it was, that beautiful chapel in flames."

"How awful."

He shook his head slowly. "That was a bad night, it was. They also hit the coal dump at Knight's Nurseries on the other side of town and killed a watchman, the father of a friend of mine at school. And the vicarage that used to sit out on the Old Vicarage Fields was hit, too. Killed the vicar and his wife. Terrible."

"The stained glass windows were blown out, weren't they?"

"Everything was blown out. But, yes, the stained glass was blown all over that area. Your grandmother told you, did she?"

"No. Why?"

"When she was a girl, she used to come here to pick up the pieces. It was her project. She wanted to reassemble them all."

"She hoped to put the windows back together?"

"A girl's fancy," he said with a gentle laugh.

"Did she come alone?"

"Not always."

"Who came with her?"

"Well, there was . . ." His voice trailed off and he suddenly look at her warily. "Why do you ask? What brings you here anyway?"

"Because of my grandmother. I'm trying to work out why she came here. In her delirium, or whatever it was, she chose to come to this place. Why? Does it have an attraction for her? A memory?" She gazed at Trevor who seemed to know something but wasn't saying. "Who came with her? Was it someone named Powell?"

Trevor stood up. "Honestly, Miss Bishop, I've lost track of the time—"

"You know who I'm talking about, don't you?"

"It would be inappropriate for me to discuss your grandmother's private life," he said, his face growing red from pained embarrassment. "It's not appropriate at all. You really must ask her."

"She won't talk. She's not saying much of anything that's helpful."

"Then I can't help you either." He began to back away toward the cottage. "It was a pleasure to meet you," he said, then abruptly turned and walked off.

Lainey sat on the log, then stooped to pick up a few pieces of stained glass.

"Right," she said to no one. "What am I supposed to do now?"

DRIVING TO HER PARENTS' HOUSE ON THE OPPOSITE END OF STONEBRIDGE, Lainey couldn't decide what to do. Perhaps she could go back to her grandmother's to see if a mere mention of Powell's name might get a reaction. She considered returning to her uncle Gerard's. If he was feeling better, he might explain himself to her. A last resort would be to try again to persuade or coerce Trevor into telling what he knew. Sadly, none of the options seemed likely to succeed. That generation tended to be very tight-lipped. It was a matter of English pride to keep personal details as secret as possible. Discussions were to be reserved for the weather.

Lainey wasn't satisfied with that and decided that if it would help her grandmother somehow, she had to learn the truth. And if it was an equal gamble about who she should talk to, then it may as well be her uncle Gerard. Had he not had that coughing fit, he probably would have explained everything. Lainey had a better chance with him than anyone. *I'll go there right after tea*, she decided as she pulled into her parents' drive.

She came to a stop behind her mother's Ford and was just about to get out when her mobile phone chirped. She picked it up and saw on the screen that it was her mother's number. Amused, she answered, "I'm in the driveway."

"Come in. Quickly," her mother said urgently.

"Why? What's wrong?"

"Your uncle Gerard has died."

CHAPTER TWO

ELAINE LAY IN HER BED, KEEPING HER EYES CLOSED IN THE HOPE THAT Serena would think she was asleep. She didn't want to talk. She didn't want to think. The pain that had begun in her heart only a couple of days ago now spread throughout her entire body. She had never imagined it could do that. It caused her muscles to ache. Her stomach was a giant knot. It was hard for her to swallow. She couldn't fix on one thought—there was a delirious randomness to her feelings. Memories flitted through her mind in patches of color, shards of jagged stained glass exploded outward, creating fissures in her consciousness. Lines like frozen lightning embedded in a wall of her mind. She could see them, as real as if they were on the stone wall surrounding the old chapel.

She concentrated, working hard to fix her mind upon that wall— and how she had crept through the crack even though her parents had told her not to. They told her it was beneath her to behave like the "common" children who went to look at the devastation.

But they don't understand how she feels, how important it is to her. She's had to wait a whole week since the bombing and now she has her chance. Her parents have gone to Southaven for a meeting of the local defense volunteers. Mrs. Edie and Mr. Fred, the two servants, are distracted with the housework.

Her tutor is busy marking papers. She's going into Stonebridge because she's bored, she tells herself. That's all. It's no lie. She's bored stiff because the war took away her horseback riding instructor and her piano teacher and the only cinema in Stonebridge and everything else she's ever enjoyed. She puts on a wool sweater and her comfortable brown leather shoes and slips away without anyone asking her where she's going.

Elaine, still lying in her bed, saw the present and the past together as she walked the half mile from her home to the town center. Before the war Stonebridge had been surrounded by fields of sheep. During the war the fields had been littered with old cars and wagons to keep enemy airplanes from landing. And since then the fields were being turned into housing estates and car parks. The thriving market area where sheep and cattle were sold every Wednesday before the war was abandoned while Hitler waged his war and, since then, had become one of the county's largest flea markets.

Oh, how it's changed! nine-year-old Elaine thinks as she walks through the town toward the old chapel. There are signs about ration books and air-raid precautions and shelters and doing one's duty to help the war effort. Keep your eyes open and your mouth shut, they say, or Adolph might hear you. Queues of people form outside of the butcher's and the greengrocer's. Women with handbags hanging from crooked arms, men with hats tipped back off their foreheads. Some still carry gas masks in small boxes. A car goes up High Street, belching the black exhaust of the ghastly paraffin some use instead of rationed petrol. Someone has the radio on and the BBC is broadcasting horrible organ music. It's so awful it's funny.

There's Mrs. Briggs. Oh, hello. She looks very pale and worried as she passes. Her husband is a pilot, Mummy says. One of the heroes in the battles overhead—the ones that streak the sky with white lines as if a giant claw has been scratching at the blue.

Sandbags. They're everywhere, it seems.

And the iron fence around the church has been taken away to be used to make weapons.

She reaches the wall to the Boswells and the wide crack in it that she assumes was made by the bomb. Slipping through, she makes her way carefully through the woods and comes upon the chapel. Oh, that poor chapel, her heart says. She's seen it before, in all of its loveliness, on a spring day three years before—before those terrible Germans began causing trouble—when she'd gone to a wedding with her parents. She was only six then, but the chapel stayed etched in her mind. It had white stones and the inside had been fashioned *out of a beautiful light wood, not the dark paneling and pews like they have at St. Mark's. On that wedding day, the sun seemed to hit the stained glass windows at just the right angle, making the altar and the statues bright and alive with color. The Catholic wedding was long and she didn't understand a word of the Latin, but she entertained herself by looking at those beautiful stained glass windows with their biblical scenes. There was a very pregnant Mary and her husband, Joseph, riding a donkey to Bethlehem, Jesus walking on the water toward a storm-tossed boat, Jesus with his disciples healing a blind man, Jesus touching a small child . . .*

They were real to her then. As real as anything in her life. At home she read her Bible and attempted to draw the scenes herself in a notebook she'd been given for Christmas. She could never get them to look like anything as wonderful as the stained glass renditions, but she persisted. Something quickened in her heart when she did. Childlike faith became belief.

She isn't prepared for the destruction caused by the bomb and now she weeps when she sees it. The walls are scorched black. The roof is gone. The windows are empty and dark, like a face without eyes. Those beautiful stained glass windows have been blown to more pieces than anyone in the world could count. They lie like confetti all over the surrounding ground. Oh, you poor thing, she keeps whispering. You poor, poor thing.

As she weeps, she feels a new hatred for the Germans for robbing her of the things she loves: chocolate and birthday candles and eggs and ice cream and turkey at Christmas and good toys and proper dolls and . . . and . . . she begins to pace and pick up the pieces of stained glass. She doesn't know why. Even at the hope-filled age of nine, she doesn't believe that the pictures can be reassembled. But she wants to pick them up anyway, to bring her own form of order to a very disordered world.

Trevor appears. His father, the caretaker of the grounds, has asked him to chase away any gawkers, and he has a stone in his hand that's raised as if he might throw it at her. Then he sees who it is. Trevor has always been kind to her, though Elaine suspects that he is merely being respectful.

Trevor tips his hat. "Hello, Miss Elaine. Didn't know it was you. What are you doing here? I didn't reckon you to be the type to come look at the damage."

Elaine quickly wipes her tears away with the back of her hand and tells him the truth. The chapel has been a very special place in her mind and she simply can't believe it is gone. She had to see for herself, she tells him. Then she bursts into tears again, clutching the shards of stained glass.

Trevor blushes at her open display of emotion and looks away. "Right. Well, you don't want my father to catch you here. Or any of the Boswells. They're very angry right now and don't want people dropping by."

He starts to walk away, but she calls after him. "Trevor, will they rebuild it? Please tell me they will."

He shrugs. "I'm no fortune-teller."

As it turns out, the Boswells never rebuild the chapel. They, like many families at the time, are sapped of their strength and prosperity because of the war. Three of the sons have already been killed. One, a pilot, gave his life by flying his plane into a German fighter. The Boswells don't have the means to rebuild the chapel or to completely tear it down. Or so Trevor later tells her. So, that autumn, they clear out what they can and leave the rest to remain in this forgotten corner of their land.

But Elaine doesn't forget and the chapel becomes her hideaway, her own haven. She goes back whenever she can. Sometimes she sits quietly and looks at the shell of the building, trying to remember its former beauty. Other times she collects the pieces of stained glass and begins to assemble them into color groups. It becomes a game, putting the puzzle back together again.

Maybe I can put together a section of one of the windows, she thinks— or possibly even an entire window! Now wouldn't that be wonderful.

Trevor comes upon her from time to time, never bothering her, hardly even speaking to her. He seems to have figured out what she's doing and leaves her alone. She suspects that he also protects her glass collection when she isn't around. The piles she makes near the chapel are kept intact, no matter how long it is between visits.

So it's an unnerving shock when, on a bright June day, she comes to the chapel and finds the Boy there. He is ten, but looks twelve, and he stands over one of her piles of glass with his thumbs hooked in the straps of his overalls. He kneels, moves a few of the pieces, then stands up again to view his work. He has thick black hair and broad shoulders, which is all she can see from where she stands.

With a voice of undisguised indignation that she's heard her mother use from time to time, she says sharply, "Just what do you think you're doing, young man?"

The Boy spins around and she sees that his fists are clenched. She guesses immediately that had she stood any closer and spoken, he would have knocked her down. When he sees that she's a girl, he relaxes. She relaxes, too, because he has a beautiful face. It's a lean face, maybe too much so, as if he doesn't eat very well. He has large brown confident eyes, a trim nose, and full lips that turn up at the ends as if he is thinking about something funny. He is tanned, which brings out the freckles on his nose, except for a tiny lighter patch on his forehead where the cowlick at the top of his hairline has blocked the sun.

Visible beneath his overalls is a checked shirt. The collar and rolled sleeves are ragged from wear. And Elaine suspects that if he unrolled the sleeves, she'd see that the shirt is too small for him.

"Good afternoon," he says politely. Then he turns his back on her and resumes looking at the stained glass pieces.

She moves closer. "What are you doing with my stained glass?"

"Oh, it's yours, is it? I saw no sign saying so," he says and gestures to the Boswell House in the distance. "Are you a Boswell?"

"No, but I'm telling you those pieces are mine and that you must leave them alone."

"I've been coming here for a week and haven't seen you before."

"I'm friends with the caretaker and he won't be pleased to have you on this land." She takes another step closer. "You must leave now."

"All right," he concedes. "But it's too bad. I was just getting the hang of it. Guess I'll clear off what I've done." He lifts his foot as if to kick at the glass.

Curiosity gets the better of her and she cries out, "No, wait."

With a satisfied smile he turns to her. He has dimples, Elaine notices. She loves dimples on a boy. Laurence Olivier has them. So does Michael Redgrave. She sees them on the covers of the movie magazines at the newsagents.

"I want to see," she says, still being bossy, as she stands at his side to see his work. She gasps, her hand flying to her mouth.

He has begun to assemble sections of the stained glass windows. Even against the dark earth, she can see that he's found part of a face with a dozen or so pieces. And, a foot away from that, he's put together another part of another scene. This one looks like a donkey. Possibly Mary's donkey.

Her heart races. "How did you do that?" she asks, breathless.

"I just looked and then I looked again," he replies. "Mostly luck, I think."

"Then you're very lucky," Elaine says. "I've been working on these pieces for ages and couldn't make a single match."

Again he shrugs.

Suddenly Elaine finds another piece, part of what looks like the donkey, and places it next to the others. "It fits!" she says.

"There," he says. "You're lucky, too."

They spend the rest of the afternoon looking for more matching pieces, with little success. Then she suddenly worries about the time and though she doesn't want to go she knows she has to or there'll be trouble at home.

"Will you be here tomorrow?" she asks, fearful that he'll say no.

"Possibly," he replies.

She takes that as a promise and runs for home, her heart racing faster than her feet.

They meet regularly at the chapel throughout the rest of the summer, talking, looking for pieces. And always, before parting, they agree to meet the next day or the day after or whenever they knew they could. The obstacles for Elaine are often her studies with her tutor, or visits to relatives, or other various family responsibilities. Since her father often travels to Bristol on business and her mother volunteers for various war duties in Stonebridge and Southaven, Elaine has more time to do what she likes.

He isn't talkative about himself. More often than not, he'll ask her a question about herself—her parents or her home, what she likes or doesn't like—and let her chatter on for ages. Only after they've gone their separate ways does she realize that he hasn't said a word about himself.

As time goes on, she gets impatient and demands to know more about him. His full name, for example.

"Adam Randolph Powell," he replies.

"Where are you from?"

"London."

Her eyes light up. "Are you an evacuee?"

He shrugs. "I suppose so."

"But my father says that the Blitz is over," she says.

"How does he know?"

"He's a sergeant in the Home Guard and he has his own gun and he even captured a German pilot once."

Adam nods appreciatively.

She continues, "He says the Blitz is over because Hitler has his hands full on the Eastern front. Do you know what the Eastern front is?"

He smiles at her and she wants to think he's fond of her. "It has to do with Russia."

"Anyway, Hitler can't be bothered to bomb us anymore because he's busy there. Aren't you glad?"

He nods.

"My father says that over a hundred thousand people have been hurt by the Blitz. Some even killed. Do you know anyone who was hurt—or killed?"

He nods again.

"Somebody close?"

Another nod.

"Someone in your family?"

"Rosemary Powell," he says and busies himself with the stained glass.

"Who is she, an aunt?"

"My mother."

"Your mother!" she exclaims and slumps down on the log. "Oh, Adam!" And two things will stay with her forever. First, how terrible she felt for him to lose his mother like that. Second, how his name sounded on her lips.

Her reaction seems to surprise him, because he looks up at her in a long, slow way as if he's seeing her for the first time.

"I came to Stonebridge because my aunt and uncle live here. Do you know the Crowthers?"

"No."

"I didn't think so," he says, and adds in a tone she doesn't like, "They're not your kind of crowd."

She's stung by his tone and is afraid to ask what he means. She doesn't think she has a "kind of crowd." But she doesn't want to appear foolish by asking and says, "But it's not still dangerous in London."

"My father is a printer and works long hours—odd ones, too. He didn't want me home alone for such long spells." Another shrug. "I think he wanted me to get some fresh air in a country village. It'd be good for me, he thinks."

"He's right!" Elaine affirms. "This is where you belong. Not in that dirty old smelly city."

"I love the city," he replies, but says no more.

He doesn't want to be here with me, Elaine thinks and feels a pout coming on.

Adam seems to sense her mood and quickly says, "But I'm happy to be here for now. I like Stonebridge, and . . ." He looks at her again—with those penetrating eyes—and it makes her feel better even if he never finishes the sentence. "I reckon you're the only friend I have around here," he says softly.

The conversation is over and they go back to their work.

When she isn't there with him, she is restless and agitated. In July, she panics because her parents want to take her away for the summer holiday. She throws an uncharacteristic fit about wanting to stay home. Ultimately, her parents agree, not because of her, but because the government gets stricter about unnecessary travel.

Adam seems to drift through the summer with no fixed obligations. Only once or twice does he ever say he can't come the next day because he has something else to do. He never says what it is and only shrugs when she presses him for an answer.

They only ever meet at the chapel and she never asks him back to her house. He is her little secret, she decides—like the stained glass pieces. She doesn't want her family to know about him.

One day she tells him this and, to her surprise, his reaction is defensive. Wiping his nose with the back of his hand, he says, "You don't want to be seen with me."

"Use your handkerchief and don't be silly," she replies. "You never invite me to your uncle's and aunt's."

"Because we're not your class," he counters. "They wouldn't know how to behave if you walked in the door, what with you being a member of the Holmes family."

"Now I know you're being silly. They could behave toward me as they would behave toward anyone. What does being a Holmes have to do with anything?"

He smiles patiently. "If the king walked through your door, would you treat him the same as you'd treat any of your other friends?"

"I should hope so," she says firmly. "I think the king would like to be treated normally. It must be terribly tiresome being fawned over all of the time. Besides, even he has to use ration books, just like the rest of us."

Adam laughs. "The way you talk. 'It must be terribly tiresome being fawned over.' Blimey, if they could hear you in Chiswick."

"Why? I don't think I sound very different than you. You talk the same as everyone else I know. Except we don't say things like 'blimey.'"

"And how do you think I sound?" he asks as a challenge.

"Well . . ." She wants to use the right word. "Educated."

He is satisfied. "That was my mother's doing," he says. "All of my life she said, 'I don't want him to sound like a ruffian. Even if we can't afford to give him a good education, he's going to sound like he's had one.' That's what she said. Word for word."

"Your mother must have loved you very much."

He turns away and lowers his head to look at the pieces on the ground. They have most of the donkey assembled now. And the face appears to belong to one of Jesus' disciples.

One day early in August Elaine's mother has insisted that Elaine accompany her on a round of errands in the town because their servants have gone away to visit family. Elaine's mother takes it upon herself to keep the house supplied with the few goods they are allowed to purchase at the butcher, grocer, and dairy with their ration books. The war is the great leveler, Elaine once heard her father say. Suddenly the wealthy have to stand in a queue next to regular laborers to get their small share of meat, bacon, cheese, eggs, tea, and sugar. Even the king and queen have to ration.

And so Elaine and her mother are standing in the queue at the butcher's and in walks Adam with his aunt, a very pretty woman who is younger than

Elaine expected. When they make eye contact, Adam and Elaine both turn several shades of red. Elaine wants to grab her mother's arm and introduce Adam immediately. But she imagines how stricken he might be, or how embarrassed his aunt might feel. She also knows she would have to explain to her mother how it is that she knows this boy—and she doesn't want to do that. Adam takes the matter out of her hands by tugging at his aunt's sleeve and whispering something in her ear. She nods and he slips out of the shop.

The next day, when they meet at the chapel, Adam explains to Elaine that he'd told his aunt that he needed to go to the toilet.

"Your aunt isn't what I expected," Elaine says. "I thought she'd be like all of my aunts—older, plump, and gray-haired. Yours is young and pretty. I think she could be an actress in one of those motion pictures."

"I think so, too," says Adam, with just a hint of red in his cheeks.

"What about your uncle? Is he rather dashing, like Errol Flynn?"

"He has a mustache like Errol Flynn," Adam answers. "But the rest of him looks more like Charlie Chaplin."

Elaine laughs at the description. But he looks at her puzzled, as if he doesn't realize he's said something funny. It is often that way, she realizes. He doesn't seem to understand what his words do to people. He can be funny without knowing it, or insensitive, or sometimes even cruel. He doesn't know his own strength. Proof of that comes late in August when they're collecting more bits of glass among the leaves and he suddenly announces, "I won't be here tomorrow. Or the day after."

"Why not?"

"I'm going back to London."

"To visit?"

"To stay."

It's like a slap in the face and Elaine stops and glares at him. "What?"

"My father has changed jobs and said I could come home to London again."

Elaine is furious. "Why didn't you tell me?"

"He only said so last night."

"But you can't!" she shouts.

There's that puzzled look from him again. He has no idea what his news has done to her.

She growls and goes back to her search for more stained glass, fuming and pouting, not believing that he's going to leave her and then telling herself that she doesn't care, why should she care? If it doesn't matter to him then it shouldn't matter to her. So she stomps around and kicks at fallen twigs and resents the songs of the birds in the treetops and wants to run home and bury her face in her pillow.

"Elaine," he says. It's the first time he has said her name.

It stops her. She looks at him, sure she's going to cry.

He opens his mouth to speak, but suddenly Trevor comes around the wall of the chapel. He looks embarrassed, as if he has something difficult to do, and Elaine's first thought is that the Boswells are going to make them leave with a warning never to return.

"Trevor?" she asks.

Trevor doesn't say anything, glancing nervously behind him.

Gerard steps from around the wall of the chapel. He is twelve and big for his age and has the volatile temper of a child with too much pampering and not enough discipline.

"What's all this, then?" he demands in a mocking voice and strides over to the pieces of their stained glass on the ground. He scowls at Adam. "Who are you?"

"Winston Churchill," Adam replies.

"Ha," Gerard says and then kicks at the section of the donkey they'd completed.

"Gerard!" Elaine cries out, moving for him, but then Adam is in the way.

"You have no business being here," Gerard says and pokes a hard finger into Adam's chest.

Quick as a flash, Adam grabs Gerard's wrist and twists his arm until Gerard has to turn around. Adam doesn't stop until he wrenches Gerard's arm upward toward his shoulder blades.

Gerard yells from the pain. Trevor is frozen where he stands, his face a mask of indecision.

Elaine is certain his arm will break. "No, Adam! Please!" she begs.

"Let go! Let go!" Gerard begins to cry.

"Say you're sorry," Adam says calmly. He holds Gerard effortlessly.

"I won't!" Gerard blubs through his tears.

Adam lifts the arm yet higher and Gerard squeals.

"Say you're sorry," Adam says again.

"I'm sorry, I'm sorry . . . ," Gerard says.

Adam gives him a hard push that sends him sprawling indignantly to the ground.

Gerard leaps to his feet, the dirt mixing with the tears, dead leaves in his blond hair. He gestures with the hand of his uninjured arm. "It's a good thing you're leaving," he shouts. "Otherwise . . ."

He doesn't get to finish the sentence because Adam takes a threatening step toward him. Gerard has the good sense to run. Trevor still looks as if he isn't sure what to do. Then, after a moment's hesitation, he follows Gerard back around the chapel.

Elaine looks at Adam with a feeling that waivers between respect and fear. But her bad mood is gone in that instant and she decides not to waste the rest of his last day pouting about his leaving.

Without a word, he begins to reassemble the section of the donkey they'd worked so hard on.

Elaine helps and chatters nervously to him about everything that comes to her mind. It is as if she wants to fill him up with memories of her. Please don't forget me, she is really saying. And finally, she really does say, "May I write to you?"

He smiles a crooked, embarrassed smile at her and then hands her a slip of scrap paper. On it is his address in London. "I had hoped you would ask," he says quietly.

Time becomes a blur now. He returns the following summer and the one after that and those days happen as if in one singular and gloriously long day. A day of sunshine and rain, of stained glass pieces and excursions into the surrounding woods and fields of Sussex, a lichen-stained gate that groans on its hinges. The dust of the country roads and the springy turf of the fields. The rugged oaks and honorable beeches. Fallow deer and gray rabbits. A riot of flowers.

When he returns at the start of that third summer, she surprises him with a long walk to a secret place. She holds his hand for the first time and guides him across a field that is adorned with old farm equipment to keep German planes from landing on it. But it is late in the war now and the German troops are busy in other parts of Europe. The Allies have invaded northern France and everyone talks like the war will be over by Christmas. Today seems normal and beautiful. The smell of salt in the air, carried up from the sea beyond the downs. The black-winged birds picking at plowed ground. The prickly hedgerows and slack-eyed sheep.

"Where are you taking me?" Adam asks.

"No one is supposed to know about this," she says. "My father will kill me if he finds out I brought you." And suddenly they are upon it—a square piece of wood covered in leaves and grass.

"What is this?" he asks. "What's it doing in the middle of a field?"

Still grasping his hand, she leads him around to one side and then bends to pull at a large iron ring. The square piece of wood lifts to reveal a hatchway. She opens it and whispers, "Come on. We have to hurry."

"But what is it?" Adam asks again and hesitates.

"It's a secret tunnel," she says breathlessly. "But we don't have long. My father may be here any minute."

They climb down a wooden ladder beneath the earth to a bunker. Using the light from above she lights an oil lamp. With flickering shadows, it reveals a three-room bunker. Adam, wide-eyed, moves ahead to look around. She can hear in his breathing that he's excited and it warms her. One room has a table with a radio and assorted books and manuals. There is also a portable gas stove, kettle, pot, and provisions for making tea. In the second room are four bunk beds. In the third is a collection of shelving lined with tins of food.

"This is for the Sussex Resistance," she explains. "My father is a member. It's all very secret. Just like the French Resistance, in case we're invaded. There are tunnels like this all over the place. Isn't it wonderful?"

His eyes tell her that he thinks it is.

"Are you glad I brought you here? I've been waiting for weeks to show you."

"Yes," he says softly. "I'm very glad." Then he leans forward, his face inching toward her.

Confused, she pulls back. "What are you doing?" she asks.

He looks embarrassed and annoyed and says, "I was going to kiss you, you simpleton."

"Oh!" she laughs, then counters his irritation with her own. "Well, why didn't you say so instead of throwing your face at me?" It's something she has thought about since he left last summer, so she steps closer, tilting her face upward and closing her eyes, just like in the movies.

It isn't so much a kiss as him squashing his lips against hers. But it is pure and innocent and stirs something in her she's never felt before. It makes her sway ever so slightly. Slowly she opens her eyes and gazes at him with nothing short of adoration. He looks a little surprised and perplexed and her heart wells up with more of the feeling and she throws her arms around his neck and kisses him again, harder.

She'd read in books and seen at the cinema how such kisses are described as taking your breath away and making you weak-kneed. She didn't believe those things really happened—until that kiss.

Suddenly there is a voice from above. "What's this? Ian, are you here?"

"Oh no!" Elaine whispers.

Adam looks around for a place to hide. "What are we going to do?"

Her mind works quickly, an idea forming instantly. "You stay here."

She rushes away and up the ladder. Mr. Gantry, a friend of her father's, peers down at her.

"What are you doing here, missy?" he asks.

"Oh, Mr. Gantry, I'm so glad you're here!" she says with all the playacting she can muster. "I was so afraid!"

"Out with it. What are you doing here?" he asks more irritably.

"I was walking through the field and saw a man in a German uniform! He must have been a pilot or something."

Mr. Gantry gasps. "Good heavens! Where is he now? Quickly, girl!"

"He ran into the woods! That way! I—"

She doesn't finish her sentence as Mr. Gantry rushes in the direction of the woods. "You stay right here. Don't move!"

Elaine rushes down the ladder and beckons to Adam, who is half-hidden behind the table. "Hurry!" she says, feeling giddy with panic. "You have to go—now!"

Adam starts for the ladder but, for reasons Elaine doesn't understand, he suddenly stops, glances around, and grabs a sheet of paper that has been taped to the wall next to the desk. He shoves the paper into his pocket, then scurries up the ladder to her. Mr. Gantry has disappeared into the woods in search of the enemy.

"Go back to the old chapel," she tells him. "But be careful. Mr. Gantry has a shotgun."

"What about you?"

"I'm all right. Go."

Adam looks as if he isn't sure, then takes a few steps backward, turns, and runs in the opposite direction from Mr. Gantry—into another part of the woods. She watches him, satisfied, until her father steps from behind a tree and grabs Adam by the collar.

"What's this, then?" Mr. Holmes shouts and drags Adam back to Elaine, who is now downright fearful by the tunnel. "What are you doing here?" he demands from Elaine.

Elaine's brain freezes and she can't speak.

"A . . . German," Adam pants, trying out Elaine's lie.

"Oh? Where?" Mr. Holmes asks calmly.

"He was in the tunnel," Adam says and Elaine instantly knows he's made a big mistake.

"The tunnel? What tunnel?"

Adam's mouth moves, but nothing comes out.

Mr. Gantry comes out of the woods, his shotgun cradled in his arm.

Elaine's father glares at her. "Well?"

"I brought Adam to see the tunnel, that's all."

"That's all?" he shouts. "A matter of national security and you think it's a playground?"

She hangs her head.

He points to Adam. "Who is this boy and what are you doing with him?"

Elaine confesses everything about Adam, the old chapel, and their friendship. Adam stands with red-faced indignation, helpless to do anything.

Mr. Holmes doesn't speak to Adam at all, but orders Elaine to go home. "This London boy, this son of a printer, has no business here with you or any member of our family. Let him stay with his own kind."

In the present again, Elaine lay on her bed, only slightly aware of the dampness on the sides of her face, hair, and pillow. She had been crying again and hadn't realized. Who could notice something as incidental as tears when her heart sat like a rock in her chest—and the memories hammered away at it, chipping it, making it crack even more.

It was so clear to her now, Elaine thought, lying on her bed. This was no illness. This was a broken dam of memories; a crystal lake pouring its clear water over her, giving her a cruel clarity about her life.

Elaine's father had forbidden her to see Adam ever again.

She didn't obey, of course. Perhaps she should have. Perhaps, had she been smarter, she would have seen the handwriting on the wall right then. Then maybe she wouldn't be suffering from this heartbreak now.

If only . . . filled her mind.

If only . . .

Then she heard Adam as a young man telling her: *Innocence can only be recognized in the past tense. Only after it's gone does one realize one ever had it.* Was he quoting someone else? He might have, not long before he left for America. At the time she'd thought it was an insightful, if unusual, statement for him to make. Now she understood. They had been so innocent. Maybe if they hadn't been, she might have known what would come next—and how to stop it. But she didn't know.

If only . . .

She rolled over onto her side and looked at her hands. They'd been clenched into fists. They hurt. The bandages felt damp. With great effort she opened them as if she was letting go of something. And hope fell heavily away from her like an old bucket into a very deep and very dry well.

How could she live now knowing what her life could have been—should have been?

If only . . .

CHAPTER
THREE

TUESDAY, THE 29TH OF JUNE

NICHOLAS POWELL TOOK OFF HIS GLASSES AND RUBBED HIS TIRED EYES. He sat at a square wooden desk in the corner of a massive warehouse filled with a dozen rows of steel shelves. Each shelf was stacked with file boxes that contained the files documenting the more than thirty-five-year history of Powell Publishing—one of the Washington, D.C., area's largest publishing houses, and one of the largest independent publishing houses outside of the New York conglomerates. One section of the shelves, the one closest to him, was dedicated to the personal archives of the publishing house's founder, Adam Powell. These were the boxes that now consumed Nicholas's time and energy, their contents the reason his eyes were so tired.

When his grandfather had moved from the large Colonial-style family house in Crockett, Maryland, to a relatively smaller but amazingly spacious townhouse in Annapolis, he'd thrown his past into boxes and had them stored in the basement of the company headquarters. Later, Nicholas's father had hired an archivist to get them into some semblance of order, with the thought that one day they'd be given to a college or university library. But Adam Powell had never attended either, and so the boxes sat.

Enter Nicholas Powell. He had been employed to compile a multi-media retrospective of his grandfather's life for an upcoming family gathering; mostly to honor the old man on his long-awaited retirement. At first, he'd been excited when his father suggested the project. He had high hopes about gaining real insight into his grandfather. But now he was a week into the project and ready to call it quits. This was sheer drudgery. Nicholas hadn't found anything interesting about his grandfather's life—it was all about the business.

The air-conditioning kicked on and breathed through the large ducts overhead. Nicholas pulled his cardigan close around him. Though it was a sweltering summer day on the other side of the windowless walls, complete with Maryland's trademark humidity, someone inside obviously thought the building should be kept at arctic temperatures. It was worse here in the basement where they kept the so-called Archive Room.

Sighing, mostly from boredom, he typed "1966—moved offices from downtown Washington to Crockett, Maryland. Powell Printing formally became Powell Publishing." He then noted: "Why the move to Maryland? Why didn't he stay in Washington?" This box didn't have those answers, but Nicholas suspected his grandfather had been drawn by Maryland's rural beauty. In 1966 the stretch of land between D.C. and Annapolis still had a lot of room for forests and fields. It was shortly afterward that the suburbs spread like a stain around Powell's house and Crockett became a bedroom community of prefab houses and shopping centers.

Back to the box. Nicholas found that year's personal letters from various family members and friends, a few birthday cards, Adam Powell's appointment book, and a handful of certificates and commendations for his civic and charitable services.

Nicholas pushed the box aside and began to wonder if there wasn't a better way to raise his tuition. Not really. Few other jobs could feed the money-eating machine that existed at Virginia Theological Seminary. Classes, books, his apartment. He was spoiled and he had to pay for the privilege.

He could tap into his trust fund, but he hated to do that. His grandfather would protest. "Don't be so lazy," he'd say. "You're a Powell, after all." Which, literally translated, meant that being a member of the Powell family didn't mean getting a free ride. He refused to let his children or grandchildren build their lives on money they hadn't earned themselves. Sure, Adam Powell would "invest" in their lives, he'd said, but he always expected a return on his investment.

Nicholas's decision to pursue a calling to the ministry certainly didn't qualify as something Adam Powell wanted to invest in. Nicholas remembered when, as a teen, he had become particularly serious about his own faith and decided to talk to his grandfather about Jesus. The result was sheer humiliation for Nicholas. His grandfather verbally slam-dunked him and made it clear that Christianity was a no-go topic of discussion. Nicholas got the impression that his grandfather was downright angry at God.

From then on, Nicholas felt cut off from his grandfather. The old man never asked how his studies were going—a conversation his grandfather regularly had with Nicholas's brother, Jeff, who'd chosen a business major. He never asked anything about Nicholas's personal life or goals. When Nicholas decided to go to Virginia Theological Seminary in Alexandria, his grandfather grunted his assent, but only because it was a prestigious school and he'd played golf with someone on the board.

So where was his grandfather's faith, if any? That was a mystery. The old man didn't seem to know much about Christianity, in spite of having been raised from the age of thirteen by a London vicar and his wife. If he'd possessed faith then, it didn't show now.

The Powell family, under Adam's guidance, would probably have remained faithless had it not been for Anna, Nicholas's mother. She had brought Christianity into the family when she and Dennis Powell were married. Nicholas and his brother, Jeff, had benefited from it, embracing their mother's active and very evangelical Episcopalian traditions. They had attended every Sunday, sang in the children's choir, and served as acolytes when they came of age. Dennis became a member of the vestry and served as treasurer for a time.

Did any of this have an effect on Adam? No.

A door slammed with a bang and an echo on the far side of room. He glanced at his watch. Noon. Kathy was on time, as always. Nicholas wryly thought that *she* was the only thing in Nicholas's life of which Adam Powell had ever given his undisguised approval. Kathy O'Connell had won the old man over the first time they'd met.

"Good Irish stock," his grandfather admitted privately, then threatened, "don't mess it up or you'll have me to deal with."

"Hi," Kathy said brightly as she stepped into the aisle and walked toward him. She was wearing a white top with colorful embroidery on the shoulders—compliments of her mother, Nicholas was sure—and white jeans. Even her tennis shoes were immaculately white. Hooked on her arm was a white picnic basket.

"You look like an angel," he said.

She stopped and curtsied. "Thank you."

"Or a very white Little Red Riding Hood," he added.

"Does that make you the big bad wolf or the noble hunter?"

"That depends on what's in the basket. I'm starving." He put the file box on the floor to make room on the table, then put his laptop computer on top of the box. She unpacked the basket, trying to push loose strands of her curly red hair behind her ear, but to no avail. It dangled with a mind of its own in front of her slender, perfectly oval face, country fresh with no need of makeup. Her eyes were an impossible green, as lush as an Irish field, her nose was dainty and turned up, her lips were predisposed to form a smile, making her countenance all the more bright when she really *did* smile, which she often did, forming dimples in her cheeks that made men stare at her in wonder. Nicholas knew that men fell in love with her daily, not only because of her beauty, but because of her uncanny ability to look at them in such a way as to make them feel important, as if they were the only ones in the world worth talking to. It was something she did sincerely. There was no artifice about her.

She could have been a fashion model, he thought, but she'd chosen instead to go into full-time ministry. Not as a minister herself, but as the wife of a minister. Everyone in their respective families seemed to assume that *he* was that minister. It was assumed that when he finished seminary in a year, they would get married, find a church to serve, and live happily ever after. The future of their relationship was understood by all.

All except Nicholas. He felt a deep affection for Kathy, but did he love her? He didn't know. He had never said so to her, nor had she ever asked him to. Maybe it was yet another assumption.

He looked at the feast spread before him—the perfectly made chicken sandwiches and potato salad, small bowls of fruit and two slices of homemade pie. The paper plates had flower patterns on them and the plastic knives and forks looked almost like expensive cutlery.

"Wow," he said. She sat down across from him and bowed her head. Taking his cue, he thanked God for the food. Afterward, he devoured the meal in an embarrassingly quick time.

"You *were* hungry," she said with a startled expression on her face, still only halfway through her own sandwich.

"I'm sorry. I was. I had no idea how much boredom could deplete my energy."

"So it's not getting any better?" she asked sympathetically.

He gestured to the shelves. "Are you kidding? I'm up to 1966 of the chronicle of my grandfather's life. Only . . . what . . . three weeks and another thirty-eight boxes to go?"

"Yes, but it'll mean so much to him at the get-together. You know it will. He'll be so surprised."

"Yeah, surprised," he said. "That's my problem about this scheme. I'm going to put together some gigantic multimedia presentation of my grandfather's life as a surprise. Men with power *hate* surprises. You know what a controlling old cuss he is. He won't thank me for it."

"Don't take it all so seriously," she said. "At least you're getting paid. More than enough to get you through the next year. Isn't that what's important, or would you rather be pumping gas?"

Pumping gas was beginning to look better all the time. "Well . . ."

"And this is perfect for you. You're the writer of the family. And who better to research a man's life? You've done it at seminary for most of the characters in the Bible. Think of him as one of those."

Nicholas laughed. "I don't think my imagination is *that* good."

Kathy leaned back and studied him earnestly. "Why do you dislike him so much?"

"I don't dislike him," Nicholas said. "I wish I could figure him out, that's all—understand what makes him tick."

"But why? Why is that so important?"

"It's important because he has singularly influenced just about every person in my family—for better or worse. More personally, he has influenced my father who has influenced me. By getting to the heart of the man, I hope to understand the rest of us a little more. Is that so unreasonable?"

"It's reasonable as long as you don't go digging up dirt on him. I don't see how that will help anything."

"I'm not after any dirt," he said. "Though I wish I could find some. It would make the job a little more interesting. Everything is boring, sterile, and factual. The only thing I've noticed of any interest is that the boxes only go back to 1955, well after his arrival in America."

"So?"

"So—what happened before that? You've probably noticed that my grandfather doesn't like to talk about it."

"I never asked," she said. "I always assumed it was something everyone in your family knows about."

Nicholas shook her head. "Here's what I know. He was born in London and his parents were killed in the Blitz when he was just a boy. He was raised by a vicar and his wife. He followed in his father's footsteps by becoming a printer. He left England and came to America where he became a hugely successful businessman. And that's it. The artifacts of his life are as cold and aloof as he is." He kicked at the box on the floor. "Honestly, Kathy, just consider the man. What is there to his life, apart from his business?"

"A marriage. His children."

"You wouldn't know it if you looked through these boxes. My grandmother was a nonentity."

"Don't be cruel."

"I'm not! Even my father has said so. You've heard him yourself. My grandmother married my grandfather out of a fear that she'd wind up an old maid. He married her because of her family connections and money. They were functionally happy, if that. I doubt they really even loved each other."

"You don't know that. You can't know their hearts."

"I see no evidence of their love."

"In what? Hearts and flowers? True love is a choice," Kathy countered. "Maybe they didn't have fireworks or romance, but they may have *chosen* to love one another over time."

"I agree that love is choice, but who does the choosing? Do we choose love or does love choose us?"

"Is this the theologian speaking or the sentimental writer?"

He groaned. "You know that I think romantic love is overrated, especially when it comes to lifetime commitments. But wouldn't you rather have it than not have it? Wouldn't you rather have love with passion?"

She gave him a Mona Lisa smile. "I don't know why we're talking about this. You know how nervous I get when you become sloppy and sentimental." She stood up and collected the basket.

"Leaving so soon?"

"I'm meeting some of the teachers this afternoon to talk about our next semester." Kathy taught at a Christian elementary school in the center of Alexandria.

He watched as she swung around and started to walk away. "What— no kiss?"

She smiled coyly at him over her shoulder, wiggling her fingers good-bye before she disappeared around the corner.

Nicholas looked at the wall of boxes and groaned.

TWO HOURS LATER NICHOLAS WAS ABOUT TO SHOVE ANOTHER BOX BACK onto the shelf when his eye caught something tucked behind the neat row facing front—a different-looking box. Strange. All the other boxes were white, with the printed content labels facing out. This one was brown and had something scrawled in Magic Marker on the side. Putting the first box down on the floor, he retrieved the brown box. A coating of dust puffed into his face, causing him to turn away. He blinked wildly and coughed.

Placing the box on the table, he eyed it with curiosity. The name "Powell" was written in his grandfather's handwriting. There was no identifying inventory number in the contents section. He glanced quickly at the inventory sheets; apparently, it hadn't been cataloged. An oversight, he supposed.

The box was taped shut. That too was unusual. All of the boxes had been kept unsealed so that more things could be added as they were discovered. Was this one here by mistake? Had a mover placed it with the wrong group when the boxes had been brought here from the house? Nicholas took his ballpoint pen and broke the seal on the tape around the four edges. He lifted the top.

This box didn't contain files or memos or the usual impersonal junk. This was a collection of keepsakes, of souvenirs. With interest, Nicholas began to pull things out one at a time.

There was a magazine called *Front Line: 1940–1941* with a black-and-white photo of a sweaty-faced fireman gazing upward with something like awe on his face. At a glance, the contents seemed to chronicle the first year of the German blitz against London through text and photos. There was also a worn paperback about how to spot German and Italian aircraft, presumably to help British citizens during the Battle of Britain. Nicholas picked up a small and colorful cigarette box with "Player's Navy Cut Cigarettes Mild" on the front. A fountain pen in a black case. An old booklet with detailed maps of the streets of London, with no copyright date, but it looked old, perhaps pre-War. There was a ration book holder containing a ration book from the Ministry of Food, a clothing book, and a National Registration Identity Card for Adam Randolph Powell. There

was another booklet, presumably from World War II, with the letters
A.R.P. in large type on the front and the subtitle: *A Complete Guide to
Civil Defence Measures.* There was a National Insurance Card from 1948,
issued to Adam Randolph Powell. A die-cast toy plane. A pack of playing
cards. A small cup with a crudely painted Union Jack on the side and the
words: *VE Day—May 8, 1945.* A small round tin with what appeared to
be chips of colored glass in it. A small vinyl record of *The Goons.* A bronze
skeleton key. Torn ticket stubs. A pocket watch with fob and chain. A red
lozenge tin with a photo of Queen Elizabeth on the cover, framed by the
Union Jack and another flag with lions on it that Nicholas couldn't iden-
tify. Above her head it said *Coronation 1953* and beneath the photo it pro-
claimed *Long May She Reign.* There was also a gold-colored program book
for the Festival of Britain in 1951. Flipping through the pages, Nicholas
assumed it was an English equivalent to a World's Fair.

And then he saw a brochure for the Billy Graham Crusade of London, 1954. *Billy Graham?* Nicholas wondered about its significance.

There was more, but Nicholas's eye fell on a bundle of letters, held
together by a rubber band that crumbled before he could ease it off. A
small sheet of paper fell out from between the letters.

In the upper right-hand corner was written in a neat, masculine style
The Vicarage and underneath that *17th of August, 1954. Dear Adam,* the
letter said, *Here are Elaine's letters, as we promised. Julie and I have discussed
the matter and believe that there has been a terrible misunderstanding. These
letters, not to mention her phone calls to us, seem to be sufficient proof of her
distress. It is our prayer that you may look beyond your own heartbreak to consider that she may be suffering as well. It is your decision, of course, but we beg
you to consider the words of our Lord about forgiveness. Respectfully, John.*

Nicholas gazed at the letter, astonished. A misunderstanding with a
woman. Heartbreak. Forgiveness. Our Lord. These were words Nicholas
had never expected to see in connection with his grandfather.

He thought through the facts of his grandfather's life he knew from
family stories. The writer of this letter—John—was probably John
Peters, the vicar Adam had lived with. John Peters and his American
wife, Julie, had taken Adam in after his parents were killed by German
bombs in London. It was Julie who later used her contacts to secure a
job for Adam in Washington as a printer.

Nicholas scrolled through his notes on the laptop. Adam Powell
left London and moved to Washington in June of 1954. The note had
been written in August of the same year. *Heartbreak . . . suffering . . .
forgiveness . . .*

His heart quickened as he turned his attention to the stack of letters. Each envelope was light blue and had written on the front in a curly feminine style *Adam Powell, The Vicarage, Bedford Road, Chiswick, London*. In the upper right-hand corner were two rose-colored stamps, each with an elaborate border underneath framing a profile of a young Queen Elizabeth II and "1D." The postmarks indicated that all of the letters had come from someplace called Stonebridge on dates in June, July, and early August 1954.

On the backs of each letter the words *Arthur House* were written over the flaps.

To Nicholas's amazement, the flaps were still sealed. None of the letters had been opened.

Without thinking, Nicholas picked up the first letter and began to tear at the top. Suddenly he stopped. Was it right for him to open the letters? There was no question in his mind that they were private, which meant the letters were none of his business. He sat and debated with himself. He was researching his grandfather's life for the family gathering. These letters were part of his grandfather's life. No one had told him that he *couldn't* or *shouldn't* be thorough in his research or that anything was off-limits to him ...

That was the letter of the law, but not the spirit, he thought. None of those reasons would hold up if he had to explain to his father or, worse, his grandfather why he'd invaded the old man's privacy.

He shouldn't open the letters.

But what was he to do? This was the first interesting find he'd had. More than that, it was the first indication he'd had that his grandfather was more than just a business automaton. He'd once had a relationship with someone that was powerful enough to break his heart. This spoke of *humanity*, of a side to his grandfather he didn't know.

Of course, he could open the letters, read them, and put them back—with the likelihood that no one would ever know. Sure he could. Why not?

He looked at the letter in his hand. It was shaking. *He* was shaking. He had to see what was in those letters.

And he would have, if his cell phone hadn't rung at that very moment.

It was his father.

"Just wanted to see how you're doing," his father said.

"Fine, Dad. I found a box—"

"More than one, I hope. Look, Son, I want to talk to you."

"Oh?"

"Are you enjoying what you're doing?"

"Enjoying—?" Nicholas began, puzzled, and then knew instantly what had happened. Kathy had probably called his mother after lunch and told about their conversation—about how unhappy he was going through the boxes. Nicholas's mother called his father. Now his father was calling him.

"Well, actually . . ." He didn't know what to say. How he felt wasn't a priority. But he had to say something. "Dad, you really need to see this box. Can you come down?"

"I'll be right there."

DENNIS POWELL SAT IN THE CHAIR AT THE SMALL DESK THAT KATHY HAD occupied only a couple of hours before. His salt-and-pepper hair—what was left of it—was slicked back as if he'd just come out of the shower. He wore a plain white Oxford short-sleeved shirt with a striped tie. Deep worry lines ridged his forehead and he had no laugh lines around his eyes.

"Well," his father said slowly and scratched his chin. He looked at the open box—and the letters—with an expression Nicholas recognized as dread.

"Well," Nicholas repeated.

"Seems like a museum would be interested in a few of these items," his father said.

"Including the letters?"

"No, not the letters. These other things, though."

"But what about the letters?"

"What about them?"

"Dad—"

"Obviously your grandfather put them in that box for a reason."

"Grandad claims to do everything for a reason. But why didn't he open them?"

His father shrugged. "How should I know?"

"You saw the letter from John Peters."

"*If* it was John Peters."

"It had to be John Peters. He mentions his wife, Julie. It came from the vicarage. What other John could it be?" Nicholas drummed his fingers on the tabletop. "Come on, Dad, you're stalling."

"I'm not stalling. I think you should put them back where you found them."

"Why?"

"For one thing, I don't think your grandfather would be very happy to learn that—"

"He's never happy anyway."

His father looked at him impatiently. "We're not having *that* conversation again."

"But don't you see? These letters may be a key to Grandad's personality."

"Maybe they are. Why is it any of your business? Why do we need keys to your grandfather's, or anyone's, personalities? Can't you accept people as they are?"

"Sure I can. But I'm also interested in the things that make people *what* they are."

"Only God knows what makes people what they are. You're not comparing yourself to God, are you?"

Nicholas groaned. "You're being evasive."

"You're being intrusive."

"You're the one who gave me this job."

"To put together a pleasant presentation about your grandfather's life. Not to dissect him. You're supposed to be a minister, not an amateur psychologist."

"Don't you want to know? Aren't you just the least bit curious? At one time in his life, Grandad was actually heartbroken, which means he must have loved someone. Do you know who she might've been? Have you ever heard of Arthur House?"

"I don't understand this warped perception you have of your grandfather," Dennis complained. "He loves people."

"Does he?"

His father looked away.

"All I'm saying is that these letters might help us to understand him."

"To what end? Do you think you're going to change him?"

"No. Maybe."

"If there's any changing to be accomplished, then God will do it. And if God wants to change him, then that's God's job. In the meantime, put these letters away and mind your own business."

Nicholas and his father stared each other down. "What if I insist on taking them to Grandad myself?"

Dennis raised an eyebrow, then called his bluff. "Go ahead."

"Are you serious?"

"If you want to take it that far, I won't try to stop you. Your grandfather is the only person who can give you permission to read those letters. So if he says it's all right, then that's up to him." His father paused for a second, then added, "With one condition."

"What?"

"You have to come up with a reasonable explanation for finding the letters. I don't want you to spoil the surprise presentation at the family gathering."

"All right," Nicholas agreed.

"After that, I want you to think about something else."

"What?"

"Announcing your engagement to Kathy."

Nicholas frowned. "My engagement?"

"At the family get-together. It would make everyone very happy—a nice addition to your grandfather's retirement celebration."

Nicholas didn't know what to say.

"Your mother has a ring, an heirloom from her side of the family. Apparently, Kathy loves it. We've had it resized for her."

"Mom and Kathy have chosen our engagement ring?"

"Looks that way."

Nicholas frowned.

"Don't be upset, Son," his father said. "It's one thing less for you to do. Enjoy the ride."

"I want to think about it."

"Don't think too long." The legs of the chair scratched loudly across the floor as his father stood up and moved away. As he left, he called back, "I don't believe for a minute that your grandfather'll let you open those letters, by the way."

"I know."

EVEN UP TO THE VERY MOMENT WHEN ADAM POWELL'S SECRETARY SIGNALED Nicholas to go into the office, he was ready to walk away. He'd practiced several approaches to the conversation, how to position his argument for opening the letters or at the very least explaining them, but nothing rang true.

This is hopeless, he kept thinking. *He'll make me put the letters back and they'll never be opened. No one will ever know what was in them.*

Adam Powell sat behind his oversized desk, an antique of rich mahogany. The walls behind him were covered with matching bookshelves displaying books by Powell Publishing. There was also another work area with a laptop computer, printer, fax machine, and other pieces of office equipment. Scattered around the shelves and walls were statuettes of publishing awards and framed certificates. But nothing personal, Nicholas always noticed. No family photos.

Without looking up, Adam Powell waved a hand at Nicholas. "Sit down," he said and kept his gaze on a large set of book galleys in front of him. He had a red pen poised above the page, occasionally circling a word, making a proofreading symbol, or jotting a note in the margin. The red gashes covered the paper. The poor thing looked as if it was being slashed to death with a small razor.

Nicholas sat in one of the visitor's chairs and placed the box on the floor next to his feet.

He watched his grandfather work, hoping to catch a clue as to the old man's mood. Adam's face held its usual calm expression, as if he held all the right cards and life was only bluffing. It smoothed out the lines and gave him a youthful countenance. At times Nicholas thought that his own father looked older than his grandfather. They were often confused as brothers rather than father and son. But, for Nicholas, it was Adam's thick bush of white hair and the leathery look of the skin on his neck that gave a hint of his real age. There was no question about it: Adam Powell was a dynamically handsome man, aging well, and was often the center of attention at social venues. Women flocked to him, drawn by his strength and charisma. And he used that appeal to meet and greet those with the most influence and power. More than once he'd told Nicholas that the biggest and most important business decisions were rarely made in the boardroom but on racquetball courts, on golf courses, or over dinner and drinks.

"Ah!" Adam Powell exclaimed and threw his pen down. "Who writes this rubbish?"

Rubbish, not *trash,* Nicholas thought. Even after all these years in America, Adam held on to his English accent and cultural phrases. No doubt he considered it an asset. It made him sound charming and urbane, intelligent and sophisticated—a far cry from the working-class London boy who began his career as a printer's apprentice. Nicholas often wondered why he didn't sound rougher with, say, a Michael Caine or Bob

Hoskins-type Cockney accent. Who taught him to speak in such a well-mannered way?

Nicholas cleared his throat and nudged the box with the toe of his shoe. Words, please. Any will do.

"Well?" his grandfather asked. His voice was a deep velvet, but not warm and inviting.

"I was doing some research in the Archive Room," Nicholas croaked. "And I stumbled onto something."

"Are you being vague on purpose? What sort of something?"

"Something from your past."

"Is that why you wanted to see me?"

"Yes." Nicholas cleared his throat again. "I need to ask you about it. Your past. I mean, what I found."

"If it's about my past, then it should stay in the archives." Adam picked up the red pen and returned to assaulting the galleys. The meeting was over.

Nicholas stood up. But rather than leave, he picked up the file box and put it on the desk. "Dad asked me to go through the company's history and I found this."

Adam looked at the box without any hint of recognition. "What is it?"

Nicholas took the top off. "Look."

Standing up, Adam peered into the box. For a couple of seconds, no more than that, his expression changed, his eyes grew wide, and Nicholas thought he saw something resembling his grandfather as a young boy. It was only a flicker, like a shadow by candlelight in a drafty room, and then he was himself again. "What are you doing with that?" he demanded.

"I found it. In the Archive Room. While I was searching for—"

He flicked at the top of the box, knocking it ajar. "Who said you could open it? Clearly it was taped shut."

"Yes. But it wasn't on the inventory sheet and didn't have any other markings apart from our name, so I—"

"Well, I'm sure you can tell that it's mine. So you may seal it up and put it away."

"But, Grandad, this is historically significant stuff. If you're only going to leave it in the basement, you may as well let a museum have the contents for display. Maybe the Smithsonian'll be interested."

He picked up the program for the Festival of Britain, considered it for a moment, and then dropped it in again. "Maybe," he conceded.

"Tell me about the Billy Graham Crusade," Nicholas requested.

"There's nothing to tell. Billy Graham came to London and preached a lot."

"Did you go?"

"I might have."

Again, a no-go subject. "Grandad—"

Nicholas didn't continue. His grandfather reached into the box and slowly brought out the collection of letters.

Nicholas said quickly, "I didn't open those. But there was a note . . . " He pointed to the edge of the paper sticking out from between the envelopes.

Adam pulled the note out and glanced at it. "You read this?"

"Yes, sir."

"No doubt you're wondering what he's talking about."

"Yes, I am."

He looked at Nicholas with a devilish fire in his eyes. The old fox could see right through him. "You don't give a toss about the junk in this box, do you? The letters are the real reason you've come to see me."

"Not, really, I—"

"You can be honest," he interrupted. "You want to know what's in these letters."

Nicholas knew he was being taunted and had no idea how to respond. "Obviously something significant happened . . . to you . . . and that girl . . . "

"Do you really want to know?"

"Yes, I do."

"I was betrayed, that's what happened. Even heartbroken by it. It happens to everyone at some point in their lives. It happened to me when I was young—and I vowed it would never happen again. Simple as that."

"But it's not really that simple. John Peters seemed to think—"

Adam's eyes were locked on Nicholas's, hard and unflinching, and Nicholas stopped himself from saying any more.

"I've told you as much as you or anyone else needs to know, Nicholas."

Nicholas wanted to argue, but his ability to reason seemed to abandon him.

"Does that answer your question?" Adam asked.

Nicholas nodded. "Yes, Grandad." He reached for the box.

"No. Leave it with me," Adam said.

Nicholas stepped back, but he didn't want to leave it. He knew he would never see the box or the letters again if he did. He shuffled, desperate to say something but not knowing what to say.

His grandfather held up the letters. "Nicholas, you're a good Christian boy. I wouldn't want these to be a source of temptation in your life."

"You don't have to worry about that," Nicholas said through a dry throat.

"But I do. A young man going into the ministry has more important things to be tempted by." He took a few steps over to a large wooden case. It had a slot in the top, not unlike a slot you might drop mail into. "To save you from temptation—and to prove that these letters are from an inconsequential moment in my life—I'll do this . . ." He dropped them one by one into the box. Instantly a high-pitched motor came to life and the teeth of the document shredder received the envelopes with shrill glee.

Nicholas involuntarily reached out. "Grandad, no!" He watched with horror and the letters were put one by one into the slot. Horror then gave way to a burning humiliation that crawled over his body like a swarm of red ants. His grandfather had played him for the sucker he was.

Adam put the last of the letters into the slot and waited until the machine finished the job. Then he turned to Nicholas again. "The sooner you realize the difference between what's important and what isn't, the more successful you'll be."

Nicholas glared at his grandfather. When he opened his mouth to respond, he felt an ache in his jaw as if he'd been clenching his teeth. No words would come.

"To succeed in life," Adam said, "you must learn to value nothing. Otherwise, someone else will always have the upper hand."

"Is that what this is about? The *upper hand?*" Nicholas choked out.

His grandfather looked at him with a cold smile.

Nicholas stormed out of the office.

CHAPTER FOUR

ADAM STOOD OVER THE FILE BOX OF HIS BELONGINGS, THE SMILE GONE, his face now ashen and his hands shaking. Alone, he felt spent and slumped into his chair. He'd put on quite a performance for Nicholas, he thought, considering what a shock it had been to be faced with this box. In one motion he scrubbed his hands across his face and through his hair.

"To succeed in life," Adam had said to Nicholas, "you must learn to value nothing. Otherwise, someone else will always have the upper hand."

That was a paraphrase of a quote by Mr. Packer, his boss and the owner of Packer & Sons Printing, Ltd., where he had followed in his father's footsteps by serving as an apprentice, and later a fully qualified printer. His nine years with Mr. Packer had been formative.

"Value nothing, my lad. The minute you value something, then someone will use it against you to get you to do what they want. Make no mistake about that. If I thought you valued this job, I'd use that value to take advantage of you. Always—*always*—be prepared to walk away. It's the only leverage you have."

He could see the old man now with his patchy bald head, ink stains on his hands, and smudges around his arms, and a cigarette dangling loosely from his lips. A black-and-white image, like a character in an old film. Come to think of it, all of his memories of London now seemed to be in black-and-white, as if the colors had faded away somehow. Only as an act of the will could he recall the beautifully sunny days, the days he remembered of his mother in a bright floral dress caring for the flowers in the back garden of their terraced house on Stavely Road, or his father coming home from his job, hands greasy and smudged, sleeves rolled up, his dark blue overalls all but covered in ink. He thought of the Thames, sometimes a deep blue, usually brown or gray, when they'd go down to the wharf, back when Chiswick had a wharf, and he and the other kids would search the banks when the tide had gone out, hoping to find anything valuable. *Mudlarks* they were called by the adults on the embankment.

But now all he could see in his mind's eye was the gray rain hitting black pavement. He saw gray chimney pots pointing like accusing fingers at the iron sky. Soot on the door of the house, black edgings to the threadbare rug in the front hall, thick fog—pea soupers, they were called—and the ongoing smell of exhaust fumes from the buses and cabs. The true colors were there in his memory, but hidden behind a dirty glass.

The countryside was another matter, though. The fields, the downs of Sussex, the shops of Stonebridge and all around it were in vivid Technicolor. When he took the train to that countryside, he traveled from grays and blacks to rich hues of green, gold, and blue. Like stained glass.

Even the rain fell in colors.

Adam looked down and was surprised to see that he'd unpacked the box. When had he done that? Everything was sitting on his desk, the scattered pieces of his life before America. He'd pulled everything out without realizing it.

It's her, he thought angrily. She still had the power to distract him, to make him behave contrary to his own impulses, his better sense. Even after all this time.

Clenching his fists, he fought against the feelings that rushed at him. He had to master them. He hadn't reached this point in his life just to be overcome by sentimentality. No, he was much stronger than that.

Leaning on the desk, he looked down at the paraphernalia of his past life and chose to defy them. He would exorcise his past by rebuking these talismans, one by one. He would shred the whole box, once and for all, and let the thin ribbons of his past be recycled in some dump somewhere. He should have done it years ago. He reached around his desk and placed the trash can at his feet.

HE LOOKED AT THE LETTER FROM FATHER JOHN PETERS. IN THE WRITTEN words, he could hear Father John's voice—the concern and heartfelt worry that only a man of his compassion could communicate. It was a voice he'd encountered during the most troubled times of his life, always breaking in with warmth and love.

He picked up and carefully unfolded a yellowed news clipping from the *London Daily Express* about a gas main explosion on Stavely Road in Chiswick. The 8th of September, 1944. Adam sighed and lowered himself back into his chair. There had been an explosion, yes, but it wasn't because of a gas main.

It had been a drizzly afternoon and Adam's father had been stubbornly trying to repair the short wall enclosing their small front garden. "It's an eyesore," he'd said again and again. "Anyone going up and down Stavely Road can see how poorly it looks. Your mother'd be ashamed." Adam didn't see what the fuss was all about. The bricks had come loose, that's all. But when his father invoked Adam's mother's wishes from the grave, there was no stopping him. So his father cursed the rain and went to work. Adam had tried to help but only got in the way. As evening approached, he realized the only way to be of use to his father was to fix their supper, so he went off to a nearby shop to buy some bread and a can of beans. Beans-on-toast was a favorite of his father's.

The neighbors said later that they'd heard a mysterious metallic buzzing overhead, which then suddenly stopped. What they couldn't have known on that rainy evening was that they were hearing a new technology—one of Hitler's newly created long-range rockets called the V2. Speeding at three thousand miles an hour, the first one hit the center of Stavely Road, the explosion heard as far away as Westminster and Piccadilly. The bomb created a giant crater, some forty feet wide and twenty feet deep. Eleven houses were destroyed, sixteen others seriously damaged, and over six hundred others in need of repair.

Twenty-four people were injured that evening. Four people died. One was a young man who'd been walking along the road to pay a visit to his girlfriend. Another was dear old Mrs. Harrison, who'd been sitting by the kitchen fire when the rocket hit. Three-year-old Rosemary Clarke had been in her cot, asleep. And, of course, Richard Powell, who had been working on the wall.

All from one rocket.

A few blocks away, Adam heard the explosion, followed by a long, low rumble. The windows of the shop rattled and Adam looked up from his purchases.

"Heavens above, what was that?" the shopkeeper with a mustache like an old broom exclaimed.

Adam ran home through the rain, a dark intuition filling him with dread. The front door of his house was blown somewhere into the house, the windows were gone, and the house inside was engulfed in flames that licked hungrily at the adjoining homes. The wall and garden and pavement his father had been working to repair were gone.

Adam screamed for his father, and raced toward the house.

A neighbor—a big burly northerner named Doolittle—grabbed Adam from behind and pulled him close, filling Adam's nostrils with the smell of last night's fish-and-chips.

"Sorry, lad," the big man said.

"I want to see my father," Adam wailed, struggling unsuccessfully against him.

"You can't."

"But I have to—"

"You can't!" A tighter bear hug.

"Let me go! I must!" Adam squirmed.

"There's nothing left of him to see!" the big man said and wept as Adam slumped to the pavement in stunned silence. He would forever remember that moment whenever he smelled smoke and deep-fried fish.

There had been no air-raid sirens, no summons to the shelters; the government even denied it had been a bomb and planted the story about a gas main explosion. Everyone knew better.

Adam's life as he'd known it was now gone. His mother, his father, and all of his possessions were no more. The Doolittles took him in, but didn't know what to do with him. He had retreated into a silent and dark place, somewhere deep inside of himself, where nothing could reach him. He spent days there. Voices were distant and muffled. His activities— eating, bathing, sleeping, staring out of the window—were all performed as if by someone else. Finally, a decision was made to send him back to his aunt and uncle in Stonebridge, but that brought no consolation.

A voice broke through two weeks after the explosion. It was a voice he'd heard every Sunday morning when his mother was still alive, and then often in the sitting room and at the funeral after she'd been killed, then only a few times with his father when they occasioned the church. It was a voice he had always liked and trusted. Father John Peters, the young vicar at St. Luke's Church, now sat next to Adam in the front room and explained that Adam couldn't stay with the Doolittles any longer—they had five children of their own, after all—and that Adam would have to come to live with him. He'd talked it over with his wife, Julie, and it's what they both wanted.

Father Peters then presented Adam a small metal box, melted and scarred. It was a box from Adam's room—containing the stained glass, a piece of crumpled paper from a secret tunnel near Stonebridge, and a few other mementos of his life.

"We found this in the rubble. I thought you'd want it."

Adam took the box and wept while Father Peters stood by, a hand on his shoulder.

The attic of the Peters's terraced house (or "townhouse," as Julie called them) became Adam's room. It was spacious and gave him all the room and privacy he wanted. In time he realized that the house—four stories high—was larger than the average Church of England vicarage. That may have had something to do with Julie Peters, a young and attractive American from a wealthy Washington family who'd come to England to work in the American Embassy just as the first blitz began. Adam didn't know the full story of how Father John and Julie met or married, and in the nine years he lived with them never asked.

He smiled as he thought of Julie. She was beautiful, poised, quick-witted, and had that particular disregard of manners and propriety so characteristic of Americans. It shocked some in the parish and may have caused Father John a few embarrassments, but Adam loved her for it. She became like an older sister to him. His strongest memories were of her fascination with all things new, especially when Britain hit the 1950s and rationing eased up a little. She was the first in their neighborhood to have an "English Electric" refrigerator with ice box, or to feed them the newly invented "frozen foods" like Birdseye fish-fingers or chicken pies. When J. Sainsbury opened the first self-service grocery store—with products on shelves that you could take down for yourself and put in a metal cart—she traveled across the city to enjoy it for herself. And she *did* enjoy it, going every week. "This makes so much sense," she announced. "What took them so long to invent it here?" She was the first to have "the television," as they called it and they watched the Coronation of Queen Elizabeth in 1953. In black-and-white, of course.

Father John and Julie made him feel at home, acting as parents, as mentors, as brother and sister, and as friends.

Yes, he'd keep the newspaper clipping. But the letter? He put it aside for now.

HE EYED THE BOX WARILY AND BEGAN THE CLEANSING.

A fountain pen—the one he'd used to write to Elaine between summers and then later, after her father had forbidden her to see him, when he responded to the letters Elaine smuggled out of the house through the housekeeper. Wasted words. Tossed in the trash can.

Train ticket stubs to Brighton. Twentieth of December, 1944. Her father had sent Elaine to a boarding school in Brighton and Adam sneaked down to see her since he was still unapproved by her family. She'd wept over the recent loss of his father and, he painfully remembered, they'd kissed—more intensely than ever before, and with a maturing passion. They professed their undying love for one another. He was only fourteen years old.

He dropped the train ticket stubs into the trash.

A "Congratulations on your 18th birthday" card from Elaine, 1949. She had delivered it to him personally, having successfully escaped her parents to come to London. But the day had been ruined when he learned that Gerard Sommersby—that wet fish he'd knocked down near the old chapel several years earlier—had become a good friend to Elaine. He was one of her kind, Adam had thought at the time; just the kind her father would want her to marry.

Adam threw the birthday card into the trash.

He picked up and studied a small black-and-white photo of himself in military uniform, with the standard short-back-and-sides haircut they required. He'd had eight weeks of obligatory training as part of the National Service at an army base in Sussex and then off to the Suez Canal for eighteen months to work in the motor pool, wearing a badly fitting uniform and earning only a few shillings a day.

He dropped the photo into the trash can and picked up a booklet for the Festival of Britain, late spring of 1951. A huge event on the South Bank in London, all to show Britain's contribution to civilization throughout history and into the future—a tonic at a time when the country was still rationing food and suffering the effects of the war with

Germany. He'd met Elaine there right after returning from Egypt. The day had been a disaster. He had gone with high hopes of working out their future together. Elaine then told him that her mother was dying of cancer and now wasn't the time to cause a family crisis by telling them of the seriousness of their relationship. He bitterly remembered how he had despaired that they would ever be together, but Elaine believed that God would help them by healing her mother and changing her father's heart. Adam believed her.

Toss it, Adam thought—and the Festival of Britain program went into the trash can. God was not interested in healing Elaine's mother or changing anyone's heart. Cancer had taken Elaine's mother in small pieces over the next two years, leaving Elaine's father a bitter and determined man. The time was never right to make their relationship known to him. And Elaine simply couldn't find it within herself then to choose between Adam and her family.

A brochure for the Billy Graham Crusade in London indicated a new milestone for Adam—the setup for his betrayal by Elaine *and* God. This one he didn't want to think about or remember. He crumpled it up and pitched it.

ADAM PICKED UP A SMALL BOOK OF MATCHES. THE MILL HOUSE, IT declared in cheap black lettering. Next to the words was a crude drawing of a wheel. Adam rubbed his finger over the wheel and wondered if the pub was still there in Stonebridge.

Perhaps this item, more than any, represented his relationship with Elaine. The hope of their love and its dismal end.

He had discovered the Mill House only because Packer & Sons had printed their menus, a job he'd supervised. When he saw that it was in Stonebridge, he arranged to meet Elaine there. It proved to be ideal for them because, though it had recently been redecorated by a new owner who hoped to appeal to a better clientele, it wasn't so upscale that it would appeal to Elaine's friends.

It was there that his relationship with Elaine came to its conclusion. These were the memories he had to master and then vanquish. So he let them come.

A Saturday in the spring of 1954, and Adam took the train to Stonebridge for his usual rendezvous with Elaine at the Mill House. He arrived at noon exactly and chatted with Mr. Soames, the owner, a cordial man who had always looked at the young couple with dewy eyes and sympathetic expressions. He always gave them the same corner booth, away from the rest of the customers. Adam waited an hour and Elaine didn't come. He wondered if, for some reason, she was busy with the Arthur children—she'd become their governess a few months before. He phoned Arthur House to find out. The maid there said she believed Elaine had gone home for the weekend.

Disheartened, Adam waited for another half hour, and when she didn't show up he found the courage to try her at her parents' home. The line chirped at him several times until he was about to hang up. Then there was a click and a man said, "Yes?"

"May I speak with Elaine, please?"

Adam knew the voice. It was Mr. Holmes. "Who is phoning, please?" he asked.

Pause. Hard swallow. "This is Adam Powell."

"She's not here. She's in Southaven."

Southaven? What was she doing in Southaven?

"Hello? Are you there, Powell?" Mr. Holmes asked with obvious irritation.

"Oh. Uh, thank you, sir," Adam said and nearly put the receiver down. Then, impulsively, he said, "Mr. Holmes?"

"What do you want?"

"I was wondering if I might come and speak with you."

"What about?"

"Your daughter."

There was a pause on the other end, then Mr. Holmes said, "Come to the house now, if you must."

"Yes, sir. I'll come right away."

Since Adam had taken the train in, he had no other means of transportation except to walk to the Holmes' house. It took him twenty minutes to get there. He had no idea what he was going to do or say, but he was determined to do and say *something*.

A maid let him in and showed him directly to the "library"—a room decorated with Romanesque pillars and white shelves covered with books and model ships and busts of British war heroes. Adam was looking at a bust of Admiral Nelson when Mr. Holmes walked in. Apart from less, or graying, hair, he looked much the same as he had over a decade before when he'd caught Adam near the secret bunker.

"Would you care for a drink?" Mr. Holmes asked.

Adam wanted to say yes, but thought better of it. "No, thank you."

"Then get to it."

"Yes, sir."

Mr. Holmes gazed at him impatiently. "Well? You said you wanted to talk with me. Something about Elaine."

"I want you to know that . . ." His mouth went dry and he struggled to contain the slight quiver he heard in his own voice. "I love her and want what's best for her."

"Is that so?"

"Yes, sir."

"Then I assume that by 'loving her' you mean sneaking around with her against our wishes and meeting up with her in strange locations. Is that what you mean?"

"Forgive me, sir, but the only reason we 'sneak around'—as you put it—is because you refuse to let me see your daughter properly."

Mr. Holmes looked aghast. "Is that an accusation? Are you saying that we've driven you to your actions?"

"Yes, sir. It was my understanding that you didn't want Elaine to see me."

"Tell me something, Powell. Would you want *your* daughter to see someone who resorts to deceit like you have?"

"You have it the wrong way around, Mr. Holmes. If there's been any deceit, it's because you wouldn't allow us to see one another openly. Your unreasonability led us to—"

"My unreasonability," he shouted, red-faced. "You arrogant pup! Wouldn't you want your daughter to marry well? Wouldn't you intervene if you thought your daughter was wasting her time?"

"I would hope to respect my daughter enough to believe in her own intelligence and wishes."

"And that's where you'll go wrong, Powell. Children think they know what they want, but haven't a clue about what they truly need. Had your parents survived the war, you'd—"

"Don't you dare talk about my parents," said Adam through gritted teeth. "You didn't know them and have no right to speak about them."

Mr. Holmes held up his hands in a gesture of conciliation. "Fair enough. I meant no disrespect to them. The point is, children need guidance about what's best for them."

"Elaine is no longer a child."

"In her heart, she is. Can't you see that? Why else would she indulge herself in a friendship with you when there are at least two—no, *three*—young men far more suitable for her. They are all reputable and financially sound. And they don't sneak around. They've been taking her to proper places in a proper manner. With my blessing."

"I see." Adam wished now that he'd asked for that drink.

"So don't come to my house, professing love for my daughter, when you haven't a clue about what love is."

"I believe I do."

Mr. Holmes snorted. "If you did, you'd stop this nonsense right away."

"If by 'suitable' you mean financial security, then I believe I have the means—"

"Not as the manager of a printing house, you don't."

Adam was surprised. He actually knew what Adam did.

Mr. Holmes chuckled. "I caught you out, didn't I? Of course I know about Mr. Packer and his firm. Do you think I'd sit back and allow my daughter to maintain a friendship—even secretly—without my knowing something about him?"

"You've been spying on us."

"Let me assure you, Powell, that your little relationship with my daughter would have ended years ago if I wasn't satisfied of your position and your association with the rector of St. Luke's. On that alone, I've allowed her friendship with you to continue."

"If you know so much about me, then why are you against me?" Adam asked, careful to keep his tone low and away from anything that might be misconstrued as pleading. "You know I'm a hard worker. I will own that printing firm one day."

"And you believe I should be impressed with that?"

"Yes."

"Then you are misguided, Powell. I don't object to you as a matter of wealth. I object to you as a matter of principle."

"What principle?"

"The class system has served this country well for centuries and I see no reason to change it now. My daughter belongs with her own kind. Just as you belong with yours."

"I can't believe you're saying that—now—in the twentieth century."

"It is undeniable. So, if you truly loved Elaine, you would leave her alone. And you may also be assured that if I thought she loved you, my intercessions would be more rigorous."

Stunned, Adam stood where he was but now at a loss for a rebuttal.

If I thought she loved you . . . rang in his mind and through his being like an enormous church bell. *If I thought she loved you . . . He doesn't know her feelings,* Adam thought. *Either he is oblivious, or she has never professed them . . .*

It was hopeless, he finally realized. Regardless of Elaine's feelings—what she has said or not said—Mr. Holmes would not change his mind. No matter what Adam did, no matter how successful he'd become, Mr. Holmes would not accept him. Status was a birthright and could never be earned.

"Well?" Mr. Holmes demanded.

"I believe we've said enough. I'll see myself out."

Mr. Holmes followed him anyway, unwilling to give Adam the last word. "If you're harboring hopes that she'll marry you, then you hope in vain. Don't confuse a childish loyalty with love, Powell. You'll go the way of Peter Pan. You already have. Right now she's in Southaven with one of those suitors I mentioned—"

Adam slammed the door behind him.

HE RETURNED TO THE MILL HOUSE AND BROODED. *IF YOU TRULY LOVED Elaine . . . If I thought she loved you . . .*

Why had he wasted all these years, all these emotions on her? Perhaps the old man was right. Elaine felt only a childish loyalty toward Adam. *Not* love.

Elaine suddenly appeared next to the table, red-faced and breathless. "What's happened?" she asked.

Adam slowly looked her over. She was dressed in a blue pullover and slacks and had her hair tied up under a scarf.

"Adam?"

"Hello, Elaine. Sit down," he said and waved a limp hand toward the bench. He nearly knocked over his drink.

She slid into the booth and undid the scarf. "Edie told me that you came to the house."

"Edie?"

"Our maid. She said you had words with Father."

"Yes, we did." He drained the glass. "Where were you today?"

"In Southaven, helping with a function at my church. I told you in my last letter. Didn't you get it?"

He shook his head.

"I'm sorry, Adam."

"So am I," he said—and the self-pity in his voice sounded childish and melodramatic even to him.

"What happened with my father?"

"Oh, we were just two old chums chatting."

"Adam—"

"I decided it was time to talk to him—man to man."

Elaine's eyes grew wide with alarm. "*You* decided?"

"Why else would I go? You didn't think he'd invite me, did you?"

She looked anxious. "What did you say?"

"I told him that I loved you and wanted what's best for you."

Elaine stared at him in cold silence.

"What's wrong?" Adam asked. "It's true. I'm not ashamed of my feelings for you. Even if you're ashamed of me."

She eyed him carefully. "We'll talk more when you aren't wallowing in self-pity."

"I'm not wallowing in self-pity," he said, and his pout betrayed him.

"I know how you are when you get like this. Anything I say now would be subject to misinterpretation."

He chuckled. "*Subject to misinterpretation.* You sound like your father."

"I wish you hadn't spoken to him. I wish you'd left it with me."

"I've left it with you for the past ten years. He hasn't changed. He hasn't budged an inch."

"You don't know him."

"I think I know him very well now, thank you. He made himself perfectly clear."

She slid out of the booth and stood next to him. "Come on."

Adam stood up and swayed a little. *Never drink on an empty stomach,* he thought. "Where are we going?"

"For a walk. I can't think for all the smoke in here."

They walked out and across the car park to the adjoining meadow where they often strolled. The sun was headed for the horizon and Adam wondered where the afternoon had gone. The birds in the trees called to them like a lamentation.

A deep sigh escaped from her.

How far they walked, he wasn't sure. They weren't on their usual path and she had taken some unfamiliar turnings along the way. They went through a gate he didn't recognize. Only when the old chapel was suddenly before him did he realize where they were.

"Ah," he said. He hadn't been here for years. Vines claimed part of the crumbling building now. The area was dense with browns and greens, a pathway gone, a fallen tree lying where they once played. The leaves were thick as a cushion under his feet. They sat down on a log.

"Adam," Elaine said softly and touched his face. "I love you. You *must* understand that."

He wanted to believe it. He pulled her close for a hard and passionate kiss, as if he could imprint himself upon her, brand her as his alone, and forever put the matter to rest. She yielded, as if she understood. The kiss became a series of kisses, breathless and yearning.

"What are we doing?" she asked, more of a gasp than anything.

He thought she was asking about them, their future together, and pressed himself against her in answer. Her arms came around him and they seemed to melt into one another with kisses and clumsy touching and then they were no longer on the log but on the soft cushion of leaves.

Somewhere in his mind he heard something like the wail of an air-raid siren, a warning, but he ignored it. There was no running from this. Let the bombs fall, let the consequences happen as they will. This was inevitable, he thought. Inevitable. They belonged together. He willed it in his mind and heart—and it was so.

Their love was secure now, as if hidden away and locked up and only they had the key now. Her parents nor her friends could touch it now.

He had misjudged *her*, though. The final betrayal came from her.

SITTING AT HIS DESK, THE AIR CONDITIONER BREATHING DOWN HIS NECK, Adam held up a ticket—his passage on the *Georgic*, a Cunard ocean liner that had taken him from Southampton to New York on the 26th of June, 1954.

Julie had returned from Washington, D.C., with a job offer from an old friend of hers with Anderson & Wyatt Printers. She thought it was a great opportunity for him, and a chance to escape the country with Elaine. It was Adam's one last hope. He would go to Stonebridge for their Mill House rendezvous and propose.

It was going to be one of those decisive moments Father John had occasionally talked about. Elaine would be surprised, yes, but she would have to make her decision. There would be no excuses left—no reasons not to accept—unless her father was right and she didn't really love him after all. This would be the day when he'd know for certain one way or the other.

In his heart Adam had believed that she loved him and would accept his proposal. If he'd been a rich man, he'd have bet his fortune on it.

The shock of what he saw when he arrived in Stonebridge was so devastating, so crushing, that he couldn't leave fast enough. Gerard had won. Adam's humiliation was complete.

Even now he felt his heart constrict. He didn't want to think about it, to relive it. He'd had enough. Those last few days and the betrayal that had led him to go to America alone was too much. He could taste the bitterness of having wasted so much time on her. Perhaps it was the one feeling that would never go away, no matter how hard he tried to put everything behind him. He wasn't so strong after all.

No, much better to think of that final moment, the epilogue, as he stood on the deck of the *Georgic* and looked down on the dock, at the people waving farewell. He saw her pushing her way through the crowd. But it was too late. The boat had set sail. She stopped and looked up, scanning the faces along the rail. She saw him. He knew she did. She raised her hand as if she could command the boat to halt where it was. She called to him.

What did she think she could say to him? Did she really believe she could assuage her guilt with a few words of apology, an explanation, more deception? Why would he give her the chance?

He had turned away and never looked back.

Mr. Packer was right after all. Value nothing.

Adam dropped the *Georgic* ticket and the book of matches into the trash.

CHAPTER
FIVE

NICHOLAS PACED AROUND HIS TWO-ROOM APARTMENT IN ALEXANDRIA, Virginia, brooding angrily about his grandfather. *Shredding those letters was not the end of it*, he thought. *Not by a long shot.*

He felt he'd been coldcocked by the old man and deeply resented it. So now he paced, praying about the sinfulness of his resentment and thinking about what he might do next to find out what those letters really meant to his grandfather.

The soles of his sneakers squeaked against the hardwood floor as he took several steps, spun, and returned again. The apartment seemed to have shrunk somehow; he felt closed in and hot. He opened a window and turned on the small box fan nearby. It didn't help. And for the first time as a student at Virginia Theological Seminary, Nicholas felt alone and wished he had stayed in one of the dorms "on the hill." He hadn't, but only because he didn't like dorm life, especially with everyone practicing their pastoral attentiveness on each other's lives—a drawback to seminary living. So he indulged himself by renting an apartment. He didn't know at the time that to live off the hill meant you either commuted because you couldn't afford to live on campus, or you were wealthy enough to afford your own place. The rest of the students quickly discovered that he fell in the latter category and rode him for it. Yet another perk of being a Powell.

He continued to pace. His grandfather had slammed one door closed by shredding those letters, but it was possible another door could be opened.

With only a vague idea of what he might do, he sat down at his desk in the corner of his living room. Booting up his computer, he logged on to the Internet and called up a search engine. He typed in the words *Arthur House, Stonebridge,* and a myriad of sites appeared containing the words "Arthur," "House," and "Stonebridge." Too many to look through them all. He tried various configurations on the words, then remembered to put quotes around the phrase "Arthur House" to help pinpoint it further. Several bed-and-breakfasts around North America and England appeared bearing the name "Arthur House." None were in Stonebridge itself. Finally, he stumbled upon a website for the National Trust in Britain and found a reference to an Arthur House in Stonebridge, Sussex. The description was terse—a Georgian house unmatched in its use of Italian art deco, blah, blah, blah . . . tours available by appointment only . . . blah, blah, blah . . . For more information, contact Serena Sanguinetti, and it gave a phone number and an e-mail address.

Before he could talk himself out of it, Nicholas typed a brief note to the e-mail address, asking if it was the home of Elaine. He felt stupid for not knowing a last name—would that cause suspicion?—but he didn't want to guess wrongly that her last name was also Arthur and figured he'd have to take a chance.

He hit the "send" button and off the message went.

When the box popped up on the screen to confirm the e-mail's departure, Nicholas suddenly doubted himself. What was he doing? Why was he persisting after his grandfather had told him that it was none of his business?

Well, it was too late now. Besides, being stubborn was a family trait. His family couldn't blame him for that. He'd inherited it from his grandfather.

"What's the worst thing that can happen?" he asked himself out loud.

"What?" Kathy asked.

Startled, Nicholas spun around in his chair. "Kathy!"

"You left the door open." She went straight to the window, closed it, then turned off the fan. "It's hot in here. Why don't you use your air conditioner?"

"Because it makes me too cold."

She disappeared around the corner. "Not if you set the thermostat properly, silly boy."

"But I like the air from outside."

"It's mostly exhaust fumes from the traffic." He heard the air conditioner kick to life. She returned to him and stood next to the desk. "What were you looking at? Supermodel web pages again?"

"Now, now," he cautioned her. "Don't put nasty ideas in my head. Half the guys I know at seminary are addicted to that stuff."

"Then what were you doing?" she persisted. "Why did you ask about the worst thing that can happen?"

He considered sidestepping the question. But Kathy was shrewd and always knew when he was being evasive. "I sent an e-mail to Arthur House in Stonebridge, England," he confessed.

Her lower lip disappeared under her front teeth as she tried to remember the significance of that name. "Arthur House?"

"It was on the back of some letters I found in Grandad's archives."

"Your grandfather *destroyed* those letters."

Nicholas's mouth dropped open and he stood up. "How do you know about the letters? Did you talk to him?" It wouldn't have surprised Nicholas at all.

"His secretary."

"His secretary!" Nicholas pressed his hand against his forehead. "Is there anyone and anything you *don't* know?"

"Yes. I don't know why you're so determined to pry into your grandfather's past, especially when he told you to mind your own business."

"What'd you expect him to say?" He shoved his hands into his pockets and looked around for his wallet. "Where do you want to eat?"

"Don't change the subject, mister." She was clearly cross with him.

"Look, something happened to him—something that I believe is the key to his whole miserable personality—and I want to find out what that is." He found his wallet on top of the small television and scooped it up.

"Nicholas, it's *none of your business.*"

"But it is! Like I told you this afternoon. It's a chain reaction. His dysfunctions have become my father's dysfunctions which are now my own. To unlock my grandfather's past could help to free us all from . . . from . . . ." He couldn't find the right phrase and lost his momentum.

"He's a sweet man and I adore him," Kathy said as if it was the final word on the subject.

"He's sweet to you and a handful of others, but to most of us he's cold, calculating, manipulative—"

"You're being overdramatic."

"Am I? When he put those letters into the shredder, do you know what he said to me? Well, of course you do. His secretary must have told you."

"Don't get snippy."

"He said, and I quote, 'To succeed in life, you must learn to value nothing. Otherwise, someone else will always have the upper hand.' I wish you could have seen the expression on his face when he said it. Moses holding the Ten Commandments never looked so smug."

"So he throws out a few platitudes every now and then. Have you listened to yourself lately?"

"Now who's getting snippy?"

She took a few steps toward the door and he started to follow. But then she turned to him again. "Why are you reacting like this? Why is it such a big deal to you? They were personal letters about an unhappy breakup. Do *you* still have the letters from your old relationships?"

"In fact, I do."

She looked surprised. "You do?"

"Sure. In a box somewhere."

"Why?"

"Because they represent a part of my life. A part that was very important to me at one time."

"But that part is *finished*, Nicholas. And when it's finished, you're supposed to let go. Most normal people do. That's why I haven't kept any of my letters."

Nicholas shifted his weight from one foot to the other. He had to choose his words carefully. He knew that this was one of those pivotal conversations that could wreck their evening if he wasn't careful. "I don't believe people can simply cut off the past like that. The things that have happened to me are now part of my journey—part of the flow of my life. I wouldn't be who I am now without those things. So I keep letters and reminders of who I once was so I can trace who I'm becoming."

"You got that from a Hallmark card."

He shrugged. "God will be very upset to hear you say that."

"What?"

"I got the idea from him."

Her hands went onto her hips, daring him to explain.

"What is the Old Testament but a collection of books, stories, poetry, and letters to help us remember the journey of God's people?"

"I wouldn't equate our old love letters with the Bible."

"No, certainly not in quality or importance, but they're similar. They're just like the signposts and altars that God commanded Israel to set up on their travels. Why? So they'd remember what he did for them. So they wouldn't forget who they were and who they were becoming."

She looked at him with disbelief. "You're going to try to justify your obsession about your grandfather with Scripture?"

He gave her a weak smile. "It's all I have."

"I'm really worried about you."

"I'm hungry. Let's go eat," he said.

THEY SAT IN THEIR USUAL BOOTH AT ARISTOTLE'S DINER, A POPULAR restaurant near the seminary. It was on odd place, really, a strange collision of cultures. Overhead the speakers played popular songs as rendered by a Greek mandolin band. Yet the walls were covered with wallpaper murals depicting scenes of Americana: an antebellum Southern mansion complete with columns and a steamboat on the river behind it; a lush Colonial garden; a New England fishing village; a country bridge leading to a distant farmhouse. Ceiling fans turned slowly like something out of *Casablanca*. The waitresses were Asian, African, and Indian. The specialty was Greek pizza, complete with the gyro meat, feta cheese, and garlic.

They ordered the Greek pizza.

"Let me put it another way," he said, resuming the conversation.

"I thought we finished," she said. "Can't you leave well enough alone?"

He couldn't. "You're an English Lit major, right? Think about Dickens. Think about *A Christmas Carol*."

"It's too hot."

"How is Scrooge redeemed?" he asked.

Her eyes narrowed as if she might not answer his question. But then she seemed to resign herself to his stubbornness. "By Jacob Marley."

"Who does what?"

She sighed loudly. "He serves as the herald for the Ghosts of Christmas Past, Present, and Future."

"Right."

The waitress, an attractive Nigerian woman, brought their drinks.

When she was gone, Nicholas continued: "And through them, Scrooge gets to see the events that brought him to his current condition, what his current condition actually is in the context of his world, and what that condition will lead to if he doesn't repent."

"Neatly summarized, Reverend Powell. I'll give you an 'A' for the class."

"Not so fast. Scrooge repents and then what happens to him?"

"He buys a very large turkey."

"He regains his humanity. He is *redeemed* by returning to his world and taking part in it once again." Nicholas leaned back in his chair, satisfied that he'd made his case.

Kathy picked at the floating ice with her straw. "So what does this have to do with your grandfather?"

"I am his Ghost of Christmas Past," he said.

Kathy groaned. "I'm afraid to ask. Just *how* are you the Ghost of Christmas Past?"

"I'm going to explore my grandfather's past to figure out his present. I'm going to help create the environment by which he'll change—or God'll change him."

Kathy sipped her soda. "One problem. Your grandfather isn't Ebenezer Scrooge."

"He's close enough," Nicholas said sourly.

Kathy shook her head.

"Consider my grandfather's life," he said. "When he's dead, how will people remember him?"

"As a successful businessman," she replied instantly.

"And?"

Kathy shrugged.

"You see? You can't think of anything else. It's all about business. No one in my family would call him a 'good father' or a 'good grandfather.' No one would venture that he was anything resembling a kind or generous man, unless he had something to gain from the effort. And what about the really important things like faith and service to God?"

"Calm down, Nicholas, you've made your point."

"No, I haven't. You're just tired of listening to me."

"True," she replied with a devilish smile.

Nicholas refused to be charmed. "Don't get me wrong. I love my grandfather. Which is why it grieves me to see him cut off from God, cut off from his humanity. I want to help him find his way back. It's all I want for him. Maybe discovering those letters will help—digging up an incident from his past when he actually had feelings in his heart for something other than his business or himself. Don't you see how remarkable it is? He once *loved* a woman named Elaine."

"How do you know that?"

"Why else would he react like he did and destroy the letters? A man only does that when he was in love—and that love has been rejected."

She gazed at him thoughtfully for a moment. He didn't know whether she was annoyed or endeared to him. "You're a real marshmallow when you get like this."

"This isn't some romantic quest," he said. "Think about it, Kathy. What if this is *God* at work? What if God wanted me to find that box?"

"You're not serious, Nicholas."

"Why not? Don't you believe that God is involved in everything that happens to us?"

"Well . . . yes . . ."

"Then why don't you believe that God is in this, too?"

"I believe that God is," she said. "I'm just not convinced about *your* role. If he's trying to reach your grandfather, what makes you so sure he wants you involved?"

Nicholas shrugged. That possibility hadn't occurred to him.

Their pizza arrived and they ate in silence.

THE NEXT MORNING NICHOLAS CHECKED HIS E-MAILS. ONE WAS WAITING from Serena Sanguinetti at Arthur House. She wrote:

> Elaine Arthur is the owner of this house, if that is the Elaine you mean. But appointments for a private tour should be directed to me. Sincerely, Serena.

Nicholas stared at the words on the screen. Elaine Arthur. Elaine. It couldn't be a coincidence.

He was on his feet again, pacing around in his T-shirt, jogging shorts, and thick white socks. He scratched at his unwashed hair. Elaine Arthur. Was that her maiden name? Was she an old maid? Is it possible that she never got over Adam and has been living alone all these years in the family home?

He returned to the keyboard, unsure what to do next.

Should he write back for more information about her? No—that would raise *a lot* of suspicion.

What if he wrote back and inquired if it's the same Elaine who once knew Adam Powell? He could explain that he's Adam's grandson, putting together a retrospective for Adam's retirement and hoped to get some good wishes from Adam's old friends in England.

He hit the "reply" button and typed words to that effect.

He hesitated.

His e-mail might upset Elaine, he thought. If their parting was so painful, then it could hurt her to bring it up, or embarrass her if her family had never heard of Adam. But on the other hand, it might be a source of joy to hear about someone she once so very clearly cared about.

Yes, that was reasonable.

He paused again.

Maybe he should ask Kathy.

"No," he said out loud. She wouldn't approve. She'd tell his father or, worse, his grandfather. He had to decide this one on his own.

Typing a few more lines politely asking for their help, Nicholas expressed his appreciation and hit the "send" button.

As he showered and prepared to drive over to Maryland, he couldn't help but wonder again about what he was doing. Kathy's challenge came back to him. Even if God is at work somehow, was it a given that *he* be involved?

CHAPTER SIX

MONDAY, THE 5TH OF JULY

LAINEY SAT ON A HARD WOODEN PEW THREE ROWS BACK FROM THE lectern of St. Mark's in Stonebridge. She leaned forward onto the back of the pew in front of her. To an observer, she might have appeared to be praying. She wasn't. She was looking at the ornate marble altar and gold screen far ahead of her, beyond the chocolate-colored choir stalls. Statues of Jesus and the saints stood in witness to the empty pews. "In this place I will give peace," said the inscription carved into the walnut base of the altar.

It was dark and cool and the rain drummed like fingers on the roof of the church. The smell of flowers filled the air and Lainey realized that there were still several baskets of flowers placed strategically around the nave. Left over from Uncle Gerard's funeral, no doubt. Amazing that they would still smell so fresh after three days.

She'd been to this church with her grandmother many times over the years. She respected its beauty, if not its faith, and had participated in the liturgy with a vague sense of distance, of not belonging. She mouthed the words and went through the motions of sitting, kneeling, standing, and singing. But that's all they were: motions. She felt as if she were trying to perform a dance routine that everyone else knew by heart and she didn't. But she did it anyway to please her grandmother.

Father Gilbert said good-bye to the last elderly couple who'd come for the noon prayer service. He then closed the side doors, shrinking the light in the nave into gray slits.

Lainey liked Father Gilbert. He had quite an unusual reputation, having come to the faith as a detective from Scotland Yard. Lainey once heard that he had spent time in a monastery as a mystic, too. Some said he was "gifted" in his discernment of people—almost as if he could read minds. She had no idea where the line between truth and gossip was found. All she knew was that he seemed to care deeply about his parishioners and had been to see her grandmother earlier in the day.

Father Gilbert signaled to Lainey with one of his large hands. "Would you like to come back to my office or are you comfortable here?" he asked in a soft but full baritone.

"We can talk here," she replied.

He scooted into the pew in front of her, sitting sideways so that his large frame was facing her. He gazed at her with eyes that seemed too narrow somehow, as if he was squinting to look inside of her. He pushed one of his hands through his thick disheveled hair, salt-and-peppered and unfashionably long. Yet he was handsome and exuded an odd mix of strength and vulnerability.

"Isn't it unusual for you to be in Stonebridge on a weekday?" he asked. "Or did you stay on after Gerard Sommersby's funeral?"

"I decided to take an extra day off," she said.

"You've been visiting your grandmother over the past few days, haven't you?"

"Yes. I've been staying with my parents, but I've dropped over every day."

"And?"

"I'd like to think she's improving. At least she's not still lying in bed all the time."

"She was sitting in the garden when I saw her this morning."

"Serena said she's been out of bed quite a lot over the past day or so. Scares her half to death."

"What do you mean?" he asked.

"Oh, you know, Serena will be tidying up and then suddenly have the feeling that she's being watched. She'll look up and my grandmother will be standing there looking at her. Serena says it's giving her the creeps. She's like a ghost." Lainey remembered her grandmother's pale face and the curtains blowing like death's veil. "She certainly looks like one. But she never says anything. Once or twice she has started to cry and simply gone back to her room."

Father Gilbert shook his head sadly.

"But the fact that she's up must be a sign of improvement," Lainey said, then frowned. "She could have come to the funeral."

"Not necessarily. People in her condition can still function physically—go through the marginal motions of life—but that doesn't mean they're well on the inside. The funeral may have been too much for her."

"You said 'people in her condition.' You mean people who are depressed."

"She shows all the classic symptoms," he replied. "Her withdrawal, her tiredness, sleeplessness, her lack of concentration and indecisiveness, regret, guilt—"

"Slow down, please. Regret and guilt?"

"When I tried to get her to tell me what's been on her mind, she answered in vague phrases. She spoke of regretting all the wasted years."

"Wasted years!" Lainey thought of all the activity that had surrounded her grandmother's life for as long she could remember. "My grandmother?"

"Apparently so. She also said something about feeling guilty, about her need to forgive."

"Guilty for what? Forgive who?"

"She wouldn't say."

Lainey mused on this for a moment. "Did she mention someone called Powell?"

"No. Who is that?"

"An old boyfriend, I think."

"She didn't mention any names."

"You know, I think my uncle Gerard triggered this problem. We don't know what he said or did, but he's probably the one she needs to forgive." She looked toward the altar, where Uncle Gerard's coffin had sat only a few days before. "It's too late for that now," she said quietly.

"It's too late to offer him her forgiveness—if he did something to hurt her—but it's never too late to forgive him in her heart. People can be eaten alive because they can't forgive. I had one parishioner who nearly went suicidal because he couldn't find it in his heart to forgive his father, a man who'd been dead for twelve years. Only when he could forgive his father could he find some semblance of hope in his life."

"So she didn't tell you what happened with Uncle Gerard."

"No. But I got a sense that she doesn't blame him alone for whatever it was," Father Gilbert said. "She indicated that she also needs to be forgiven."

"By whom and for what?"

"I don't know. When I asked her to explain, she got angry."

"Angry?"

"As if she was annoyed with me for not already understanding what was wrong with her. That's not uncommon when someone is depressed."

Lainey's gaze went up to the statue of Jesus at the altar. He was dressed in robes of white and purple and his arms were outstretched. She wished she could go to him, get him to make some sense of this problem. He was supposed to be the great healer, right? Did the Gospels record anyone going to him to be healed of a broken heart or a troubled mind? Turning back to Father Gilbert, she asked, "If she won't talk about what's troubling her, then what are we supposed to do?"

"Those of us who are inclined to pray are certainly doing that. And I've cleared my schedule to visit her every morning. I hope she'll eventually let me further in on her darkness."

"Darkness," Lainey repeated softly.

"Yes. She's skirted the edges of it before, but now she's in the thick of it."

Again, Lainey looked at Father Gilbert with obvious perplexity. "Skirted the edges of it? What are you talking about?"

"For as long as I've known her, your grandmother has struggled with depression."

"What? That's impossible."

"Why is it impossible?"

"Because she's a strong woman!" Lainey protested, upset. "She always has been. Obviously you don't know her as well as you think."

Father Gilbert smiled patiently at her. "Of course I don't presume to know her as well as you."

Lainey felt her cheeks turn crimson at his rebuke. "I'm sorry."

"Your grandmother isn't as tough as she'd like everyone to think. She's subject to the same doubts and worries that most of us have."

"She never showed them to me."

"No, I don't suppose she would."

"But why not?" Lainey pleaded. "We never asked her to be Super-woman."

Father Gilbert rubbed his forefinger on the wood of the pew. "At some point in her life she decided she had to be strong for those around her. I don't know when or why—but she did. And she's been playing that role ever since."

"If my grandmother has been playing a role, then she played it to perfection. Now tell me about her darkness."

"Whatever is troubling her now has veiled her ability to see clearly. The fight has gone out of her. She's given in to it."

"Do you think she's suicidal?"

"I don't know. I'm speaking as a priest, not a psychiatrist. But we'd be fools to ignore the symptoms."

Lainey sat back in the pew. "You're not very encouraging."

"Sorry. I thought you'd want me to be honest with you."

"Yes." Lainey lowered her head onto her crossed arms, still resting on the back of the pew. "But I'm terribly frustrated."

Father Gilbert tipped his head up toward one of the stained glass windows. "Lainey, I don't know what your profession of faith is—if you have any at all—so what I'm about to say may not make any sense to you."

"Please say it anyway, Father."

"If I were to offer words of encouragement, I'd tell you not to despair."

"Why not?"

"Because I believe that God never wastes anything. Good experiences or bad, he is at work somehow. Sometimes you can see it clearly, there's no doubt he's right in the middle of things. Other times it seems as if he's working around the edges."

"Now try to say that same thing to someone who isn't a churchgoer," she challenged him.

"That's a bit more difficult." He rubbed his chin thoughtfully and tapped his lips with his thick forefinger. He gestured to the stained glass windows. "It's like looking at one of these windows. If you stand very close to one, you might see colors that look random, without purpose or design. Then you move back and realize that they're not random or without purpose at all. They form a much bigger picture—an intended image by the artist."

Lainey gazed at one of the stained glass windows—Jesus holding a child—and tried to take in what Father Gilbert was saying. "You're saying that what's happening to my grandmother is part of some cosmic bigger picture?"

"I think we're all part of a bigger picture, though I wouldn't call it cosmic." Father Gilbert smiled ever so slightly. "Have you read the Bible?"

"Not really."

"When you go back to your mother's house, have a look at hers. I know she has one. Jesus talks about this idea quite a bit. So does St. Paul and the rest of the apostles. When they were in the midst of great tragedy and suffering, they were able to cope because they saw the big picture. They knew that God was at work in all things."

"Are you preaching to me?" Lainey asked playfully.

Father Gilbert shrugged. "Whatever it takes."

"But what's the picture, Father? What are we supposed to be seeing? What if my grandmother is seeing it and that's what has thrown her into depression. Have you thought of that?"

"Unless there's a physiological reason, most people who wind up depressed get that way because they're looking only at the tiny pieces of the picture, their immediate circumstances, and can't make sense of it. They're stuck in the moment, trapped in their own perspective, and can't see beyond it. I believe that seeing the big picture—looking at things from God's perspective—brings freedom, even joy. But it isn't easy. When the waves are crashing around the boat, it's hard to believe that Jesus can calm the storm. But he can. He did, in fact, if the Gospels are to be believed."

"So how do we get my grandmother out of this moment when she won't even tell us what it is?"

"We pray that she will—or God will show us another way. Perhaps through someone else."

She eyed him skeptically. "Fifty years after the fact? No. I'm afraid the secret went to the grave with Uncle Gerard—and will go to the grave with my grandmother, too, if we don't do something soon."

GUILT AND REGRET . . . REGRET AND GUILT . . .

Lainey turned them over and over in her mind as she walked from the church, through Stonebridge, and down the narrow lane to her parents' house. Father Gilbert's words were a bombshell to her. To think that her grandmother had been putting on a show of strength all those years . . .

Overhead a canopy of thick branches formed a short tunnel, nature's dividing line between the town and the rural area that stretched out to the east. She loved the momentary darkness that then gave way to the golden light on the other side—the fields of green and the four-legged cumulus clouds of wool drifting over those fields like shifting weather patterns, bleating as they went. On the other side of the lane were the houses, "newer" homes built in the late fifties with fat beams arranged in the Tudor style that had been popular then. Her parents owned the third house on the right.

She paused at the end of the driveway and wondered what her grandmother could possibly feel guilty about. Had she hurt the mysterious Powell, or had she been hurt by him thanks to whatever Uncle Gerard had done? Lainey could easily imagine her grandmother as a recklessly beautiful girl who had destroyed the hearts of many suitors. But that didn't line up with her personality. She seemed so levelheaded and beyond such whimsical behavior. Or had that levelheadedness come later? Perhaps she'd hurt one too many young men, and that's why she feels regret now. Or was the regret tied to something else?

Lainey shook her head. Regret didn't make sense, because it was Uncle Gerard who had done something—something her grandmother had known nothing about until the other day. So what was it? What could Uncle Gerard have possibly done to put her into such a tailspin?

He *saved her*, he'd said. Presumably from Powell. But how—and why would it upset her grandmother *now*?

She strolled up the twenty yards or so of driveway, past the obligatory garden gnome in the center of the front garden, and onto the short stone porch. As she reached for the door handle, her mother yanked it open.

"Where have you been? Dr. Gilthorpe is waiting. He was just about to leave."

Lainey glanced back at the drive, only now seeing the unfamiliar Volvo sitting there. "Sorry. I didn't realize."

Her mother whispered as they walked down the front hall. "He stopped by unannounced. The house is a wreck. I've given him a gallon of tea waiting for you to come." They turned left into the sitting room, and Dr. Gilthorpe pulled his huge frame out of the pink wingback chair and extended a hand to Lainey. "Hello, Lainey," he said softly. He had platinum hair and a full beard, making him look like Santa Claus. His eyes even twinkled.

"I hope you didn't make a special trip," she said. "I thought we were going to meet you in your office."

"I was in the area," he explained. "Just as well to drop in, I thought. Though your mother was put out. No time to polish the floors," he teased.

"I was not put out!" Margaret Bishop protested, clearly put out.

Lainey's father sat on the sofa and winked at her. He was dressed as if he'd been working in the garden when the doctor arrived. His cheeks were flushed and his graying hair was matted from sweat.

Lainey sat down next to her father on the sofa and wasted no time getting to the point. "What can you tell me about my grandmother?"

Gilthorpe's expression seemed to change rapidly, like the shadows of clouds moving across a rugged field, as if he didn't know how to frame the answer. Then he said directly, "There's no doubt in my mind that Elaine is suffering from depression. Perhaps it's related to an event, as you've described, or it's biochemical. I don't know for certain. But she needs help. More help than I can give."

Lainey thought her mother might speak up, but she sat with a deer-in-the-headlights look, as if someone had just spilled red wine on the sofa. Her father grunted thoughtfully.

"What kind of help?" Lainey asked.

"Medication, at the very least. Regular counseling. Hospitalization, if necessary."

Lainey frowned. "Do you think she's suicidal?"

"I don't believe so, but I wouldn't take the chance that she *isn't*."

Suddenly Lainey's mother stood and retrieved the teacups as she spoke. "Good heavens. Listen to this nonsense. Medication. Suicide. This is absurd. My mother doesn't need anything except a few days' rest. That's all." Her lip was quivering and the china cups were rattling on the saucers as she left the room.

Dr. Gilthorpe nodded sympathetically to Lainey's father. "This is difficult, Tim. I know."

"Are you sure it isn't Alzheimer's?" Tim Bishop asked.

"As sure as I can be of anything at this point. At her age, it can be hard to distinguish between the symptoms of being old and the symptoms of a mental illness."

"She is *not* mentally ill!" Lainey's mother shouted from the kitchen.

"What do we do now?" asked Lainey.

"I want to talk to Dr. Harrison."

Lainey lifted her shoulders. "Who is he?"

"He was your grandmother's doctor before I came along. Maybe there's something in her history that'll be helpful." Dr. Gilthorpe pulled a small sheet of paper out of his pocket and handed it to Lainey's father. "Here's a short list of qualified doctors who'll be helpful. I wouldn't try to prescribe anything myself. So you need to get Elaine to one of these doctors for evaluation. Though I'm sure that getting her there will be a problem. She won't do it willingly."

"Why not?" Lainey asked, already knowing the answer. "Is she afraid?"

"No."

"Then why?"

"I don't think she wants to be helped. She doesn't *want* to get better."

LAINEY FELT RESTLESS AND COULDN'T BEAR THE THOUGHT OF SITTING around the house. There were too many questions to be answered. Shouting good-bye from the front door, she stepped into the afternoon heat and strolled back into Stonebridge. She went directly to the only bookshop on High Street. Considering how small the shop was, it seemed to carry a lot of books on a variety of subjects. She went to a section identifying "Self-Help & Personal Care" and scanned the titles to find the ones dealing with mental health or, more specifically, depression. There were three on depression and one that served as a guide for those who have a depressed family member. It was a large volume, filling Lainey with despair that this battle—if it could be called a battle—wouldn't be quick or easy. And for all she knew it was a battle that wouldn't be won. But she had to try.

There was a light touch on her shoulder and she turned to face Serena.

"It looks as if we had the same idea," Serena said, gesturing to the book.

Lainey caught the sadness in Serena's eyes and was struck by the realization that she—not Lainey—had more of a burden to bear than anyone. Serena lived at Arthur House and had to watch over Elaine constantly. *Constantly.* Lainey frowned. "Where is my grandmother?"

Serena looked puzzled. "She's at home."

"But if you're here, who is with her?"

"No one. She's sleeping, so I thought—"

"*Serena,*" Lainey said, alarmed. She threw the book back on the shelf and took hold of Serena's arm. "You can't leave her." She firmly led her through the shop.

"What in the world is wrong with you?" Serena asked loudly. Heads turned. An older woman behind the counter glared as they went through the front door.

"Where is your car?" Lainey asked.

Serena pointed to the car park behind the shopping area. With her arm crooked through Serena's, Lainey pressed forward.

"Lainey, calm down."

"Don't you understand? She's *depressed*—perhaps even suicidal."

"Suicidal? No one said anything to me about . . ." She gasped. "Good heavens—"

They found Serena's car—a sporty little Fiat—and climbed in. Serena looked as if she might burst into tears as she started the ignition and tore out of the lot.

How do people kill themselves these days? How would her grandmother do it?

Lainey imagined the worst. Slashed wrists, knotted sheets hanging from the upstairs banister, a limp hand next to a tipped pill bottle.

Within five minutes they were pulling to a stop near the front door of the house. The stones crunched beneath their feet as they raced from the car. Serena fumbled for her keys, nearly dropped them once, then got the lock turned. Inside the front hall, they instinctively stopped—each knowing how distressing it might be to Elaine if they both burst into her room in a panic. They took off their shoes to keep the soles from tapping against the hardwood floor and walked softly down the hall to Elaine's bedroom. The door to the bedroom was partially closed. The entire house seemed to be holding its breath. The blood pounded in Lainey's ears.

Serena allowed Lainey to take the lead, hanging a step back as they reached the doorway. The drapes were pulled, the room washed in a dark gray. As her eyes adjusted to the light, Lainey could see that the bed was empty. She turned to Serena, who indicated that she'd look outside if Lainey wanted to search inside. Lainey nodded. As they were about to leave, they heard water rush through the pipes in the wall. The adjoining door to the bathroom opened and Elaine drifted like a ghost across the room to her bed. She'd didn't look at Lainey or Serena. She seemed oblivious to their presence.

"Gran?" Lainey whispered.

Her grandmother didn't turn, didn't respond. Slipping under the covers, she rolled over with her back away from them. Lainey circled the bed to see if there was any indication that she'd taken something—for an overdose—or anything else with which she might hurt herself. Nothing. Lainey looked in the bathroom. Nothing out of order on the shelves, nothing in her medicine cabinet that could hurt her, no empty pill bottles in the bin. All seemed well.

Back in the hallway Lainey closed her eyes and took a deep breath. "Put the kettle on, will you, Serena?"

IT TOOK TWO CUPS OF TEA TO SOOTHE THEIR NERVES.

"I wish people would tell me these things," Serena said. "Someone should have called. Never in my wildest dreams would I think of Mrs. Arthur as a possible suicide. Never."

"I'm sorry," Lainey said softly. "I should have called you right after we talked to Dr. Gilthorpe."

Serena shuddered, drawing her arms around her. "If anything had happened to her . . ."

The rest of her statement hung in the air between them.

"This is going to take some thought," Lainey said, then drained the last of her tea. "We need more information. We need a plan. You can't watch her alone." Her mind raced with the options. "I could take an extended vacation, a leave of absence. I could come and live here for a while, until she gets on the other side of this problem."

"*If* she gets on the other side," Serena said.

Lainey looked at her as her heart sank. "If."

"I should talk to Dr. Gilthorpe," said Serena. "I have a dozen questions about what I should do until she gets medication or help or is institutionalized or—"

"She won't be institutionalized," Lainey said firmly.

Serena didn't answer, but gazed at Lainey with a *you can think that if you want* expression.

Lainey gazed back at her defiantly. "She *won't* be institutionalized."

Serena held up her hands in surrender.

Putting her face in her hands, Lainey groaned, running her fingers through her hair, around to the back of her neck, and then forward to her chin. "I'm sorry," she said, not sure what she was apologizing about.

"It's all right." Serena came around behind her and began to massage her shoulders. "We'll figure this out. But you won't help your grandmother if you're a wreck, too." Serena's fingers worked nimbly on the knotted muscles and Lainey began to feel like melted butter.

"You're right. This is a bad time to panic."

"You can panic later."

Lainey's head dropped onto her crossed arms. "Much later."

Serena stopped the massage with a small gasp. "Oh dear, I almost forgot!" she said.

Without lifting her head to look, Lainey could hear Serena pad out of the kitchen. She kept her eyes closed and wiggled her shoulders a little, as if to confirm that the muscles were still in working order. Serena padded back and there was the slap of paper on the countertop. Lainey looked up. A white sheet stared at her. She picked it up, looking to Serena for an explanation.

"You'll see," Serena said.

Lainey had to focus her eyes on the small inkjet print. It was an e-mail of some sort. Still unsure what she was looking at, her eyes scanned the page—then she sat upright as if she'd been electrically shocked by what she saw there.

Powell.

LAINEY AND SERENA WERE AT THE COMPUTER IN SERENA'S OFFICE. THE e-mail from Nicholas Powell was on the screen. Lainey read and reread it to see if there were any useful clues. It was terribly straightforward.

> Thank you for answering my last e-mail. I'm the grandson of a gentleman named Adam Powell. I believe he was friends with an Elaine Arthur when he lived in England (until 1954). I know it's a wild stab in the dark, but I thought that maybe it's the same Elaine Arthur as yours at Arthur House. I am putting together a collection of reminiscences and tributes to my grandfather for his impending retirement. If this is the right Elaine Arthur, would she be interested in sending a few words of greeting or good wishes?
>
> Sincerely, Nicholas Powell

"You said he first wrote a couple of days ago?"

"Yesterday morning. This came later."

"This is amazing," Lainey said, then tapped the screen. "But my grandmother wasn't Elaine *Arthur* until 1956. Adam Powell would have known her by her maiden name—*Holmes*."

"So?"

"So how did he know to contact her as Elaine Arthur?"

"You're right." Serena leaned forward to type onto the keyboard. "Maybe he didn't give her full name . . ." She navigated from one screen to another until she found the folder where all her e-mails were kept.

She pulled up an e-mail from Nicholas Powell, dated from the day before. It simply inquired if a woman named Elaine lived at Arthur House.

"That's also strange. To ask about an Elaine without giving the surname. But you gave her full name in your answer to him, right?"

Serena nodded. "Yes. It makes me feel foolish now. What if it was some sort of scam?"

"I might think so under different circumstances, but this . . . well, I don't know."

"Are you going to write back, or would you like me to?"

"I don't mind," Lainey replied, and began to type.

Dear Mr. Powell,

Thank you for contacting us about Adam Powell and his possible connection to Elaine Arthur. It would help for us to get more information, to be certain that we're talking about the right people. How did you find Elaine Arthur's name?

Lainey reread her words.

Serena *hmmed* thoughtfully. "He's bound to think it strange that Mrs. Arthur isn't writing back herself."

Lainey then wrote:

Mrs. Arthur is not in good health at the moment, so we don't want to ask her to write a greeting unnecessarily. Any further details would be much appreciated.

With thanks, Lainey Bishop.

She scanned the letter again. "What do you think?"

"It has all the charm of a late notice from the telephone company."

"Good. I don't want to give anything away."

"Why not? He may be the answer we need for your grandmother."

"He may be," Lainey conceded. "But I'm suspicious."

"Suspicious of what?"

"The timing of this e-mail. It's an enormous coincidence, don't you think?"

"Yes, it is. What's wrong with that?"

"It makes me nervous," she replied, fumbling for her words. "As if something is going on behind my back."

"That sounds awfully paranoid."

"Still . . . what are the chances that the grandson of Adam Powell—the very person we've been wondering about—just *happened* to write to us *now* about my grandmother?"

"I couldn't give you strict odds."

"They must be astronomical."

Serena pointed to the screen. "But it happened."

"Yes," Lainey said. "That's what makes me nervous."

"Is this you talking—or your mother?" Serena asked.

Lainey turned to face her. "Resorting to insults won't change my mind." She hit the "send" button and the e-mail disappeared into the wondrous workings of the Web.

"What time is it in America?" Lainey asked.

"Depends on what part. Their East Coast is five hours behind us, the West Coast is eight. I don't remember where they draw the lines in between."

Lainey glanced at her watch. It was a little after six in the evening. "So, if he's in New York, it's early in the afternoon."

"Right."

"Then we may hear back from him tonight."

NICHOLAS ARRIVED AT HIS APARTMENT AND WENT STRAIGHT TO HIS bedroom to get ready for bed. He slipped into a T-shirt and some jogging shorts, brushed his teeth, and then went back to the living room to turn off the lights. The mind-numbing exercise of compiling his grandfather's life had gone on the entire day—he'd worked twice as hard to make up for the long Fourth of July weekend—and left him exhausted. After that he had dinner with Kathy and then they went to a movie, a romantic comedy that Nicholas thought was neither romantic nor a comedy. Kathy seemed charmed by it and called him a snob for his disapproval.

The truth was, Nicholas only half watched the film. In his mind he kept thinking about his grandfather and those mysterious letters.

Too restless to sleep, he went to his computer and logged on to check his e-mails. There was one from "Arthurhouse" with a ".co.uk" server. A surge of adrenaline shot through him. Maybe this time it was a note from Elaine Arthur herself.

Dear Mr. Powell,

Thank you for contacting us about Adam Powell . . .

Nicholas reread the note twice, musing on its formality and distance and wondering who *Lainey Bishop* was. Presumably a relative. He decided to answer right away.

"How did you find Elaine Arthur's name?" she'd asked.

Drumming his fingers on the edge of the desk, he tried to decide how to reply. Should he tell the whole truth—how he'd found the unopened letters in a secret box and his grandfather had destroyed them? That sounded ridiculous. And it would certainly raise alarms.

Dear Miss Bishop . . .

Miss? What if she's *Mrs.* Bishop? So which should he assume, *Miss* or *Mrs.?*

"I hate this," he said out loud. *How are we supposed to address women these days? Ms.?*

Dear Lainey . . .

Do the British resent American informality? Who knew anymore? "Stop second-guessing yourself," he reproved himself. "Just write the letter."

I hope you don't mind if I call you Lainey. I have no idea how to address people anymore. Are you a Miss, Mrs., or Ms.? Whatever you are, thank you for responding to my e-mail.

To answer your question, I learned about Elaine from a few letters I found among my grandfather's keepsakes.

Was "keepsakes" too strong? Might it imply more than he intended? "Shut up and write," he said.

The letters didn't indicate her last name, but the address was 'Arthur House, Stonebridge.' I used that information to find Arthur House and, in turn, your e-mail address. If it's of any help, the letters were written in 1954 and addressed to my grandfather's former home in London. They were then forwarded to America, where he had moved.

Does that help at all? It would be helpful to confirm that the Elaine at Arthur House is the same person who wrote the letters. Maybe she'll remember them, if it's not too much trouble to ask her.

I'm sorry to hear that she isn't feeling very well. I hope she's up and around soon.

Sincerely, Nicholas

Looking over the e-mail, he was satisfied that he'd said as much as he needed to say. All of it was the truth. He hit the "send" button, logged off his computer, and went to bed.

It was some time before he was able to sleep. He pondered the name *Lainey,* which he recognized as a variation on *Elaine,* and wondered if the writer was a namesake. Maybe Elaine's daughter.

He dozed off with the name Lainey flitting around in his mind like a butterfly.

CHAPTER SEVEN

TUESDAY, THE 6TH OF JULY

DRESSED IN A THICK ROBE AND CARRYING A LARGE MUG OF COFFEE, Serena sat down at her computer and opened Nicholas's e-mail. She read it quickly and then forwarded it to Lainey's e-mail address in London. She dialed the number at Lainey's flat.

The phone rang several times before Lainey, sleepy voiced, picked up and growled a "hello."

"Nicholas Powell wrote back," Serena said.

Lainey came alive. "He did? Well, it took him long enough."

"Maybe he has a life," she chided her. "I've forwarded it to you."

"I only have one phone line in my flat. I have to hang up." And she did. Seven minutes later Lainey called back.

"Well?" Serena asked. "Are you Miss, Mrs., or Ms.?"

"I don't care about that. He has *letters*," she said with girlish excitement. "Keepsakes! Why would Adam Powell keep the letters unless . . ."

"Calm down, Lainey. Don't jump to conclusions."

"I'm going to write back to him now."

"And say what?"

"I don't know. I haven't had my coffee yet."

"Are you going to tell him what's really going on here?"

"Good heavens, no. What would I say? That my grandmother has lost her marbles and we think it has something to do with his grandfather?"

"That may be a decent place to start."

"And he'll never write to us again. Somehow I've got to get him to tell me a little about those letters without alarming him."

Serena glanced at the door just to be sure that Mrs. Arthur hadn't drifted in unawares. She lowered her voice. "Before you do, I was wondering . . ."

"Wondering what?"

"Should we tell your grandmother about this?"

Lainey hesitated. "Why?"

"It might help her. If this Adam Powell was so important to her, maybe it will pick up her spirits to hear from him."

The line hissed with the silence. "No. Not yet, Serena. I don't want her to know, especially if all of this leads to nothing. Or worse, it leads to something bad."

"What could be worse than the way things are now?"

"I don't know. But it worries me. I want more information."

"What kind of information?"

"I want to know what's in those letters!"

Dear Nicholas (fair is fair),

My grandmother's condition isn't fatal, as far as we know. But I thank you for your concern. I'm hesitant to approach her about your grandfather's retirement until we know more.

You wrote that the letters were sent to Adam Powell's former address in London. Do you know where, specifically? I know that Americans aren't renowned for their knowledge of geography, so I mean no offense when I explain that London is a very large city.

It would also be helpful to us if you'd make copies of the letters and send them to Arthur House. Or you could attach a scan of them to an e-mail. Her handwriting will most certainly tell us if we're barking up the right tree, or simply barking mad.

With thanks, Simply Lainey (not Miss, Mrs., or Ms.)

P.S. Please note the change of e-mail address. We decided that it would be better for you to write to me here.

"IT'S HER GRANDMOTHER!" HE SAID OUT LOUD. *THEN SHE MIGHT BE MY age, or thereabouts.*

He reread the e-mail and felt a hint of pleasure that she had called him by his first name. The cold formality of the previous e-mail had worried him, so the familiarity of this one gave him hope that he might have an "ally" on the other side of the Atlantic. He read through the letter once more, trying to glean what he could from what she'd said—and what she didn't say.

"No offense?" he laughed. *London is a very large city,* she said and she meant *no offense?*

He thought dismally, *The letters! How did I know she'd want the letters? Because I don't have them, that's why. Because it was the last thing I wanted them to ask about, that's why.* He leaned forward on his desk, his face only an inch or so away from the screen. "What am I going to do?"

Clasping his hands behind his head, he leaned back again and reread the e-mail.

They're awfully protective of Elaine, he thought. Is she so ill that they don't dare mention Adam's name to her? Or are they afraid that it might make her worse? Then again, this whole thing might be an annoying inconvenience to them. (But if that's true, then why did Lainey bother to write back?)

He wrote:

Dear Simply Lainey,

Is London large? I had no idea! I assumed that all of the cities and towns in England consisted of about twenty-seven people living in thatched huts and raising sheep. But thank you for meaning no offense. The answer is: Chiswick. The vicarage on Bedford Road, to be more exact.

Unfortunately I won't be able to send you copies or scans of the letters since we've had a mishap and they have been destroyed. But surely we have enough information now to know that Elaine Arthur once knew my grandfather. I know it's presumptuous to ask her to write a few words to him on the occasion of his retirement—for all I know the two of them parted on questionable terms—but I'd like to believe the best.

Sincerely, Nicholas

IN HER GRAY, FELT-COVERED CUBICLE AT CARPER & HOLLINGS, LAINEY stared at the computer screen. Nicholas had given her a little more information about Adam Powell. He had lived at a vicarage in Chiswick. But what did that mean? She'd have to ask.

The news about the letters was a disappointment. And a mystery. How on earth could they have been destroyed—especially if Nicholas only recently found them, as implied in his other e-mail?

With a guilty glance at the manuscript she was supposed to be proofreading, she pulled the computer keyboard closer and wrote:

Nicholas,

Ah, Chiswick! That's not far from my flat in Shepherd's Bush. And if he lived at the vicarage, should I assume he was a vicar?

I'm trying to imagine what kind of "mishap" could have destroyed the letters. They were walking across the street unescorted and were knocked down by a bus? You were using them to sharpen a lawn mower? They slipped from your hands and fell into a vat of acid?

Surely your grandfather could tell you whether his relationship with my grandmother was amicable or otherwise. Perhaps you could ask him directly?

Lainey

She reread the e-mail, nodded in approval of its tone, and sent it off. Since she had no idea of Nicholas's schedule or how long it would take him to answer, she turned back to her work—a novel about Jack the Ripper traveling to New York and murdering prostitutes there. Riveting stuff, to be sure. But she found it very hard to concentrate.

Nicholas was proving to have some personality. *Twenty-seven people in thatched huts and raising sheep.* She enjoyed that answer. Not too touchy, able to give back as good as he got.

The phone rang. *It's him,* she thought and then realized how ridiculous that was. Picking up, she gave her department and name. Without the warmth of any hellos and how-are-yous, Serena informed her that her grandmother had an appointment to see a psychiatrist that afternoon. Lainey's mother and Serena would take her.

"Have you told my grandmother?"

"Yes."

"What did she say?"

"Nothing. I honestly don't think she cares."

"Do you want me to come?"

"Only if you want to, but there's really no need," Serena replied. "We'll take her to the doctor, she won't say anything, and the doctor will prescribe some medication that I'll have to force down her throat. It'll be easy."

"Oh, good," Lainey said. For the tenth time that day she wondered if maybe she should take a leave of absence and move back to Stonebridge for a while. She hated to be so far away. "Let me know what happens," Lainey said and they hung up.

A symbol appeared on her computer indicating that she had an e-mail waiting. She went to the file and opened it up.

It was from Nicholas. She stole a glance at her watch, wondering what time it was where he lived—*where did he live?* If he was on the East Coast of the United States, it was eight in the morning.

Dear Lainey,

No, my grandfather wasn't a vicar. Just the opposite, some might say. But he lived with a vicar at that house for several years after his parents were killed in the Blitz.

The work I'm doing for my grandfather's retirement is supposed to be a surprise. If I ask him questions about your grandmother, then he'll know I'm up to something. That's why I hoped your grandmother would help. Is she feeling better? Is she able to send a note to my grandfather for his party?

I have found London on a map and am startled. You're right, it is big! Two whole pages! I also found Shepherd's Bush. Brings to mind large fields and gambling sheep. Is that how it is?

Sincerely,
Nicholas

Lainey smiled and immediately wrote back:

Nicholas,

Your grandfather must have had quite a life in London, to have been there during the Blitz. Now I'm curious why you say he was "just the opposite" of a vicar. What do you mean by that cryptic phrase?

I'm afraid that my grandmother's condition hasn't changed, so we haven't been able to talk to her about your grandfather.

I hate to disappoint you, but Shepherd's Bush is a crowded, congested area with a lot of houses and flats. But it's near to Hammersmith, which is the headquarters of the publisher for whom I work. You won't find a sheep within miles of here, except the bits of ones they serve at the local kebab restaurants. And sheep don't gamble, by the way. They gambol.

Where do you live? We seem to be talking in real time right now.

Lainey

She sent off the e-mail and then wondered if it would be an indulgence to wait for his answer. For all she knew, he'd sent his last e-mail and then went away from his computer. Within minutes, however, an e-mail came back from him.

Dear Lainey,

I've heard about the betting shops you have in London, so naturally I assumed that the sheep . . . oh, never mind. So you work for a publishing house! Which one? My grandfather is the founder of a publishing house: Powell Publishing. What do you do for yours?

Since you asked, my grandfather has been/can be a very determined, aggressive, and stubborn man. Certainly not the stereotype of a vicar—and not the kind of person you'd expect to glean spiritual wisdom from. Business wisdom, maybe, but not spiritual.

I currently live in Virginia, but grew up in Maryland. I don't want to insult your intelligence, but Virginia and Maryland surround Washington, D.C. I assume you know where Washington, D.C., is.

May I ask what your grandmother's condition is?

Sincerely, Nicholas

Powell Publishing, Lainey thought. She'd definitely heard of them. Grabbing her mouse, she navigated out of the e-mail function and into the Internet server. She found a search engine and typed in "Powell Publishing." Within seconds, a listing of over a thousand sites sprung up. Many of them were useless, merely listing the word *Powell* or *Publishing*. But Powell Publishing itself had its own website. She clicked on that and went instantly to a corporate logo and a variety of menu choices for the company's products, customer service, and contact information. There wasn't anything about its history or Adam Powell himself. She went back to the search engine and tried another site. It contained a press release from the year before explaining that Powell Publishing had purchased another small publisher called Milestone Books.

Lainey scanned past the details of the purchase and found toward the bottom of the article a sidebar about Adam Powell. It explained that he was a Londoner who'd come to America as a printer in the mid-fifties and, within a decade, had become the founder and head of one of the fastest-growing publishing houses in the country. The article told little about the man, but chronicled the increasing fortunes of his company; how it had begun as a printing company with large government contracts, then acquired an editorial staff to develop manuscripts, mostly specialized technical books, which grew to a broader list of titles, and now it was number twelve in a list of the top twenty publishers in America.

As she read the article, she remembered another tidbit about Powell Publishing: Carper & Hollings had wanted to buy it at one time. She now felt stupid for not remembering the name of Adam Powell. But who could've guessed such a thing?

Lainey went back to Nicholas's e-mail and smiled at the jab at her about knowing where Virginia and Maryland were. The truth was that she knew they were somewhere in the middle of America's East Coast, but she would have failed an exam to say where exactly.

She looked at the screen with the expression of a chess player preparing for her next move. She could respond to the revelation about who Adam Powell was, but Nicholas had also asked directly about her grandmother. What should she say? She still didn't feel comfortable telling him yet, not while he hadn't told her how or why the letters were destroyed. There was something behind that. But what?

There's no diversion like a total diversion, she thought as she began to work the keyboard to reply.

Nicholas,

I work for Carper & Hollings Books as a copy editor. Nothing exciting, but it gets me close to books, which are a passion for me.

I know about Powell Books and never imagined that you were the grandson of THE Adam Powell. He's legendary! A living case study of the classic "rags-to-riches" story, isn't he? A poor printer's apprentice who created a publishing dynasty through hard work and the sweat of his brow. Though he could only have done that in America. Had he stayed in Britain, he'd still be a printer's apprentice. We don't tend to reward initiative in this country. It's considered crass and unseemly.

So, as his grandson, are you the heir apparent to the "throne"? And do you have a grandmother (does Adam have a wife)?

Lainey

She wondered about that last line. Was it over-the-top to ask a question like that? But she wanted to disarm him by being blunt in that way Americans seemed to like. She decided not to second-guess herself and sent it off.

Again, his answer came back within a few minutes.

Lainey,

No, I'm not in line to take over Powell Publishing when my grandfather retires. That honor goes to my father and older brother. I'm the failure in the family, choosing instead to become an Episcopalian minister. I'm in seminary even now.

I'm sorry to hear that England doesn't reward initiative. If that's true, though, then what about all the great minds, talents, and advancements that have come from your country? I happen to be a big fan of England.

My grandmother—Adam's wife—passed away several years ago.

Sincerely, Nicholas

A minister!

Sinking into her office chair, she stretched her legs out and kicked back and forth, swinging the seat left and right, left and right, while twirling a lock of her hair in her fingers.

He's studying to be a minister. But what on earth was an "Episcopal" minister? Weren't they the American equivalent to the Church of England? Lainey shuddered as she imagined a wet-lipped, chinless vicar with an Adam's apple the size of a large pear and all the charm of a dead trout.

Though Father Gilbert wasn't like that, Lainey corrected herself. So maybe Nicholas wasn't either. His written "voice" certainly didn't evoke a cold-blooded vertebrate in a priest's collar.

More than that, she hoped his being a minister meant he would tell her the truth about the letters if she pressed him a little harder. But not too fast, or he might notice that she'd dodged his question about her grandmother.

She looked over the e-mail again. Adam's wife was no longer living, so that was one door closed to find out what had happened. Assuming, of course, that Adam had ever told her. Lainey opted to follow up on the vicar in London. Maybe there was a lead.

Nicholas,

You wrote: *I'm sorry to hear that England doesn't reward initiative. If that's true, though, then what about all the great minds, talents, and advancements that have come from your country?*

Accidents. All accidents.

And if you're a fan of England, then that probably means you've never been here. You Americans are notoriously sentimental and romantic about your former mother country. It's just as drab and dismal as anywhere else. Am I right in believing that an Episcopalian minister in your country is the same as an Anglican (Church of England) vicar in ours? Is it really filled with "failures" who couldn't do anything else with their lives?

Do you know who the vicar was that your grandfather lived with in London? Is he still alive? Will he be coming to your grandfather's retirement party?

Lainey

She sent off the e-mail and pretended to work on the manuscript in front of her. But she found herself constantly watching for the e-mail icon. The minutes ticked by. This time he didn't answer.

NICHOLAS'S HEART WAS POUNDING FURIOUSLY, BUT HE COULDN'T HAVE explained in a rational way why. He had been at his computer reading Lainey's last e-mail to him when Kathy arrived at the door. Her knock made him quickly bail out of his e-mail account. He felt like a teenager who'd been caught thumbing through the lingerie section in the Sears catalog.

Why did he feel guilty? He wasn't doing anything wrong. Even though Kathy didn't want him investigating his grandfather's past, there was no reason to jump. He wasn't doing anything wrong.

Technically.

After he'd let her in and she stood chatting cheerfully in his living room about their plans that day, he worked to calm himself. He kept glancing at the computer as if it might choose to betray him and suddenly shout "You've got mail!" Kathy would look. Kathy would be upset.

It was a perfectly innocent exchange. She's across the Atlantic. It's strictly business. Strictly about my grandfather.

In all of the time he'd dated Kathy, he'd never kept any secrets from her. Now he was keeping one. And he was keeping it for two different reasons.

They had a full day ahead of them. Both were taking a break from their work to meet up with another couple in Washington. Friends of Kathy's from the University of Maryland where, in fact, they had led several campus Christian groups and were now married. Indiana natives, they'd never seen Fonzie's jacket at the Smithsonian and had promised someone back home—a mother? a friend?—that they would get a photo.

It was a beautiful summer day; the heat wave had given over to something far more bearable. Nicholas played the charming host, but spent most of the day wondering how Kathy had become friends with these two. The girl, Fran, was skinny as a rail, with masterfully applied makeup and a horrible habit of diverting every conversation with a horrible pun.

Driving past the U.S. Mint, Nicholas—in an attempt to make conversation—mentioned that he'd heard how the government was going to abolish pennies because they had become superfluous. "They've been superfluous for years," Nicholas said.

"I'm sure the U.S. *mint* well when they created them," Fran said.

And so it went the entire day.

Ron was a techno-wizard with a very large forehead, a monosyllabic conversational style, and a laugh like a goose calling its mate. Unfortunately it was a noise he made every time his wife made one of her puns. His interest in conversation changed only when Nicholas asked him about his vocation. "Programming for NASA in Greenbelt now," he said. "But that's only a means to an end."

"To what end, then?" Nicholas asked.

"I want to get computers into the hands of children in Third World countries. Then, while delivering those computers, we'll preach the gospel to them. It's too late for our generation. So we need to reach the next. And computers are the way to do it."

A noble effort, Nicholas agreed.

"It's something we think we can sink our teeth into," Fran added. "One *byte* at a time."

Ha, ha. Honk, honk.

They walked through the Smithsonian, and Nicholas was hopeful that the pop culture displays would give them something to talk about. It didn't. Fran and Ron gave a cursory acknowledgment to Howdy Doody, Oscar the Grouch, and only a brief glance at Dorothy's ruby-red slippers.

How did they ever reach any of the students on campus? Nicholas wanted to ask, but didn't.

When they reached Fonzie's jacket, Ron pointed: "They don't make shows like *Happy Days* anymore." He sighed deeply. "An age gone by."

Fran took a picture, tried to work a pun with the name *Fonzie*, and gave up.

When Nicholas failed to find something about them of any interest, he began to fill the gaps by rattling on about himself and anything that came to mind. It was no less boring, but at least he was doing something.

They went to the mall at the Old Post Office for lunch. When the couple excused themselves to go to the bathroom, Kathy took the opportunity to whisper, "What are you doing?"

"What am *I* doing?"

"You were talking about *hermeneutics*, Nicholas."

"I was trying to make conversation."

"You brought up hermeneutics to make conversation? Even Christians don't care about hermeneutics! Not everyone is in seminary, you know."

"I was getting desperate. You didn't warn me about the puns or the honks."

"What?"

He shook his head. "Just tell me—who are these people *really* and why am I spending my day off with them?"

"They're my friends."

"I know that. But I don't understand *why*."

"I wanted us to spend some time with another Christian couple, that's all. We're always alone. Sometimes it's like we don't have any friends."

"We have friends," he protested, but couldn't think of any that they actually socialized with. The couple returned and they went off to find something to eat.

The afternoon dragged on.

Only when Ron mentioned that they had been to England for a vacation recently did Nicholas come alive, asking where they went and stayed and what they thought of the country.

More monosyllables and bad puns.

"Did you go to Shepherd's Bush in London?" Nicholas asked.

They had no idea what or where that was. But Fran mentioned proudly that she became very fluent in speaking British while she was there.

"You mean you spoke with an accent?" Kathy asked.

"No," Fran answered. "I became adept at using their words."

"They speak English, don't they?" Nicholas asked.

"They use different words than we do," Fran explained. "For example, what we call an elevator, they call a *lift*. We say *exit* and they say *way-out*.

What we call a subway, they call the *underground*. A *subway* in England is a pedestrian walkway that goes under a road. And a *flat* is an apartment."

"Really?" Kathy said, feigning her interest.

Nicholas winced. *She thinks she's bilingual because she speaks English in two countries*, he thought, and resigned himself to a very, very long afternoon.

LAINEY FINISHED UP HER DAY AT THE OFFICE. AS SHE CHANGED HER NICE low heels to a pair of trainers for the walk to the Hammersmith tube station, she felt strangely disappointed that she hadn't heard from Nicholas. She was pleasantly distracted by his e-mails, she had to admit.

She said good night to her coworkers, turned down an offer to go to the pub, and began her journey up Fulham Palace Road toward the station. It began to rain.

"No, no, no . . . ," she said to herself and picked up her pace.

While waiting for the light to change at a crosswalk, she became aware that a car nearby was blaring its horn. Then someone called out, "Lainey!" She turned and saw a black BMW. A man inside was waving at her—Steve Winchell, her former boyfriend.

Approach with caution, she thought as she made her way to the car. He pushed open the passenger door. "You'll get soaked," he shouted. "I'll give you a lift."

She hesitated. But the choice between his dry car and the rain without an umbrella seemed obvious. She got in. "Thank you," she said.

The car, which looked brand-new, was gorgeous. Leather seats, dark wood, a dashboard to make a pilot drool.

"Like it?" he asked.

"Very impressive."

"It came with my new job," he explained. "Managing director."

"Congratulations."

He guided the car through the traffic and Lainey stole glances at him. He had a lean, dark face with dimples on both sides of his mouth. His eyes could melt butter, so some said, and his brown hair had just the right amount of wave to it to make most women yearn to run their fingers through it. He was a good looker and he knew it. Exploited it.

"You look fantastic," he said, eyeing her.

She self-consciously pulled her skirt down over her knees. "Thank you."

"Seeing anyone?"

"No. You?"

"Not really." Which was Steve's code for: *I am, but she's not important enough to keep me from doing what I want.* "It seems like ages since we talked," he said.

"Oh?"

"How do you fancy a meal? I know where we can find a great curry." That was more code from Steve meaning: *We'll get take-away, go back to your place, and mess around for a while.*

She looked out at the rain, the deep gray and loneliness of it, and considered how nice it would be if . . .

If what? It would be meaningless. A temporary respite from her loneliness, but shallow and filled with regret tomorrow morning. *Regret.* She thought of her grandmother and said, "No thanks, Steve. I really need to go home."

"You *need* to? What—have you got a cat there or something you need to feed?"

"No, I'm . . . I'm expecting some important e-mails from America." She bit her lower lip, telling herself that she wasn't really lying. She was hoping to hear from Nicholas, after all, in order to help her grandmother. Right? Right.

"A book project with America, huh?" Steve concluded and she didn't deny it. "I could pick up the food and bring it back while you—"

"Steve, it's not a good idea," she said firmly.

"What's not?"

"We split up. For some very good reasons, I believe. And as far as I can tell, those reasons haven't changed."

He was all innocence. "What do you mean? We're still friends, aren't we? I only wanted to treat you to a meal, catch up on things . . ."

She didn't believe a word of it. "I'm grateful for the ride, Steve. But, honestly—" She stopped herself. There was nothing else to say.

They rode on, the wipers scraping at the window.

"Why do you always have to be such a cow?" he asked sourly.

She'd forgotten about his temper, which was reason number four for their breakup, if she got the order right. "Don't pout."

"I'm not pouting," he said, "and don't tell me what to do."

"Look, you don't have to take me home. It's not as if I asked. Drop me off anywhere along here, if that suits you better."

"Yeah, you're right," he said as he signaled and then quickly pulled to the curb. An unappreciative driver behind them hit the horn. "I don't know what I was thinking."

"I know what you were thinking," Lainey teased, without anger, as she opened her door. She felt strong and in control, for some reason. She got out and then leaned back in. "Good-bye, Steve. Thanks for the ride."

"Yeah. Whatever."

Lainey closed the door and he pulled away to a renewed chorus of offended horns. The rain came in a downpour now and she knew she'd be drenched by the time she walked the remaining four blocks to her flat. She looked around for shelter and spotted a cybercafé only two doors away. She ordered a large coffee, paid for one of the computers, and sat down at the counter in front of one of the screens. She logged on to her server and went to her e-mails. There were the usual spams, copied jokes, and a few from some friends. Still nothing from Nicholas.

Disappointed, she fell into her chair and watched the rain fall on the commuters outside.

MERCIFULLY, RON AND FRAN WEREN'T AVAILABLE FOR DINNER. NICHOLAS could barely hide his joy. But Kathy was annoyed by the time they got back to Nicholas's apartment.

"What did I do wrong now?" he asked as they walked in.

"Nothing," she said, meaning *something*. She closed the windows and turned on the air conditioner. "I had no idea you were so interested in England."

"You said I couldn't talk about hermeneutics anymore."

"But you wouldn't let it go. You kept going back to it, bombarding them with questions. Bed-and-breakfasts. The currency exchange. How they planned to travel. Airfares. No matter what we were talking about, you went back to their trip to England. I was beginning to think that you've planned a trip for yourself and forgot to tell me."

"I was making conversation," he explained. "I was trying to be your charming boyfriend—to show them what a good couple we are. Isn't that what today was all about?"

She didn't look at him. "What are you talking about?"

He shrugged. "Maybe I'm wrong."

"Tell me what you mean, please, and I'll tell you if you're wrong."

"You wanted to impress them with us." He waited. She mouthed the word *wrong*. "*Or*," he said, taking another stab, "you wanted to impress me with them."

Her expression changed ever so slightly. Bingo.

"I get it," he said as the light dawned. "You wanted to go out with this couple because they're what you want *us* to be as a couple."

She looked at him with annoyance. "I'm tired. I think I'll go home."

In three quick steps he was between her and the door. "Kathy . . ."

"They had a big impact on me," she said.

"And?"

"And I remember thinking: This is how I want to be when I'm a couple."

"Telling bad puns and laughing like a bicycle horn? Or converting the innocent through technology."

She turned away from him and sat down on the sofa. "Don't be glib. I'm serious."

"Then you better tell me what you admire so much about them. I'm willing to learn."

"Their spirituality, first and foremost," she explained.

"We're spiritual."

"We don't pray before our meals."

"I thought being spiritual is more than that." Nicholas wondered where all of this was leading. "Do you want me to pray like Ron did over his French fries? Is that it? A full-fledged pray-out-loud sermonette with altar call and benediction? My hamburger got cold and my milkshake melted."

"A short prayer would be nice."

"But I'm an Episcopalian! You know I can't pray unless it's written down for me."

She didn't laugh.

He sat down next to her on the sofa. "Is that what this is about? Praying before we eat?"

"No. It's . . ." She paused. A small wrinkle in her forehead. "I want us to aspire to be more than we are. I want you to motivate me to be a better Christian. I want to motivate you."

He opened his mouth, but closed it again.

"We should be reading our Bibles together, praying together . . ."

"But we do," he reminded her. "We've done *three* Bible studies for couples in the past six months. We've learned how to experience God, read through the prayers of obscure Bible characters, and discovered how to be purposeful and driven. Then we pray before saying good night."

"Not in the last week or so."

He nodded. "Okay, so I've been distracted."

"We should never be distracted from our faith."

His eyes went wide and he had to restrain himself from what he wanted to say. "I won't be glib if you promise not to be trite."

"Trite!"

"A momentary distraction from praying together isn't the same thing as being distracted from our faith, Kathy. This isn't a crisis. What's the big deal?"

"I worry about our discipline, about being a Christ-centered couple."

"What does that mean?" Nicholas asked sharply. "I try to keep Christ at the center of my life and you try to keep Christ at the center of your life. We're a couple. Isn't that Christ-centered enough?"

"It's not the same."

He shook his head. "I'm not following this conversation at all."

"You're studying to be a pastor. What's so hard to follow?"

"This *ideal* you seem to have about us. I don't think I can meet it."

"Of course you can," she said. "We must."

"Or?"

"Or I don't see any point in going on."

He scrubbed his chin. "That's pretty serious."

"I've been thinking about it a lot, Nicholas."

Thoughts bounced around his mind like moths against a lightbulb. It was a struggle for him to grab a single one. He could be defensive in how he answered, he could overreact to what sounded like an ultimatum, or he could try to accept what she was saying and work toward something better for both of them. Finally, he said, "You're right."

Silently, she looked at him with those big, gorgeous eyes. He saw great expectations there. But rather than shrink away from the challenge, he knew he had to exceed them.

"Let's pray," he said softly.

AFTER A MEAL OF TAKE-AWAY CHINESE AND A HOT BATH, LAINEY CRAWLED into bed, expecting to fall instantly to sleep. She didn't. Couldn't. Plucking one of the half-finished books on her bed stand, she began to read, all the while wondering how long she'd have to wait for Nicholas to write back.

Around one in the morning, she went to her computer and logged on to check her e-mails. Nothing. She was about to sign off again, when suddenly the mail symbol came alive. An e-mail had arrived from Nicholas. Lainey glanced at her watch. It was a little after eight in the evening for Nicholas. Perhaps he was sitting at the computer right now.

She opened the e-mail.

Dear Lainey,

Yes, Episcopalians are Anglicans with American accents. Same group—or at least we were last time I checked, but it's hard to tell these days.

And, yes, some would argue that our denomination is full of the "failures" that couldn't succeed at any other vocation. Or maybe I'm the only one, having turned to the priesthood after failing to make a living as a rock-and-roll star.

I will confess that I have never been to England. But I'm always surprised when the English bad-mouth their own country the way they do. Why is that?

The vicar I mentioned was John Peters, of St. Luke's Church in Chiswick. I believe he passed away some years ago. (Again, I can't be too inquisitive or my grandfather will get suspicious—and my family seems to know very little about my grandfather's pre-America years and friendships.)

By the way, you haven't told me what your grandmother's condition is. Is it a secret?

Sincerely, Nicholas

Lainey replied:

Nicholas,

I love England, actually, but it's "not British" to say so. It's in our genetic code to complain about everything here: the rain, the trains, the rain, our government, the rain, the traffic, the rain, our lack of identity, the rain, the close proximity of the French, the rain, our cricket teams, the rain, the weather . . . the rain. It's a harmless habit, like biting one's nails.

You wanted to be a rock-and-roll star? Was it glam-rock, punk-rock, alternative-rock, or "rock" in the Air Supply vein? Any photos of you onstage would certainly help me to understand just what you gave up to be a priest. And if you hoped to be a rock-and-roll star, then you should be Nick, not Nicholas. Maybe that contributed to your lack of success.

Oh, and when you say "priest"—is that the celibate kind or are you married?

I'll tell you about my grandmother when you tell me how her letters were destroyed.

Lainey

Lainey sent off the e-mail and wondered if he was really there to receive it. She looked out the front window at the rain and the traffic lights turning their colors whether anyone was watching or not.

Dear Lainey,

Air Supply? What's that? (And, no, I have no photos that I can show— ever—of when I sang onstage.)

I hadn't thought about the name thing. I've always been Nicholas and didn't think to change it to Nick. Of all the luck! Where were you ten years ago when I needed this kind of advice?

As an Episcopal priest, I can marry if I want—females, males, small farm animals, you name it. Our denomination is all about inclusion, you know. I think we got that from you guys.

Tell me about your grandmother and then I'll explain what happened to the letters.

Sincerely, Nicholas

Lainey smiled, harrumphed, and then wrote:

Nick,

Ten years ago I was wearing a school uniform and wondering why I was born with such limp hair.

I asked about the letters before you asked about my grandmother, so you have to go first.

Lainey

P.S. So you were a singer! Were you any good?

The answer came a moment later:

Dear Lainey,

I thought I was a good rock-and-roll singer. Apparently no one else agreed.

And aren't we being a little childish to play this game of "you first"?

Nicholas

Lainey responded with:

Nick,

Yes, it is very childish. So go ahead and tell me.

Lainey

Dear Lainey,

No, really—after you.

Nicholas

Nick,

An impasse! How sad. And just when I thought there was hope for us. Oh well.

Lainey

Dear Lainey,

This is silly. We're adults. And time is passing ever so quickly. Don't you realize what time it is?

Nicholas

Lainey looked at her watch. Nearly nine for him.

Nick,

I know exactly what time it is. And I'm sleepy. So you should stop fiddling about and tell me.

Lainey

The rain had stopped and the street lamps cast light into the pools on the black tar of the roads. She debated fixing herself a cup of coffee but knew the caffeine would have her up for the rest of the night. She'd be worthless at work tomorrow.

Nicholas is thinking about it, she thought. Why else would it take him so long to reply?

Dear Lainey,

The letters were shredded.

Nicholas

Shredded! What in the world did that mean?

Nick,

I don't think cryptic answers count as answers at all. That would be the same as my saying that "my grandmother is in bed." How or why, pray tell, were the letters shredded?

Lainey

Then:

Dear Lainey,

They were shredded because my grandfather put them in the shredder in his office.

Nicholas

She sat, staring at the words on the screen, then hammered at the keyboard.

Nick,

This could take a very long time if you don't simply spell out the details in one go. Why, she asks with strained patience, did your grandfather put the letters in a shredder?

Lainey

Blink, blink, the cursor flashed. Why did Adam Powell shred the letters? It had meaning and significance—Lainey knew that, or Nicholas would have mentioned it before.

Maybe it was an accident, she thought. Hoped. Like throwing out an important piece of mail without meaning to.

But how did one accidentally *shred* something important?

The answer came.

Dear Lainey,

Because they were unopened when I found them and, being the *expletive deleted* that he is, he decided to shred them rather than allow me to be tempted to read them. He claims that they were part of a time of his life that is gone and unimportant. I don't believe him—which is why I have persisted in trying to find your grandmother and learn what really happened between them. There. You have the whole truth. Are you happy now?

Nicholas

No, she wasn't happy at all. The letters from her grandmother were unopened. Why didn't Adam open them back in 1954? What had happened between them? Why didn't he want Nicholas to read the letters? *He claims that they were part of a time of his life that is gone and unimportant. I don't believe him. . . .*

This was far more complicated than she could have imagined.

But she felt a peculiar relief that Nicholas had put his side of things out into the open.

Lainey sent off another e-mail and made the mistake of lying down on the sofa while she waited for his answer.

THERE, NICHOLAS THOUGHT. IT'S DONE. WHAT'S THE WORST THING THAT *can happen for telling the truth?*

Her e-mail arrived and he opened it.

Nick,

Why didn't you say so in the first place? My grandmother has recently sunk into a deep depression and we believe it's due in part to whatever happened between your grandfather and her back in 1954. It was a defining moment, for some reason. But she won't talk about it and I'm trying desperately to learn the truth to help her.

This e-mailing back and forth simply won't do. Let's exchange phone details. I know it's late for you, it's even later for me. But we have to talk.

Lainey

What in the world is going on here? Nicholas wondered. Elaine Arthur had *recently* sunk into a depression because of his grandfather—some fifty years after they'd last seen each other? And it was happening just as he found those letters in the box?

"I don't believe in coincidences," Nicholas said out loud. *Coincidence is nothing less than a providential accident,* one of his instructors had once said. God was up to something.

A *deep* depression, Lainey had written. That's why Lainey couldn't or wouldn't talk to her about Nicholas's questions. Did "deep depression" mean she was suicidal? *Over his grandfather?*

It was two thirty in the morning in England. When Lainey said she wanted to talk, did she mean now? He typed his phone number and e-mailed it to her. Then he slowly spun in his chair to face the room. Not two hours ago he'd sat on the couch with Kathy and prayed for their relationship. But here he was continuing with this secret. And giving Lainey his phone number seemed to make it worse.

You're doing nothing wrong, he reassured himself.

But he didn't believe it. He was enjoying these e-mail exchanges too much. He liked the playfulness, the flirtation. Though he knew very little about the woman on the other end, he knew that he liked her.

Was she going to call tonight?

Tomorrow was Wednesday and he was due at the company at ten for the weekly "update" meeting with his father and brother about his research. He needed to get to bed soon. But he would wait for a little while. That much he would do.

CHAPTER EIGHT

WEDNESDAY, THE 7TH OF JULY

THE PHONE WOKE HIM WITH AN ELECTRONIC CHIRP. HE SAT UP ON THE couch, confused. Why wasn't he in bed? It was dark outside. He rubbed his mouth and tried to swallow away the dryness. More chirping from the phone.

Stumbling, he went to his computer desk and picked up the slender white receiver. A glance at his watch told him it was one fifteen in the morning.

"Hello," he said in a low croak.

"Did I wake you?" a woman's voice he didn't recognize.

"Yes. I think so. I'm not sure."

"I'm so sorry I didn't ring you straight away," the voice said and he discerned the accent. It was British. A pleasant one, cultured, not like Dick Van Dyke in *Mary Poppins*.

"Is this Lainey?"

"Who else would it be?" she asked, a teasing in her tone. "Do you often get calls from English women in the middle of the night?"

He looked at his watch again and did the calculation. It was six fifteen in the morning in England. "But it's not the middle of the night for you."

"You're right!" she gasped. The sound of curtains being thrown aside. "Good heavens! I'm so glad I phoned you, otherwise I'd have never known."

He was perplexed now. "I thought you were going to call earlier."

"I was. But I fell asleep on the sofa. Then, when I woke up, I was afraid you were waiting there, wide-awake, wondering what had become of that strange girl in England while your night ticked away. Do you see how considerate I am?"

"Yes. Impressive."

"Then I said to myself, 'This Nicholas fellow is a hardworking vicar wannabe, so he's probably awake anyway, saying his prayers, genuflecting, and doing all the things that a pagan like me would never think about.'"

"Yeah, right," he said as he went into his kitchen to make coffee. "Let me roll up my prayer mat so we can talk properly." He pulled out a jar of instant from the cupboard. He filled the kettle.

"You're making coffee, aren't you?" she asked, and her voice had a soft, warm, in-bed-with-a-blanket kind of sound.

"Yes. I'd offer you some, but ..."

"It's all right. I prefer tea anyway," she said.

"I have some Lipton's."

"Oh, *please*," she groaned. "I tried some American tea once. Foultasting stuff. You must have Typhoo or PG Tips or don't bother."

"Fix me a cup sometime and I'll let you know," he said and immediately grimaced. He was flirting with her and shouldn't. He cleared his throat. "Let's talk about your grandmother."

"Let's talk about your grandfather."

"Oh no. We don't have time for this 'you first' game."

"Then get on with it."

She wins again, he thought. "I'm not sure where to begin."

"Start with the letters," she suggested. "And don't be boring or I'm liable to fall asleep."

"I'll be as exciting as I can be."

"Good boy."

He explained about working on the presentation for his grandfather's retirement, finding the box with the letters, his discussion with his father, and then that decisive moment when his grandfather took the box and shredded the letters. He was aware, but only as a nagging sense, that he had carefully avoided mentioning Kathy. Why?

"He sounds like a nasty piece of work," Lainey said. A pause on the line with a distinct overseas hiss that cut in and out. "There's something I don't follow, though."

"What?"

"Why are you persisting? He clearly wants you to leave things alone. It's none of your business, right?"

"Well, that part's a little more complicated," he replied.

"I'm good at complicated," she said. "I do complicated really well."

"But I'm not very good at articulating complicated at this time of night. It's enough to say that I want to find out the secret of those letters and everyone else wants me to leave it alone."

"*Who* wants you to leave it alone?" she asked indignantly. "Let me have a word with them."

"My father. My girlfriend." There, it was out.

"You won't listen to them, though," Lainey said firmly.

"I won't?"

"You can't."

"Why can't I?"

"Because I'm about to tell you what's happened with my grandmother. And as I speak you'll be touched to the core of your being and will see that your grandfather seems to have some connection to my grandmother's state of mind. You must help me to help her."

"Then I guess you better tell me what's going on," he said.

Lainey obliged, explaining about her grandmother's mysterious conversation with Gerard Sommersby, her subsequent breakdown, the old chapel, the stained glass, and the lead from Gerard to his grandfather.

And she was right. Nicholas was touched *and* fascinated to think that, after all these years, the lives of their grandparents were once again intertwined in some strange way. His faith demanded that he believe this wasn't mere coincidence or bizarre chance—there was something to this. What it was and why it was happening now, Nicholas had no idea. But he couldn't help but think again about Scrooge and the Ghost of the Past coming to bring redemption.

"What's our next step?" Nicholas asked, hoping she understood that he was determined to stay involved. For his grandfather's sake, and her grandmother's.

"What's next? I haven't the foggiest."

"Maybe you should tell your grandmother about my grandfather."

"I'm not sure it's wise, considering her condition."

"Is there a doctor you could talk to?"

"Yes. Good idea."

"Okay."

An awkward pause, then: "Right. Well, some of us have real jobs to go to. We'll talk soon. Good night, Nick."

"Good-bye, Lainey. Nice to meet you. But I'm—"

Click.

"Nicholas," he corrected the empty line.

LAINEY LAY IN BED, STARING AT THE CEILING, FOLLOWING THE HAIRLINE cracks to the corners. She hoped she hadn't overplayed her hand with Nicholas. She had been very feisty and forceful—even a flirt. But preeminent in her mind was the need to help her grandmother. And to do that, she suspected she would need Nicholas's help. There was no getting around it now.

So why did it disappoint her to hear that he had a girlfriend?

LAINEY CALLED SERENA LATE IN THE MORNING, AS WAS HER HABIT NOW that her grandmother was ill.

"Any changes?" she asked softly, not wanting her coworkers on the other side of the cubicle walls to hear.

"No," Serena replied, also speaking softly.

"What happened with the psychiatrist?"

"Nothing. She didn't say anything to him. She didn't react to him at all."

"What's his name?"

"James Watson."

"Did he venture a guess about what's wrong with her?"

Lainey could hear the sound of papers shuffling on the other end. Had Serena taken notes? She had, and spoke with careful precision: "Dysthymic Disorder. That's his guess."

"Sounds impressive. What does it mean?"

"Sad, down in the dumps for more days than not."

"I wonder how much he gets paid to come up with that diagnosis? I could have told him that. Was there anything else?"

"That's all he would say until he can spend more time with her."

"When's that?"

"I don't know. He said he'd have to find room in his schedule for regular visits."

"Bloody National Health," Lainey said. "Do you have Watson's phone number? I want to talk to him."

Serena gave Lainey the number.

"Thank you," she said after scribbling it down. "You sound tired, Serena. Are you all right?"

"Yes, I suppose." Her voice was now a whisper. "This is harder than I thought."

"Is my mother helping?"

"She comes by every day for an hour or so. But it's very uncomfortable for her. She doesn't know what to say or do. It's *messy*. And you know how your mother feels about messes."

"I know. I'll see about getting some time off." Hadn't she promised to do that before? She'd taken a couple of days for Uncle Gerard's funeral. Clearly that wasn't enough.

"No, Lainey. Honestly, I'll be all right. It's only that ..." Her voice trailed off.

"It's only what?"

"I find myself getting angry at her. At her silence. *Really* angry. I want to shake her and tell her to snap out of it."

"That's normal," Lainey said. She'd read it in a book.

"It drains me. It takes a lot of energy to stay cheerful for her, to keep from upsetting her, to bottle up my own emotions."

Tracy, one of the office assistants, appeared in the doorway of Lainey's cubicle. She mouthed that a bunch of the editors were going to the pub after work. Was she interested? Lainey shook her head and said into the phone. "I'll come down tonight."

Tracy frowned at her and walked away.

"You can't do that. What about your job?"

"I'll sort that out," Lainey said. "I'll come down and you go out. Take the night off."

"Are you sure?"

"Yes, of course I'm sure. You can't carry this burden alone." Lainey leaned forward so as not to be heard. "I talked to Nicholas on the phone."

"Did you? When?"

"Last night. Early this morning, I mean. I called him."

"You spoke in person?"

"Yes. I think he's going to try to help us."

"Did you ask about his grandfather and the letters?"

Lainey quickly told Serena about their e-mails and conversation and suddenly felt like she was back in school. She was almost giggly with excitement.

"At least we're a few steps closer," Serena said when she finished. "Let's pray we're on the right track."

"I certainly hope so."

Hanging up the phone, Lainey stared at the piles of manuscripts on her desk. Too much work. But she had to do something to help Serena. She tapped her pencil against the top page of a manuscript about a woman who finds the Fountain of Youth in a sewer beneath a Birmingham bus station. The gray taps looked as if a bird with dirty feet had been hopping on the page, skittering across the title and the author's name.

Glancing at the manuscript, computer, and the rather Spartan cubicle in which she worked, it struck her that she could do her job from just about anywhere—even Stonebridge. Have laptop, will travel.

She went to have a chat with her boss.

NICHOLAS WAS FIFTEEN MINUTES LATE FOR HIS MEETING WITH HIS FATHER AND brother. They didn't seem to notice. As he walked into the conference room, they were engaged in a very serious conversation about paper stock and print-buying and how to cut costs without compromising quality. Nicholas offered thanks to God that such discussions weren't a regular part of his life.

"Dad tells me you've found some interesting stuff about Grandad," Jeff said, signaling the start of their meeting. Jeff was always a get-to-the-business kind of person. Not unpleasantly, since everyone seemed to like him, but he didn't waste time with small talk. In that, he was like his grandfather. He was like his grandfather in appearance, too. The same thick hair, determined good looks, keen eyes, a dimple on the left side of his mouth. And whereas their father—and Nicholas—always looked frumpy wearing suits, Jeff looked sharp and intelligent.

It was a good thing that Nicholas loved Jeff deeply, or he would have been bitterly jealous.

"You told him about the letters?" Nicholas asked his father.

His father nodded. "And he agrees with me."

"Now wait a minute," Jeff said. "I agree that you should forget about them. But not for the same reason."

Nicholas sat down. "Dad thinks it's none of my business. What do you think?"

"We're family—and, as far as I know, we've never drawn lines about what's our business and what isn't. If it involves one of us, it involves us all."

Nicholas gave his father a *so there* look.

His father smiled at him.

"But," Jeff said, holding up his hand. "I think it's a distraction for you. We have only a couple of weeks until the family bash and I want to make sure our tribute to Grandad is the best tribute anyone has ever done anywhere in the whole history of tributes. If you start spending time on the writer of those mystery letters, you won't get your work done."

Sheer practicality, Nicholas thought. "You'll get the best I can do. I promise."

"Then tell us what you've done," Jeff said.

Nicholas opened his backpack and pulled out a folder. From that he went through a lengthy explanation of the photos, letters, awards, and overall history he'd unearthed. He was working with the graphic arts department to turn it into a multimedia presentation, incorporating images, sound, and music to capture his grandfather's life. He was working to keep everything at ten minutes, no more than twelve.

"Why ten to twelve minutes?"

"Any more than that and I'll be worried about being indulgent or boring," Nicholas replied.

"Good point."

Nicholas's father produced a schedule of the day's events. There would be a presentation from the mayor, a plaque from Congress, a videotaped appreciation from the president of the United States, Nicholas's presentation, and then a few words from Adam himself.

"Oh, and we have to make room in here for your announcement," Dennis said.

"What announcement?" Nicholas asked.

Jeff laughed. His father slowly shook his head.

Nicholas looked from one to the other, waiting for an explanation.

His father reached over and tugged at Nicholas's ear. "Hello? Anyone home? Your *engagement*."

"Oh. That," Nicholas said. "I haven't actually asked her, you know."

"Details, details," Jeff teased.

"Don't mess it up, Nicholas," his father warned. "Or you'll have the whole family to contend with."

Nicholas forced out an embarrassed chuckle. "Are you kidding? You'd drop me before you'd ever drop her. I have my inheritance to think of."

"And don't you forget it," his father said with a serious smile.

Back in the bowels of the building, Nicholas began going through his grandfather's boxes again. He told himself he wouldn't be distracted by Elaine Arthur, or missing letters, or family mysteries, or even Lainey. Jeff was right. It's all a distraction.

But after only an hour, he got fidgety and went to a computer in the corner of the room. It had an Internet link, so he typed in his name and password to get past the company's firewall and went to his own server to check e-mails. There were a dozen offers for mortgages, drugs, and physical enhancements. Nothing from Lainey. He was about to log off when, on a whim, he decided to do a little hunting. He went to a search engine and typed in *Lainey Bishop*, putting the name in quotes to isolate the results.

Why hadn't he thought of it before?

Within a couple of seconds a handful of websites popped up. One was for a Lainey Bishop who taught at an elementary school in Michigan, there was another Lainey Bishop in Los Angeles, a would-be model and actress, and an obituary for one in Melbourne, Australia. And then there was a result for a Lainey Bishop on the Carper & Hollings website. Nicholas clicked on that. It instantly took him to a section on the publisher's website dedicated to author relations. Lainey Bishop had been chosen as "their favorite proofreader" by some of the authors. *See photo*, it said. Nicholas scrolled down and came upon a photo of a small group of people at a luncheon. The caption identified the woman at the center as Lainey Bishop.

Shazam! Nicholas thought.

Lainey stood wearing a baseball cap with the words "I Be Good" on the front. A gift at the luncheon, no doubt. She had long brown hair that framed her slender face—dark, expressive eyes that seemed to penetrate out of the photo and directly to him. A gentle slope of a nose. Full lips, drawn up into a broad smile. She wasn't beautiful, not in that stop-on-the-street-to-look-at way, but pretty in a natural, unaffected way. She wore a yellow top and had her arms folded in front of her as if to feign an attitude of great pride in her award. *Lithe* was the only word he could think of to describe her physique, but even that word didn't seem right.

He rested his chin on his hand and gazed at her face again. Those eyes. *Yes*, he thought, *this is the woman I talked to on the phone*. The voice was right for the person he saw in front of him.

By the time he returned to the boxes, the guilt came. He was being unfaithful to Kathy. Maybe Jeff was right. Elaine, Lainey, and the letters were a distraction. He had to stay focused, get the job done. Only two weeks left. Everyone was depending on him.

His intentions were good.

The photo, however, remained burned into his mind.

NO JOY, LAINEY THOUGHT AS SHE ENDURED THE TRAFFIC FROM LONDON to Stonebridge. She was approaching the three-hour mark since she'd left her flat around four o'clock.

During her drive she tried to call Dr. Watson to talk about her grandmother. His answering service took a message. *No joy.*

She tried to phone her mother and father. Another message left on a machine. *No joy.*

"I hope I haven't made you late," Lainey said to Serena as she fumbled with her suitcase through the front door of her grandmother's house.

"Not at all," Serena said. "I'm meeting some friends in Southaven for dinner and a movie."

Lainey eyed Serena—done up in a very nice silk blouse of blue, with black jeans and matching high heels. "Must be some special friends."

Serena's smile held a secret. "Do you need help?"

"No," Lainey said over her shoulder as she went back to the car to get her box of work and briefcase.

Serena followed her. "Your grandmother is having supper in her chair."

"Does she eat much?"

"She pecks at it."

"All right," Lainey said, then impulsively hugged Serena. "You're great. Now go. Have a good night."

"I put my mobile phone number on the counter in the kitchen. If you need me."

"Thanks."

"I put a plate of food in the oven for you."

"Thanks."

"And if anything—"

"Go, Serena. We'll be fine. Honestly."

Serena smiled, nodded, and walked around the house to her car.

Lainey slung the strap to her briefcase over her shoulder and carried the box of manuscripts with both hands. Her grip wasn't strong and as she went through the door, the briefcase strap caught on the doorknob, dropping the briefcase down her arm, which yanked her hand away from the box. Everything crashed to the floor and the manuscripts spilled into the hall.

Lainey muttered some very unkind phrases and stooped to pick up the mess. Reaching for some of the scattered pages, she caught sight of a pair of slippers out of the corner of her eye. She looked up. Her grandmother stood over her, a look of bemusement on her face.

"You shouldn't swear," Elaine Arthur said.

"Sorry, Gran."

Her grandmother turned and drifted back down the hallway to her room.

ONCE SHE HAD TAKEN HER THINGS TO THE GUEST ROOM THAT WAS REALLY her room when she stayed, Lainey quickly unpacked and then selected the manuscript she was going to proofread tonight. She thought of her grandmother's face, looking down at her. Gaunt, it was, with dark circles under her eyes, a sure sign of her sleeplessness. One of the books about depression talked about that, the insomnia, the nighttime demons that afflicted the sufferer.

With the manuscript in hand, Lainey went back downstairs to her grandmother's bedroom. Elaine Arthur was sitting in the wingback chair near her bed. A tray of food rested on a stand in front of her. Small bits were missing from the slices of roast, the roasted potatoes, and the York-shire pudding. The peas and the corn looked as if they'd been pushed around. Elaine had pecked at her food, just like Serena had said she would.

"It looks delicious. You really should eat, Gran," Lainey said and was immediately aware of her tone of voice. She was speaking as if to a child. *Don't do that*, she told herself. *She's not mad. Speak to her like you always have.*

Her grandmother looked out of the French doors at the vanishing day. Long shadows filled the garden.

"I've come to stay for a few days. I hope you don't mind."

No response.

"I'm going to do some work while I'm here." She held up a manuscript. "A novel."

No response.

"This one's about three women who went to university together and reunite ten years later in a small village in Lincolnshire." She put the manuscript down on the dressing table.

No response.

Lainey looked at her grandmother, who was still gazing out of the French doors. "I'm going to fix myself a plate. Would you like some tea or coffee?"

No response.

This is the silence that makes Serena so angry, Lainey thought with new sympathy. "I'll be back in two ticks. Just call if you need anything."

Lainey walked to the kitchen. *This is going to be a long night.*

When Lainey returned from the kitchen, her grandmother had moved from the chair to the bed. She lay staring up at the canopy. Lainey sat down in the wingback chair, balancing her plate on her knee while she ate. "This is excellent. Are you sure you don't want more? I could warm it up."

No response.

"Are you ever going to talk to me again?" she asked.

No response.

"I saw Steve. You remember Steve?"

No response.

"He wanted to take me out to dinner. I said no." Lainey was talking, filling the silence, but began to wonder how far she could push her grandmother. What could she say that might trigger a response? She wanted to probe, like a dentist searching for an exposed nerve.

Her grandmother didn't move.

"The truth is, he wanted to take me back to my flat and do wild things to me," she said.

Lainey glanced over at her grandmother. Was there a flicker of something? Did Elaine's expression change? Lainey hadn't looked quickly enough to be certain.

Finishing her dinner in silence, Lainey debated with herself about what to do. Should she indulge the silence and get her proofreading done, or should she test her grandmother even further? She picked up the plates, took them to the kitchen sink, and put on the kettle. She prepared a tray with a pot of tea, two cups, and a small jug of milk and a bowl of sugar.

Her grandmother was now lying on her side, facing away from the chair. Her eyes were open.

"I've made us some tea," Lainey announced and put the tray on the stand where her dinner had been. She put her grandmother's cup on a coaster on the bed stand. "Yours is right here."

No movement, no response.

Lainey sat down in the chair again and sipped her tea. "I've met a very interesting young man," she said. "He's an American. His name is Nicholas."

No response.

"What makes him so interesting is that he's the grandson of someone you once knew."

No response.

Lainey put the cup to her lips, but her hand was trembling ever so slightly and she put it down again. "His name is Nicholas Powell. He's the grandson of Adam Powell. You knew Adam Powell, didn't you?"

Her grandmother seemed to go rigid. She straightened her back and stretched her legs out. But she didn't turn or respond.

"Does that name ring a bell? Adam Powell?"

A muffled cry, a stifled sob, came from the back of her grandmother's throat. Soft enough that Lainey almost didn't hear it. Then her shoulders began to shake, ever so gently, and she drew her legs up, curling within herself.

Lainey put her cup of tea down on the bed stand, knowing she'd done the wrong thing. "Gran?"

The shoulders shook, a loud sniff as she brought her arms up over her face.

"Gran, I'm sorry," Lainey said as she crossed to the bed. She lay down next to the old woman and tried to pull her close. Skin and bones. Nothing but skin and bones. "Please tell me," Lainey whispered into her ear. "We can't help you unless you tell us."

Elaine Arthur swung her arm backward, hitting Lainey in the side without effect.

"Gran—"

"Go away," her grandmother whispered and threw her arm at her again. The blow was a little harder, but not enough to hurt.

"Please, Gran—"

Elaine's arm came back again, glancing off of Lainey's hip, but this time staying firm and rigid, held straight like a traffic policeman's. "Leave me alone," she said louder, her sobs increasing. "Leave me alone."

Backing away, Lainey grew alarmed. What was she thinking? What was she going to do if her grandmother became overwrought, violent, or even suicidal? It was sheer stupidity on her part, Lainey thought. "Never mind," Lainey said, as calmly as she could. "Forget I mentioned it."

Her grandmother wept loudly now. A wail.

"Gran, please. It's all right."

Lainey now stood by the side of the bed, stroking her grandmother's outstretched arm. "Please, Gran. Calm down."

"Leave me alone!" came the cry.

"I will, I will," Lainey said, backing out of the room, panicked, her own tears starting to fall. "I'm sorry, Gran. I'm sorry."

In the hall, she spun to go to the kitchen—to call Serena—and ran straight into her parents.

"What's going on here?" her mother demanded.

"Gran's upset."

Her mother glanced nervously past Lainey into the room. "About what?"

"I . . . I mentioned Adam Powell."

"Stupid girl!" her mother snapped and turned to her husband. "What should we do? Call Dr. Gilthorpe?"

Tim Bishop looked at his wife and his daughter with an expression of exasperation. "We can't bother the doctor every time she sheds a tear. Let me see her. Make yourselves useful and put the kettle on." He went into the room, pushing the door closed behind him.

IN THE KITCHEN LAINEY HAD TO DEAL WITH A DIFFERENT KIND OF SILENCE: the silence of her mother's disapproval. Without saying a word, Margaret Bishop voiced a series of accusations. Lainey dabbed at her eyes, accepted her mother's silent rebuke, and then silently rebuked herself as well.

She felt thoroughly beaten up by the time her father walked into the kitchen ten minutes later. He was carrying the tea tray, which he put down on the counter. "She's asleep," he announced.

"What did you say to her? What did you do?" Margaret asked.

"I merely told her to sit up and drink her tea before it got cold. It was tepid, but she didn't complain."

Margaret took charge of the tea tray and began to clear it up. "Did she tell you why she was crying?"

"No. She didn't say anything. She drank her tea and then lay down to go to sleep. At least, I *think* she was asleep. Her eyes were closed in any event."

"Oh, Daddy, I feel so stupid," said Lainey, ready to cry again.

"I should think you would," he said gently. "What were you up to?"

"I wanted her to say something, *anything* really, so I mentioned Adam Powell."

"Ah. The old boyfriend," he said. "Where's my tea?"

"Under the cozy," Margaret said and gestured to the small flowered cozy next to the electric kettle.

"Thanks." He poured himself a mug and sat down at the island. "Well? You wanted a reaction and you got one. Did it serve any purpose?"

"No. I don't know what I was thinking. I suppose I'd hoped she would be shocked into talking to me about him."

"A bit naïve, I'm afraid," her father said.

"I know."

"It's dangerous to play amateur psychologist," her mother chimed in.

"I *know*, Mother."

Tim Bishop held his mug in both hands, as if warming them. "We got your message on the answering machine. That's why we came over."

"You could have told us you were coming to stay," said her mother.

"I *did* tell you. That's what the message was."

"*Before.*"

"There was no 'before,' Mother. I only decided to come down this afternoon. To give Serena a night off. She's wrung out, you know."

"Why did you have to come all the way from London? She only needed to tell me. I would have come over so she could go out."

"You know Serena. She's not going to say she can't handle something. You have to offer."

"That's silly."

"As if you aren't the same way."

"I'm not. I ask for help. Don't I, Tim?"

Eyes closed with a *God help me* expression, Tim asked, "May we forgo this argument for a few years? I want to know about this fellow in America. The one you mentioned in your message." He struggled for a name. "What's he called?"

"Nicholas. He's Adam Powell's grandson," Lainey explained.

"Does he know anything useful?"

"Not much, but he's trying to find out. His grandfather won't talk about what happened."

"Don't tell me *he's* lying in bed, curled up in the fetal position, too?"

"No," Lainey replied. "He's thriving. But he's bitter."

"Bitter? About my mother?" Margaret asked indignantly.

"It would seem so. He won't talk about her, or their relationship, or whatever happened between them."

"So it's a dead end," her father said.

"No." Lainey said firmly. "It can't be." And then an idea seemed to strike her from nowhere.

Her father raised an eyebrow. "Your grandmother won't talk. His grandfather won't talk. That sounds like a dead end to me."

"Adam Powell won't talk to Nicholas. But he might talk to someone else."

"Like who?"

"Like me."

"Oh?" her father asked. "And how will you get him to do that?"

"By going to America and *making* him talk."

Mid-gulp, her father choked on his tea.

Her mother turned to face her. "This man has been keeping a secret for fifty years and you think you'll simply walk in and get him to tell you what it is?"

"Why not?"

Margaret looked at her husband. "Oh, Tim. The doctor said she didn't get enough oxygen at her birth. Now I believe him."

Tim smiled, and nodded.

Lainey wasn't amused. "Look, you can sit around and watch Gran waste away. But I can't. I won't. I have to do *something* to save her."

CHAPTER NINE

SATURDAY, THE 10TH OF JULY

IT WAS A MATTER OF SHEER WILL AND DETERMINATION ON NICHOLAS'S PART to keep away from his e-mails and to concentrate on the presentation for his grandfather. He worked twelve-hour days on Thursday and Friday, had dinner with Kathy Friday evening, fell asleep next to her while watching a video in his apartment, felt guilty when he awoke later and the video had finished and Kathy had gone. He glanced at his computer on his way to bed. He wondered if Lainey had written. How was her grandmother? Had they talked at all about Adam? He almost went to look for an e-mail, or to write one asking those questions, but opted for bed instead. It's not that he was so sleepy, but that he wanted to heed Jeff's advice not to be distracted.

He woke up early on Saturday morning and felt drawn to his Bible and Prayer Book. He read a few chapters in Isaiah and took assurance in God's repeated declarations that his will shall be accomplished.

"I will go before you," God promised somewhere in chapter 45. And then he reminded those who might resist his will: *Woe to those who argue with their Creator. Does the clay pot say to its potter: 'What are you doing? Your hands are useless!'"*

I don't want to resist you, Nicholas prayed. *Give me a clue about what you're up to. Give me the wisdom to deal redemptively with my grandfather. Heal Lainey's grandmother. Guide my steps if I'm to play a part. Thy will be done.*

Thy will be done.

The phone rang, startling Nicholas as if God himself might be calling. It was Kathy.

"Did I wake you up?"

"No," Nicholas said. "I'm sorry I fell asleep last night."

"You've been working hard. Are you awake enough to go out? It's a beautiful day."

"I need to take a quick shower and get dressed."

"All right. I'll be there in about fifteen minutes."

As he had the night before, Nicholas glanced at the computer. He really should look at his e-mails, he thought. *Later.* He took a shower and, while he was getting dressed, he could hear Kathy in the other room.

"Kathy?"

"I'm here. What do you want to do today?"

"I didn't make any plans. Let's go to a movie."

"Which one?"

"I don't care. Check the listings online."

"All right." He heard her at the computer while he pulled on a pair of shorts and a T-shirt. He retrieved a pair of socks from the dresser drawer when she called out, "You have a stack of e-mails. Haven't you been checking them?"

"No. Too busy."

"Let's see what you have here . . ."

He was pulling on one of the socks when he had a sudden and very sharp sense of panic. Hopping on one foot toward the living room, he said, "Don't worry about them. I'll—"

It was too late.

Kathy was reading something on the screen. "Who is Lainey?" she asked.

"Lainey?"

"She says she has an idea," Kathy said. "She says she needs to talk to you about coming to America."

Nicholas was stammering even before he spoke. "Really," was as much as he managed.

"Who is this?" she asked, turning to him, scrutinizing his face.

"I'm sure I mentioned it to you," he said, not sure at all. "Lainey is Elaine Arthur's granddaughter."

"Elaine Arthur. The woman in England that your grandfather knew?"

"Yes." He tried to be calm and casual as he approached the computer. "What does she say?" He leaned over Kathy's shoulder and looked at the e-mail. Find out the damage.

In the subject line it said *Idea: we must talk about my coming to America.*

"Hmm," he said and went on.

Dear Nick—

"She calls you Nick?" Kathy asked as she tapped the screen with her forefinger.

"It's a joke," Nicholas explained.

"You know her well enough to joke?"

"We've written a few e-mails."

I should have phoned you. I probably will now.

"You've talked on the phone?" Kathy asked. Her tone was hardening.

"Just once. It made sense once we established that there was a connection. Between my grandfather and her grandmother."

My grandmother's condition is getting worse.

"What condition?" Kathy asked.

"She's sunk in a deep depression—because of my grandfather."

"How do you know that for sure?"

"It's the only thing that makes sense."

I believe if I could talk to your grandfather and get him to explain what happened then we might understand better what to do. Help! It may be an absurd hope, but there's a chance he'll talk to me. Once I win him over with my English charm, I doubt he can resist me.

"Her English charm?" Kathy asked. "Does she have a lot of that?"

"Oh, you know how it is," he said.

"No, I don't."

"The accent. Everyone is charmed by the accent."

"Your grandfather has that accent, Nicholas. I don't think he'll be charmed. But you are, is that it?"

"She seems nice, if that's what you mean. But no, I'm not 'charmed' in the sense that I . . . uh . . . ."

Kathy already turned back to the screen and wasn't listening anymore.

We need to talk right away. I'm looking into the airfare to come, if you agree. Time is of the essence.

She signed off with a simple *Lainey*.

Nicholas scanned the e-mail for a date. It had come sometime yesterday. He should have looked at the e-mails last night, he reprimanded himself.

Kathy leaned back in the chair, but didn't look up at Nicholas. "So she's coming to see you."

"To see my grandfather," Nicholas corrected her. "Things must be getting desperate with her grandmother."

"Desperate? Do you think she's going to *die* because of something that happened with your grandfather?"

"Maybe."

Kathy looked up at him skeptically.

He raised his hands in surrender. "I don't understand it myself. But Elaine Arthur is in a deep depression. She has withdrawn completely. She won't talk to anyone."

Kathy shook her head. "People don't withdraw because of something that happened—when did you say?—fifty years ago?"

"Obviously some people do."

"I don't believe it."

"What's not to believe? Whatever happened between my grandfather and Elaine Arthur must have been extremely intense. And when it fell apart, it impacted both of them—enough that he sank into bitterness about it—"

"You don't know that."

"I think I do."

She folded her arms defiantly and said in her teacher voice, "*Nicholas.*"

"She was panicked about writing to him. It was a *stack* of letters, Kathy. She was desperate to reach him."

"There's that word again. Desperate. Why is everything suddenly so desperate? Two weeks ago, everyone was just living their lives. And now you're caught up in desperation."

"I don't know why it's all come back now. But it has. And the poor old lady is suffering. Just like my grandfather is suffering."

Kathy now stood up. "Your grandfather is *not* suffering!"

"Like I've told you—"

"I know your theories and rationalizations, Nicholas, but this—," she gestured to the screen, "this seems weird and meddlesome. A woman wants to fly herself here—a complete stranger—with the idea that she'll get him—a complete stranger—to talk about something painful from his past—"

"Ah! So you admit it's something painful—," he interjected.

"It might be. I never denied that. What I've denied is your right to get in the middle of it."

"Why shouldn't I? He's my grandfather!"

She shook her head, not hearing him. "I've read about e-mail relationships. How intense they get. How they create artificial impressions of people, of emotions. There was a girl I used to work with who became infatuated with a man who turned out to be married with three kids."

"This isn't like that. And it certainly isn't an infatuation."

"Then what is it? Why are you so obsessed?"

"I've explained all that. I want to help my grandfather. And now I have to help Lainey's grandmother. It's all interconnected, don't you see? I can't do one without the other."

Silence for a moment. Nicholas could feel that Kathy's mind was working it out. She then said, with a tone of resignation, "Your family isn't going to be happy about this."

"Then don't tell them."

"Oh, you're going to surprise them with this British chick?"

"I don't know. But I don't want you to tell them, Kathy. Not yet. Not until I figure out what to do."

"Do you think she should come to see your grandfather?"

"I don't know how to answer that. I just got the e-mail. I have to think it through."

"Maybe you should talk it over with *her*," Kathy suggested. "Discuss it between yourselves."

He had no idea she could be so sarcastic. "Kathy—"

She brushed past him for the door. "I'm going."

"I have to put my shoes on."

"I'm not hungry now."

"Come on. You're making this into something it isn't."

"No, I think *you're* making this into something it isn't."

"Let's have breakfast and talk it through."

"There's nothing to talk about. In spite of the fact that your family—*and I*—have asked you to leave things alone, you haven't listened. And you won't listen to anything I have to say at breakfast either. So why bother?"

"We don't have to talk about that. We can talk about lots of other things. Please, Kathy. Don't leave."

She was not to be persuaded. At the door she turned to face him again. "Tell me something. If I hadn't stumbled onto that e-mail, would you have told me about it?"

"That's not a fair question."

"I'll take that as a 'no.'" She opened the door and left.

Frowning, Nicholas dropped his head and growled. He was still wearing only one sock.

NEEDING TO THINK, NICHOLAS SHOVED A FEW THINGS INTO HIS KNAPSACK and drove east on King Street until it stopped at the waterfront of the Potomac River. It was still early—the tourists hadn't crawled out of their beds yet—so he easily found a parking place near a corner coffee shop. He got a cup of something strong and a cheese Danish and sat at one of the tables on the sidewalk. The Old Torpedo Factory sat opposite. It had served the city well in the first and second World Wars, bringing jobs and much needed growth to the area. All that had changed in 1946 when it was shut down, putting thousands out of work. No one had known what to do with the site until someone got the bright idea to move the entire catalog of Nazi archives there. Thirty years they sat— thousands of documents shoved into old and dented filing cabinets. Then, in the 1970s, some local fellow launched a campaign to renovate the derelict old monstrosity and it became an arts center, a haven to painters and sculptors who worked and displayed their creations.

Nicholas mused on the transformation. From bomb-building, to a warehouse for one of the most evil regimes in history, to a site marked for demolition, to a purveyor of beautiful art. He thought: How's *that* for redemption?

He wished Kathy was with him now. He wanted to point to the building and say, "There. That's my grandfather."

Good thing she wasn't there, he thought. It would have been a stupid thing to say.

He tilted his head up at the deep blue sky, the clouds like ostrich plumes. Boats drifted on the Potomac. A sailboat here, a speedboat there, a large touring boat making its way down the middle. What a day. Young couples pushed their little ones in strollers. Dogs pulled their owners on leashes this way and that. People said hello, acted like they knew one another. Maybe they did. Occasionally he could hear a plane coming in for a landing at Reagan National Airport.

I should be walking with Kathy. On a day like this we shouldn't be quarrelling. Everyone is probably right. I'm being obsessive. Who am I to think that my grandfather needs to change? How can I be so presumptuous to think I can help an old woman on the other side of the Atlantic?

Lainey shouldn't come. What purpose would it serve? The old man might not agree to see her, let alone speak to her. And, as it now stood, everything had become so complicated with Kathy's reactions and his brother's and father's warnings.

No. He had to tell her not to come.

Nicholas drained the last of his coffee, pitched the cup into a trash can, and went back into the coffee shop. They had wireless Web access, so he found a corner, took his laptop out of his knapsack, and got connected. He then typed an e-mail to Lainey.

Dear Lainey,

Sorry it's taken so long to write back. I've been very busy preparing for the family gathering on the 17th.

Well, I've given it some thought and don't think you should come to talk with my grandfather. It will only make things more difficult for all of us.

Maybe there's another plan. Or maybe we're on the wrong track completely.

Nicholas

With grim determination he sent it off, packed up his things, and left the shop. He walked up King Street, not wanting to let go of this beautiful day. The shop owners were beginning to open their wooden doors, relics of the eighteenth and nineteenth centuries. The morning light caught the large windows and brick fronts—some red, some painted gray or blue. He stepped into one entrance that led left to an ice-cream parlor and up a staircase to a second-floor antique shop. He went up, dodging a blow-up Spiderman that hung by a web from the ceiling. Betty Boop adorned the walls, along with a masthead of someone who might've been Napoleon. French doors led into a small hallway crammed with old books and a front room congested with glass cases of antique jewelry and nostalgic toys, yellowed newspapers and magazines,

Revolutionary and Civil War memorabilia, and only God knew what else. Nicholas had to sidestep antique furniture scattered around the room. An elderly woman with a jet-black wig and heavy black eye mascara sat behind a small counter and nodded to him.

Drawn to the shelves of books, he saw an old copy of *A Christmas Carol* and thought of the moment in the story when Scrooge came face-to-face with his own mortality. He had seen his own name carved into a headstone. The moment was dramatic enough to shake Scrooge out of his smug complacency about his life and to beg for a second chance. Maybe that's what his grandfather needed. A dramatic moment. And maybe Lainey's arrival might be dramatic enough.

Lainey should come, he suddenly thought.

His cell phone rang on his hip and the woman behind the counter looked at him with disapproval.

Nicholas retreated toward the back of the shop and flipped open his phone. "Hello?" he asked in a forced whisper.

"Son?"

"Oh—hi, Dad."

"Where are you?"

"In an antique shop in Old Town. Where are you?"

"Home. Are you coming this way?"

"Maybe later. I have a few more boxes at the office I want to go through."

"Are you dropping by here?" Meaning, the house.

"I wasn't planning on it. Why?"

"I want to talk to you."

Uh-oh. "About what?"

"Your mother talked to Kathy a few minutes ago."

More uh-oh. "Why did she do that?"

"I think she wanted Kathy's mother to bring some cookies or something to the family get-together."

That made sense, Nicholas thought. Kathy's mother was renowned for her homemade cookies. "Chocolate chip," Nicholas said.

"Come by and we'll talk."

"Now is a good time."

His father paused to make a decision. Then: "What's going on with you two?"

"What do you mean?"

"Kathy was upset. She told your mother that you're bringing that English girl over to see your grandfather."

"I'm not *bringing* her over, Dad. Lainey thought it might help if she spoke to Grandad personally."

"You tell her it won't. It'll be a waste of time—and it'll stir things up needlessly. I thought we told you to drop it."

"I *did* drop it. Sort of."

"I don't understand you, Son," his father said. "Don't you care about Kathy?"

"Of course I do." He felt himself getting irritated. "This isn't about Kathy."

"She seems to think so. She's really upset."

"That's *my* business," he said. He took a deep breath to control his anger. "Look, I don't appreciate her running to you guys every time we have a little problem."

"This isn't a little problem."

"A big problem, then. I don't care. We're supposed to work it out between us. Not the whole family."

"You need to straighten yourself out, Son."

"I *am* straightened out."

"Then make it clear to that English girl that she mustn't come."

"Lainey, Dad. Her name is *Lainey*. Not 'that English girl.'"

"Tell her not to come. Do you understand?" A firm, unequivocal command in a tone inherited from Adam Powell himself. No negotiation, just listen and obey.

"I understand," Nicholas said, not wanting to admit that he'd already done just that.

His father waited, then softened his tone and said, "I know you're angry. But it's for the best. Why would you want to ruin your grandfather's party?"

"No one wants to ruin the party, Dad. She wasn't coming for the party. She probably would have arrived afterward."

"Afterward? Then that's even better."

"What do you mean?"

"You grandfather won't be here afterward."

"I don't understand. Why not?"

"He's decided to take a few weeks to travel. I think he plans to go fishing in Canada somewhere."

"He's going fishing?" Nicholas asked, his voice rising. "For how long?"

"Aren't you listening? A few weeks. He didn't say exactly."

"Oh, great."

"Come by later," his father said. "I think your mother has the engage-ment ring ready for you to see."

CHAPTER TEN

LAINEY DIDN'T EXPECT TO BE BACK IN LONDON SO SOON, BUT HER SUCCESS on the phone the day before motivated her to return quickly. Who knew that one could navigate the Church of England's bureaucracy so effectively? A call to Lambeth Palace, a connection to another department, then another, until she was talking to some dear old soul who had access to the records for retired and deceased priests, vicars, canons, and every other officer in the church hierarchy. Pensions was the key, she'd said. If John Peters, who was the vicar of St. Luke's Church in Chiswick until he retired in 1988 and then died in 1993, had a proper pension, then it went to his surviving spouse, if she were still alive . . .

Lainey scribbled notes and waited while, on the other end of the line, papers were being shuffled, a book dropped and opened, and then the tap-tap-tap of long fingernails working the keyboard.

"Yes, I see now," the dear old voice said. "Mrs. Julie Peters is still living at number 32, the vicarage on Bedford Road in Chiswick."

"Still?"

"Hmm. Yes. That's unusual, I think. She must have bought the house from the diocese. We allow that from time to time . . ."

That was Friday. On Saturday morning Lainey left her grandmother in the care of Serena and enjoyed the clear morning weather, and traffic, to get into London. She stopped by her flat in Shepherd's Bush to get some additional clothes, then headed for Bedford Park, just north of Chiswick.

Bedford Park Road was tree-shaded and lined on both sides with rustic Victorian houses. Developed in the early 1880s, it was the first of the "garden suburbs," famous for its architecture and its connections to the countercultural artists of that time. They lifted up ideals of simplicity, of beauty and harmony. The irony now, Lainey thought as she drove up the street searching for number 32, the vicarage, was that this anti-materialistic haven of Victorian England was now one of the most expensive areas in which to live in all of London.

As Lainey drove down the leafy street, past the semidetached homes with ornate gables and colorful stained glass windows on the doors, she began to second-guess her decision not to phone Julie Peters first. Lainey had reasoned that it'd be easier for Mrs. Peters to put the phone down on her than to slam the door in her face. A personal visit was the better option. But now she wasn't so sure. Even as a wild guess, Lainey figured that Mrs. Peters must be approaching ninety years old, if not older. What if she was senile or bedridden or institutionalized, the house now being lived in by a relative? What if she didn't remember Elaine Arthur at all?

Lainey found the number on the left side of the road and parked as close as the other cars would allow. The vicarage was a terraced house, set back from the road, with a white gate and a well-tended front garden, brilliant with flowers. Lainey opened the gate and walked toward the front door. Out of the corner of her eye, she saw a small figure off to the right, a woman dressed in rough gardening clothes and a large straw hat kneeling next to a rosebush. The hat moved back and forth as the woman yanked weeds from the bed and dropped them in a small basket next to her.

"Hello?" Lainey called out.

The woman didn't move.

Lainey came within a few feet of her. "Hello?"

Still no reply.

Perhaps she's hard of hearing, Lainey thought, and reached out to touch the woman's shoulder.

The woman turned around quickly, lost her balance, and would have fallen over if Lainey hadn't grabbed her arm.

"I'm so sorry!" Lainey cried out.

"Oh dear," the woman said after she had steadied herself. "Help me up."

Lainey obeyed, drawing the woman to her feet.

She wasn't hard of hearing. She was listening to music through a headset. Pulling them from her ears, the woman said, "I'm sorry," and reached for the small CD player attached to her belt. Lainey heard a short piece of something that sounded like big band music before it suddenly cut off.

"Well, *that* was dramatic," the woman said with a smile. She was taller than Lainey had expected, almost the same height as Lainey, lanky and scarecrowlike. Strands of white hair poked out from beneath the hat. Her face was pale and wrinkled, but Lainey recognized the beauty that had once been there. Her eyes shone bright; keen, yet calm.

"I didn't mean to startle you," Lainey said.

"I shouldn't play my music so loud," she said in a low voice. "I get lost in it while I do the garden. Someone could kidnap me and it'd be an hour before I'd know what had happened." She tipped her hat back a little and eyed Lainey more closely. "Your face looks familiar, only I don't remember your name. Do I know you from church?" She had an American accent, with just a hint of English inflection.

"We haven't met," Lainey replied. "You're Julie Peters, aren't you?"

"I am." Her eyes narrowed. "You're not an estate agent, are you? I'm not selling the house."

"No, no," Lainey said quickly. "I'm here about Adam Powell."

"Adam?" she asked, surprised. "Oh dear. He's not dead, is he?"

"No."

"Good. I'm getting tired of people younger than me dying before I do."

"He's very much alive and—" Lainey squinted against the sun. "May we go inside to talk?"

"I suppose so. As long as you promise that this isn't some kind of sales pitch."

"I promise."

"Then come in."

At the front door, Mrs. Peters retrieved a cane and used it to make her way up the two steps and then inside. Lainey had to adjust her eyes as she followed Mrs. Peters down the front hall, between a staircase and a front room, then past a dining room, then a third room with a bed in it. Mrs. Peters slowed down and gestured her cane toward the room. Lainey peered in, took in the scent of something sweet, the floral wallpaper, the very feminine decor. "That used to be John's office. It's my bedroom now," she explained. "Getting up and down those stairs is a little harder than it used to be." She chuckled softly. "You can be sure it wasn't that girly when he was alive."

Lainey smiled. Her eye caught a gold-framed photo on the dresser. It was a posed head shot, probably from the forties or fifties. Longish black hair, combed back. Montgomery Clift in a clerical collar, she thought. He was definitely handsome, with a dreamy-eyed expression, as if the heavens had opened up to him right before the photo was taken.

"That's my John," Mrs. Peters said. She abruptly tapped a door under the stairs. "The loo is in there if you need to use it."

The hallway deposited them into a large kitchen area. Mrs. Peters removed the straw hat and hung it on a hook next to a side door leading to the back garden. Her hair was thick and white and with a few deft strokes of her fingers, it took on a fashionable shape, as if she'd been out to lunch rather than working in the garden. Cupboards, appliances, and counters lined both sides of the kitchen. At the end a small table and chairs sat next to tall windows, a conservatory that had been added at some point in the house's history, giving a stunning view of the garden. Like the front, it was well-tended, the grass perfectly manicured. Sparrows lit upon a bath in the far corner. Mature trees dotted the sides and the far end, giving strategic shade to lawn chairs and a bench.

"Please sit down," Mrs. Peters said.

Lainey sat at the table, a solid pine. Gazing at the kitchen and then the garden again, she said, "This is beautiful."

"It's not for sale," Mrs. Peters reminded her.

"I'm not an estate agent," Lainey promised again.

Mrs. Peters shoved her cane into a nearby umbrella stand and leaned against a counter. "So, how do you know Adam?"

"I don't know him, actually. But I know his grandson."

"Which one? Jeff or Nicholas?"

"Nicholas."

"I've never met them in person," Mrs. Peters confessed. "I know of them from the photos that Adam occasionally sends with my birthday and Christmas cards. I doubt they know I exist. Does Nicholas?"

Lainey felt embarrassed. "No, he doesn't. I'm sorry."

"Don't apologize." She sighed. "That's Adam for you."

"What do you mean?"

"Tell me why you're here and then maybe I'll explain."

Lainey hadn't rehearsed this part and could feel a stammer coming on. "Well . . . ," she began, then stopped. "I'm not sure where to start."

"Is it that complicated?"

"Yes."

"Oh dear. I better put the kettle on. Or would you prefer lemonade?"

"Tea, please." Lainey started to rise. "I can make it myself."

Mrs. Peters waved her down. "I'll get it," she said and poured water from the tap into the kettle. "Why don't you tell me who you are. That's a good starting point."

"My name is Lainey Bishop. I'm Elaine Arthur's granddaughter."

"Elaine Arthur," she said slowly, as if stretching out the syllables might jog her memory.

"I think you knew her as Elaine Holmes."

"Elaine! Oh, yes. Of course. Good heavens. No wonder you look so familiar." Mrs. Peters turned the electric kettle on, then came closer and took a good look at Lainey's face again. "Yes, I see it now. Oh my. This is a blast from the past."

"I'm sure."

She sat down across from Lainey and folded her hands in front of her. Her fingers were slightly twisted from arthritis. "Tell me about Elaine and why you're here."

Lainey did, beginning with her grandmother's walk in the rain to the old chapel, Uncle Gerard, her depression and the search for reasons, finding Nicholas and through him Adam Powell, and up to her current desire to fly to America to talk with Adam personally.

By the time she finished, the kettle, an old metal one, had come to a boil. Mrs. Peters looked at her thoughtfully. "Well, now," she said and got up to pour the water into a china teapot. "I hope you don't mind bagged tea. I used to insist on leaf alone, but it's too much bother."

"Bagged is all right."

The teapot and cups were put on a tray, along with a small pitcher of milk and pot of sugar. With some difficulty, Mrs. Peters carried the tray to the table and set it down. "I often wondered how it would all turn out," said Mrs. Peters as she took her seat again.

"How what would turn out?"

"Adam and Elaine. I remember thinking when Adam went to America without her that the story wasn't finished. Mind you, I didn't expect it to take *fifty years*."

"Do you know what happened? Why Adam left?"

"He left because of me," Mrs. Peters said. "I got him the job in America. But the plan was for Elaine to go with him."

Lainey shook her head. "The plan? I don't understand."

"Of course you don't. How could you? Let me tell you what *I* know."

SHE FOLDED HER HANDS IN FRONT OF HER AND LOOKED OUT OF THE WINDOW at the back garden. "We took Adam in after his father was killed by one of those German rockets. Such a blow, considering his mother had died in the Blitz. We felt terrible for him and gave him the room in the attic."

"Did you often take in strangers?" Lainey asked.

"No, not often. But his mother was a member of our church and had dragged Adam and his father along. Then she died and we hardly saw them. He spent a couple of summers in Stonebridge."

"We think that's where he met my grandmother."

"Yes. That first summer after his mother died. I seem to recall him saying something about meeting at a church."

"A bombed-out church."

"That's right. They were trying to put the stained glass windows back together, bless them." She sipped some of her tea. "By the time we entered the picture, they were in love. And I don't mean just a child's crush. There was something almost mature about their affection. I knew the minute I met her that they had something remarkable."

"When did you first meet her?"

"Just before Christmas in 1944. I escorted Adam on the train to meet up with her in Brighton. Travel was difficult in those days, because of the war. There were a lot of restrictions. Having an adult made it easier for him to go."

Lainey tried to think through what she knew of her grandmother's life. "Why Brighton?"

"She was attending school there."

"I thought she went to a school in Southaven."

"Perhaps she did. All I know is that her father had sent her to a school in Brighton for a while. He probably thought it would discourage their relationship." Her eyes flared up like a striking match. "Her parents didn't approve, you know. It was sheer, unreasonable snobbery! They had the poor girl cross-eyed with it. I came from a wealthy family, so I'd seen that kind of arrogance."

Lainey didn't respond, unsure what to say. She took a drink of her tea. "You were telling me about your first impression of my grandmother."

"Thank you," Mrs. Peters smiled. "I'm prone to wander and pontificate. Your grandmother met us at the station in Brighton and I remember vividly how poised and beautiful she was. She made an instant good impression on me. A lot like you."

Her cheeks turning crimson, Lainey glanced away.

Mrs. Peters continued. "Your grandmother raced up to Adam and unashamedly kissed him right in front of everyone—and then began to cry."

"Cry?"

"It was the first she'd seen Adam since his father had died. The dear girl, she took his loss to heart so." Mrs. Peters now smiled at the memory. "We had tea together and Elaine and I bored Adam stiff by talking about the latest fashions and what was going on in London. She was also fascinated about my being a vicar's wife. She'd experienced a spiritual awakening at school because of reading her Bible as part of her studies. She'd decided that Jesus was remarkable, certainly a lot more interesting than the churches allowed him to be. She told me that she wanted a faith that was truly a matter of the heart. In that, I knew John would like her. And he did." Another sip of tea. "I made excuses to leave them alone. We met up at the station for the last train back to Victoria. They were both so young and innocent. He shook her hand good-bye before he got on the train."

Lainey imagined the scene, like something out of an old movie.

"I confess that I made it my personal mission in life to help arrange their meetings, even though her parents disapproved."

"How often did they see one another?"

"Not often, sadly. But they wrote. Oh! The letters from her. Once, sometimes twice a day. And when he wasn't in school or working at the printer's, he was in his room at the desk, writing everything to her."

"Like e-mails," Lainey observed, and thought of Nicholas.

"E-mails!" Mrs. Peters exclaimed. "Aren't they wonderful? I can't tell you all the old friends I get to talk to now. The ones who aren't dead, I mean."

"So what finally went wrong?" Lainey asked, guiding them back to the subject at hand.

"What went *right*?" asked Mrs. Peters. "Whoever said 'Love conquers all' didn't know Adam and Elaine. It was an uphill battle for them, every step of the way. For over *ten* years."

"Because of her family," Lainey said, just to clarify. Then thought: *my* family.

"Your generation has no idea what it was like. The pressure from her family to be with friends of her own class was tremendous. Your grand-mother loved her parents very much—and that put her in direct conflict with her love for Adam. She was in constant turmoil about it. And your uncle Gerard, as you called him, was no help at all."

"Why? What did he do?"

"Adam seemed to have one run-in with him after another. I suppose you could call him a rival."

"A rival? For my grandmother's affections? But they never went out together."

"No. Perhaps he was just a good friend."

"What's so bad about that?"

"Under normal circumstances, nothing. But in these circumstances it brought out all of Adam's insecurities. Gerard was one of her kind, after all; just the kind her father would want her to marry."

"But they *didn't* go out," Lainey said defensively.

Mrs. Peters raised her hands in surrender. "Regardless, Adam was very suspicious of Gerard's intentions. More than anything, he probably resented that Gerard had the freedom to see your grandmother when *he* couldn't. Surely you understand. He *loved* your grandmother so very much. But, toward the end, he despaired about their future. He had us all praying for them."

"*Adam* did?"

"Why are you so surprised?"

"Well," she replied. "Nicholas talks as if his grandfather isn't a Chris-tian at all."

"How would he know?" she asked—a challenge.

"He's studying to be an Episcopal priest."

"Ah, then I suppose that makes him an expert, doesn't it?" she said, with a twinkle in her eye. "You tell Nicholas to come talk to me about Adam's faith. He looked up to my John, and was very active in our church's youth group. And I know personally that he made a profession of faith at Billy Graham's Crusade here in London in 1954. I saw him go forward. So Nicholas had better be careful before passing judgment."

"I'll tell him," Lainey said, uncomfortable about the subject. "So my great-grandparents somehow succeeded in splitting them up? Is that what happened? Or was it my uncle Gerard?"

"It was likely a conspiracy of them all," Mrs. Peters replied, "*and* circumstances."

"What do you mean?"

"Well, eventually Adam decided it was time for them to take charge of their lives. He didn't want to sneak around anymore. He wanted her to announce their love and their intentions to get married one day." She held up a finger, as if pinpointing the memory in the air. "It was right after he returned from Egypt, his military duty there. He'd gone back to his job at the printers and, of course, we insisted he return to his room in the attic. Anyway, they met at the Festival of Britain here in London. Do you know about the Festival of Britain? 1951?"

Lainey shook her head.

"I suppose you could think of it as a huge Disneyland to commemorate Britain's greatness. It was an incredible effort to give the English something to celebrate. To forget about the war debt and the rationing and how bleak everything had been for over twelve years. The South Bank was packed with pavilions, displays, entertainment, restaurants, rides, and activities—you name it. John and I saw almost all of it ..." She looked as if she might go on with recollections of the Festival, but then stopped herself. "What I'm trying to say is that the future seemed bright, if only for the Festival. So it seemed appropriate for Adam and Elaine to meet there. But it all went wrong. Just as Adam wanted to press the issue of their future together, your grandmother informed him that her mother was dying of cancer."

Lainey remembered. "My great-grandmother *did* die of cancer."

"God rest her soul," Mrs. Peters said. "It was horrible news, apart from the obvious reasons. Elaine simply couldn't bring herself to add to her mother's pain by forcing her relationship with Adam on the family. Not then. Oh, how she wept over that. We talked several times and I had to confess that I saw no other solution. So Adam had to be patient yet again."

"That was 1951? My great-grandmother didn't die until 1953."

Mrs. Peters nodded sadly. "Another two years of writing and clandestine meetings."

Lainey sighed. "I don't think I could have done it."

"Perhaps not," Mrs. Peters said. "Or perhaps you haven't met someone worth working that hard for."

Lainey gazed at the old woman's youthful eyes. They were alight with the memory of her own love, presumably for John. "But their love didn't survive," Lainey finally said. "To be honest, the whole thing sounds rather miserable."

"Oh, no—it wasn't," she said quickly. "I'm giving you the short version. In those last few months they had settled into something resembling peace. They weren't together like they wanted, but they had found a place to meet every Saturday. The Mill House, right there in Stonebridge."

"I've been there."

"Oh? Is it still there? I'm glad. It was perfect. Elaine had begun working as a governess for the Arthur family and had Saturdays off. So the two of them would eat lunch at the Mill House and then take long walks through the fields surrounding Stonebridge. He was always aglow when he came back to London from those meetings." She giggled. "I still imagine them walking those meadows, holding hands and daydreaming of the future."

"It sounds romantic," Lainey said.

"Romantic, maybe, but it was only a respite. Adam was still very frustrated, and he seemed to channel it into his work at the print shop. He was made a manager there in no time at all. I know he felt that his success should impress Elaine's father. John and I began to worry about it."

"Why? Is it so bad to want to be a success?"

"It is if it becomes all-consuming, as it did for Adam. I saw his spiritual life suffer as a result. He didn't have time for church. His view of the world simply wasn't Christian any more. Then the Billy Graham Crusade came and we saw a glimmer of hope. Sadly, soon thereafter, things went awry."

Lainey looked at Mrs. Peters expectantly.

"I'm getting hungry," she said abruptly. "Are you hungry?"

"A little," Lainey replied, perplexed by the sudden change.

"Let's order some pizza. I think it's absolutely *brilliant* how they bring it straight to the house."

THE PIZZA ARRIVED AND MRS. PETERS AND LAINEY RELOCATED TO THE dining room with plates, knives, and forks. As they did, Lainey encouraged the old woman to continue the story.

"There came a turning point, around the time of the Billy Graham Crusade," the old woman said between bites. "One night, Elaine had a heart-to-heart with her father and felt the time was right to talk about Adam again."

Lainey guessed the outcome, concluding as she had that her great-grandfather was really a nasty piece of work. "I suppose he demanded that she stop meeting him?"

"No. Surprisingly, he didn't speak against Adam at all. He acknowledged their relationship, but then expressed that his only wish was for Elaine to see other people before making her mind up about a future with Adam."

"Was he serious—or was it a ploy?"

Mrs. Peters shrugged. "I don't know. But Adam was wary. He thought it was a trick to drive Elaine into the arms of Gerard Sommersby, or someone like him. Elaine was more hopeful. She wanted to believe that her father would let her marry Adam if he saw that she'd truly considered her options with others. She honestly thought it was a sign from God."

"From God!"

"Yes. For her father to go from a complete denial of Adam to allowing the possibility of a relationship with him—well, that was nothing short of a miracle. So she agreed."

"Adam couldn't have been very happy about it."

"No, he wasn't. In fact, he told her that if she saw other men, he didn't want to know about it."

"That's reasonable."

"He also told her that if she fell in love with someone else, he'd never forgive her—*or* God."

Lainey gazed at Mrs. Peters. "That's quite a thing to say."

"So it was." Mrs. Peters swallowed a mouthful of pizza. "It was all coming to a crashing conclusion, I can see that now. My father had passed away late in May and I went back to Washington for the funeral. I saw old friends. One was in the printing business and he complained about not finding good printers, men who knew the machines. I thought of Adam and recommended him. I was scheming, you see. I thought that it was a way for Adam and Elaine to run off together. The only problem was that my friend needed an answer from Adam quickly."

Putting down her knife and fork, Lainey turned her full attention to Mrs. Peters.

The old woman continued, "Adam decided to take the job and then formed a plan to surprise Elaine. He'd go to Stonebridge early the next Saturday and arrange with the owner of the Mill House to decorate their favorite table with flowers and confetti. He would ask Elaine to marry him. They would have champagne. He would give her a token ring— something cheap from the jeweler's on High Street until he could buy her something better later. Then the next week John and I would serve as witnesses at the registrar's office."

"Why the registrar's office and not a church?"

"Because of the bans. They had to be announced for three weeks preceding the wedding. There was no time for that. So it had to be a civil ceremony."

Lainey nodded to say she understood.

"Adam was very excited as he made all the preparations. In his mind, this was the moment of truth about their relationship. If Elaine truly loved him, she would have to say yes."

The picture began to come clear to Lainey. "Did she say no? Is that what happened?"

Pushing her plate aside, Mrs. Peters leaned forward and rested her arms on the table. "You're going to be terribly disappointed."

"Why?"

"Because I don't know exactly what happened. And what I do know doesn't put your grandmother in a very good light."

Lainey held her breath.

"Something went wrong," Mrs. Peters said. "I don't think it was a matter of a 'no' or a qualified 'yes' or any of the most obvious possibilities. Adam came back from Stonebridge in an absolute fury. He was as angry and hurt as I'd ever seen him. Neither John nor I could get him to talk. All he said was that he'd been betrayed. All that time wasted on *her*, he said. I don't think he ever said her name again. Your grandmother became 'she,' 'her,' and 'that woman' after that."

Lainey bit her lip. All of her loyalty to her grandmother rose up, wanting to deny it, to claim foul play or a misunderstanding. She managed only: "I can't believe she would hurt him, not purposely."

"If you love your grandmother as much as I suspect then, yes, it's hard to believe. To be candid, I don't believe it myself. I didn't believe it at the time. When Adam came back and said what he said, then refused to talk about her ever again, I felt deep inside that it wasn't right. Like you, I thought he'd misunderstood."

"But where does Uncle Gerard fit into it?" Lainey asked. "Did Adam say anything about him?"

"Not a word. He wouldn't talk and he wouldn't listen to reason. There were no other chances to be given, he wouldn't let us get involved. You don't know how many times I almost phoned your grandmother, but John said I mustn't. Adam had to work this out himself. But Adam refused. He took the job in America, booked his passage, and left."

"My grandmother wrote to him. Clearly she wanted to explain."

"Yes, she did. She wrote, she phoned. But to no avail. She phoned on the day he was booked to leave for America, and I told her he was sailing from Southampton. That was as much as I could do. We didn't hear from her after that. And we didn't feel it was our place to press the matter."

"But the letters . . ."

"Yes, they came and eventually John forwarded them to America when we had Adam's address." She took a deep, mournful breath. "I was confused about it all. And sad. Such a sad end." Her eyes drifted away, going to some distant place. "John was distraught, I know. All the Christian love in his heart yearned for reconciliation. But Adam wouldn't consider it. He wasn't the same after that. We both realized it, as his letters to us became shorter and shorter, less and less frequent. There was a certain tone to them. It was all business."

"That's how Nicholas describes him."

Mrs. Peters went on as if she hadn't heard Lainey. "It was as if his heart died," she said softly. "He wanted to forget his past."

"You stayed in touch with him, though."

"A little," she said. "We were invited to his wedding. But we were very busy at the church and, to be brutally honest, I didn't want to go. I felt it was a sham. I don't believe he loved her, nor she him."

"Then why did he marry?"

"Their marriage made good business sense. It was an ideal merger." Mrs. Peters paused again. Another distant gaze. "Adam did us the honor of coming back for John's funeral. But I hardly knew him by then. He wasn't the Adam I once knew. And losing John was very hard for me. I couldn't be bothered to try to sort out Adam's life while dealing with my own."

Lainey sat quietly, drained now. She wasn't sure what to say or do.

Mrs. Peters began to clear up the plates. "I remember seeing an announcement in the newspaper. About your grandmother getting married to James Arthur. I thought then that things didn't seem finished. There was more to the story, I said to John. It couldn't really end with them simply going on with their lives. John said I was a hopeless romantic and that Adam and Elaine had every right to get on with their lives, even with other people."

Lainey could see that Mrs. Peters was getting tired, her movements slowing down, her eyes heavy-lidded. Lainey insisted on helping with the clearing up. This time Mrs. Peters agreed and said proudly, "I have a dishwasher."

As Lainey put the last plate into the machine, Mrs. Peters suddenly exclaimed, "Where is my mind going?" and raced out of the room. A moment later she returned with a small box and a black book. She beckoned Lainey back to the table and handed her the book. It was a small leather Bible with "Adam Powell" engraved in gold on the lower right-hand side of the cover.

"The *Revised Standard Version*," she said. "I got this for Adam in 1953. It was a new version then, easier to read than the King James."

Lainey flipped through the pages and saw that many of the verses were underlined in pencil. And a few had writing next to them, in the margins. "His writing?"

She nodded. "Adam read this book a lot after he went to the Graham Crusade."

Lainey glanced at one of the underlined verses. *Do not be deceived; God is not mocked, for whatever a man sows, that he will also reap. For he who sows to his own flesh will from the flesh reap corruption; but he who sows to the Spirit will from the Spirit reap eternal life.* Another on the opposite page: *But God, who is rich in mercy, out of the great love with which he loved us, even when we were dead through our trespasses, made us alive together with Christ (by grace you have been saved)* . . .

"They used to have some lively conversations," Mrs. Peters said. "Adam and my John, I mean."

"Why do you have it?" Lainey asked, holding up the Bible.

"Adam left it behind when he went to America. A symbolic gesture, I assumed." Lainey tried to hand the Bible back, but Mrs. Peters refused. "No, no. Please give it to him when you see him."

"If I see him."

"Then give it to Nicholas. You said he's studying to be a priest, right?"

"Yes, but I'm still not sure if I should go at all."

"You must go, my dear. There's no question about that now. If only to tell Nicholas what I've told you." Mrs. Peters touched Lainey's arm gently and she whispered. "Your being here has given me goose bumps. This is God's doing. He's at work somehow."

Lainey gave an embarrassed shrug. She wasn't convinced that God had anything to do with it at all. But, still . . . *I must go,* she thought. *There's no other way.* She tucked the Bible into her handbag. "All right."

Mrs. Peters took the lid off of the small box. Inside were photographs, mostly old, all black and white. "I know I have one or two," she muttered.

"Of Adam?"

She pulled a snapshot out. "Here he is." The picture shook in her fingers as she handed it to Lainey. "Taken at one of our youth events, I think."

Kids sitting on folding chairs along a brick wall. Two girls with plates of cake, one with her fork caught forever in the air. A blurred image of a teenage boy to the far right laughing. He was moving when the photo was taken. At the center was young Adam Powell, around twenty years old. Long-legged and languid, he was sitting on a folding chair with his body stretched out, in danger of tripping any passersby who weren't looking. Like John Peters, he had his hair combed back in a distinct fifties style and had movie-star good looks. He wore a checked shirt and baggy trousers, his hands shoved deep in the pockets. One of his shoes, perhaps they were work boots, was untied. He had an *I dare you to take my picture* look.

"He never liked having his picture taken," Mrs. Peters said. "I was the only one who could get away with it."

"I must've been born in the wrong decade," Lainey lamented. "The men were more handsome then."

"Yes, they were, weren't they?" Mrs. Peters agreed. She pulled out another photo. "Aha. This is the one."

It was Adam Powell in a suit and tie, perhaps a couple of years older, standing at the front door of the vicarage. His hair was shorter and his body erect, as if he were uncomfortable. Yet there was a hint of a smile—the cat who'd just swallowed the canary. "What's he thinking?" Lainey asked, amused by his expression.

"He was thinking about your grandmother."

Lainey looked at Mrs. Peters for an explanation.

"I took this the morning he went to Stonebridge to ask her to marry him."

That explained it. He had a look of victory, a promise about to be fulfilled. "May I borrow these?"

"If they'll help."

"They might."

"Take care of them."

"I'll have copies made and bring the originals back to you."

"Personally. Don't mail them," said Mrs. Peters.

"You don't trust our mail service?" Lainey teased.

"It isn't that," she said. "I'd like you to have an excuse to come back."

Lainey smiled. "It's something I'll look forward to."

At the door, Mrs. Peters kissed Lainey on the cheek and held her face in her hands for a moment. "You do look like her," she said.

"So I've been told."

"Go see Adam personally," said Mrs. Peter firmly, as if she'd made a decision about it. "Let him look at you. I defy him to refuse you. And when you do, give him a message from me."

"Oh?"

"Tell him that St. Luke's is going to install a plaque to honor John's service to the church. Next month. I'll be sending him an invitation with the details." Her eyes were suddenly bright again as she smiled. "Tell him he'd better not disappoint me."

"I'll tell him."

IT'S LIKE A RUSSIAN NOVEL, LAINEY THOUGHT AS SHE REPLAYED MRS. PETERS' story in her mind. *Over ten years, they had to sneak, scheme, and connive to be together. I couldn't have done it. What kind of relationship would be worth that sort of trouble?*

Rather than drive all the way back to Stonebridge and arrive at a late hour, she decided to stay the night at her flat. She opened the windows to let some air in and called Serena to tell her where she was. Serena assured her that all was well, though her grandmother seemed even less responsive than she'd been. She hadn't touched her dinner or tea. Lainey felt a sharp stab of guilt. Mentioning Adam Powell to her may have made things worse.

Lainey turned on the television, watched nothing for a few minutes, and turned it off again. Though she now had more of her grandmother's story, she was still missing an important part. What happened on that day to send Adam back to London in such a fury? What had her grandmother done to him?

Or perhaps she hadn't done anything, Lainey corrected herself. It had been Uncle Gerard. But what could Uncle Gerard possibly do that her grandmother wouldn't know about? How could he spoil their engagement?

She considered the possibilities, moving them back and forth from one hand to the other.

What she refused to believe was that Elaine Holmes really had done something to betray Adam. She couldn't. It wasn't in her nature. Surely his bitterness was displaced, a terrible mistake.

But . . . what if Elaine Holmes did hurt him? Perhaps that was why her grandmother now felt such deep regret and the need to be forgiven.

There was no doubt in Lainey's mind about one thing: She had to see Adam Powell personally. He was the only one who could shed light on this subject—a light that might help lead her grandmother out of the dark tunnel she was in.

Lainey logged on to her e-mail account, wanting to see whether Nicholas had got her message. There were a dozen uninteresting e-mails—and one from Nicholas in the middle of them all. She clicked on it to open and read the short message.

He was telling her not to come.

He was telling her not to come!

"No!" she cried out. "No, you can't back out now!"

She leaned forward, her face in her hands, her forehead against the screen. Anger and despair fought for a place of prominence. *He's given up. He's not going to help me.*

Glancing at the phone, she considered calling him. He didn't know all she'd learned from Mrs. Peters. If he knew, then he'd realize how important it was for her to come.

I have to call him.

She lifted the telephone handset to her ear, but a computer tone screamed back at her. She'd forgotten that she had to sign off the Internet to free up the phone line. Just as she was navigating the mouse to do that, she spotted another e-mail from Nicholas. It had come later. She apprehensively clicked on it.

Dear Lainey,

It's later and I'm writing to retract my last e-mail. My grandfather is leaving for an extended vacation directly after the party. Which means the party is our only hope. You must come if you want to talk to him.

Nicholas

Lainey breathed a sigh of relief.

CHAPTER ELEVEN

FRIDAY, THE 16TH OF JULY

FOR THE NEXT FEW DAYS, NICHOLAS PUT HIS PERSONAL LIFE ASIDE TO finish the retrospective on his grandfather's life. He worked twelve, sometimes sixteen-hour days, going through the boxes, then going through them again, looking for just the right photo or clipping or document to fill in gaps or evoke a particular period of the company's history. He met with staff from the company's graphic arts department, a sound engineer with their video department, and a host of other employees who'd been secretly pressed into service. He dug through compact discs of sound tracks and commercial libraries to find music to complement the visuals. He secured the services of a friend who specialized in voice-over work to narrate passages where needed. And then on Thursday he did a twenty-hour crash-and-burn to make sure all of the elements were finally assembled and mixed together to create an eight-minute tour-de-force of a man and his accomplishments.

He hardly saw Kathy. A lunch early in the week. A late dinner after the crash-and-burn. She was still aloof—an unspoken question hung between them—but she didn't ask about Lainey and he didn't volunteer any information. Maybe he was being naïve, but he wanted to believe that if Lainey came and the truth emerged about their respective grandparents, then Kathy would understand. She would see that he was right. And then life could go on.

In the midst of this tension, his mother had shown him the engagement ring he was expected to present to Kathy during the family get-together. He knew nothing about rings, but had to admit that it looked impressive. A white gold band with a brilliant oval diamond with six single-cut diamonds orbiting it. It had belonged to his grandmother, been bequeathed to his mother, and was now handed to him to secure the eternal love of his future bride. With a ring like that, he figured it was a done deal. But he left it with his mother—for safekeeping—until the night before the gathering. That way, he wouldn't have to think about it.

Lainey hadn't written since her last e-mail saying she would try to come. In moments when he stopped to catch his breath he was tempted to write to ask about her grandmother or her job or if she was indeed coming. But he feared that Kathy or his father might somehow find out—was it possible to "bug" e-mails?—so he didn't. Besides, if they asked about "that English girl" he could honestly say he hadn't spoken to her.

There were moments when he thought she wouldn't come. Surely it wasn't worth the risk in money or time, considering that Adam Powell might turn her out without comment. And she now knew that Nicholas's family didn't want her there. So why bother?

She'd have to be a particularly brave girl to make the journey. Or crazy.

Still, he checked his phone machine and e-mails every night, expecting to hear from her. *Hoping* was more like it. But he didn't know why. Maybe she was his fantasy, the ever nagging *What-if?* What if his life suddenly took a new and unexpected turn? What if he surprised everyone and ran off with this strange and mysterious woman? He suspected that most men tortured themselves with those kinds of questions—a sweet, blissful torture because they knew they'd never get the answers. *In the end*, Nicholas concluded, *we're levelheaded and practical creatures, we don't take new and unexpected turns. We don't pull the rugs out from under our lives to run off with strange and mysterious women.*

That's the adult reality that snapped Nicholas out of an adolescent fantasy.

He knew nothing about Lainey or her life. She knew nothing about his. They were three thousand miles apart. They could be pen pals, maybe (but not likely). One day he might make a trip to England and have a *proper* cup of tea. But it was ridiculous to flirt and speculate about an English phantom. Mature people don't think that way.

For his life, for his goals, for his future, Kathy was the right one. He knew that. Why fight the obvious?

And by Friday morning he began to believe that Lainey was nothing more than a strange whim, a diversion. A *distraction*, to borrow his brother's phrase. By Friday morning he was beginning to doubt that his quest for the truth about his grandfather was even important. Okay, maybe the old man wasn't a saint. Who was? Sure, there was Lainey's grandmother to think about, but for all he knew she was predisposed to depression and her condition had nothing to do with Adam at all.

By Friday morning he had it all figured out.

And on Friday afternoon Lainey called from the airport.

"HELLO, NICK. I DON'T WANT TO BE PRESUMPTUOUS—"

It was definitely her voice on the phone and his heart went into overdrive. "You're *here?*" he asked.

"I'm at Washington-bleeding-Dulles and we have to talk about those silly-looking trams. They're grotesque."

Suddenly he didn't know what to say. About the trams, about anything. "You're here."

"I'm not entirely here. The rest of me hasn't landed yet."

"Do you have a car or should I come get you?"

"I have a hire-car. I'm in it now. In the car park. I thought I'd better ring you first. Which meant I had to go back in to the counter and hire a phone. For some reason my cell phone won't work over here. Must be the difference in accents."

"Do you have a map?"

"Do I have a map? Are you joking? I'm overwhelmed with maps. Every friend I've ever had has been to America and given me maps. I have more maps than your Congress has brain cells."

"How many maps?"

"Six."

"Oh."

"I won't be anywhere near Colorado, I assume?"

"No."

He heard a loud rustle of paper. "Good. That one's banished to the backseat. New Mexico?"

"No."

Another loud rustle of paper. "Gone."

"Look, you want the Washington, D.C., Northern Virginia, and Maryland map."

More rustling of paper. "That leaves me with just this one. I had no idea Washington was shaped like a diamond. Do you play baseball on it?"

"Only if that's a euphemism for politics. What do you want to do?"

"I want to drive directly to the hotel and get checked in. It's called The Olde Towne Inn. The extra *e*'s sold me on the place."

"Do you know how to get there?"

"It looks straightforward, if these big fat green lines are anything to go by. This one goes east, then drops down to that one, then over to the river and follows it down."

"Exactly what I would have told you."

"You drive on the opposite side of the road, don't you?"

"Depends on which way you're going."

"I mean, you drive on the opposite side than the British do."

"Yes. But don't worry. You're on major roads the whole way. Just do what the rest of the drivers do."

"And if one of them suddenly runs into a lamppost?"

"Do the same and you won't have to worry about driving anymore."

Suddenly a soft beeping in the background. "Oh! It's one of those direction thingies."

"What is?"

"This little television next to the steering wheel. What a relief. I know Americans are addicted to the telly, but I couldn't imagine that they expected me to watch *The Simpsons* while I was driving." A few more beeps as she pushed the buttons on the console. "I just program in where I'm going and the satellite will lead the way. Brilliant. Perhaps it will drive for me, as well."

He chuckled. "Call me if you get lost or have any trouble."

She didn't reply.

"Lainey?" He thought the phone had gone dead.

With a clear change of tone and a gentle clearing of her throat, she said, "Nick, I know my being here will cause you problems. But I want to say up front that I don't expect you to do anything. Well, not much of anything. Just point me in the right direction to talk to your grandfather.

You don't have to do anything else. You mustn't be blamed for my being here. Do you understand?"

Nicholas laughed. "Lainey, it would be rude not to be a good host now. We Powells pride ourselves on being hospitable."

"Let's hope your grandfather remembers that."

That was at six minutes past two o'clock.

AT SEVEN MINUTES PAST TWO O'CLOCK, NICHOLAS WAS PACING THE length of his apartment. *She's here*, he said. *She's here she's here she's here she's here she's here* . . .

In so many ways it had been a game up until now. A theoretical exercise. Now it wasn't. Now she was here.

He thought quickly through the logistics. Kathy was—he looked at his watch—on her way to Crockett to help his mother with something-or-other for the get-together. He was supposed to join them later and spend the night.

All right. The rest of his family was on *that* side of the Beltway. Lainey was on *this* side.

They were safe enough until he could think things through.

But there was no thinking anything through until he could talk to her and find out what her plan was. *If* she had a plan.

AT 3:34, THE PHONE RANG AGAIN. NICHOLAS SNATCHED IT UP. "HELLO?"

"Is *everything* named after George Washington around this place?"

"Hi, Lainey."

"I had no idea the man was so egocentric."

"I think they used his name *after* he died."

"Oh. That's all right, I suppose. Though I hope you realize that the English don't behave that way. There was no *Bill London* after whom London was named. Or Ferdinand *Winchester*. Or Horatio *Liverpool*."

"What about the actor Michael York?"

"Oh, well, yes. It's true. We named the city of York after Michael York."

"So where are you now?"

"At the hotel."

"Did you have any problems?"

"No. Well, just one. But you'll see that on the news later tonight."

"What?"

"A minor international incident. Nothing to worry about."

"Are you hungry?"

"Yes, now that you mention it."

"I'll come and get you. We'll eat—and talk."

"Alone?"

"Yes."

"Not your girlfriend?"

"No. She's at my parent's house, helping to set up for tomorrow."

"And you aren't? You slacker."

"I'm going later."

"I don't want to hold you up."

"You won't."

"Did you tell anyone I'm here?"

"No."

"Just as well."

"Give me about ten minutes and I'll meet you in the lobby."

She gasped. "There's a lobby? Oh dear, I just walked into the first room I found. The door was open, so I—"

"Lainey—"

"That would explain the clothes in the closet. I was so impressed with American hotels for a minute there. I thought they provided an entire wardrobe with the price of the room."

"Lainey, I think you're jet-lagged."

"Probably. Hurry, will you? I want to take a nap."

NICHOLAS CHANGED SHIRTS, CHANGED AGAIN, AND THEN USED THE DRIVE from his apartment to the hotel to try to quell his nervousness. He couldn't shake the feeling that he was going on a blind date. He had to tell himself again and again that he was meeting a woman in trouble who needed his pastoral help. A distant stranger. An overseas guest. A new friend. That was all she was.

He reminded himself over and over that this encounter was *not* about unanswered questions. There was no *What-if?* to be found here. They were on a mutual mission to learn the truth—to help Lainey's grand-mother and Nicholas's grandfather. That was it.

Keep your eye on the goal.

The Olde Towne Inn was in the north section of town, nestled between a new development of townhouses and an old development of offices. A bus dominated the main parking lot, with a harried driver standing amidst a gaggle of suitcases. A large group of tourists milled around the front entrance and well into the lobby, talking about their plans, where did the camera go, will we see the Washington Monument today, should we do the boat tour? It was chaos.

How would he find her? *Dope*. He would recognize her from the photo on the Internet, of course.

He saw her standing against the far wall, gazing at the sea of strangers with an amused look. Her long brown hair was pulled back and fastened with a small ribbon. Her eyes scanned the room—those dark, penetrat-ing eyes that he'd seen in the photo. The slight nose and full lips. She wore a blousy white short-sleeved shirt, blue jeans, and white sneakers.

Shazam, he thought, and then rebuked himself soundly for thinking it.

Someone spoke to her and she smiled back. *Radiant*, he thought, and then rebuked himself for thinking that, too.

He didn't know how long he stood there looking at her, but he was suddenly aware that she was looking back at him. Their eyes locked on one another for only a second. Maybe a fraction of that. It was enough.

She mouthed, *Nick?*

He then smiled and forced his way through the tourists.

She met him halfway and said, "This happens every time I travel overseas. People find out where I'm staying and they show up by the hundreds."

Nicholas put out his hand. "Hello, Lainey."

"Hello, Nick." She took his hand and he noticed how soft her skin was, and how long her fingers were.

He blushed and was momentarily speechless. She was flesh-and-blood. "Well—"

"Shall we stand here for a few moments or make our way out?" she asked, teasing him.

He came to his senses. "Out," he said and took her arm. He guided her through the crowd to the door.

Out in the sunshine, they crossed the parking lot to his car. "How did you know me? Do I really look so British?"

He didn't understand. "How did I know you?"

"You were looking straight at me."

He opened the passenger door, turning his head away so she wouldn't see that he was blushing again. Confession time. "Your photo."

She looked puzzled. "What photo?"

"On the Internet. Some occasion at your work. I looked you up."

She cocked an eyebrow, a moment's hesitation, then said: "It's a horrid picture."

"Do you still have the hat?"

"*No.*" She got into the car. "There should be a steering wheel here!" she exclaimed as he walked around to the driver's side.

He climbed behind the wheel and opened his mouth to ask what she wanted to eat, but she cut him off.

"It was very rude for you not to have one," she said.

"Have one what?"

"A photo. On the Internet. I looked, too."

He laughed and pulled out of the parking lot. Following Second Street in the direction of the Potomac, he turned right to go south into Old Town. They passed hotels, offices, and endured the speed-up-and-slow-down of the stop signs at every corner.

He pointed to the left at a large patch of trees and green lawn, parents with strollers, joggers with headsets, and a volleyball game going on at the net. "Oronoco Bay Park," he said, playing the tour director. "And the beautiful Potomac River beyond."

"Not the *Washington* River? Somebody slipped up there."

"The Indians would put up with only so many name changes."

Silence, and then she asked softly, "It's very strange, isn't it?" She had turned a little in her seat and was looking directly at him.

"What is?"

"The difference between e-mails and real life. I mean, I knew there was a real live person on the other end of the line, but . . ." She giggled. "I think I'm rather nervous."

"You? Nervous? I don't believe it."

"Oh, but I am. I'm a chatterbox when I get nervous. Though my mother would say that I must be nervous a lot. I go on and on about silly things and try to be clever. And here I am, doing it again. I think I'm trying to impress you."

He glanced at her, not sure of what to make of her frank admission. "Impress me? Why?"

"I don't know. I think because you're cute."

He let out an embarrassed laugh. "You're not so bad yourself," he said in his best Groucho Marx.

She ignored it. "I expected you to be wearing a dog collar."

"A what?"

She gestured to her neck. "A priest's collar."

"Some of the students at the seminary do," he explained. "I think it's a lot like wannabe doctors who wear stethoscopes all the time. I only wear a collar when I'm at church. Maybe I'll wear one more often when I'm working full-time. And now I'm doing it, too."

"Doing what?"

"Chattering. You don't really want to know about clerical fashions."

"I want to know about food."

"Then you're in luck." He turned right onto King Street.

"IMAGINE COMING ALL THIS WAY FOR FRENCH FOOD," SHE SAID.

They were in a corner café on King and North Pitt, a cafeteria-style place that advertised a variety of dishes, but seemed to serve mostly quiche.

"There's a McDonald's further up the street," he offered.

"This will do." She shoved a petite portion of Quiche Lorraine into her mouth.

He jabbed at his Quiche Florentine, having ordered it before he realized he wasn't hungry at all. It was getting awkward, he thought. His eyes drifted back to her. Her face—*those eyes*—kept hold of his attention. He forced himself to look outside at the people walking past the window. "How's your grandmother?" he asked.

"Not well." A cloud crossed over her face. "I made the mistake of mentioning your grandfather's name to her the other night and, well, her response wasn't what I'd hoped."

"What did she do?"

"Cried. Wailed, is more like it."

"Did she say anything?"

"Not a word. My father had to calm her down."

Nicholas shook his head slowly. His mind raced back to the mentally ill patients he encountered during his pastoral training at a nearby hospital. "Is she on medication?"

"The doctor has prescribed Prozac. But it takes awhile to work, I've heard. Lithium has come up as a possibility. I don't know. I get impatient with their fiddling around." She shrugged, her knife and fork unmoved over the plate. "It doesn't matter. My grandmother refuses to take anything. Serena sneaks it into her food."

"No wonder you came."

Her eyes settled on his. The seriousness of the situation showed in them. "I can't sit around and do nothing." She tore into her food again. It was something to do. A way to change the mood. "Julie Peters says hello," Lainey said casually with a coy expression.

"You found her?" he asked, impressed.

She nodded. "She still lives in the same place. The vicarage in Bedford Park. Chiswick."

"Was she helpful? Did she tell you what happened?"

"I got a lot of the story from her. Not the important bit, unfortunately, but a lot of the rest of it."

"Are you going to tell me or do you intend to keep me in suspense?"

She leaned over and picked up her purse. Opening it, she rustled around and then pulled out a stiff cardboard envelope. From that she produced two photos and handed them to Nicholas.

He reached into his shirt pocket and put on his glasses to see.

"Oh. You wear glasses," Lainey said.

"To read. Why?"

"I didn't imagine glasses."

He grinned, embarrassed again, and looked at the photos. He recognized his grandfather immediately. But they could have been black-and-white photos of his brother, Jeff, the resemblance was so strong.

"From Mrs. Peters's private collection," Lainey said proudly.

"These are great," Nicholas said—and then smiled as an idea struck him.

"What?"

Nicholas looked up at Lainey.

"Your expression. You have the look of him," she said. "The cat that swallowed the canary. What are you thinking?"

"Hold that question." Nicholas snatched his cell phone from his belt. He hit the speed dial, a number in Maryland.

Paul Murphy, the media editor, picked up his extension at Powell Publishing. "This is Paul."

"Paul, it's Nicholas."

Paul groaned. "What now?"

"Two more photos. Are we too late to include them?"

"But I just finished the master."

"These are *good* photos, Paul."

A conceding sigh. "How soon can you get them to me?"

Nicholas grimaced and asked sheepishly, "Uh . . . eight o'clock?"

"Not a chance. I'm going home now."

"How about first thing in the morning? Is there time before the party starts?"

"If you know *exactly* where you want them to go, then I can drop them in and redo the master. It'll take an hour."

"Nine tomorrow morning, then."

"Okay. But they better be *great* photos, Nicholas. I don't care if you're the owner's grandson."

"You'll see," Nicholas said and hung up.

"Yes, you have my permission to use them," Lainey said and took another bite of food.

"Sorry. I think they may aid our strategy."

She held up her hand to beg time to swallow. "Our strategy? My strategy, you mean. You have to keep out of this as much as possible. Just tell me the best time and place to see your grandfather and I'll take care of the rest."

"It's not that easy," he said. "And I can't just throw you to the wolf like that."

"Yes, you can. And I'm used to wolves. You should see the ones I have to deal with in London."

He shook his head. "They're nothing compared to Adam Powell. Besides, I have an idea."

"Oh?"

"I'll show my masterpiece about his life, *including* the two photos of him from England. He'll be amazed. He'll wonder how I got them. That's our setup."

"Our setup for what?"

"For when I introduce you to him later, when he's relaxed and appreciative of all the attention. I'll say you've come as a representative of his English past. To wish him well."

"Isn't that awfully close to a *lie* considering you're studying to be a priest?"

"It's not a lie. You *are* a representative from England and you plan to wish him well, right?"

She eyed him warily. "You Episcopalians behave a lot like our Anglican vicars with your rationalizations."

"It's the only way." He picked up his fork, took a few more pokes at his food, then put his fork down again. His mind was racing with anticipation of what would happen and how his grandfather might react.

"Actually," Lainey quickly said as if her mind were buzzing along, too. "I do have a message to deliver to him. From Mrs. Peters."

"Oh?"

"She wants him to come to London next month for a special presentation. They're putting a plaque about John Peters in St. Luke's Church."

"He'll have to go."

"*She* thinks so."

Nicholas pushed his plate to the side and leaned forward onto the table. "Enough small talk. Tell me everything Mrs. Peters told you."

"WELL? WHAT ARE YOU THINKING?" LAINEY ASKED.

"There's so much to consider," Nicholas replied, his brain spinning.

Lainey had recounted Mrs. Peters's story as they'd finished their meal, and continued as she and Nicholas strolled down to Strand Street—an alley more than a street—and around to a small park with a bench facing the Potomac. The sky was overcast and the choppy water a hard gray. A cooling breeze blew from the northwest and gave some relief from the humidity. Commercial jets flew overhead at regular intervals to land at Reagan National. When Lainey had finished, they sat silently.

Hearing the story helped Nicholas focus on his original intentions for his grandfather. *If* Mrs. Peters was right and Adam Powell had had a true encounter with God through the Billy Graham Crusade, then there was hope for him. Unless he'd been faking it. Nicholas wouldn't have been surprised.

"It fills in a few blanks about your grandfather and my grandmother, but it doesn't help explain what happened that day," Lainey said. "Did my grandmother really do something to betray your grandfather? And where was my uncle Gerard? Your grandfather said *nothing* about his being there. What could he have done that my grandmother wouldn't know about until just a few weeks ago?" She put her face in her hands and groaned. "The same bloody questions keep circling around the drain."

"Isn't 'bloody' supposed to be blasphemous?" Nicholas asked, a less serious question to get them away from circling the drain.

"I understand from a very good source that 'bloody' has nothing to do with God, Jesus Christ, or Mary. No one knows the etymology."

"What source told you that?"

"I got it from a book by some American writer."

"I'm not sure I'd believe him." He stood up to begin the journey back to his car.

"Time to go?" she asked, also standing.

"Yeah." He led her up the tree-lined and cobblestone Prince Street.

"*Gadzooks*, on the other hand. Now that's the one you want to watch for blasphemy," she said.

"Why?"

"It means 'God's hooks.' So when people say it, they're actually swearing by the nails that attached Jesus to the cross."

"I didn't know that."

"Oh, yes. I'm an amazing source of useless information."

"WHO'D HAVE THOUGHT THAT ONE AFTERNOON COULD CHANGE THE course of two people's lives so significantly?" Lainey said thoughtfully as Nicholas brought the car to a stop in front of the hotel. The bus was gone, the tourists either in their rooms or doing other things that tourists like to do.

A jet passed over with a high whistle, jet stream trailing.

"Let's hope that tomorrow will change it again," she said, almost as a toast.

"What are you expecting to happen tomorrow?" he asked her. He had become afraid that her hopes might be set too high. It was ever-present in his mind that the encounter could end in utter failure.

She undid her seat belt and turned to face him. "Ideally? I hope that your grandfather will give me a deep and profound insight about what happened that day so I can figure out how to help my grandmother."

"Lainey—," he began, his voice a caution.

She pressed on. "Realistically? I'm fully prepared that he'll say nothing and throw me out on my ear. At which point I'll either catch the next flight home or spend a few days sightseeing. One can't come all this way and not see *everything* named after Washington."

"That's right. You can't go home without seeing some of the area," he insisted. "I'll be happy to give you a grand tour."

She smiled at him. A *you poor deluded boy* smile.

"What?" he asked defensively.

"Nick . . . *if* your family hasn't disowned you for your part in our little scheme, then they certainly won't allow you to play tour guide for me. And I'm sure your girlfriend will have a thing or two to say about it."

"You've got the wrong impression of her. She'll like you. She'll want you to enjoy yourself while you're here."

Again, that *you poor deluded boy* smile.

"You don't know her," he added.

"No," Lainey said, "but I know how I'd feel if I were in her shoes."

"But you're not," he protested. *Why do women always think they know so much about other women?* he wondered. Then he said, "There's something you don't know."

"Oh dear. What now?"

"I'm supposed to give her an engagement ring tomorrow. At the get-together. A big announcement."

"Congratulations," Lainey said pleasantly. "If I'd known, I would have brought a gift."

"It's supposed to be a surprise," he said.

"You used the word *supposed* twice just now," she observed. "Was that intentional?"

"I said it's supposed to be a surprise, but she knows it's going to happen."

"Go back one *supposed*, please. You said you're *supposed* to give her the engagement ring. Does that mean you might not?"

"I didn't realize you were going to proofread my sentences as I say them."

"It's in my blood."

He tried to clarify his statement. "I shouldn't have said *supposed*. It will happen. It's all arranged."

"Arranged," Lainey said, as if she wasn't sure of the word's meaning. "Have you set a date for the wedding?"

"Next June. After I graduate from seminary."

"Good for you," she said with a polite amount of enthusiasm. "Well done. Do priests' wives wear clerical collars, too? It's quite common in England, you know."

"It is *not*."

"Isn't it?" Another coy smile. "My mistake."

A moment of expectant silence, the hum of the car's air-conditioning.

"Your invitation!" he suddenly remembered.

"Invitation?" she asked.

"To the get-together. You'll need one to get in." He sprung into action, reaching to the backseat and retrieving the white envelope. "All the information is right here. Including a map."

"Who needs a map when I've got an onboard navigational system?"

He scribbled his cell phone number on the envelope. "I'll have this with me the entire time. Call me if you get lost or need help or . . ."

"Lose my nerve?"

"Yeah. Something like that."

She patted him on the leg. "Thanks for your help, Nick. I don't take it for granted, you know."

He smiled. "I'm glad to do whatever I can. For both of our families."

She opened the door, but turned to take one more look at him. She feigned exasperation and said, as if continuing some other thought. "But you are so *cute*."

He watched her go inside. *Lithe*, he thought and expected her to turn around to wave, just once more. Willed it, in fact. But she didn't.

Oh boy. I'm in trouble.

LAINEY LAY IN BED WITH A DISTINCT, JET-LAG FUZZINESS OF THE BRAIN. IT was only half past seven, but that was half past midnight London time. Her day had begun well before dawn in England. The last of her packing, the drive to Heathrow Airport from her grandmother's, the six-hour flight on which she couldn't sleep—a long day.

The air-conditioning in the room was only a little better than the average fan, blowing warm and humid air around. The sheets felt damp. She'd drawn the curtains, but she was still aware of the light outside. The television was a poor distraction. She considered having a bath, but the tub was too small and too old, the porcelain rough and chipped.

Her bravado with Nicholas was one thing. Her feelings now that she was alone in her room was another. She was anxious about tomorrow.

She knew what Nicholas had been after when he'd asked the question *What are you expecting . . . ?* He was worried for her, about her expectations being set too high. What a sensitive soul he was to think about it. How could he know that, though she told herself repeatedly that Adam Powell might refuse to see her, she also harbored a very deep hope.

She had a scene in her mind—like a movie—where she would meet Adam Powell and he would look at her, see the resemblance to her grandmother, and suddenly melt before her, all resistance gone, the bitterness washed away in a river of newly remembered love. "Yes," he'd say. "I can tell you about that day. Happily! And perhaps I should go back to England with you to see your grandmother personally, to tell her to come out of her shell, that all is well, there is nothing to regret." And there would be forgiveness and peace.

Silly old bear, she said to herself.

Turning over, she considered reading the book she'd brought. A mystery thriller set in post-World War II Berlin. A man searching after four years away for a woman he'd once loved and had lost.

No. It would only fuel her false hopes.

Four years. What was that, really? Nothing compared to the ten years, no, the *fourteen* years that Adam and Elaine spent with clandestine rendezvous, of hoping against hope, of clinging to a love that might never be fulfilled. How tragic. For a love to endure that long and then prove to be so fragile. It was horrible. Like the marathon runner who stumbles and falls only yards away from the finish line.

Fourteen years. And now here they were *fifty* years after that and there was still a connection, a thin strand, the tiniest of threads running between them.

She got up and went to the window. The air in the room was stuffy, oppressive. She threw the curtain aside and raised the window, forgetting that she wore only an oversized T-shirt and briefs. The small courtyard below was empty. She breathed in the air, but it was no different than the air in the room. She felt the sweat slide along the small of her back. *How did people cope with the humidity?* she wondered, and closed the window again.

Facing the room, her mind raced back to the same questions. Circling the drain. Going around and around but never going down.

Adam Powell's Bible—the one Mrs. Peters had given her—was on the dresser. She picked it up and thought about her conversation with Father Gilbert. What had he said about the big picture? She flipped the cover open, her knowledge of the book a vague recollection from her religion classes in school. She found the New Testament. Underlined passages, Adam's notes. Her eyes fell on a page, a section he'd underlined in pen rather than pencil and an exclamation mark next to it. She read the passage and, in her mind, she heard the headmaster of her school, Mr. Phillips, reading in his clear, clipped BBC accent: "Second Corinthians, fourth chapter, beginning with the sixteenth verse . . ."

> *So we do not lose heart. Though our outer nature is wasting away, our inner nature is being renewed every day. For this slight momentary affliction is preparing us for an eternal weight of glory beyond all comparison, because we look not to the things that are seen but to the things that are unseen; for the things that are seen are transient, but the things that are unseen are eternal.*

These were words that had particular meaning for Adam at one time. *We do not lose heart.* Was he thinking about his relationship with Elaine? *This slight momentary affliction* . . . The little picture, the pieces of stained glass that Father Gilbert had talked about . . . *preparing us for an eternal weight of glory beyond all comparison* . . . *we look not to the things that are seen but to the things that are unseen* . . . *the things that are unseen are eternal* . . .

The big picture.

So what had happened to Adam on that day—and all the days following? He'd walked away from Lainey's grandmother, gone to America, and left his Bible behind. Had he really walked away from God, too?

The big picture, she thought again. Fifty years later and Lainey was going to see Adam Powell. Was that also part of the big picture?

Sitting down on the bed, she wondered if there was a spark from the past, a living ember, if not of love then of compassion, buried somewhere under the dust of time. Was it so wrong to believe that there might be?

Then there was her flirting with Nicholas to consider. What was she thinking? *It's because he's safe*, she thought. She always flirted with men who couldn't or shouldn't reciprocate. A bad habit, perhaps, but it kept her at arm's length from getting into anything serious. Most of the single men she knew had either a desperate look—they were beside themselves to get married—or that hungry look—they were nearly cross-eyed from blatant desire.

But Nicholas was cute. More than cute, really. She'd only said that to tease him. But she could easily fancy him—that much she knew. Hazel eyes and wavy brown hair—the kind of hair you wanted to run your fingers through and get properly messed up. His hazel eyes exuded a certain sensitivity and understanding, almost feminine in a way, but they were balanced by a very masculine jaw that conveyed strength and purpose. He was a little taller than her, with a slim build. He certainly wasn't an Arnold Schwarzewhatsit. But he had broad shoulders.

Shoulders you could count on to hold you up when you slow danced or needed to have a good cry.

It was a moot point, she reminded herself. He was studying to be a priest, after all. What did she know about that? That was a different world from hers.

And he was going to announce his engagement tomorrow. A reminder that she had invaded his life. She was the guest here—the momentary interloper—who would be gone again in a few days. If her mission with Adam Powell was successful, there was nothing else for Nicholas to do. She would go back to England and have no reason to talk to him ever again.

Pity.

NICHOLAS ARRIVED LATER THAN HE'D PLANNED AT THE "POWELL PALACE," as it was called by the locals. He'd missed dinner with his family, Kathy, and two other distant relatives from his grandmother's side that he could never keep straight. No one asked why he was late, so he didn't have to explain. And Adam Powell wasn't there, choosing instead to stay at his home in Annapolis that night. Thank God.

He took a couple of minutes to update his father and brother about the presentation but didn't mention the two new photos he planned to add the next morning. His mother kissed him, complained that she never saw him much anymore, then scurried off to entertain Uncle So-and-So who'd just arrived from Chicago.

Kathy signaled that she wanted to take a walk, so he slipped out with her into the warm evening. The air was thick again with moisture. In spite of the lateness, there were still a half-dozen people busy with preparations for the next day's event. The twenty-acre property, normally just an expansive lawn at the edge of a small forest, now contained an enormous white pavilion on the east side of the Georgian house.

"Amazing," he said to Kathy as they strolled the grounds. "The house has thirty-two rooms and it's in danger of being dwarfed by a tent."

"There are a lot of people coming tomorrow," Kathy said. "I heard your mother say there'd be close to four hundred."

"Who in the world are they all?"

"Employees, friends, your relatives."

"Mine? Hardly. My relatives are my mom, my dad, my brother, me, and my grandfather. That's all."

"You're forgetting your grandmother's family. There are a lot of them who've come down from New York and New Jersey."

"That's right," he conceded. "The esteemed Aldriches of Red Bank, New Jersey. I always forget about them."

"Why?"

"Because they never had much to do with us. Or we didn't have much to do with them. It's hard to tell which. My mother was very good about staying in touch, but the men in the Powell family didn't."

She took his hand and they walked around to the east side of the house where caterers were busy unloading food from vans. A wiry, high-strung man was shouting orders at the other men about hurrying up, about the late hour, about how little time there was until tomorrow. Nicholas didn't notice that anyone's pace improved for all of the cajoling.

The workers were using an entrance to the house that he'd forgotten about. He and his family had spent almost all of their time on the west side, with Nicholas's teen and early adult years spent going in and out of a separate door to his room in the basement. For a moment, Nicholas felt like a stranger as he looked at the mansion, the vast lawn, and the iron fence that seemed to appear and disappear from his view around the perimeter.

He had no heartfelt sense of ownership of the house. Looking at it now, he realized it was always someone else's—his grandparents', his parents', eventually Jeff's. Never his own. If he felt an affection for any part of it, it was for the old barn, half-rotted, falling apart, that stood just on the other side of the woods bordering the property. He and Jeff had their best times there. It was where they'd played and talked and hid their comic books and practiced shooting the BB gun their father didn't want them to have and, in general, grew up together. He smiled to think of it now. A mansion in which to play and they had created a boy's paradise in an old barn.

They walked around the back of the house to the edge of the woods, where a tire still hung from a tree. The crickets were beginning their nightly serenade. A path led in one direction to a pool, and there was a separate path to a tennis court. Neither were used much now, but the pool would get some use tomorrow.

"Hey," Kathy said, moving in on him and invading his thoughts. "Where are you?"

He gave the old tire a nudge, making it sway slightly. "I'm right here."

"But what are you thinking?"

"I don't know. A lot of things."

She pulled him close for a hug. "It's been a very stressful week. I know that. And I want you to know that I understand."

"You understand what?"

"How hard it's been for you."

"Oh."

"After tomorrow let's give ourselves a break. Let's take a few days and go down to the bay—Easton or St. Michael's—or drive to Ocean City. Wouldn't that be nice?"

He pulled her close, burying his face in her neck. He didn't reply—he couldn't.

"Aren't you glad she didn't come?" Kathy asked.

Nicholas stiffened. "What?"

"That woman from England."

"Oh. Yeah." He moved away from her as if to give the tire another playful push. *Tell her*, his conscience screamed. *If you don't tell her now and she finds out tomorrow, she'll never forgive you.*

"You don't agree," Kathy said, looking closely at his face, trying to read him.

"I feel bad about her grandmother," he said carefully, attempting an indifferent tone. "And if talking to my grandfather'll help, then why not do it?"

A deep sigh. "You're probably right."

"I am?"

"I'm sorry I overreacted."

"You are?"

"I don't know why, but I felt—" She turned away from him. "You've never given me a reason to be jealous. But there was something about her. The way you seemed to be keeping her a secret from me. It made me feel . . . threatened."

"Kathy . . . ," he began, but didn't know what to say.

She turned to face him again. "Actually, this is the moment when you wrap your arms around me and tell me that I had no reason to feel threatened."

He obeyed and put his arms around her. But rather than feel warmth and affection, he felt like he wanted to pull back from her. He was confused. And all the while his conscience was calling him a coward and a cheat.

God, what am I doing? How had he become so turned around? Three weeks ago he'd known nothing about Elaine or Lainey Bishop, his grandfather's past, or a box with mysterious letters. Now he was a coconspirator with a virtual stranger, deceiving his family and his almost-fiancée.

He should have been able to tell Kathy about Lainey. He should be able to tell her now. Why couldn't he?

"Loyalty," he said out loud, a thought rather than a statement.

"Loyalty?"

"I didn't tell you about Lainey because sometimes I think you're more loyal to my family than you are to me."

She stood back from him. "One of us needs to be loyal to them."

"Ah." He moved away from her.

"I love your family, Nicholas. Just like I love my own. I like hanging out with your mom, joking with your dad, playing with Jeff—and even flirting with your grandfather. You think he's Ebenezer Scrooge and I think he's wonderful."

"Yes, I know."

"So what's going on? Your family is terrific, but you always position yourself as an outsider, like you're embarrassed or ashamed of them."

"It's nothing like that."

"Then what is it?"

He was momentarily speechless. No one had ever challenged him about this before.

"Well?"

"We're not the same," he said clumsily.

"Meaning?"

"Their interests aren't my interests. We don't have the same goals."

"What are you talking about?"

"I've dedicated my life to God, not the family business. That makes me different. Weird. Jeff and my father talk about work. My mother goes on about the inner workings of the Annapolis, Baltimore, and Washington elite. What room is there for my life? I don't fit."

She moved close again for a cuddle. "That's why you need me as a bridge," she said, and he noticed she hadn't denied his statement. "I won't let you be the outsider. I have it all figured out."

"I'm sure you've got it all arranged with my parents," he said, and it sounded more sarcastic than he'd meant.

"Please don't be like that," she said. "Not on the eve of—" She stopped herself and smiled.

He gazed at her. *The eve of our engagement*, she'd almost said. The *arranged* surprise. Everything according to plan.

But not *his* plan. Someone else's.

"I'm sorry." But she wasn't.

"Let's go back to the house," he said.

"Are you sure you're all right?" she asked as they walked.

He took her hand, as if to answer; hoping it was enough of a gesture of affection, praying that he wouldn't have to speak for fear that she might finally expect words from him that he couldn't say.

God, what am I doing?

HE WAS READING IN HIS ROOM WHEN HIS MOTHER CAME TO SEE HIM. SHE brought the engagement ring, which she placed reverently on the bedside table, next to his wallet and keys.

"Thank you," he said, putting his book aside.

She sat down on the edge of the bed, the mattress hardly moving because she was so slight. *Pick*, her friends in high school had called her. Short and skinny like a toothpick. Both of her pregnancies had required special care and, in Nicholas's case, hospitalization, because she had bordered on the anemic. "The baby weighs more than she does," was the common family joke at the time.

She smiled at him. Lines around her eyes, around her mouth. But he could see the beauty that had attracted his father when they were in college. A Princess Diana. Even the blonde hair, now cut and styled especially for the family get-together.

"You look tired," he said.

"Do I? Oh. Well," and then waved her hand toward the door. A sweeping gesture to encompass all the work and entertaining she was doing for the big event. "I'm going to bed shortly. How are you?" she asked. It was a leading question. Her emotional radar for him was uncanny.

"I'm fine," he said.

She didn't believe him. "Are you ready for tomorrow?"

He assumed she was talking about his presentation. "As ready as I'll ever be."

She frowned. "Only as enthusiastic as that?"

"How enthusiastic should I be?" And then he realized that she was talking about becoming engaged. "Oh. No. I was talking about the presentation."

She waved it away like an annoying bug. "I don't care about that. I'm sure it'll be wonderful."

He watched her, wondering what she was really after.

She tugged at the bedcover, straightening it, then pressing it with her hand. "We're not a demonstrative family, as you know. But we're very proud of you. *I'm* especially proud. To give your life to God, to marry a girl like Kathy. Those are significant things. I hope you know that I'm not taking them lightly."

"No."

"Then what's wrong?"

"Why do you think something's wrong?"

She gave him her motherly eye—her *don't insult me with such a stupid question* look.

"Pre-engagement jitters, I guess," he replied. It was the only reasonable thing to say. Everything else—his grandfather's reactions to the presentation, to those two photos, to Lainey—had to remain unspoken.

"You want to marry her, don't you?"

"Why do you ask that? Why wouldn't I?"

She eyed him again, as if scanning him, reading his contents. "You answered my question with two more questions. You're either unsure or being evasive for some reason. Which is it?"

For a second—a mere flicker of a second—he thought he might tell her everything. A little boy with his mother. He could simply pour out his feelings in the hope that she might be able to sort through them, like she had with his toys or his math problems, and make sense of them. Instead he said, "Marrying her is the right thing to do."

"I hope it's more than a mere sense of duty."

"She's terrific. Amazing. She'll be a perfect wife—a perfect *pastor's* wife."

She smiled at him, patted his knee, and stood up to leave. Thinking it was the end of their conversation and she was satisfied, he picked up his book. But at the door, she turned and lingered.

For a moment he hoped she might intuitively know to say, "Look, if you're not sure about Kathy, then don't give her the ring tomorrow. It'll keep until you know it's what you *want* to do, not what you *have to* do."

She glanced into the hallway, then looked back at him and sighed. "They're calling for rain tomorrow." And then she was gone, the door gently bumping closed.

CHAPTER TWELVE

SATURDAY, THE 17TH OF JULY

THERE WAS AN UNDERCURRENT OF ANXIETY ABOUT THE FORECAST OF rain throughout the morning. It hung over the remaining preparations like the dark fat clouds overhead.

Kathy, who looked stunning in a white skirt and pink top, had been pressed into service to help arrange flowers—a last-minute addition by Nicholas's mother who wanted some of the posts holding up the tents to be decorated.

Nicholas stayed clear. His priority was to make sure that everything was set up for his presentation, come rain or shine. It was the perfect distraction.

Paul Murphy showed up around ten thirty for a final check of the master and the equipment in the pavilion. A stage had been set up at the far end with a large screen and projector hanging from the rafters. Nicholas sat with Paul at the control board near the rear. They watched the retrospective of Adam Powell's life. The two photos had been included as planned and, for Nicholas, added a nice twinkle of magic to the whole presentation.

By eleven o'clock, the clouds had lost interest and moved on to the south. It looked as if they'd have sunshine and blue skies after all. Nicholas could feel the collective sigh of relief.

The guests began to arrive around eleven thirty. First, the family cars and compacts of the employees, then the Volvos, BMWs, and Mercedes Benzes of the dignitaries from Washington's social elite, the statesmen, and business executives.

Nicholas fidgeted nervously, pacing back and forth behind the booth, his thoughts ricocheting between Kathy, Lainey, her grandmother, and his grandfather. Lives intertwined by choices and consequences. How different would things have been if his grandfather and Elaine had married? Would Adam still have become the determined success that he was? Would he have fathered more children? Might this reunion be taking place in England with ten times the number of family and significantly less employees and contacts? Would Nicholas Powell even exist to ask such questions?

What if? What if that was the source of Elaine's depression? What if Uncle Gerard hadn't *done* anything at all, but had simply told her something that triggered the torturous *what might have been?* Maybe it was as simple—and hard—as that. She was imagining the life she didn't have, and it was driving her to despair.

What if? was a question that created a hell of its own. To know what might have been. Or, worse, to have to live with the consequences of one's wrong decision while knowing how good the other decision would have made things. Sheer hell.

So maybe it truly was an act of God's grace not to know, and to accept his grace for the things that are.

Nicholas glanced around, wishing Lainey were there so he could talk to her. He glanced at his watch, fiddled with his cell phone. Was she on her way? What if she was lost somewhere? Or maybe she was on the grounds already. Suddenly he felt anxious for her—for what was going to happen this afternoon with his grandfather—for his own future. He was expected to announce his engagement to Kathy. What if he didn't?

At one o'clock, Jeff climbed onto the stage and grabbed the microphone. He was dressed in expensively casual jeans and polo shirt. Blowing into the mike once or twice, he said a big welcome to everyone, via speakers strategically placed around the grounds. He announced that the food was ready to be enjoyed, and if everyone would fill their plates and come to the tables in the pavilion, there was a fun program planned.

"Eat and enjoy!" he shouted and then, with loud pops and bangs, put the microphone back onto the stand.

Nicholas stood and was thumped on his back. He turned to face a platinum-haired gentleman with milk-white skin, sparkly eyes, and a purple clerical shirt and white clerical collar.

"Bishop Jackson!" Nicholas exclaimed, genuinely surprised. Bishop Jackson was the bishop of Virginia and the head of the Board for the seminary.

"Nicholas. Just wanted to say a quick hello. Are you well?"

"Yes, I am. Thank you, sir."

"I meant to have my office call you this past week."

"Oh? Why would your office need to call me?"

"To give my permission, of course."

"Your permission?"

"About getting married. Aren't you going to announce your engagement today?"

Nicholas was flustered. "Well, yes." Who on earth told the bishop? "But how did you know?"

"I believe my wife had a conversation with your mother or something like that. You know that as a student at the seminary you must have my permission to get married."

"Oh. I didn't know."

"Don't worry, son. You'll have my blessing. From what I've seen, Kathy is a suitable girl. Pretty, too."

"Thank you, Bishop," Nicholas said, swallowing hard. "It's kind of you to tell me."

"Congratulations." He started to walk away, then pointed upward. "Glad the weather held up for today," he said as an afterthought.

"Thank you."

"It has nothing to do with *me*," he said with a laugh and was gone.

Nicholas choked back a feeling of annoyance that even the bishop was in on his engagement. It made him feel pressured, manipulated somehow.

He made his way to the line for the food tables—a lot of "hellos" and "how are yous" to various acquaintances along the way. A great-aunt from God-knows-where gave him a kiss on the cheek, called him Jeffrey, and then marveled at how much he'd changed. There were aunts, uncles, cousins, and second cousins—a plethora of strangers to Nicholas.

Jeffrey then appeared at Nicholas's elbow, which confused the great-aunt beyond repair. They left her standing, shaking her head in bewilderment. They strolled across the lawn, going nowhere in particular.

Jeff gestured to Nicholas's torn jeans and T-shirt. "Don't you get the feeling like everyone is dressed for an occasion that you weren't invited to?"

"It's a picnic, isn't it?" Nicholas asked.

"Of sorts. But you might want to put on some nicer pants. Maybe a shirt with a collar."

"Why? It's not as if I'm going to be up on the stage."

"You aren't?" Jeff asked. "Did you change your mind about announcing your engagement?"

Nicholas stopped in his tracks and said angrily. "Now I'm being told what to wear?"

Jeff held up his hands. "No offense. I assumed you didn't want to stand up there with your bride-to-be looking angelic and you looking like a dung beetle who's really let himself go. That's all."

Nicholas backed down. "I'll change after we eat," he said.

"Good plan. Though you should know that we decided not to make the announcement during Grandad's retirement show."

"*We* decided?"

"We'll do your announcement at the smaller dinner this evening, when it's just our family and closest friends."

"Thanks for letting me in on the decision," Nicholas complained, though he was actually relieved.

"No problem."

Jeff was called away and Nicholas found himself standing in the middle of a sea of people, none of whom he knew. A stranger in a crowd. A hand slipped onto his arm and Kathy kissed him on the cheek. "Hello, Nicholas," she said.

"You look very nice today," he said.

"Thank you."

She looked him over, but didn't return the compliment.

"I know. I'm going to change after we eat."

Though he wasn't hungry, he went with her to the serving line. The table was laid with barbecued ham and beef, potato salad, baked beans, corn on the cob, garden salad, rolls, and every other "picnic" food imaginable. She fixed herself a plate, frowned when he declined, and followed him to a table in the pavilion. He chose an empty one near the soundboard at the back.

"Shouldn't we sit with your family?" Kathy asked.

Jeff glanced at the table near the stage. Jeff was there with a date Nicholas hadn't met yet. His father and mother were chatting with elderly relatives in wheelchairs. Other cousins, aunts, and uncles took their places nearby. Still no sign of Adam Powell himself.

"It looks crowded," he replied. The rest of the pavilion had filled up, too.

She shot him a look of displeasure.

She ate while Nicholas kept looking around impatiently, drumming his fingers on the table.

"Nervous?" she asked.

"Not really."

Silence again. He wondered where Lainey was. And his grandfather. *Dear Lord, what if they've bumped into each other and are talking even now?*

Kathy nudged him with her elbow. "If I'd known we weren't going to talk, I would've insisted that we sit with your family. At least they're having a good time."

"I'm sorry."

"Who were you looking for?"

"My grandfather. He's not here."

"I saw him earlier. He must be 'working the crowd,' as usual."

Nicholas was relieved.

"You haven't even asked about my family."

He looked at her, blank. "Your family?"

She sighed, deeply and with great exasperation. "Aren't you wondering why they're not here?"

"Were they invited?"

She glared at him. "*Yes.*"

"I didn't know. Nobody told me."

"You didn't ask."

What's the point of asking anything, it's all arranged, out of my control, he thought irritably. He said: "Where is your family?"

"There was some kind of accident on Route 50. The traffic is all backed up."

Ah. That would explain why Lainey wasn't there. She'd have come the same way.

"You can't do your presentation without them," she warned.

"You'll have to talk to Jeff about that."

"I will. Right now." And suddenly she was out of her chair and moving away from him to the front of the pavilion.

Watching her go, he felt a weight off his shoulders. He wouldn't have to make conversation with her.

I'm supposed to announce our engagement today and I don't even want to talk to her? It was wrong—so very wrong, as if everything had suddenly gone out of alignment and off balance. He needed to come clean with her about Lainey, his grandfather, everything. *Now. It'll be so much worse when she finds out later.*

He stood up to go after her, but took only a few steps before he stopped again. There was a sudden drop in the volume of chatter around the pavilion. Adam Powell had entered, carrying his food and greeting people on the left and on the right as he made his way to the front table. Heads turned, tilted, nodded with the physical equivalents of "there he is!" A celebrity in their midst. Nicholas watched him as he took his place at the head table. He put his tray down, scanning the audience with a smile, and then his gaze fell on something off to the right. His smile faded, replaced by a look of puzzlement.

No one but Nicholas seemed to notice the change—and he followed his grandfather's gaze. A woman stood next to a tent pole, her chestnut hair pulled back, her light summer dress blowing ever so slightly in the summer breeze, the sunglasses veiling her eyes and evoking cool detachment.

Lainey.

She did nothing to draw attention to herself, but Nicholas was aware that the men in the pavilion were subtly turning to look at her. Her head moved only a little, as if she was lost and searching for someone. Jeff saw Lainey, too, and was now leaning in the direction of his father, no doubt to ask who she was. Adam, Nicholas noticed, was still watching her.

Does he recognize her? Nicholas wondered. *Is the family resemblance enough to make him think of Elaine?*

Lainey suddenly turned, as if whoever she was looking for wasn't to be found in the pavilion, and walked away toward the food tables. Grabbing a cup, he followed her.

She was at the drink stand pouring herself some water. Nicholas walked up next to her and picked up a pitcher of iced tea. "May I offer you some fresh American iced tea?" he asked.

She didn't turn to him, but said, "No, thank you. It's an abomination."

"Only for a country that hasn't learned the recipe for ice."

She smiled, but still didn't face him. They looked like a pair of spies from a movie, heads down, trying to be nonchalant. "You shouldn't be talking to me. You're not supposed to know me."

"Says who?"

"Does your fiancée know I'm here?"

"No."

"Did you tell her I'm coming?"

"Not yet. I was just about to."

"Until you do, I suggest you hedge your bets and keep clear. As it is, I'm tempted to walk back to my car and drive away. I'm not cut out for dramatic encounters."

"You can't leave. Not without talking to him."

"That was him in the tent, wasn't it? I think he saw me."

"I'm *sure* he saw you."

"I'm scared, Nicholas."

Saying *Nicholas* instead of *Nick* made him look at her. "Lainey—"

"Nicholas!" Kathy called from a few yards away. "Hurry. They're starting the program."

"Okay," he called but held back, wanting to say something to Lainey, but coming up with nothing except, "Don't go."

She didn't respond.

He guzzled the tea and then jogged to where Kathy stood. He took her elbow to guide her inside, but she pulled back, only for a second, looking at Lainey. Nicholas knew the question was there, right on the edges of her lips—*Who is that?*—but she didn't ask. Instead, she said, "My parents just arrived. They're inside waiting for us."

They walked into the pavilion. There was no turning back now.

JEFF PLAYED EMCEE, POURING ON HIS PUBLIC CHARM AND HANDLING THE program with a masterful mix of warmth and humor. *Mr. Personality*, Nicholas thought affectionately.

After the welcomes and the traditional games and prizes for who traveled the farthest, who is the oldest, who is the youngest, and who has floss in their pocket, Jeff asked Adam Powell to come to the stage.

Nicholas's grandfather feigned suspicion and shouted, "I'm retiring. I refuse to make any speeches" as he took his place on the stage.

"Come on up, Grandad. All you have to do is sit and listen."

Adam Powell sat down on a folding chair that mysteriously appeared behind him and looked as if someone was about to play a trick on him. Was it possible that they'd pulled it off—that he really had no idea that this day was more for him than anyone?

"Grandad, you know we couldn't let your retirement happen without some acknowledgment of you and your work."

Adam pursed his lips at Jeff. "What have you been up to, young man?"

"Relax and enjoy yourself." Jeff said, and gave a signal. Employees quickly dropped all of the side flaps so that the pavilion was enclosed in as much darkness as could be expected.

"We're on," Paul Murphy whispered to Nicholas and hit a switch on the board. Suddenly the Seal of the President of the United States appeared on the large screen overhead. Then it was the man himself saying, "I wish I could be there today, Adam, to witness this special day. It's a miracle, some think. Your *retirement*. Personally, I never believed you'd do it. But now that you are, I'd like to go on record to say . . ." The effusions came about Adam Powell as a businessman, as a benefactor, as a vital part of the Washington and Maryland community, as a success, as a giant among men. It was warm, eloquent, and short, concluding with, "And, Adam, don't hog all the best fishing spots for yourself. There's an election coming and, to be honest, I might decide to join you."

The audience laughed and applauded as the picture faded. Then came a message from the governor of Maryland, then the mayor of Crockett, then a parade of other government and business associates who presented certificates and plaques and general warm wishes.

Eventually Jeff took the stage again and announced that they'd be taking a break from all the speeches for something truly entertaining. "A little something put together by Nicholas Powell." Then, with grand flourish: "Grandad—*this is your life*."

With that cue, Paul Murphy started Nicholas's presentation. Bright Aaron Coplandesque music began with the words "Adam Powell. A life."

Nicholas swallowed hard and prayed as the life of Adam Powell played out in a panorama of images, words, and music. Nicholas had assembled photos of pre-War London, culled from news archives. He tried to evoke the kind of life Adam might have had as a child in the thirties. Then England went to war—the Blitz—the fires—the Allied victory—and then post-war Britain, a collage of ads and newspaper headlines to get the viewer quickly to Adam's journey to America. The first photo of Adam with the church group appeared. A few people laughed at this uncharacteristic image of the man they knew.

Nicholas watched his grandfather.

Adam, who'd been sitting back in his chair, slowly sat up.

A few other images came and went, and then the second photo—the one of Adam dressed up to go ask Elaine to marry him—appeared.

Again, a few titters from the audience. Someone did a wolf's whistle. And now Adam Powell sat as straight as his chair back. His face betrayed nothing, but his body language was like an exclamation point to Nicholas.

The rest of the presentation showed the rise of Powell Printing and then Powell Publishing and a series of photos of Adam with various presidents, kings, queens, actors, and celebrities, with the music building to a crescendo and everything ending with a still of Adam Powell in a recently taken photo, and a final "Congratulations on Your Retirement."

There was wild applause from the audience.

"You're getting a standing ovation," Kathy gasped from behind Nicholas.

"It's not for me," Nicholas corrected her. "It's for him."

Jeff offered the microphone to his grandfather, who was now standing. Nicholas held his breath in anticipation of what he might say or do.

"Ladies and gentlemen, I'm not a man of few words, as you know. But today I will be." He lowered his head briefly, then cleared his throat. "I'm touched deeply by all I've seen and heard today. Thank you for not eulogizing me before I've died, but making me feel that the years I've spent at my work have been worthwhile. Thanks to my family for their love and patience, to my coworkers and employees for their professional contributions, and to the many other friends who've come together today to see me off—or to make sure I go." Laughter and more applause. "In any event, thank you so much. And now I'm going fishing!"

He handed the microphone back to Jeff and walked off the stage, making his way through the crowd—shaking hands, giving quick embraces. Jeff made announcements about the activities on the grounds, including the availability of the pool for everyone's enjoyment, but his voice seemed to fade away as Nicholas watched his grandfather. He'd been momentarily diverted by well-wishers, but there was no question in Nicholas's mind where he was headed.

Nicholas felt his heart pounding wildly in his chest. Kathy was saying something to him, and so were her parents, and Paul Murphy was shaking his hand, but Nicholas could only see and hear his grandfather—walking this way.

"Well," Adam Powell said, only a few steps away.

Kathy went up to him, hugged him and said, "Congratulations. Didn't Nicholas do a wonderful job?"

As if to answer, Adam stepped forward and pulled Nicholas to him in a bear hug. Nicholas was stunned. He couldn't remember the last time his grandfather had hugged him, if ever. Was his grandfather actually pleased?

Just as Nicholas began to think that all might be well, his grandfather whispered in his ear. "In the study in five minutes. And bring *her* with you." He let Nicholas go, clapped him on the shoulders in a visual display of approval, and then moved on to others who wanted to speak with him.

Kathy looked proudly at Nicholas. "I wish I had my camera," she said. "You see? You were worried for nothing."

GETTING AWAY FROM KATHY AND HER FAMILY WAS ONE PROBLEM, FINDING Lainey was another. He had no idea how he was going to do either.

After a moment's chitchat with Kathy's father, Nicholas abruptly turned to Kathy and said, "I have to go talk to my grandfather."

"You do? Why?"

"He just said he wants to see me in the study."

"Was he angry?"

"I think so." He began to back away, gesturing apologetically to Kathy's mother and father. "I'm sorry."

"But—*why?*" Kathy asked.

Nicholas leveled his gaze at her. "There's something I have to tell you, Kathy. But not now. Not here. I'll see you later."

"Nicholas—"

But he left her before she could get her questions out.

He scanned the crowd for Lainey, but with no luck. Maybe she'd gone after all. That would be an interesting twist to this misadventure. He'd get stuck pleading with his grandfather on Lainey's grandmother's behalf.

Making his way across the lawn, Nicholas bumped into Jeff again.

"You did a great job on the presentation," Jeff said.

"Thanks," Nicholas replied, but wasn't looking at his brother. He was craning his neck one way and the other to find Lainey.

"Who are you looking for?"

"The girl you saw earlier at the pavilion. Pretty dress, sunglasses."

Jeff instantly remembered, and smiled. "Who is she? Don't tell me you know her from the seminary."

"No."

"You didn't bring a *date* to your own engagement announcement!" he said.

"No!" Nicholas said, annoyed.

"Good." And in that one word was a world of implication and opportunity. Jeff fixed his collar. "Now, who is this girl and why are you looking for her?"

"Don't get your hopes up. Have you seen her?"

"Yes."

"When? Where?"

"By the old tire swing, a minute ago."

Nicholas was about to go, but had a better idea. "Do me a favor and go get her."

"What?"

"Grandad wants to talk to her—and me—in the study. Right now."

"Why in the world would Grandad—?"

"Just do me a favor and bring her to the study," Nicholas said firmly. "That'll give me a chance to cool him down."

Jeff cocked an eyebrow. "What have you done, Nicholas?"

"The girl is Lainey Bishop."

Jeff looked blank.

"The girl from England," Nicholas said.

Suddenly Jeff's face lit up. "Oh!" Then it went very dark. "You didn't."

"Just *go*, will you?"

Nicholas headed for the house.

"You are *so* dead," Jeff called out behind him.

ADAM POWELL SAT IN THE THICK GREEN EXECUTIVE CHAIR BEHIND THE LARGE oak desk that dominated the study. Nicholas crossed from the door, noting anew how the room still maintained the British flavor his grandfather had originally brought to it. Framed paintings of the English countryside, fox hunts, and snow-laden fields covered the paneled walls. Hand-built cabinets and shelves contained leatherback editions of classics.

Nicholas chose not to sit down in one of the matching leather guest chairs, but stood directly opposite his grandfather. He could feel the adrenaline throbbing in his ears. "You wanted to see me, Grandad?"

His grandfather's voice was quiet, but clenched. "Just what kind of game are you playing?"

"Game, Grandad?"

Adam glared at him. "Where did you get the photos?"

"Lainey got them from Julie Peters. Last week."

"*Lainey*, is it? And where is she now?"

"She's coming."

"What is she, a granddaughter?"

"Yeah. How did you know? Is the resemblance that strong?"

His grandfather shot him a *stupid question* look. "How did you find her?"

"The Internet. The return address on those letters I found. Arthur House."

"Her *husband's* estate."

"He's dead." Nicholas sat down on the arm of the guest chair and tried to sound calm and in control. "Look, Grandad, there's a lot you don't know."

"There's a lot *you* don't know, you stupid boy." He slammed both palms down on the desk. A sound like a gunshot. "What right do you have to meddle in my life—past or present?"

Nicholas stood up again. "A woman's life is at stake."

His eyes narrowed. "Whose?"

"My grandmother's," came Lainey's voice from the door.

Adam looked up and Nicholas turned. Lainey was framed in the door, as if choreographed for a cinematic entrance. Jeff stood in her shadow like a walk-on part, a comic doorman. Normally assured and confident, he looked as if he had no idea what to do.

Adam stood up. "Come in, young lady."

"I'm Lainey Bishop," she said as she walked in slowly, with a measured stride. Her sunglasses were off and her eyes were bright. If she was nervous or afraid, it didn't show.

"I think you know that I'm Adam Powell." Adam gestured to a chair. "Please sit down."

"Thank you," she said as Nicholas held the chair for her. She looked at Nicholas, her head slightly turned from Adam so he couldn't see her face. With a wink she sat down.

Jeff lingered until his grandfather said, "I'm sorry, Jeff, but this is none of your affair. Please close the door." Then, as an afterthought, "And tell your parents not to worry. We'll be out shortly." Translation: Keep the family away until we're done.

Still the doorman, Jeff nodded and backed away, closing the door.

"Right," Adam said, sitting down again. "So we have a crisis of some sort, is that it?"

Lainey sat on the edge of the chair, her back erect, her hands in her lap. "My grandmother is very ill—and we think it has something to do with you."

"With me? Impossible."

"See if you think so after I tell you what's happened."

"Then do," he said and leaned back in his chair, his hands prayer-like under his chin.

Lainey told him everything: about her grandmother's breakdown after talking to Gerard Sommersby, the pieces of stained glass in her hands, her withdrawal from life, the concerns of the doctors, and her reaction to Adam's name. She spoke with a strong, level voice, never betraying what she was thinking or feeling. She was articulate and concise. Nicholas marveled over her ease and eloquence. When she finished, she sat back in her chair; the lawyer resting her case and now waiting for the jury.

Adam listened quietly, his face solid, giving away nothing. Nicholas felt his hope wane. His grandfather seemed unmoved by what he was hearing. Nothing could penetrate the years of scar tissue that had covered his heart.

When Lainey had finished, Adam stood up and walked to the large picture window with his hands clasped behind him. *Captain of the ship*, Nicholas thought. *He's about to give his orders.*

With his back to them, he said, "That's remarkable."

"So you understand why I've come all this way to see you," Lainey said.

"I think I do," he replied and turned to face them again. "And the little trick with the photos?"

Nicholas held up a hand. "It wasn't meant to be a trick, Grandad. I honestly thought the photos might make you think about your past."

"It has, Nicholas," he said. "You succeeded in that much."

"Then you'll help?" Lainey asked.

The question. Everything now hung on the answer to that question. Nicholas shifted in his chair. He wanted to take Lainey's hand.

"Lainey," Adam said as if beginning a thought, but then lowered his head and walked back to the desk. "You were named for her, weren't you?" he asked.

"Yes, I was."

"Why aren't you called Elaine?"

Lainey shrugged. "I've always been called Lainey. Perhaps it was to avoid confusion in the family."

Adam nodded, as if it was important. Then he began again, his voice low, almost soothing. "Lainey, I want to make something clear. I don't approve of the way you and my grandson have behaved. He told you how I shredded your grandmother's letters, which was as strong an indication of my thoughts about the past as I wished to make. In spite of that, the two of you have persisted—"

"Only to help my grandmother," Lainey interjected.

"I'm not saying that *your* motives weren't good," he said, a jab at Nicholas. "However, I consider it nothing less than emotional *blackmail* for you to corner me in this fashion."

"Blackmail!" Nicholas rose from his chair.

"Yes," Adam said. "How am I supposed to respond now? You've come all the way from England with your tale of woe. You have my grandson savoring every morsel of my past heartbreak—"

"That's not fair," Nicholas said. "I'm not savoring this."

Adam ignored him, speaking to Lainey. "To be perfectly candid, I think you'll be disappointed."

"Why?" Lainey asked.

"You seem to think the events of that day fifty years ago are important to your grandmother's health. I don't agree. And once you hear what happened, I think you'll be even more confused and wonder why she's behaving as she is."

"You may be right," Lainey said. "But I won't know until you tell me." It was a challenge.

"*Will* you tell us?" Nicholas asked, slipping back into his chair.

There was fire in Adam's eyes as he replied, "You won't like what I have to say."

"WE WERE DOOMED FROM THE START," HE BEGAN. "IT WAS SHEER FANTASY to think that we ever had a chance together. Her parents were against me, so were her friends. I wasn't one of them. I was a London working-class boy, after all. But she was naïve enough to believe that it didn't matter. And I was arrogant enough to believe that it *shouldn't* matter."

Nicholas and Lainey waited.

Adam cleared his throat, his eyes focused on the ceiling. "We were from different classes, you see. It's not so important here in America, but it was still extremely important in England back then. Marrying the right sort, knowing your limitations, never rising above your station. We had to sneak around, meet when we could. It was a roller coaster, to use the cliché. Up one day, wanting to think we had a future, and down another day, wanting to give it all up as impossible."

Another pause. Nicholas didn't move, fearful his grandfather might change his mind and not continue. Lainey remained frozen where she was, as if she had the same fear.

"We used to meet on Saturdays at the Mill House," he continued. "You know it."

Lainey nodded.

This seemed to soften him. "Is Mr. Soames still the proprietor?"

"He retired. I think his son now runs it."

"So it hasn't been grabbed up by the corporations."

"Not yet."

"Good." He pondered that for a moment, then continued. "Julie Peters arranged a job for me in Washington, D.C. Her contacts with the United States Embassy in London got me the proper papers to go. Her plan was for Elaine and me to go together, out of the reach of her family and friends."

"She told me," Lainey said.

Adam nodded. "After all those years of fighting for our relationship, I believed at last we were going to be together. So I rang Mr. Soames at the Mill House and told him I wanted to come earlier than usual. I told him why. He decorated our favorite table—the one in the corner—with flowers and colored paper. I planned to get on bended knee and ask her there, in front of everyone."

He fell silent, then slowly leaned forward, resting his elbows on the desk.

"When I arrived around eleven o'clock, everything looked wonderful. But then I saw that fellow at the bar—the one who hung around Gerard Sommersby—the troll-looking one."

"Trevor Mann?"

"Right. He was *very* inquisitive about what I was up to. Kept annoying me with questions, all very friendly, but persistent. He kept calling me 'old chum' and I thought he'd had too much to drink."

"He was drunk before noon?"

"No, not drunk. Nervous, more likely. I kept wanting to tell him to get lost, but I was in such good spirits that day that I didn't want a fight. We'd had some run-ins before. Then he disappeared and I got on with making sure everything was ready. And then he came back."

"Trevor?"

"Yes. He was buzzing around like a little bee, taking in what I was doing." Adam put on an accent, which Nicholas assumed was Trevor's. "'Special day, eh? Got something planned, have you?' and that sort of thing. Then he started shaking his head and making *tsk, tsk* noises. 'Are you sure about this, old chum? I'd hate to see you embarrassed.' I asked him what he was talking about. 'Things aren't always what they seem, you know,' he said. He was being very cryptic. Finally I got annoyed and told him that if he had something to say, then say it. Otherwise, get lost.

"He pulled me aside and said very quietly, 'It's none of my business, but you may be making a mistake. A misunderstanding, perhaps. I don't know. All I know is what I see. I'm not one of their crowd, but I can tell you how it is.' That's how he talked.

"I asked, 'If you're not one of their crowd, then how can you tell me anything?'

"'I'm like a pet for Gerard,' he said. 'I'm only the son of a groundskeeper, you know. We played together as kids and now he keeps me around as a mascot, of sorts. They like that. Associating with the lower classes, like me—like you. It makes them feel like they've got the common touch. Makes them feel good about themselves.'

"'What's your point?'

"'I've known Elaine since we were children. She's got suitors here, you know. She's very cozy with Gerard. You know Gerard. I mean, it's not for me to say, but they're very close. Everyone around here assumes they're going to be engaged.'

"'I don't care what everyone around here thinks.'

"'I don't want to see you get hurt, old chum. But think about it. She's got the pick of the crop here and you think she's going to chuck it away for a working-class Londoner?'

"I found the man offensive and told him so. Then he said, 'I can prove it to you, right? For your own sake. I can show you what I mean.'

"'How?'

"'She meets you here at noon, yeah?'

"'Yeah.'

"'Where do you think she is now?'

"'I don't know. At Arthur House.'

"'No. I know where she is. Not far from here. A short walk. I'll show you. They're there now. They always meet before she comes here.'

"I didn't want to believe him. But how could I refuse to go? To refuse would have been to show my fear, my doubt. It was like a dare between schoolboys. So I said I'd go with him. And threatened him if he was pulling a prank. He said he wasn't, and led me out. By now it was around eleven thirty.

"We a followed a path that cut through the woods and skirted around the edge of the town. Elaine and I had walked it a few times. I remember that Trevor had picked up a stick, which he occasionally used to thrash at an overhanging branch or a tall weed. I remember that only because he reminded me of a puppy, playing with that stick. Then we came upon a small grove along the path that had been set up by the local council for parking. I saw a car sitting alone in the middle of the grove—a convertible with the top down. Gerard was in the driver's seat. Elaine was on the passenger's side. They were turned toward one another and chatting. I couldn't hear what they were saying. But I was aware that his arm was on her seat, around her. And she was leaning in to him—very close. Trevor nudged me and pointed. A *you see? I told you so* nudge. And then he snapped the branch in two and it cracked loudly."

"Why did he do that?" Lainey asked.

"I don't know. He was nervous, fidgeting. The crack made me jump and I instinctively stepped behind a tree, afraid that Elaine would see me and think I was spying on her."

"But you *were* spying on her," Nicholas observed.

"At Trevor's insistence. But I'd seen enough. They were two friends talking, that was all. I had a jealous streak, but I wasn't going to make an issue of the two of them having a chat alone. It meant nothing. They had no idea I was there, so I turned to leave and then Trevor stopped me. He gestured toward the car." Adam paused to swallow, as if his throat had gone dry. He scowled at Nicholas. "Here's your moment, Nicholas. The chance to hear about my great humiliation."

"Grandad—"

"Be quiet and listen," he said sharply, then rushed on as if he thought speaking quickly would lessen the difficulty of saying it. "Elaine laughed—I can hear it now—and then Gerard kissed her. Or she kissed him. It was hard to tell from where I stood."

Lainey sat up straight, her eyes wide. "A friendly kiss, surely. Nothing more."

"*Not* a friendly kiss, I'm afraid. A lover's kiss. And an embrace."

"Are you sure?" she asked.

He gave her a stern look in response.

She wisely gave him the benefit of the doubt and said, "All right. They kissed and embraced. Did you confront them?"

"Have the English changed so much since I was a young man?" he asked her. "Confront them? What was to confront? They kissed, they embraced. Everything Trevor had told me looked to be true. And even if I wanted to go up to them and do something dramatic, I didn't have the chance. Gerard started the car and drove away." He fell silent.

Lainey looked at Nicholas. She seemed at a loss for words. Then she asked Adam, "What did you do?"

"I left. I went back to the Mill House, paid Mr. Soames—who refused to take my money. A decent man."

"What about Trevor?"

"Oh, he was with me every step of the way, apologizing, so sorry that he had to show me the truth. But that's what happens, he said, when people get mixed up with the wrong class. Don't try to go above your station, he said. Know your place. He gave me a lift to the train station. I returned to London. I know it sounds clichéd to say so, but that was the end of it for me. I felt stupid and foolish for ever believing that we could have had a life together."

"Mrs. Peters said she tried to ring you. She wrote, as well."

"So? There was nothing to say."

"Why not?"

"I had given up—and didn't want to be persuaded otherwise. What was the point? I went to America as planned. But alone." He sighed, then added as a postscript. "Later I heard—through Julie, I think—that she had married James Arthur. I was surprised. I would have put my money on Gerard. But there you are. End of story."

THEY SAT QUIETLY FOR A MOMENT AND ONLY THEN WAS NICHOLAS AWARE of a clock ticking somewhere. He was speechless. He didn't know Elaine at all, and wanted to feel sympathetic, but if everything had happened as his grandfather had said, then this was an entirely different situation. It was true humiliation for his grandfather.

"But that doesn't make sense," Lainey finally said. "That doesn't sound like her at all."

"I wouldn't know what she's like now."

"But you knew what she was like *then*," Lainey responded. "Didn't the whole thing seem strange to you?"

"Strange? Not at all." He gazed at her, a stern look. "When I'm feeling cruel and cynical, I think Trevor was right. Elaine Holmes strung me along for some warped pleasure of her own, to claim me as her little rebellious working-class fling on the side. Or perhaps I was her mascot."

"No!"

He pressed on. "When I'm feeling more kindly, for the sake of something I once felt, then I believe that she was unsure and confused. In the end, she succumbed to the will of her class. It was inevitable. She couldn't—*wouldn't*—leave them for me."

"Then why, fifty years later, is she suddenly besieged with guilt and remorse?" Lainey asked, a plea more than a question.

"I have no idea," Adam said and stood up, indicating the end of their conversation.

Nicholas stood up slowly. But Lainey wasn't to be dismissed so easily. "She tried to contact you, Mr. Powell. *Repeatedly*. Why do all that if she didn't care?"

He spread his hands in a shrug. "Perhaps she felt guilty then. I never imagined that she was completely heartless. Just the opposite. Perhaps she felt pity toward me, as one would a stray puppy."

Lainey's voice was beginning to rise, her calm starting to crack. "Pity? It can't be as simple as that. All those years of going behind her parents' backs, of seeing you, writing to you, all because she felt sorry for you? That doesn't make sense. She *loved* you."

"I never said these things were simple, young lady. People do all kinds of things for very complicated reasons."

Lainey shook her head. "It was a setup. Uncle Gerard set it up somehow."

Adam raised his eyebrows. "Quite a setup," he said. "With a full kiss and hug?"

"I don't pretend to know *how* he did it," she said, exasperated.

"Perhaps it wasn't her at all!" he taunted Lainey. "He'd had an inflatable doll made to look like her! All to fool *me*."

"All right, Grandad," Nicholas interceded. "You don't have to be cruel."

He gave a low chuckle. "You're accusing me of being cruel? You two are the ones playing amateur psychologists, cornering me into reliving painful memories for your own pleasure. And I'm cruel."

"There's no pleasure in this, Mr. Powell!" Lainey cried out. "I'm trying to save my grandmother!"

"Maybe you should stop and leave it for the professionals," he said coolly.

"But the professionals don't know what to do!" she exclaimed. Then, as if the sound of her own voice had startled her, she withdrew. With an air of defeat, she also stood to leave.

"I've told you what I can. That's as much as I can do," Adam said and moved around the desk. He was going to usher them to do the door.

"What if you told her you forgive her?" Nicholas abruptly asked. "If you wrote a letter, or went to see her."

"That's asking too much."

"Why? Because you haven't forgiven her?"

Adam spun on Nicholas. "I'm not here to let you play spiritual counselor or therapist for me, young man. Practice your priestly mumbo jumbo on someone else."

"This isn't some kind of exercise for me, Grandad," Nicholas protested. "Don't you see the connections, the significance of what happened then and who you are now? It affected *everything* for you. Your whole life turned on that moment."

"So?" he countered. "All lives turn on moments like that."

"But not all lives wind up like yours," Nicholas said angrily. "Obsessed with money, void of any real relationships with those around you—or God."

"You don't know what you're talking about," said Adam.

Nicholas kept going. "You were in touch with your faith then. Through Father John and Julie, and even through Elaine. Julie Peters said that you had a spiritual experience at the Billy Graham Crusade. What happened to that faith?"

"My faith is none of your business." His voice was bigger, commanding now.

"Why not? As your grandson, I care. As a fellow Christian, I care. Someone has to. Why did you walk away from your faith?" Nicholas said.

"We're finished with this conversation," Adam said.

"Was it because of Elaine?" Nicholas persisted. "Is that why you gave up on God?"

"Why, you presumptuous, arrogant—"

Lainey was suddenly between them, her hands up. "Stop, please. Back to your corners."

Adam moved away from them. "Get out."

Lainey stayed where she was, speaking gently. "Mr. Powell, I'm not here to dissect you or to figure out the intricacies of your life. I don't care if you believe in God or not. If you don't believe in him, then I'm appealing to your basic humanity, to whatever you once felt for my grandmother, to please help her now, in whatever way you can. If you *do* believe in God, then I'm appealing to you on the basis of this—" and she withdrew an old Bible from her purse and placed it on the desk.

She had played it like an ace up her sleeve, Nicholas thought. Her last chance.

Adam turned and looked at the Bible with an expression that Nicholas had never seen before. Was it surprise? Pain?

Lainey continued. "Christians espouse things like forgiveness and compassion. That's what I'm asking for. A little forgiveness and compassion for my grandmother. Like it or not, you're at the center of her crisis. If somehow you could find it in your heart to reach out to her, then I believe it will bring her back to us."

Adam's eyes were fixed on the Bible. Nicholas thought he might reach out for it. But he didn't. He said sadly, but firmly, "I'm sorry, Lainey. There's nothing I can do." He turned his back on them again.

Lainey waited, perhaps with the hope that he might qualify his statement or change his mind. Adam said nothing. "Thank you for your time." She spun on her heels and walked out of the study.

"Grandad, you're not going to leave it like that," Nicholas said. *"Please."*

"I've said all I'm going to say."

CHAPTER
THIRTEEN

NICHOLAS WENT AFTER LAINEY. SHE WASN'T IN THE HALL, NOR ANY OF the main passages leading outside. He stepped into the sunshine, squinting against its brightness and looked around. Family members and employees were still eating, some playing at the volleyball nets that had been set up. Squeals and shrieks carried across the lawn from the pool. He saw his father, brother, and mother near the pavilion, waiting—a look of expectancy. They started toward him. No sign of Lainey, nor of a way to escape.

"Nicholas," his father called.

He held up his hand. "Give me a minute," he said and jogged toward the part of the lawn where the cars had been parked. Still no sign of her.

Then he heard an engine rev and turned in time to see Lainey pull out of a spot on the far side. She didn't look at him, looking instead toward the gateway. He was about to sprint after her when a hand caught his arm.

"Nicholas," Kathy said.

"Kathy."

"Was that her?" she demanded. "The English girl?"

"Lainey," he replied, watching her car disappear down the drive, leaving plumes of dust. "Yes. She *was* here."

"You brought her over after all."

"I didn't bring her over," he said, now facing her. "She came on her own."

"But you knew she was coming."

"Yes."

"Even though everyone said she shouldn't come."

"That's right."

"And you didn't tell me."

"For obvious reasons." He glanced at his watch. It was a little after three. Was there another flight back to London tonight? Would she take it? Or maybe she'd have to catch one tomorrow.

"Nicholas—" She tugged at his arm to get his full attention.

"Kathy, let's talk about this later. I have to go."

She was furious. "You're going after her?"

"You don't know what happened in there—what this means to her."

"And what was today supposed to mean to me?" she asked. "How are you going to announce our engagement if you leave?"

Nicholas's head was buzzing now. He didn't have the patience for this. "Why announce it? Everyone already knows. It's been a preplanned surprise. You don't need me. You and my family have it all settled without my participation."

"What's wrong with you?"

"Us," he said. He felt sick, but he couldn't stop. "Our goals, the ring, even our announcement. We're perfectly prearranged. The committee was formed, action items given, and plans laid out." He took her hands in his and pulled them close to his chest. "I have an idea. Let's do something spontaneous, Kathy. Come with me now."

"Now?"

"We'll go talk to Lainey *together*—to figure out if there's any hope left of helping her grandmother. Get involved, Kathy. With me. Come on."

"We can't leave the picnic."

"Sure we can. Come on. I'm going."

"But my family—"

"They'll understand."

"*Your* family—"

"They *won't* understand, but I don't care right now."

She resisted, pulling her hands away. "No, Nicholas. Stay here. Let her go home and figure out her own problems."

"I can't do that. Not now." He gestured toward the house. "*He* won't do anything. So I should. I feel morally obligated."

"That's crazy."

"I'm going."

"I'm not."

He suddenly kissed her on the cheek. "Then have a good time. I'll talk to you later." He took off.

His father called impatiently from the pavilion. *"Nicholas!"*

Jogging backward, Nicholas raised his hands, as if he couldn't help himself. *Have to go, Dad. Gotta run.* He spun and dashed for his car.

DRIVING DOWN ROUTE 50 TOWARD WASHINGTON, NICHOLAS KNEW FOR certain that he would spend the rest of his life apologizing for today.

He tried to call Lainey on the cell phone, but was diverted to a message service. Either she'd forgotten to turn the phone on or had purposely left it off. His own sense of paranoia told him it was the latter.

It was a Saturday, so Nicholas decided to cut through Washington, taking shortcuts to the Parkway, then down to Alexandria. Using his cell phone's directory assistance, he got the number for the Olde Towne Inn and confirmed that Lainey hadn't checked out. That was good news. Even if she wanted to catch a flight home, she'd have to go back to get her things.

His cell phone rang and he snatched it to his ear. "Hello?"

"Nicholas," his father said. "Have you lost your mind?"

"No, Dad."

"I think you have. You're completely out of control."

"Wrong, Dad. I'm not out of control. I'm making decisions every step of the way. I'm doing the right thing. Gotta keep the line open, though. Talk to you later." He hung up.

I'm doing the right thing, he thought. *Or am I?*

His mind went back to a conversation he'd once had with his grandfather. Well, not a conversation, as such, but a lecture his grandfather had given him back in high school. He'd said, "Every man has moments in life that test who he really is and what he truly believes. They come when you least expect them. The question is, Nicholas, what will you do when the moment comes? Will you even recognize it when it arrives? I hope so. Those are the moments that change your life—and only the fool fails to see it."

Nicholas pounded the steering wheel. Why hadn't he thought of those words an hour ago when he was with his grandfather? They might have made a difference, given his grandfather a chance to think twice about what he was doing. *This* was one of those moments.

But, as a Christian, he didn't believe those moments were random or haphazard. God was in them. Somehow. Testing us, guiding us, giving us roles to play *in this moment.*

Though, he had an awfully hard time imagining what his role could be. *Healing.*

The word came to him in a whisper.

Healing.

And then a prayer he'd memorized from the *Book of Common Prayer* came to him.

Heavenly Father, giver of life and health: comfort and relieve your sick servant Elaine, and give your power of healing to those who minister to Elaine's needs, that she may be strengthened in her weakness and have confidence of your loving care; through Jesus Christ our Lord. Amen.

A warm feeling rushed through him. The same feeling he often had when taking communion, the wine working like a pleasant fire from his lips to his belly. A genial tranquility. A sense of peace and well-being filled him completely.

He thought, *Either God is in this, or I've just gone into shock.*

HE MADE IT TO LAINEY'S HOTEL IN UNDER AN HOUR. PARKING THE CAR, he raced inside to the front desk. Lainey was standing there in a heated discussion with the desk clerk.

"It's policy, ma'am. Nothing I can do. Twenty-four-hours' notice or you have to pay for the room."

"Lainey," Nicholas called out.

She swung around, surprised. "Nick!"

"You thought you could make a dramatic exit and then leave without talking to me?"

"But what are you doing here? Your family get-together—your engagement announcement—"

"I told them to go ahead without me."

"No!" she cried. "You can't. You *mustn't*." She tried to physically move him toward the door. "You have to go back—right now."

"It's too late. Going back now won't accomplish anything."

"Oh, dear," she said. "This is a mess."

He walked her back to her room. It was a plain box with a double bed, a dresser, a desk, faded wallpaper, and a painting of Mount Vernon on the wall. It was meant to have a Colonial feel to it—and that may have been true during the Revolutionary War—but now it looked worn and shabby.

Her suitcase was on the bed. It was little more than an overnight bag. "You never intended to stay longer than a couple of days, did you?"

She looked at him sheepishly. "No. If the trip was a success, I knew I would want to go straight back to my grandmother. If it wasn't a success, then I knew I'd be too disappointed to stay."

"So you were arguing with the clerk about checking out."

"I could catch the last flight out of Baltimore tonight."

"Don't go tonight," he said. "Wait until tomorrow."

"Why? What's the point?"

"It gives us time to figure out what to do next."

"We? What 'we'? You've done all you can. This isn't your problem anymore."

"But I haven't done anything."

"It's not your responsibility, Nick."

He shook his head. "I can't just walk away. I can't let you walk away either. I'm part of this now, whether you like it or not. We're going to figure it out together."

She looked at him as if he'd surprised her with a dozen roses. "You're so kind," she said. Her eyes filled with tears.

Without thinking, he put his arms around her. "Now, don't do that." Her head rested against his chest and she wept fully.

"I'm sorry," she said, but couldn't say more. She put her head down and cried again. This time her arms came up around his waist, pulling him close. "You're a good man," she whispered.

He felt her against him, took in her smell, her softness, and fought hard to remember his reason for coming there. *Healing*, he thought. *This is about healing.* She lifted her head and they faced one another for only a second, maybe two. Did she want him to kiss her? He couldn't be sure, but felt the power of his desire to do it.

She's vulnerable, he told himself. I'm *vulnerable. Too many unanswered questions. Don't do it.*

He stepped back with an awkward smile.

She lowered her head, then turned away from him to dab at her eyes and blow her nose. "I'm not usually so emotional. I didn't realize until now how much I'd hoped your grandfather would help."

He considered her again, feeling a stab of regret that he didn't kiss her. Looking around the room, he was aware of how alone they were. How easy it would be to . . .

"Let's go," he said.

"Go?"

"There's a strange little tavern you should see. We can talk there."

THE MIDDLE EARTH TAVERN, JUST A FEW BLOCKS FROM KING STREET, WAS an eighteenth-century inn that had been renovated in the 1970s by an avid fan of J. R. R. Tolkien's *Lord of the Rings*. It had been decorated in a hobbitlike style, with Tolkien's characters hand painted on the walls; Frodo, Sam, Gandalf, Aragorn, and even Shadowfax the Wonder Horse were represented. A large fireplace took up the entirety of one wall, with iron rings and large steins and chalices covering the mantel.

It was too early for the dinner rush, so the place was empty. They chose a corner table. After ordering drinks, Lainey looked around. "I can't decide if this is wonderful or wholly inappropriate," she said.

"I'm never sure either," Nicholas said. "But it's cozy and quiet."

"Do you come here with Kathy?" she asked.

"No. She doesn't care for it."

"She's not a Tolkien fan?"

He shook his head. "Tolkien—or taverns. I come here alone. Sometimes to read, sometimes just to think."

"A tavern?" she asked, a wry challenge. "Not church?"

"I do a lot of thinking and praying there, too. But I love quirky places like this."

"Then you'd love England. We have hundreds of them."

Their drinks came and Nicholas used the gap to change topics of conversation. "Look, Lainey, try not to despair about what happened with my grandfather."

"I'm not in despair," she said quickly. "Honestly, I don't know what came over me in the room. I'm thinking a little more clearly now."

"At least we know why he's so bitter."

"From *his* perspective, yes. But I simply can't believe that my grand-mother would be so deceitful."

"Maybe it wasn't purposeful. Maybe it's like he said, she got confused and gave in to her class."

"I don't believe that either. It's not like her."

"Not like her *now*. But how can you know what she was like when she was younger. Lots of girls can be flighty when they're young, and then become very strong and sensible later."

"Flighty is one thing. But to have a relationship with your grandfather for almost *fourteen* years and then two-time him for my uncle Gerard—a man I know she didn't love—well, that's not flighty, that's downright malicious or stupid. And my grandmother isn't either." Her cheeks had turned red, her eyes alight with the passion of making her case.

"I'll have to take your word for that."

"I suppose you will," she said with a frown. "Or you can believe your grandfather's account and there's nothing left to discuss."

He held his hands up defensively. "Whoa, now. I'm on your side." *This girl's got a fiery spirit,* he thought.

She looked down at her drink. "I know," she said softly. "But we're still circling the drain. Your grandfather's story raises more questions than it answers."

"But it answered quite a few, too. Between everything Julie Peters told you and what my grandfather said today, we've got a pretty good picture of what happened. The biggest question, though, is what we do now."

"Trevor. He's the one I want to talk to next."

"Is he still alive?"

"Yes. I saw him recently. Now I understand why he got so nervous when I mentioned your grandfather. He's got the missing pieces to this story. He's my first port of call when I get back to England."

"TELL ME HOW YOU'RE GOING TO FIX THE MESS WITH YOUR FAMILY—AND your intended," she said as they drove back to the hotel.

"I don't know," he said, and the enormity of the day crashed upon him again. He'd defied his family, confronted his grandfather, and deceived his fiancee-to-be—all on the day he was supposed to announce their engagement. *Yeesh!*

"It's all my fault."

"They don't blame you for anything. They blame me for letting it happen. I disobeyed. I didn't act according to plan. Unforgivable."

"Is it really?"

"I've always been a good boy. This is the first time in my life I ever went so completely against their wishes."

"If they disown you, then you'll have to come to England. There's plenty of room."

Nicholas eyed her, trying to discern her offer. Was this outgoing friendliness, or was something else going on? His heart quickened as he wished that maybe, just maybe, she liked him, that the moment in her room when he thought of kissing her was something she wanted as well. He decided to play it safe, not to assume wrongly. "You better be careful. I might take you up on that offer."

"I hope you do," she said, her eyes on his. "I still owe you a proper cup of English tea."

He hoped she hadn't noticed, but he was taking a long way back to her hotel. He enjoyed her company, listening to her talk, looking at her expressive eyes, her enthusiastic gesturing with her hands, her lack of self-consciousness with her opinions, the way one corner of her upper lip turned up when she was being ironic, a tiny scar—probably from childhood—that appeared just below her right eye whenever she smiled.

She glanced out of her window. "Funny, I don't remember the hotel being so far away."

"It's just around this corner," he said.

She glanced at her watch and sighed. "It's eight o'clock."

"Already?"

"You were so captivated by me that you simply didn't realize the time—or where you were driving."

He blushed. "That's right."

In the hotel lobby, they were left with functional chitchat. She explained that she hoped to get onto a flight leaving at eight o'clock the next morning, but she had to phone to make the arrangements. If she succeeded, she'd have to be at the airport no later than six, which meant leaving at five, which meant getting packed tonight.

"You could avoid all that by staying tomorrow and catching a flight tomorrow evening," Nicholas suggested. "I could show you around Washington."

She rebuked him with a glance. "*You* have to spend tomorrow mending your various relationships."

There was another moment of awkwardness as he tried to decide whether to say good-bye in the lobby or walk her back to her room. He wanted to go back to her room, to be tempted again by a kiss. His better judgment won out and he stopped at the elevator. "This is where I'll say good night," he said.

"Oh," she said, and again he couldn't tell if she was glad or disappointed. She summoned the elevator, then faced him. Close. "Thank you, Nicholas, for everything."

"E-mail when you get back. I want all the news."

"I will." The elevator arrived with a discordant chime. The doors opened to an empty chamber.

He put out his hand. "See you later, Lainey."

"Okay, *Nick*." But she brushed his hand away and threw her arms around him, kissing him on the cheek. He pulled her close, gratefully. She tilted her head back and kissed him lightly on the lips. "Good-bye." She slipped away from him and stepped into the elevator, wiggling her fingers at him, a coy expression on her face. The doors closed.

Nicholas didn't move. His reflection in the metal of the doors was a blur of colors. But he believed the burning of his cheeks showed bright red against the silver.

Shazam.

As Nicholas pulled away from the hotel, he knew he had a stop to make before going home. He didn't really want to, but he felt duty-bound.

He stood on the small porch and rang the doorbell, shifting nervously from one foot to the other. A curtain moved in one of the front windows. From somewhere inside Kathy shouted, "I'll get it," and then the door opened a moment later and there she was. She'd exchanged her dress from the afternoon for jogging pants and a T-shirt.

"Well, look what the cat dragged in," she said. Rather than invite him in, she pulled the door behind her as she stepped out onto the porch.

"Hi."

"Well? Did you get Lainey's life figured out?" A sarcastic tone.

"Only a little. She's going home tomorrow morning."

She folded her arms, a defiant posture. "And then what?"

"Then we hope to take what we learned from my grandfather and use it to help her grandmother."

"You're still going to help her?"

"As I can, sure."

"And what if I asked you not to? What if I said that I really don't want you to talk to her again?"

"I'd have to ask you why."

"Why? *Why?* It's obvious why. Everyone seems to understand why, except for you."

"Kathy, do you trust me?"

"I thought so."

"You don't now?"

"I think you're suffering from a lapse of judgment. Your sense of priorities is askew."

"Ah."

"Or, as a worst-case scenario, you've decided that you like English crumpets."

"Don't be crass."

She continued to hold her posture, her eyes on him. "What happened today has made me wonder about you. I've been asking myself very seriously if I know you at all. I'm trying to imagine if this whole incident is an aberration or if it's how you'll behave for the rest of our lives."

He stared back at her, suddenly unsure how to answer. Was it an aberration—or was this a serious change in him? Or was he developing a taste for English crumpets?

"That's what I thought," she said, as if his silence was his answer. "You need to decide what you want to do. About your life. About us."

"I know what I want to do," he protested, and it sounded feeble to his own ears.

She put up a cautionary hand, a teacher's gesture. "Don't say anything tonight, Nicholas. Take some time first. A few days, even more if you want. Make up your mind and tell me what you want to do."

"Make up my mind?"

"About who you are. The Nicholas I knew before today, or the Nicholas I saw today."

He shuffled uncomfortably. "What if it's the Nicholas you saw today?" he asked.

"Just think about it," she said. Not waiting for a reply, she stepped back through the door and closed it on him.

"Ouch," he said softly to the moths flitting around the porch light. It turned off and he stood alone in the darkness.

NICHOLAS DROVE BACK TO HIS APARTMENT AND WONDERED HOW OTHER people felt when their relationships hit a *let's take a break and think about it* moment. Did they feel relieved, sad, hurt, confused, or annoyed—all the things he was feeling at that very moment?

The only feeling he couldn't dodge was guilt. He had no one to blame but himself.

His apartment door was slightly ajar and the smell of coffee wafted out at him.

"If you're a burglar, I hope you made the French roast," he called out.

Jeff stepped out of the kitchen with a large mug of the dark stuff.

"Oh, you're home," he said casually, then held up his mug. "You want some?"

"Yes, please," Nicholas replied and followed his brother back into the small kitchen.

Jeff made another mug of coffee without a word of explanation about his being there. As he handed it over to Nicholas, he said, "Dad wants you to call him right away. But I suggest you wait until tomorrow. Give him time to cool down." Jeff went in to the living room and sat down on the sofa.

A companionable silence while the two brothers sipped their coffee, until Nicholas asked, "What are you doing here? Are you the delegation from the family?"

"Are you kidding? You don't think I wanted to stay home and answer questions I don't have the answers to," he replied.

Nicholas nodded appreciatively. "That's fair."

Jeff tipped his head toward the bedroom. "I put your overnight bag in there. I assumed you weren't coming back."

"Thanks."

"The engagement ring is on your nightstand."

He'd forgotten about the ring. "Thanks."

Another sip. "Have you talked to Kathy?"

"Yeah. We're taking a break while I decide what my priorities are. Or something like that."

"Smart move," Jeff said. "Pretty gracious of her, considering you brought a strange girl to your own engagement party."

"My engagement party? It was everyone else's party, everyone else's idea, right down to the engagement ring. I was a walk-on part."

Jeff cupped his coffee with both hands. "It would have helped if she wasn't so good-looking."

"Her looks have nothing to do with it. I'm trying to help her grandmother."

"I believe you," Jeff said without an ounce of belief. "No one else will, but *I* do."

"I appreciate that." Taking another drink of coffee, he settled into the chair. "Today I did something I felt was the right thing to do—even though the family didn't approve. I didn't play by their rules."

"You surprised us all, that's for sure."

"More than that, I *liked* it," Nicholas admitted. "I *liked* the feeling of freedom."

Jeff put his coffee mug down and sat on the edge of the seat. "Okay. I have an idea."

"What?" Nicholas asked warily. Call Dad? Send flowers to Kathy? Toe the family line?

"It's the only thing you *can* do," Jeff said. "You're on a break from Kathy. You want to help Lainey's grandmother. You *don't* want to see the family for a few days."

"What are you suggesting?"

"Go to England."

Nicholas nearly choked on his coffee. "*What?*"

SUNDAY, THE 18TH OF JULY

IT WAS REMARKABLE TO NICHOLAS THAT HE COULD DECIDE AT TEN O'CLOCK on a Saturday night to leave on a flight for England first thing Sunday morning. He had his passport, enough clothes to last for at least a week, and money from the ATM. Jeff made the flight arrangements, leveraging his kajillion frequent flyer miles to get Nicholas on a British Airways flight the next morning—Lainey's flight.

"Amazing," Nicholas said. It was a little before six in the morning and they were at the curb in front of Dulles. Even for the hour, it was busy. A policeman shouted and waved at those drivers who lingered a little too long. Keep 'em moving in the name of national security. Nicholas turned to Jeff, who'd slept on the couch and still didn't look awake.

"Thank you, Jeff."

Jeff shrugged. "My brother's keeper."

Nicholas opened the door to climb out.

"Get it out of your system, Nicholas. Whatever this is. Then come back, get on with your ministry, and live happily ever after."

Nicholas was touched and leaned over. They hugged briefly.

"*Go* before I get arrested as a terrorist."

Nicholas got out, pulled his carry-on knapsack and suitcase from the backseat, and waved as his brother pulled away. Jeff blew him a kiss.

LAINEY SAT AT THE TERMINAL GATE, HER HEAD NUMB FROM TOO MUCH thinking and too little sleep.

She'd gone to bed not long after Nicholas had dropped her off at the hotel, but she woke up every hour, fearful that the alarm wouldn't go off and she'd miss her flight. Each time she awoke, her brain engaged and she found herself thinking quickly and randomly, like she had slight delirium from a fever. Her mind shot to Trevor—how she would approach him, how she'd coax the information out of him, role-playing the scene in her mind. Then, her thoughts bounced to Nicholas and the feelings she couldn't deny having. He'd been so heroic throughout the day, standing by her with Adam Powell and rushing away from his own family to see to her. His arrival at the hotel touched her deeply. Her tears, she knew, weren't from any disappointment about the meeting with Adam but from Nicholas's kindness toward her. And when he held her in his arms, all of her resolve had dissolved.

It wasn't in her nature to mess around with men who were about to become engaged. She never wanted to be "the other woman" in anyone's relationship. Nicholas was with Kathy. He was three thousand miles away *and* studying to be a priest.

Back off, she told herself. It doesn't matter that he's thoughtful, sensitive, intelligent, gentlemanly, and good-looking. He *was* a gentleman, too. He'd nearly kissed her in the room. He wanted to, but he didn't. His restraint only made her appreciate him all the more.

Naughty girl, she'd then teased him with that kiss at the elevator. It wasn't something she'd planned to do. In those last moments with him, she'd suddenly had the desire to leave him with an impression of her, to make him think about her after she'd gone. Now it seemed to have backfired. Instead, it left *her* with an impression. It made her knees go weak and heart race every time she thought about it.

How clichéd, Lainey thought. She'd read of such things, women turned into puddles by a man's embrace or kiss, but she didn't really think it happened that way in real life. It certainly hadn't happened to her until last night. Such a schoolgirl thing to have happen.

She sighed and looked out the large window. The Triple-7 was parked at the end of the causeway. A truck had backed up to a side door and two men loaded the catering. Below, a man and woman were throwing luggage onto the ramp that led into the belly of the plane. Other planes taxied past, their tails like shark fins rising in and out of view. She glanced at her watch. 7:20. They should be boarding soon. The gate was getting crowded, the rows of dull gray seats filling up.

Closing her eyes, she thought of Nicholas and felt the feather-light touch of his lips again.

Silly girl. Stop thinking about it.

She was jolted from her thoughts by someone clumsily sitting down next to her. Annoyed, she looked over at the invader—a heavyset man with ginger hair and unfashionably long side whiskers. He nudged her elbow off of the armrest and replaced it with his own. *I hope I don't get stuck next to him on the flight.*

She looked around for another seat. Or maybe she'd stand, since she'd be sitting for several hours anyway. Getting up, her eye caught sight of a man standing next to the agent's desk. It stopped her. The man was looking directly at her, smiling, while the agent typed on the computer.

"Nicholas?" she whispered, her heart leaping into her throat. She felt frozen where she was, sure that she was gaping at him like a fish at feeding time.

He held up a *wait a minute* finger and turned his attention to the agent. He was handed a ticket folder. He said thanks and then moved toward her. She was on her feet now, moving toward him.

"Nicholas?" she said again, still not believing nor comprehending what he was doing there.

His cheeks were tinged with red, his face the expression of a boy who'd been caught with his hand in a cookie jar. "Surprise," he said.

"What are you doing here?"

He laughed, then put his hand over his mouth to stop and looked sympathetically at her, appreciating her confusion. "I don't want to be presumptuous," he said, "but I decided to take you up on your offer for some proper English tea."

"That's *brilliant!*" she shouted and threw herself into his arms.

CHAPTER FOURTEEN

NICHOLAS WAS RELIEVED THAT LAINEY WAS SO HAPPY TO SEE HIM AND delighted she'd hugged him. He pulled away quickly, though, and turned to the gate agent. With some maneuvering of their seat assignments, they were placed together in two seats next to a window.

As the plane left Dulles and roared into the azure blue sky, he confessed, "I was afraid that you'd call security and demand a restraining order. I had no idea whether you'd be pleased or alarmed."

She looked at him, surprised. "Honestly? You had no clue at all?"

He shook his head. "I'm not very smart about these kinds of things."

"What about your family?" she asked.

"I haven't spoken to my family, except Jeff—and this trip was his idea, so he said he'd take the heat for that."

"A great brother if ever there was one."

"Yeah." He thought of Jeff blowing him a kiss. "Weird, but a good brother."

She randomly pushed the buttons on her seat control. The small screen in front of her flickered, but she didn't seem to notice. "And Kathy?"

"She suggested we take a break."

"A break from what?"

"From us," he replied. "She's worried that I'm not who she thought I was."

"And who was that?"

"Certainly not the kind of guy who impulsively jumps on a plane to England."

Lainey hung her head. "I feel responsible, you know."

"You're *not*," he said firmly. "I'm a big boy. I made my own choices for reasons that I still think are right. If Kathy can't understand that, then it's better to get it out in the open now. I wouldn't want to marry her if either of us had a false idea of who the other person really is."

"Very sensible."

Sensible, yes. Or was it a smokescreen to avoid the feeling that was growing with every second he sat next to Lainey. With her, he felt he could be—and do—just about anything. "Let's talk about England," he said.

In-flight movies came and went, so did snacks, drinks, and a meal. They hardly noticed. Lainey made suggestions and Nicholas made lists in a notepad he'd brought. He *had* to see the usual sites in London, she said, like Big Ben, Westminster Abbey, Buckingham Palace, Trafalgar Square, the Tower of London, and St. Paul's—and those sites outside of London like Windsor Castle, Oxford, maybe Brighton. She was also adamant that he should stay at her grandmother's house. It was huge, she said, and he'd be no burden to anyone, certainly not her. Why pay for a bed-and-breakfast, or a hotel? She pointed out that the train system, for all of its faults, still operated well enough to get him to most places. She'd happily drive him wherever else he wanted to go.

Playing tourist was okay, he said, but his first priority was to help Lainey's grandmother. Other than that, he was more interested in seeing how the real people lived than seeing some postcard façade. And, if it wouldn't be too boring for her, he wanted to visit some of the more interesting churches and cathedrals. She instantly suggested Winchester, Salisbury, and Canterbury.

"I assume you'll want to drop in to see the archbishop," she teased.

"A personal friend of yours?"

She laughed, "Not a chance. I couldn't even tell you his real name."

"You mean, not everyone in England knows?"

"I don't mean to shock you, Nicholas, but Christianity is irrelevant to most of the British population."

Nicholas frowned at the news, though he'd heard as much in seminary.

"The Church of England is like an embarrassing old aunt that you hope will sit in the corner of the room and keep her mouth shut," Lainey explained. "And even if she does speak, most of the people don't listen, because they don't care. They respect her only because she's been around for a long time, not because they think she has anything important to say."

"Then what do the British care about?"

"They care about the weather, the commute to work, how long until the next holiday, going to the pub, sports, and gardening. Not in that order."

"They don't yearn for more, a desire for something more transcendent? The afterlife? Eternity?"

She shook her head. "Not at all."

"That's terribly sad."

"Only because you think about such things. But it isn't sad if it's not part of your reality, how you think."

"Is that how *you* think?"

"Oh, dear. I had hoped to avoid this conversation with you."

"Why?"

"Because I don't want you to know what a pagan I am."

"A pagan? You don't believe in anything?"

"Sometimes I think I do, when I go to church for some reason, or meet with a priest like Father Gilbert in Stonebridge. I feel—" She stopped for a moment, looking for the words. "I feel something, but I don't know what it is. A spark."

He nodded and felt encouraged.

She eyed him. "You're smiling."

"I think I know what that spark is," he said.

"Do tell."

"It's a spark from God. A piece of him, like a homing device that beckons us to come back to him, to come home. But we follow it in the wrong directions, or bury it with all kinds of clutter and garbage, or work hard to ignore it. Every now and again, though, it lights up. Maybe in church, or because of a song or a moment in a movie or the beauty of nature. All of those things point to God, reminding us of the spark. And then one day it hits. That *zing*—the thunderbolt—that quiet voice— and he's standing in front of you and you think, 'Oh, you're the one I was looking for the whole time.'"

"*Who* is standing in front of you?" she asked.

"Jesus," he replied.

"I'm out of my depth here, Nicholas." She looked truly bewildered.

Nicholas suddenly felt self-conscious. "I'm sorry. I don't mean to preach at you."

"Is that what you were doing?"

"You didn't know?" he teased.

"You need to raise your voice and pound the tray table a little more," she suggested, smiling.

The light faded outside the small square windows as they flew toward evening. Lainey dozed and Nicholas was content to gaze at her.

THEY LANDED AT HEATHROW'S TERMINAL FOUR. IT WAS WELL PAST NINE at night now, and closer to ten by the time they cleared immigration, got their luggage, and made it through customs. In spite of himself, Nicholas had the wide-eyed look of a tourist as he gazed at the illuminated yellow signs directing people to "meeting points" and toilets, signs indicating "Way Out" rather than "Exit." Lainey guided Nicholas out to the taxi stand.

"My car is at my flat," she explained. "It's only twenty minutes from here."

Nicholas was cheered to see the line of traditional British black cabs with the drivers on the right side, just the opposite side from American cars. A red double-decker bus drove past with a belch of black fumes and shrill brakes. A light rain began to fall.

"So this is England," he said.

"Oh, *please* don't let this be your first impression," she said woefully.

"Why not?" he held his hand out to the rain before getting into the cab. "I love it."

The cab driver was like a sketch from a Dickens novel. Thin with a birdlike face, large Adam's apple, and a thick, nicotine-saturated Cockney accent. He was a forty-year veteran driving cabs in London and regaled them with his opinions about the monarchy, the current government, American foreign policy, and Frank Sinatra, whom he had driven once back in the '60s and thought no man on earth a finer singer or gentleman.

Nicholas stared out of the cab window, catching glimpses of old Tudor pubs and Victorian houses along the modern stretch of highway that took them in to Hammersmith. Concrete office blocks came and went. Skyscrapers of glass dwarfed nearby churches and apartment complexes. Hotels and supermarkets were ablaze with light. Dark patches of trees hid parks and historic mansions, now set up as tourist attractions. This certainly wasn't the England of Dickens, no horse-drawn carriages or cobblestone streets, but he was entranced anyway.

They drove through Chiswick, which Nicholas remembered as the place where his grandfather grew up. Lainey assured him that they would see it properly during his visit. To avoid a traffic jam, the driver suddenly diverted down some back lanes and avenues, bringing them into Hammersmith and Lainey's apartment building. She called it a "block of flats, a flat being what you'd call an apartment." The building was nestled down an alley, behind two Georgian-looking offices, and looked rather plain in the dimly lit streetlights.

"Let me grab a few things," Lainey said after she'd paid the cab fare.

Nicholas followed her up a flight of stairs to Number 6, and she warned him as she opened the door to watch for the post. He looked around, thinking he'd run into one—but then she stooped for letters scattered on the floor and he realized she meant the mail. It had been slipped through a slot in the door.

The apartment was small, cozy rather than cramped. There was a curtained window on the far wall of the living room. A functional kitchen sat off to the right.

Lainey pointed to a door on the left. "That's the loo, if you need it."

"Loo?"

"Bathroom."

He was suddenly aware of just how Americanized his grandfather had become. He'd kept some of his British accent and a few of the phrases, but there was a lot Nicholas had never heard him use. "I'm okay."

"I need some extra clothes," she said and disappeared into the bedroom. "Won't be but a moment."

"All right," he said, standing in the middle of the living room.

She called out, "I'd offer you that cup of tea, but I'm afraid I don't have any milk. Anyway, I'd rather you have it when we can make it properly—and when we're not in such a rush."

"Are we in a rush?" he called back.

"It's an hour and a half to Stonebridge from here. Longer if there's traffic." She appeared at the doorway. "Unless you'd rather spend the night here and we drive down tomorrow."

He gazed at her, trying to discern what she was actually suggesting. "We should go tonight," he said. "It wouldn't look right if we stayed here alone."

She smiled at him, satisfied, as if he'd passed some sort of test. "Such an old-fashioned gentleman," she said playfully and disappeared back into the bedroom.

Oh, if she had any idea of what he'd *like* to do, Nicholas thought. But that was the difference between desire and action.

The apartment was decorated in modern furniture. Nicholas spied a desk in the corner, with a computer dominating the surface. Like the rest of the flat, it was organized and tidy, everything exactly where it belonged. He imagined Lainey sitting there writing her e-mails to him. It gave him a different perspective somehow, as if he should now go back and fill in the missing images of their previous exchanges in his memory.

Lainey said something from the bedroom, so he went to the door. "What did you say?"

She stood next to the bed, a phone to her ear. "All right. Thanks, Serena. It'll probably be close to midnight before we get there. Good-bye." She put the phone down and looked at him with lines of worry across her forehead.

"What's wrong?"

"My grandmother's in the hospital," she said. "Dr. Gilthorpe admitted her today. Apparently she's been cheating."

"Cheating?"

"With her food. Serena found that she hasn't been eating after all, but stuffing it under the bed, shoving it into the closet, or flushing it down the toilet."

It was worse than he imagined. "I'm sorry." He offered a quick and silent prayer for Elaine.

"She's given up." Lainey went to her closet and yanked a few shirts from their hangers. Clutching them, she turned to Nicholas, her whole countenance one of distress. "What are we supposed to do when she's completely lost her will to live?"

"Help her to find it again."

THEY TOOK THE STAIRS FROM THE FLAT DOWN TO AN UNDERGROUND parking garage, squeezed their luggage into Lainey's Mini—one of the fashionable new BMW versions—and drove off for Stonebridge. They sped along motorways and A-roads and B-roads. Lainey tried to explain the differences, but Nicholas lost track of which was which. The rain and darkness obscured their vision to the degree that, apart from driving on the opposite side of the road and the roundabouts, Nicholas could have been on any road anywhere in the U.S. The real England was, for the time being, only distant lights on pitch-black fields.

It was well past one by the time they pulled into the drive in front of a large and impressive mansion, maybe twice the size of the Powell home. "Is this a hotel?" Nicholas asked as he craned to take it all in through the little passenger window.

"This is Arthur House."

"The queen must be very envious."

She laughed at him.

They leapt out of the car. Nicholas wrestled with the luggage while Lainey got the front door open. In no time at all, they were standing in the front hall, drops of water falling from the luggage and onto the hardwood floor.

Nicholas looked around with open astonishment. It was like stepping onto the film set of a British costume drama. He walked up to one of the gold-framed portraits, set against the dark wood paneling of the hall. "If I tilt this a little to the left, a secret door will open up, right?"

"Right," Lainey said. "But watch out for the poison darts that'll shoot out from the painting just opposite."

He nodded appreciatively. *This* was the England he imagined. Any moment a bald butler in a black tux—or even a wigged one in breeches—might appear.

He looked down the hallway, half expecting it to happen. Instead, a woman with jet-black hair and wearing a fluffy white bathrobe came around a corner.

"You made it," she said, stifling a yawn.

"Did we wake you? I'm sorry," Lainey said.

"No, I was reading," she replied. "You must be Nick." She stretched out a hand to him.

Nicholas shook it gently. She must be his parents' age, he thought as he looked at her face, but she was beautiful in an exotic way. Her black hair, dark skin, and deep eyes contrasted against the white robe. "Hi," he said.

"This is Serena," Lainey explained. "The keeper of the castle."

"In my robes of state," she said. "Would you like some tea?"

"Not for me, thanks."

Lainey shook her head. "We won't keep you up. But I want to hear the latest about my grandmother first thing in the morning."

"Nick is going in the Waterhouse room," Serena said.

"I'll show him up, you go back to bed."

"See you in the morning," Serena said and turned to go back down the hall. "Good night."

"Good night," Lainey said, then gestured to the luggage. "Sorry we don't have a porter."

"No problem." Nicholas slung his knapsack over his shoulder and lifted his suitcase. Lainey grabbed her small bag and led the way.

They walked up the wide staircase to the floor above. A long, carpeted hall took them past several rooms with white doors. She tilted her head toward one. "That's my room."

"Does it have a name?"

She looked at him, puzzled. Then she realized. "Oh. No. That's just *Lainey's* room, I suppose. I don't know what they call it when I'm not around. Your room is called the Waterhouse Room because it has a few paintings by J. W. Waterhouse. I hope you don't mind."

Nicholas didn't, especially since he didn't know what kinds of paintings J. W. Waterhouse produced. It sounded to him like the name of an accounting firm.

The room was at the end of the hall on the left. Lainey opened the door and turned on the light.

Nicholas let out a low whistle. The room was breathtaking. A large four-poster bed took up the center, with ornate French-looking bedside tables, dresser, and tallboy to fill out the rest. A small desk sat in the corner. An inset bookcase took up part of one wall and contained a selection of hardbacks, along with vases, busts, and framed photos of classic paintings. The walls were dominated by more than just a few Waterhouse paintings. He recognized the artist's work immediately, the Victorian style, having seen some of the paintings in art galleries, postcards, and calendars. The subjects of the paintings hanging before him were varied: women dressed in loose Grecian outfits pouring from large pots of water, a knight on horseback kissing a maiden good-bye, nymphs and goddesses cavorting in green pastures, medieval damsels in distress, and ancient scenes that may have been biblical in nature. Nicholas looked closer and realized that the model in the most of the paintings was the same woman.

"Is it too much?" Lainey asked.

"Not at all." At least these models wore clothes. Some of those Victorian artists were pretty racy.

She threw open a door off to the side. "You have your own bath-room—which actually has a *bath* in it rather than just a toilet. The light switch is on the outside wall, though. British law, I'm afraid. They like to keep the electrics as far away from water as possible."

He looked at her, realizing only now how tired she looked. "You should go to bed."

"I will. Shout if you need anything." She moved for the door, but he touched her arm as she passed.

"Thank you for putting me up."

She smiled faintly and nodded. "I'm glad you're here, Nick. You give me hope."

"There's always hope," he said lightly, but prayed quickly that it would be true.

MONDAY, THE 19TH OF JULY

HIS DREAMS RAN LIKE FUGITIVES FROM HIS CONSCIOUSNESS. HE DREAMED he was still on the plane, reading a novel. The words were vivid: *She stumbled into the situation not knowing that he'd ordered the same thing. "Let me finish my thought, I've never managed to do that," she said.* Then he was in a large empty room arguing with his grandfather, later he was lost in the woods—the ones near his parents' house—trying to find Kathy and feeling the entire time as if he had to tell her some bad news, then he had a half-waking worry that he'd left the engagement ring sitting in the open in his apartment where it would be stolen. He woke up, not sure of the time since there didn't seem to be a clock in the room. He thought it must be the middle of the night, until he slowly realized that the cur-tains on the two windows were very heavy and thick and bright light now framed them. Just as he was gathering the energy to get up and open the drapes, there was a knock at the door.

"Room service," Lainey said from the other side.

"Come in," he called out as he sat up.

Lainey walked in, dressed for the day in a black-and-blue rugby shirt and jeans, and carrying a tray with two mugs of tea on it, a sugar bowl, and small pitcher of milk. "Properly made, as promised." She slid the tray onto the bedside table. "Milk? Sugar?" she asked.

"Both, please."

She gave him a look of feigned disgust. "I was afraid of that. Serena said you were the sugar type. You Americans like everything so sweet."

"Yes, please," he smiled. She put in a spoonful, making it clear by putting the lid on the sugar bowl that she would not give him any more than that.

"Very nice," he said after a taste. "The difference from American tea is downright startling."

She went over to the window and threw open the curtains. Bright sunlight poured in. "It's a gorgeous day."

"What time is it?"

"Nearly nine o'clock."

"Nine! Why did you let me sleep so late? The day is wasting away." Putting his mug down on the tray, he threw his bedcovers off and dropped his legs over the side of the bed. He wore a T-shirt and jogging pants. "What's our plan for today?"

"I have to go visit my grandmother."

"*We* have to visit your grandmother."

She acknowledged her error with a slight nod.

"And Trevor," Nicholas added.

"And Trevor," she agreed.

"Your parents?" he asked. "Am I going to meet them?"

She looked as if she wasn't sure of the answer. "Yes, I suppose so."

"What's wrong?"

"Mum thinks I've been making too much of a fuss about my grandmother. I'm not sure how she'll react to my bringing reinforcements from America."

"She'll love me."

"Not in a T-shirt and jogging pants."

"What would you prefer, my clerical collar?"

"I'll leave it to your discretion. And if you have any trouble with the shower, let me know." Lainey left, closing the door behind her.

Nicholas stood up and wondered why she thought he'd have trouble with the shower.

IN FACT, HE DID HAVE TROUBLE. THE SHOWER WAS UNLIKE ANYTHING HE'D ever seen. It consisted of a handheld showerhead that hung from a small hook on the wall. A metallic hose ran from the head to a small box attached to the wall above the faucet for the bathtub. The box had two dials on it. After some fiddling around, Nicholas realized that one dial controlled the water pressure—which wasn't very strong even turned up as high as it would go. The other dial controlled the temperature, which seemed to jump from skin-shriveling cold to skin-shriveling hot within the tiniest fraction of a turn. It was a matter of great finesse and artistry to get it just right.

After shaving he dressed in black jeans and a white Oxford, waved a brush in the direction of his hair, and went to the window to see just how gorgeous the day really was.

His room faced a large, carefully tended garden with strategically placed shrubs and flower beds filled with an amazing spectrum of reds, purples, yellows, and whites. The garden stretched maybe fifty yards away to a low stone fence. Beyond the fence was a bright green field and, further on, a forest that rolled away to the distant hills and horizon of blue sky. The vividness of the colors made him gasp. And in an instant he understood what the British writers meant when they wrote of a "green and pleasant land." This was Tolkien's Middle Earth and Lewis's Narnia. It was the Hundred Acre Wood. Here before him was the vision from which the great British authors drew their inspiration.

He felt a quickening in his heart that told him he'd come home.

BY THE TIME NICHOLAS ARRIVED IN THE KITCHEN, SERENA HAD ALREADY left for the hospital and Lainey was busy making breakfast. She moved between three different skillets and a pan on the stove, the toaster to the side, and the kettle.

"You didn't have go to so much trouble."

"This is your first breakfast in England. You must have a fry up."

"Fry up?"

"Traditional English breakfast." She waved at him to sit down. "Prepare to be amazed."

A few minutes later she put a plate before him that contained fried eggs, fried tomatoes, fried mushrooms, fried bread, sausages that looked like hot dogs, bacon, and a large helping of baked beans. She also presented him with a large mug of tea.

"We don't do pancakes for breakfast," she said apologetically. "We English find the mix of sweet and savory rather revolting."

"I like all of these ingredients individually," he said. "It never occurred to me to put them all together." At first, if only out of politeness, he dug in.

Lainey sat across from him with her own plate and they ate in silence.

"Well?" she finally asked.

"I love it," he said sincerely. "That's what surprises me."

He finished before her and sat back, drinking his tea with an unusual sense of contentment. *I'm a stranger here*, he thought. *But I feel as if I've always been here.*

"What are you smiling about?" Lainey asked.

"I'm smiling?" he asked and pursed his lips.

"Yes. Like you've got a secret." She tilted her head slightly and a lock of hair fell across her face. "Have you got a secret?"

He reached across the table and pushed the wayward hair away. "No secret," he said. "I'm just enjoying myself."

She smiled, pleased with his answer.

"Where's Serena?" he asked.

"She's gone to the hospital ahead of us."

"Did you talk to your parents? Do they know I'm here?"

"I'll call them after we see Gran. Or they might be at the hospital." She finished her breakfast and looked as if she was bracing herself for a difficult task. "Are you ready?"

"Let's roll, Dan-o."

A blank expression.

"*Hawaii Five-O?* Reruns on television? Steve McGarrett?"

"Sorry," she said. "I was a *Dukes of Hazzard* girl."

THEY DROVE TO SOUTHAVEN, A LARGE UNIVERSITY TOWN WITH A HOSPITAL where Elaine Arthur was now being kept as a patient. Nicholas stared out the passenger window, marveling at the beauty of the scenery going past.

"Do you have any idea how incredible this country is?" he asked.

She glanced in his direction and shrugged. "I suppose. If you like that sort of thing."

He turned to her, not wanting to believe that she—or anyone— could ever get tired of those fields, those hills, even those sheep.

Chuckling at him, she lightly tapped his knee. "Don't look so horrified. Of course I know how incredible this country is. I *love* our countryside.

And wait until you see Hampshire and Oxfordshire. There are some breathtaking sights up north, too, if you have time."

"I'll make time."

"How long are you staying, if I may be so bold to ask?"

"Didn't I tell you? I have an open ticket. I can stay as long as I want."

"Honestly?"

"Yeah. But don't worry. I'm not going to take advantage of your hospitality."

She waved the statement away. "You can take advantage of me for as long as you like."

"Oh?"

She realized what she had said and laughed. "That's not exactly what I meant to say."

Blushing, he turned toward the passenger window to take in the view, which was now deeply wooded. Then the countryside gave way to more and more houses, built closer together, then townhouses and office complexes, then high-rises and traffic. Like London, Southaven was a mixture of ancient and new. At one point they drove through a stone archway that had once been a gate in a medieval wall encircling the original city. On the south end of town they reached Southaven District General Hospital.

Inside, they had trouble finding the psychiatric wing even with instructions from the blue-haired volunteer at the information desk. One corridor seemed identical to another. Finally they found the secured double doors. Pressing the intercom button, Lainey gave their names and explained whom they'd come to see. There was a soft buzz and the doors unlatched. Nicholas pushed one open and they stepped through.

He instantly felt depressed. The walls were an uninspiring pale green and completely unadorned. The air stank of sweaty clothes, old food, and urine, reminding him of his work at the hospital in Alexandria. Apparently old age, decay, and death were the same no matter which country you lived in. Nicholas wished he hadn't had that fry up.

They walked to a stark nurses station directly ahead, their heels clicking against the floor like a clock.

Serena appeared from a side doorway to intercept them. "We're in here," she said softly. "Good morning, Nick. How did you sleep?"

"Great, thanks."

"Did Lainey explain the shower?"

"I figured it out, thanks." He had no idea that showers were such a big thing here.

"Any sign of Mum and Dad?" Lainey asked.

"They're coming later this morning."

Serena stepped aside so that Lainey could go into the room. Nicholas hesitated, but Lainey took his hand to pull him along. She didn't let go of it, clutching it tightly and nervously, as they approached the foot of the bed.

The woman in the bed was little more than a white face and white hair, the rest of her body small bumps under the blanket. Tubes and wires connected her to bottles and monitors. Her eyes were open and they drifted lazily across the ceiling with little comprehension that anyone else was in the room.

"Hello, Gran," Lainey said, and Nicholas could hear a slight tremble in her voice.

Serena was at their side. "She's sedated," she whispered.

"Why?" Lainey asked.

"She decided last night that she didn't want to be here and made quite a fuss about leaving."

Lainey turned to her. "She was violent?"

"The doctor said she was *insistent*," Serena replied. "So they drugged her."

"Where was she trying to go to?" Lainey asked. "Back to the old chapel?"

"No. Home. To get something out of the closet, she said. She insisted she needed to go to the box for her confession."

"A box," Lainey repeated.

"A confessional box? They're like closets," Nicholas said. "She's not Catholic, is she?"

"No," Lainey replied. "Church of England."

Another mystery.

Nicholas gazed at Elaine Arthur, so still, but her eyes moving around the ceiling as if watching a screen. She was a skeleton, a slight figure, a shadow pressed onto hospital sheets like a stain. He was filled with sadness for her.

Lainey moved around the bed to her grandmother's side and gingerly picked up her hand. She held it like a child's and said, "I'm going to help you, Gran. We'll get you out of this trap."

The eyes didn't acknowledge her.

Lainey looked as if she might say something else, but quickly turned her head away. A telltale sniff told Nicholas to grab a tissue and hand it over, which he did. She wiped at her eyes and then turned and left the room.

Serena and Nicholas exchanged glances—a good-bye—and Nicholas followed Lainey out.

"This is hard," Lainey said, wiping her eyes again.

He put his hand on her shoulder. He wondered what he should say to her. What comfort or consolation could he give at a time like this? He had his faith to fall back on—a stubborn belief that God was at work, even in old age, infirmity, and mental illness. But to say so would have sounded trite. She had to be shown somehow.

"SO THIS IS WHERE IT BEGAN," NICHOLAS SAID AS HE GAZED AT THE OLD bombed-out chapel.

They had driven there to see it, but also with the hope that they might talk to Trevor Mann.

"So it was," Lainey agreed.

Nicholas could imagine his grandfather there as a boy, chatting with a young Elaine, becoming friends as they tried to reassemble the stained glass windows. Nicholas reached down and picked up a few of the fragments.

"Should we give it a try?" he asked Lainey as he tried to put a couple of the pieces together.

"And come to the same end as they did? No, thanks." She walked on toward the open field that spread out like a carpet to the Boswell mansion and, off to the side, a small cottage.

Nicholas walked with her, musing on what she'd just said, feeling the sting of it and wondering to what end she hoped they *would* come.

The walk to the cottage was farther than it appeared from the old chapel.

"What's our plan?" Nicholas asked with a slight breathlessness.

"My impression is that Trevor's the kind who's overly eager to please his superiors."

"His superiors?"

"The upper class. He's from that generation your grandfather talked about. He would have respected the class system and his place in it. If he was friends with my uncle Gerard, it would have been a friendship of convenience. He would have considered himself a servant, there to do my uncle's bidding in exchange for companionship. Of course, it would have given Trevor some prestige among his other friends, to be hanging around someone like Gerard Sommersby."

"That's not a class system," Nicholas observed. "That's the kind of pecking order that exists everywhere."

She shrugged and continued, "I got the impression when I met him that he felt deferential to my grandmother—he respected her position. He clammed up about your grandfather, probably out of loyalty to Uncle Gerard. So my appeal to him now is that Uncle Gerard is dead and he needs to think about helping those who are living."

"Do you think he'll buy it?"

"I hope so."

The cottage could've been taken straight from a David Winter collection, or one of those scenic calendars with pictures of rural England. It had a high, sloping roof made out of thatch. Chocolate-brown Tudor beams supported the yellowing walls. The leaded windows looked uneven, or maybe it was the shutters that made them look uneven since they hung loose and crooked. The front door seemed small. Brightly colored flowers lined the length of the front of the house.

"It's straight out of The Hobbit," Nicholas said softly as they approached the door.

"Wait until you see Trevor," Lainey said, then knocked.

Nicholas thought he saw a shadow move in the window, but no one came to the door. Lainey knocked again. Still no answer. She sighed.

"I think someone's in there," Nicholas whispered.

Lainey pounded harder. "Mr. Mann?" she called, stepping back to be clearly seen from inside. "It's Lainey Bishop, Elaine Arthur's granddaughter. We met the other day. I need to talk to you. It's rather urgent."

They waited. The house was still, and Nicholas wondered if he'd imagined the movement in the window.

"Should we have a look around?" Nicholas asked. "If he's the caretaker, he might be working somewhere on the grounds."

"No," she said, deflated. "I should have brought pen and paper to leave him a note."

"Do you have some in the car? I can run back."

"Don't bother. We'll come back around suppertime. He's bound to be home then." Then she added with a mischievous smile. "Hobbits don't miss their meals."

BACK AT THE CAR LAINEY PULLED OUT HER CELL PHONE AND TRIED TO CALL her parents. There was no answer. "Let me show you around Stonebridge," she suggested.

Clouds had somehow sneaked up on them, covering the sky with an ominous blanket of gray. The wind came in small gusts, puffing as if it were having trouble getting over the downs. It felt like rain.

Stonebridge was a charming town, Nicholas thought, and seemed to encompass a diversity of history. On the south end of High Street, there was a Georgian house and a building that had been a hotel dating back to the early eighteenth century. Victorian buildings dominated the center of town, with newer structures filling out the north end.

Nicholas was also aware of the cultural differences from America. There were several small shops that sold newspapers, magazines, stationery, and candy. They were called *newsagents*. They passed two small pharmacies, which the signs indicated were *chemists*. There was a shop dedicated to vegetables and fruits, another for fish and meat, and even an *ironmonger*. Everything seemed so specialized, evocative of another time in history before supermarkets and mass production.

Nicholas gestured to St. Mark's Church. "I'd like to see the inside of that."

They stepped through the large arched doors at the front and into a cool dark. Nicholas immediately noted the Gothic architecture that he'd seen used in so many Episcopal churches—the strong vertical lines, the pillars and high vaulted ceilings, window and door openings all pointing heavenward.

Nicholas's attention was drawn to a group of young people dressed in shirts and jeans, standing in a circle in the area just in front of the altar. A tour of some sort. Then they lifted their heads and began to sing a motet by Palestrina. They sang a cappella and the voices seemed to come from heaven itself, the parts unfolding one over the other, the notes winging gently around them, cascading upward to the very rafters of the church, the echo making the sound all the more ethereal.

The piece was achingly beautiful. Nicholas slid into the closest pew, leaning forward, closing his eyes to take it all in. He could feel Lainey slide in next to him.

The words were in Latin, but it didn't matter. The voices conveyed the emotion, the song stirred in his heart the longing he always felt when he encountered God. There was always a yearning for more.

The song ended, the notes ringing out and disappearing into the deep reaches of his soul.

He opened his eyes and turned to Lainey. Her eyes were moist with tears.

"What was that?" she asked in a stunned voice, more tears coming.

Thinking that she was crying because of her grandmother, he put his arm around her. "It's all right, Lainey."

She didn't pull away from his embrace, but said in a voice so close he could feel her breath touch his cheek, "No, this isn't about my grandmother. This is about . . ." She stammered, struggled with the words. "The beauty of it."

"Sparks," he said, and gazed at her. Some people carried their scars in the open—like Serena, whose face seemed to reflect a very deep pain. But Lainey's freshness, her wit and playfulness, made it easy to forget that something was happening to her inside. He now recognized in her eyes the conflict of her life as she'd always known it suddenly coming in contact with the whisper of another life.

The choir began another song, one in English and probably by Byrd, or so Nicholas guessed. *Sing joyfully*, they sang.

"Well," someone said softly from behind them.

They turned to face a large barrel-chested man in a priest's collar. He smiled at them. "Incredible, aren't they?"

"Father Gilbert," Lainey said. "Is this your choir?"

"Heavens no," he said with a slight chuckle. "They're a youth choir from Hungary. They were driving through Stonebridge on the way to a concert in Southaven and stopped in to see the church. They asked if I minded if they rehearsed a little. I certainly didn't mind." He put out his hand to Nicholas. "We haven't been introduced."

Nicholas stood up and shook the man's hand, aware of how his own was enveloped by Father Gilbert's. "Nicholas Powell."

"Nick is from America," Lainey explained quickly. "He's studying to be an Episcopalian priest."

"Ah! Where are you studying?"

"Virginia Theological Seminary in Alexandria, Virginia."

"I've visited there. A lovely campus," Father Gilbert said. "You're getting your M-Div?"

"Yes. I'm about to start my final year."

"Well, don't let it destroy your faith." Father Gilbert winked at him, then seemed to make a connection. "Powell? You aren't by chance related to . . ." He looked at Lainey without finishing the question.

"He is Adam Powell's grandson," Lainey confirmed. "I went to America and dragged him back."

"If by *dragging* you mean that I came along willingly and without telling you until we got to the plane," Nicholas said.

"Yes. That."

"If you have a few minutes, I'd like you to come back to my office," Father Gilbert said. "We need to compare notes."

"I'VE JUST COME BACK FROM SEEING YOUR GRANDMOTHER," FATHER GILBERT said once they were seated in his office. It was a small room with a fire-place on one wall that was blocked by an electric heater. A painting of a shepherd and a flock of sheep on a pastoral English countryside hung directly above the fireplace. There was a small arched window of stained glass—a knight battling a dragon. The wall just to their left was covered with old wooden shelves, each buckling under books of various sizes. Nicholas noted that the books covered a broad range of theological and biblical subjects and authors. There were also several shelves dedicated to fiction—classic and contemporary, including recent thrillers. Nicholas also spotted several books about police procedures, criminal investiga-tion, and case histories tucked away on a bottom shelf.

"We saw her this morning, too," Lainey said. "Was she still sedated?"

"Yes. The doctors think it's best, particularly while they try to get some nourishment back into her. Serena was terribly distressed to realize your grandmother hadn't been eating. I was distressed, as well. I'd been to see her every day and never would have guessed what she was up to. Your parents certainly had no idea. Your mother is extremely upset. She asked me to drop by this afternoon."

"She *must* be upset if she asked you to come by."

"Exactly."

Lainey turned to Nicholas. "Oh, dear. She'll kill me once she finds out I've been back all this time and haven't spoken to her."

"Right again," Father Gilbert said. He then looked from Lainey to Nicholas and back again. "So, which one of you is going to tell me what happened in America?"

Nicholas deferred to Lainey, who went into a full account of her visit with Julie Peters, the conversation with Adam Powell, and how touched she was that Nicholas returned to England with her.

Father Gilbert listened thoughtfully. After Lainey finished, he said, "Quite an adventure."

She nodded.

He turned his gaze to Nicholas. "If you handle your parish work with as much diligence as you're handling this, then you'll make a great priest."

Nicholas didn't reply, blushing a little. He knew—as he was sure Father Gilbert did—that he wouldn't treat all of his parishioners the same way he was treating Lainey.

"I had an interesting conversation just yesterday with an elderly gentleman called Dr. Chaney," Father Gilbert said to Lainey. "Have you heard of him?"

"No."

"He was your family's doctor before you were born. I mentioned him to your mother this morning and she remembers him from when she was a child. He's now living at the Pevensey Retirement Home. Some of my church members go there once a month to meet with the residents, sing a few songs, conduct a short service. We were there yesterday."

"Did he tell you something about my grandmother?"

"He spoke very affectionately about her."

"When was Dr. Chaney my grandmother's doctor?" Lainey asked.

"When she was a young girl—and even after she married into the Arthur family."

"Then he knew my grandmother in 1954."

"Yes."

Lainey's voice became more excited. "Did you ask him about her? Does he know what happened?"

Father Gilbert held up his hands. "Calm down, Lainey. I explained to him that I knew Elaine and about her condition now. He didn't seem surprised. Just the opposite, in fact."

"Why?" Lainey asked.

"Because it's happened before."

"*Before?*"

"What did he mean?" Nicholas asked.

"Dr. Chaney remembered that your grandmother was a very strong woman, but had a difficult time in the summer of 1954. He remembers it because it seemed so contrary to her character and was one of the few times he felt helpless to do anything for a patient. General practitioners were simply that back then: men who dealt with the most general complaints. Mental and emotional problems were beyond his knowledge."

"What kind of mental and emotional problems did my grandmother have?"

"He said she suffered from stress and anxiety."

"Did he know why?"

"He wouldn't say so directly. But it became clear to him that it was because of a failed love affair."

Nicholas and Lainey exchanged looks.

"What were her symptoms then?" Lainey asked. "The same as now?"

"Similar. She was quiet and withdrawn, couldn't sleep, wouldn't eat. Dr. Chaney went to see her several times at home. They talked a bit, but she was always vague with her answers."

"How did she snap out of it?" asked Nicholas.

"It's Dr. Chaney's opinion that if James Arthur hadn't been head-over-heels in love with Elaine, she wouldn't have made it through that period. He was the one who persuaded her to go to a specialist in London—one of the Harley Street crowd."

"All the really posh doctors were on Harley Street," Lainey explained to Nicholas. "Which doctor did she go to?" Lainey asked Father Gilbert.

"Either he couldn't remember or he didn't know, but he drew a blank on the name," Father Gilbert said. "Your mother knew nothing about it, when I asked her. Neither did Dr. Gilthorpe."

He's more like a detective than a priest, Nicholas thought.

"There must be a way to find out," Lainey said.

Father Gilbert scratched at his chin. "There must be physician lists and registers from that time. I still have a few contacts with Scotland Yard. I can see what they know. Meanwhile, you should see if your grandmother has any diaries. She was a governess. Perhaps she kept appointment books with her lesson plans and personal schedule."

"We can go back to the house and look now."

Scotland Yard? Nicholas thought, a delayed reaction. He glanced at the police manuals on the shelf, then back at Father Gilbert. The question was written all over his face.

"Father Gilbert was a detective with Scotland Yard," Lainey explained.

Nicholas looked at the man with astonishment.

"It's a long story," said Father Gilbert.

SERENA WAS BACK AT ARTHUR HOUSE WHEN LAINEY AND NICHOLAS returned. It was now mid-afternoon, but she looked very tired.

"Are you all right?" Nicholas asked her.

"I need a drink," she said with a sad smile.

Lainey shot her a worried look.

"I'm joking," Serena said quickly.

Lainey's expression told Nicholas she was unconvinced. "Does my grandmother have any appointment books from 1954?" she asked.

Serena thought for a moment, then indicated for them to follow her down the hall. "They're in the office. But I looked through them when your grandmother first became ill. I saw nothing about Adam Powell."

"Not Adam Powell," Lainey explained. "We're looking for doctor's visits. My grandmother had a breakdown like this one back in 1954."

Serena stopped in her tracks and turned to Lainey. "Did she?"

Lainey explained about Dr. Chaney and the mystery doctor on Harley Street. "We hope his name is in her diary somewhere."

They stepped into the office and Serena went to a small door at the bottom of a large cherry cabinet. "The diaries are here." She knelt to open the door. "Let me see ...," she muttered as she pushed a few file boxes around on the shelf. Finally she exclaimed, "Here" and pulled out a black rectangular box. It was made of heavy cardboard and had a small latch on top. It clicked against her thumb and the thin lid lifted. Inside were several appointment books, all the same in appearance, except each one had a year stamped in gold on the front. Serena picked out 1954 and handed it to Lainey.

Nicholas moved in close, looking over Lainey's shoulder. Serena leaned against the corner of the desk, her arms folded. Starting with January, Lainey flipped the pages to June. It was a day-by-day diary, with each day and date indicated at the top in bold black. Along the left-hand column were times broken into half-hour segments. At the bottom were lines for additional notes. Most of the days were filled with Elaine's neat handwriting indicating books and assignments for her students, scheduled times to study certain subjects, and extracurricular lessons for things like piano or horseback riding. Occasionally there were notes in the evening hours for a dinner or party somewhere, a film every now and then. Gerard's name seemed to pop up every couple of weeks.

Throughout the early spring many of the evenings were filled with "B.G.C."

"Who is B.G.C.?" Lainey wondered aloud.

"Billy Graham Crusade," Nicholas speculated. "Did she go all those times?"

Lainey shrugged.

Pages turned and the spring months became summer. "Some of the dates are circled," Nicholas observed.

"I wonder if those are days when she met Adam," Lainey said. "Most Saturdays are circled."

In late June and thereafter the circles disappeared. Though they flipped the pages back and forth, they could find no indication of that fateful Saturday when her life changed. The pages were blank, as if Elaine's life had suddenly stopped. Then Dr. Chaney's name appeared at various times on days in July and August.

"Now we're getting somewhere," Nicholas said.

There was a notation at the beginning of August about the Arthur family going on holiday to Spain. Elaine didn't go. On Tuesday, the 10th of August, the page was blank except the entry "Dr. Sheaf/London."

"That must be it," Lainey said with restrained excitement. She turned the pages and two more entries for Dr. Sheaf appeared on Tuesday, the 17th and on Wednesday the 25th of August. The name didn't appear again until late in September, twice in October, and then no more.

"She hardly did anything in the autumn," Lainey observed. "No appointments, no lessons, nothing at all."

"She'd left Arthur House then," Serena said.

Nicholas and Lainey looked up at her together.

"I remember her telling me once that she had resigned as governess at the end of August. She'd moved back home."

"Did she say why?"

"No. Only that the change in weather between August and September always reminded her of it."

"These three months may be empty because she was in the midst of her breakdown," Nicholas suggested. "We don't know how long it lasted, do we?"

"She married James Arthur in the spring of 1955, so she must have been on the mend," Lainey said.

"Or he was part of her mending," Nicholas added.

Lainey put the diary down and moved around the desk to the phone. "I'll call Father Gilbert to give him the name."

"The number is on the pad," Serena said. "I rang him this morning before I went to the hospital. Why do you have to tell him?"

"His friends at Scotland Yard might be able to find Dr. Sheaf," replied Lainey. She pointed to the number and then started to dial. Then she suddenly put the phone down again and said as a reprimand, "What was I thinking? I don't need Father Gilbert to check with Scotland Yard. I know exactly who to call."

"Who?" Nicholas asked.

"Penelope Young."

"And who is that?" asked Serena.

"She's the author of a book I'd proofread about post-war London medical practices and physicians. It covered 1945 to 1961. It was thoroughly researched—boringly so."

"Great. Let's go buy the book."

"It's not published yet. But if anyone could help us, she could."

IN THE PUBLISHING WORLD, PENELOPE YOUNG WAS KNOWN AS A *HIGH maintenance author*. Lainey remembered getting calls from her day and night about her manuscript. Ever the diplomat, Lainey did the appropriate amount of schmoozing on the phone and secured the author's help. The name of Dr. Sheaf was familiar, she'd said, but she needed time to go through her files to be sure. Lainey arranged to meet her at two o'clock the next day at her home in Richmond, a well-to-do borough on the western outreaches of London.

Lainey beamed as she put the phone back on the receiver. "This is brilliant."

Serena had gone off to another part of the house and Nicholas now sat on the opposite side of the desk from Lainey. He watched as she scribbled a note about Penelope Young's address, smiling as she wrote. To her, this undoubtedly felt like a little victory in the two-steps-forward-three-steps-back experience she'd had since her grandmother was found in the rain by the old chapel. Others would have given up long before this and stuck with conventional help at the hands of the doctors. Not Lainey. She was going to save her grandmother one way or the other. Nicholas admired that kind of tenacity and determination, and appreciated the love that drove it forward. Nicholas felt a deep affection for her—even a pride he had no right to feel.

Lainey glanced up at him, saw him looking at her, and frowned self-consciously. "What's wrong?"

"Nothing," he replied. "I'm watching you, that's all."

"That's nice," she said, then returned to her scribbles.

"I'm getting hungry."

"Yes. And I have an idea about where to eat."

Six fifteen was a little early for the usual dinner crowd at the Mill House, so Nicholas and Lainey had no trouble getting a table. Nicholas was impressed with the pleasant combination of English pub and stylish restaurant. And the menu had everything from hamburgers and sandwiches to more elaborate dishes like duck and prime rib. Nicholas ordered the duck with a cherry sauce, Lainey ordered a chef's salad. They limited their drinks to Coca-Colas.

Nicholas was going to ask Lainey about Father Gilbert's conversion from detective to priest when he saw that something had caught her attention behind him . . .

He leaned forward and whispered. "You look like you've seen a ghost."

"Better than that," she whispered back. "A hobbit. Trevor is sitting at the bar."

"Perfect," he said. "Let's invite him over for a friendly drink."

"Do you think we should? What if he runs away?"

"Then we follow him back to his house." Nicholas craned his neck around to look at the bar, which was on the other side of a waist-high set of dividers. Nicholas spied Trevor at the far end of the bar, dressed in a countryman's tweed, even including his cap. He wore green rubber boots. Nicholas spun back around to Lainey and laughed. "He *does* look like a hobbit."

She grinned. "I'll ask him."

"Maybe *I'd* better," Nicholas suggested. He stood up and casually strolled to the bar. Trevor was sitting with his back to the bar, surveying the room. He was smiling, but Nicholas guessed he'd spotted Lainey because his expression changed to one of consternation. Before he could turn away from her, Nicholas was at his side.

"Hi," he said.

Trevor eyed him with suspicion. "Hello," he said and clutched his drink as if Nicholas might try to steal it. His nose and cheeks were red and he swayed ever so slightly. He'd been sitting at the bar for a while.

Nicholas pointed to the pint glass, now nearly empty. "May I buy you another one of those?"

"You may," Trevor said, his speech slurred. "But I'd like to know why."

Nicholas signaled the bartender and ordered another pint for Trevor.

"I'm here from America and learned that you're the groundskeeper at Boswell—"

"Are you one of the investors? They said you were coming."

"Actually, I'm—"

"'Be watchful, Trevor,' they said to me. 'The investors will want to talk to you. You know more about that property than anyone alive.'"

"I imagine you do."

"I do. What would you like to know?"

"I want to know if you'll come sit at my table so we can chat."

Before Trevor could answer, the bartender returned with the pint. Nicholas picked it up. "Add it to my bill," he said quickly to the bartender and took the drink, heading back for the table. Trevor followed with great expectation, like a hungry puppy going after a steak.

Only when they reached Lainey did Trevor suddenly stop. "You're together?" he asked, his voice anxious.

"You know Lainey," Nicholas said.

He tipped his cap politely to her. "Hello, Miss Bishop."

"Sit down, please," Lainey said and pushed a chair away from the table for him.

He looked at the chair as if he didn't know what to do. Nicholas guessed that his good manners and deference to his superiors demanded that he not be rude. A drink had been bought for him, after all. He couldn't rush away until he'd had some of it.

"Yes, sit down," Nicholas said, clapping him on the back.

Trevor obeyed. Nicholas put the drink down in front of him, which Trevor took gratefully. Nicholas sat down opposite.

"Are you hungry?" Nicholas asked.

"No thank you, sir. I have stew at home," he answered. "But I'm curious. How is it that you're involved with the investors, Miss Bishop?"

"What?"

"A case of mistaken identity," Nicholas said quickly. "You assumed I was an investor," he said to Trevor. "I'm not."

"Ah." He took a drink from his pint. "Then what's this about, if I may be so bold as to ask?"

Lainey took the lead. "You know about my grandmother."

"Yes, I do. I'm very sorry to hear she's in the hospital."

"It's sad, yes. But I think you may be able to help her."

"Me? Oh no, Miss Bishop. What could someone like me do for Mrs. Arthur?"

"You could ease her mind about something that happened years ago."

"Ha. As if I could remember anything that happened past a fortnight ago."

"You may remember this," she said, coaxing him. "You and my uncle Gerard played a little prank on someone my grandmother knew. Adam Powell."

Trevor was visibly shaken to hear the name. He pursed his lips and glanced toward the door. Nicholas knew the odds were very good that the old man might bolt. He squirmed in his seat and then took another drink.

Lainey leaned toward Trevor, putting a hand lightly on his arm. "We're running out of people who can help," Lainey said in a measured tone. "My uncle Gerard is dead, as you know. You're the only other person on the face of the earth who can tell us what really happened between my grandmother and Adam Powell."

Trevor shook his head miserably. "No. I'm sorry. It wouldn't be right. It's not my place. You'll have to ask your grandmother."

"I *can't*," Lainey said, a little too emphatically. It startled Trevor. She calmed her voice. "My grandmother won't talk. The doctors are bewildered about how to help her. It's as if she's given up, Mr. Mann. And we believe if we could find out exactly what happened fifty years ago, we can help her."

Trevor lowered his head as if offering a silent prayer to the god in his beer. When he spoke a moment later, his voice was so low that Nicholas had to strain to hear him. "It was Gerard's idea. He's the one who arranged everything."

"He arranged for you to meet Adam at the Mill House or what happened afterward?"

Trevor's head came up, his eyes lifted high upon his forehead. "The Mill House," he said with a look of relief. "Right. The Mill House."

Nicholas was puzzled by his change of countenance. *It's as if he thought we were going to ask about something else, then was relieved we didn't,* Nicholas thought. *Or is it just part of the cultural barrier?*

"It was for her own good," Trevor said. "You have to understand that we were doing her a service."

Lainey offered no comment. "What did you do?"

"I came here for a drink, as I often did around noon on a Saturday. That's all. Came early that morning. I'd been chasing poachers, I think."

"If you came here every Saturday, then you knew my grandmother and Adam Powell met here."

"I knew. But it was none of my affair."

"So what happened?"

"On this particular day, I could tell something was up. They were decorating, making a fuss. So I asked the owner, Mr. Soames, I asked, 'What's going on?' and he said, 'I think Powell is going to ask Miss Elaine to marry him.' Well, that was news."

"Something to call Gerard about," Nicholas said.

"Oh, yes," Trevor said, then took a long drink from the glass. "I rang him, I admit it. He was protective of Miss Holmes, you see. Liked her a lot. So I rang him and told him he better come down right away. Well, he said he had a better idea and asked if Elaine—I mean, Miss Holmes—had arrived yet. She hadn't. So he told me what he wanted me to do."

In characteristically bad timing, the waiter arrived with their food. He put the tray down on a stand and delicately placed the plates in front of Lainey and Nicholas.

"Would you like something to eat?" Nicholas asked Trevor.

"No, no," he said. "I have a rabbit stew at home. But thank you anyway."

After making sure they had everything, the waiter left. No one touched their food.

"What was the plan, exactly?" asked Lainey. "What did Uncle Gerard tell you to do?"

"To try to talk Powell out of it," Trevor replied. "He wanted me to say it was a mistake. She was well-to-do and he wasn't. That sort of thing. And then he wanted me to persuade Powell to walk with me to a clearing at, I think, eleven thirty. Somewhere around that time."

"He told you to get Adam Powell to that parking area at a specific time?"

Trevor nodded. "Yes. So Powell could see what he saw."

"That was a long shot, wasn't it?" Nicholas asked, surprised by the sheer adolescent nature of the plan.

"That was Gerard for you. He'd try anything. I was a nervous wreck. I never believed I could get Powell to go with me. But he did." Another drink. "I played to his fear, you see. Deep down we knew we didn't belong with people like Gerard and Elaine Holmes. And it worked. He came with me."

"How did Gerard get my grandmother into his car? Surely he couldn't have planned that."

"He knew which way she walked from the Arthur House to here."

"You seem to have known an awful lot about Elaine and Adam," Nicholas said. "You two had been spying on them."

"Not *spying*. Protecting. It was for her own good, as I've told you."

"So Gerard picked up my grandmother somewhere along the way," Lainey said.

"Right. They were friends. Why not? So she got in and instead of bringing her here, he took her to that little car park place in the clearing."

"But she was due to meet up with Adam Powell. She must have been worried about being late."

"Gerard told her that he was having problems with—" He stopped, trying to remember a name. "Oh, blast. What was her name? Some girl he was seeing at the time." He frowned, losing himself in trying to recall the name.

Lainey spoke to get him back on track. "I've got the idea. He feigned some sort of problem so my grandmother would take the time to talk with him."

"Yes. So I took Powell to the place and—what did I do?—I made a noise so Gerard could see me in his wing-mirror. Oh, I know. I snapped a branch. That was it. It was loud enough so that Gerard would know we were there watching." Trevor smiled. "He should've been an actor, Gerard. He made a real drama out of his problems with whatever-her-name-was."

"My grandmother really fell for it, didn't she?" Lainey asked.

"Hook, line, and sinker," Trevor replied. "Gerard played it up to get her sympathy and then, just for added measure, he confessed that she was the one he truly loved."

"He confessed that he *loved* my grandmother?" Lainey was shocked.

Trevor nodded. "He claimed he had always loved her. It was nonsense, of course. They'd been friends too long for that. But your grandmother was alarmed and tried to let him down gently, you see. That's how he worked it. When he knew we were watching he told her that if he could get one good kiss from her, he'd never mention the subject again."

Nicholas was aghast. Suddenly the scheme didn't seem adolescent so much as downright malevolent.

"Oh, he could be a charmer when he wanted," Trevor continued. "She agreed and he kissed her and they hugged. Then they drove away. That was enough."

"A clever little plan," Lainey said, with dripping sarcasm.

Trevor missed her tone and agreed. "It certainly did its job on Adam. He was livid. That was the end of it. Good-bye and good riddance." Trevor drained his glass with smug contentment.

"But how did he convince her to stay in the car when she was expected here—to meet Adam?" Lainey asked.

"What could she do?" he said with a shrug. "He was driving and kept taking turns in the other direction. She got very annoyed with him, but he ignored her. Finally, when he thought he'd stalled long enough to make sure Powell wouldn't be here, he dropped her off around the corner so she could walk up as usual. It was a terribly simple plan—and Powell fell for it."

"What happened when my grandmother arrived and Adam was gone?"

"She was very upset, as one would expect. That was the most difficult part for me. To see her so distraught. I offered her a lift to the station, to see if she could catch him, but I made sure she didn't get there in time."

Nicholas couldn't read from Lainey's face what she was feeling at that moment. She gazed at the old man quietly, then asked, "Didn't you feel badly for deceiving her?"

He rubbed his eyes wearily. Nicholas knew that he was done with this conversation by the impatience in his tone. "It was for her own good. I told you. We had to save her."

"Save her from what?" Lainey asked, her voice a sharp edge.

"From a disastrous life. The *wrong* life. She would've married the wrong man if we hadn't helped her."

WITH NO OFFERS FOR ANOTHER DRINK, THE OLD MAN SAID GOOD NIGHT. With cap in hand he bowed to Lainey as if he'd been dismissed, and left. Nicholas pushed his plate of cold food away, leaned on the table, and put his face in his hands. The wrong life, Trevor had said. What kind of arrogance must a man have to make that determination with such conviction?

But it wasn't just Elaine's life, it was Adam's as well. Nicholas's grandfather still bore the scars, carried them like a suit of armor around his heart and soul—all because two men decided he wasn't worthy of Elaine.

And what of Elaine's life? Nicholas had no idea where her scars were, but she'd obviously withdrawn into the safety of a cocoon to keep from receiving any more.

"God have mercy," Nicholas whispered.

Lainey sat with her arms folded, her eyes steely, her face set around clenched teeth and white lips. "Now we know," she eventually said.

"That must be what my uncle—" She stopped herself, the intimacy of the title more than she could bear just then. "That must be what Gerard Sommersby confessed to my grandmother."

"What do you do with that kind of revelation? How are you supposed to react when you're told that the course of your life had been changed by a . . ." Nicholas couldn't find the words, and he slumped a little from the burden of his inarticulation. "Little wonder she was thrown into a depression."

What must she be feeling? Nicholas wondered. Anger at Gerard? Foolish for having been duped? Self-recrimination for not reaching Adam in time? Loathing for being part of a class that would do such a thing? Helpless because she had no way to tell his grandfather that it was all a mistake?

The waiter returned and looked with disapproval at their untouched plates. "Not to your satisfaction?"

"I'm sure it was the best meal I never had," Nicholas said.

"Would you like me to warm them up?"

Nicholas had lost his appetite but looked at Lainey. She shook her head. "Let's go home," she said.

"Box it up, we'll take it with us," Nicholas told the waiter. Though he couldn't imagine when he'd want to eat it.

The waiter said a brusque "Yes, sir" and walked off.

Lainey stood up. "I need some fresh air."

Nicholas stood as well. "I'll pay the bill. You go on ahead."

Lainey stood under a clear sky, the setting sun dragging yellows, blues, and reds behind it. Stars appeared, then the moon.

Elaine and Adam had looked at this same sky. Then as now, Lainey mused, the universe went through its slow steps, a dance it has performed for years and years, ages and eons, indifferent to the dramas beneath it.

The bells in St. Mark's chimed for some evening service. She listened to their distant peal and thought about God. If he existed, then where was he as two of his children were wrenched apart by circumstances beyond their control? Hadn't he heard Elaine's prayers—or Adam's? Why had he sat idly by while Gerard and Trevor hatched their little scheme? Where is he now?

Leaning against the hood of her car, Lainey felt a fury like she'd never known. It bubbled up, feeling as if it might explode from her in a scream.

Maybe God would notice *that*. Maybe the moon would hesitate for only a second and glance her way.

She turned and, folding her arms on the roof of the Mini, dropped her head on them, the metal of the car cold against her forearms. Oh, her poor grandmother. Did she really believe that she had lived the wrong life? Was she tortured now with the *What-ifs* of a life she hadn't been allowed to have? Regret. Recrimination.

And Uncle Gerard, that stupid, insensitive man.

How does one forgive a thing like that?

She heard footsteps on the gravel, then the crunch of a paper bag being put down. Nicholas appeared next to her, mimicking her posture on the car, their faces mere inches away from each other. "A penny for your thoughts."

"Just looking at the sky," she said. "And then I didn't want to look anymore. It's too big. Too indifferent."

"When I was a kid I used to look up at the sky and wonder if God was out there. I mean, *way* out there, even to the farthest point. And if he was, did he stretch from here to there like something massively elastic, or was he merely there *and* here at the same time?"

"Interesting thought," she said.

"Then I wondered *why* he would want to be way out there when all the human beings were here. *This* is where the action was, this is where he was needed the most, so why bother with all those big glowing rocks out there? I wanted him right next to me all the time. Nowhere else."

Lainey took in his half-shadowed face, handsome and innocent and sensitive. "You must have been a laugh-riot with your friends," she teased.

"I'm a Powell. I didn't need to have friends," he said.

She lifted her head. "Nicholas."

"Hmm?"

His head was tilted slightly toward her, his face shadowed, and she wished that he would kiss her. But that would be foolish. Why would she entertain a kiss *now*? Especially at a time when love seemed nothing more than a reason for pain. Look at her grandmother. Look at Adam Powell. What had love done for them? What did it do for anybody?

"Lainey?"

"Shut up," she said and reached over, her hand on his warm neck, and pulled him toward her. His lips were on hers and this was no quick tease in a hotel lobby but a full, hot kiss that made her close her eyes as if she were swimming in a warm pool, floating, being carried away. His hand gently touched the side of her face and their lips parted ever so slightly and then a car door slammed somewhere nearby and a voice came crashing in on the moment.

"It *couldn't* be our Lainey, I said. Surely she'd have better manners than to be doing *that* in a public place."

"Mother," Lainey said, feeling every bit like a caught schoolgirl.

Margaret Bishop stood pinch-lipped, her hands on her hips. Timothy stood next to her and had an unduly amused look on his face.

"Nick," Lainey said, her voice gone. "I'd like you to meet my mother and father."

Red-faced, Nicholas held out his hand.

"WELL, IF NOTHING ELSE, I MAKE AN INCREDIBLE FIRST IMPRESSION," Nicholas said with a loud groan after Lainey's parents had gone into the Mill House. Their exchange had been awkward and mercifully quick, with a promise to talk tomorrow.

Lainey put her arms around him, kissing him once more.

He felt like he was in high school again, his heart pounding, excitement going through him like forked lightning. Then the thunder of guilt followed, making him self-conscious. He gently pulled away. "They'll come back," he said. "I just know it."

A wistful smile from her. "Right," she said. "Good thinking." Then she turned and climbed into the driver's side of the car. He picked up the bag of food and got in the passenger side.

"Where to now?" he asked, wanting to be tempted by a provocative answer, but knowing he mustn't.

"You're going to ring your grandfather," she said, instantly killing the mood.

BACK AT ARTHUR HOUSE, LAINEY LEFT NICHOLAS ALONE IN THE OFFICE to call America. "I'll make us some tea," she said. "Double-oh-one, and then the number," she added before closing the door.

The old man had said he was going fishing after the party, but Nicholas couldn't imagine he'd cut himself off from all communications.

Picking up the receiver, he slowly dialed the 001, then his grandfather's cell phone number. The phone rang in his ear.

How was he going to handle this? How should he break the news to his grandfather that he'd been played for a sucker all those years ago? And would it make any difference now? Nicholas imagined himself explaining everything Trevor had said, then a stone-cold silence followed by "so what?" Maybe his grandfather was too cut off from his heart to care anymore.

After the fourth ring, voice-mail picked up. An automated voice said that no one was available and to leave a message. At the beep, Nicholas said quickly, "Grandad, I'm in England and I have some important information for you. Call me at—" and then he realized he didn't know the phone number to Arthur House. He scrambled to see if it was on the phone itself. It wasn't. "Oh, I don't know what it is," he said to the machine. "I'll call you back."

Nicholas slammed down the phone. His eye caught part of the Arthur House letterhead near the edge of the desk. The phone number was beneath the address. "Aarrgh," he said and considered calling his grandfather to leave the number. He decided instead to call his father's cell phone. Maybe he'd know how to reach his grandfather.

He punched in the numbers and waited. The connection was slower, but finally there was a ring on the other end. After three rings, Nicholas's father answered.

"Hello?"

"Hi, Dad. It's Nicholas."

Silence. "Well. The prodigal phones home."

"That was E.T., Dad. Look, I was wondering—" He stopped himself. His father wasn't listening. He was shouting for Nicholas's mother. "Dad," Nicholas said again, trying to get his father's attention.

"So you ditch your girlfriend and run off to England with that other girl, is that what happened?"

"Not exactly."

"Kathy seems to think so."

"She does? How do you know?"

"She said that she thought you were taking some time to think about your future together," he said. "But when she heard that you'd gone off to England, she took that as your answer."

Nicholas didn't speak, feeling annoyed that once again Kathy seemed to go to his family, working them behind his back.

"Is that your answer? Have you broken up with her? Because if you have . . ." His father didn't finish the sentence.

"If I have then *what*, Dad? Are you going to threaten me to marry her?" This was all wrong. He shouldn't be angry. He needed to stay calm.

"We were under the impression that you cared for her, that you were a good match—"

"She's great, Dad. She's terrific. This isn't about that."

"Then what's it about? Why would you treat her so poorly?"

"I didn't—"

"You ran off, Nicholas. It was your engagement party and *you ran off.*"

"It wasn't supposed to be an engagement party, remember? That was a surprise. Planned by everybody but me, I might add. And, forgive me for being so insensitive, but I thought it was more important to help Lainey. Her grandmother is ill and—"

"There's no point in trying to play the Good Samaritan card, Nicholas."

"I'm not playing anything. I'm trying to explain, but you won't listen."

"Speak sense and I'll listen."

Nicholas rubbed a hand over his eyes and groaned.

"You've made a real mess of things, that's all there is to say. So you better get on the next plane home and get it fixed. Do you understand?"

Nicholas swallowed back all the things he wanted to say. "I'm doing the right thing, Dad. That's all *I* have to say. Now, where's Grandad?"

"Your grandfather's gone fishing. You knew that."

"Where exactly did he go? I have to talk to him."

"I have no idea where he is. If he calls in, I'll tell him you're looking for him. But believe me, you don't want to talk to him. He's absolutely furious with you. He's ready to cut you off completely."

"Okay, Dad. Thanks."

"Here's your mother."

"No, wait—"

Too late. A jostling of the phone, then his mother's voice: "Nicholas? What on earth is going on?"

"Don't worry, Mom. I'm all right. I know what I'm doing."

"But poor Kathy—"

"Kathy isn't poor, Mom. She's a sharp girl who knows exactly what she wants, from the clerical collar right down to the well-trimmed cuticles."

"What?"

"I know you're disappointed but, trust me, I don't think I'm what she wants anymore. We would've realized that sooner or later. I'm sorry it took us this long."

"But she was so good for you."

"Maybe, but I wouldn't have been good for her. I don't think I would have behaved up to her standard."

"That's an odd thing to say."

"I know. I'm sorry."

"You've fallen in love with this English girl, haven't you?"

"*Lainey*, Mom. Her name's *Lainey*, and—"

There was a soft knock at the door and Lainey walked in with a mug of tea.

"You beckon and I come," she whispered and put the mug down in front of him.

"Thank you," he mouthed back to her. She slipped out again and he watched her go, that high school feeling coming back again.

"Nicholas?" his mother said down the line.

"I have to go, Mom. We'll talk more later. Here's the phone number where I am."

"No, wait," she said, flustered. "I need a pen and paper." More jostling of the phone, then: "All right. Go ahead."

He gave her the country code and phone number for Arthur House.

"Those are a lot of numbers," she said as if the effort of writing them down had fatigued her.

"I know," he said sympathetically. "They get longer the farther away you have to dial."

"Really?"

"No, I'm joking."

"Silly boy."

"Mom, please tell Grandad that I have to talk to him."

"If we ever hear from him, we will. But you're only asking for trouble."

"Trouble seems to be my middle name these days."

A motherly sigh. "But I love you, you know."

"I know. I love you, too. And tell Dad that I love him, even though he's completely wrong."

"Oh, heavens. I can't tell him *that*."

"WHERE'S SERENA?" NICHOLAS ASKED AS HE ENTERED THE KITCHEN. Lainey was sitting on the counter, flipping through a magazine and drinking her tea.

"She's at her Alcoholics Anonymous meeting."

"Ah." Now Nicholas understood the significance of that earlier exchange.

"How is your family?"

"Just fine, thanks." He would've liked to tell her the truth but didn't see the point.

"Did you talk to your grandfather?"

"No. He went fishing, as planned, and nobody knows how to get in touch with him." He looked at her for a moment, his mind going back to their kiss.

As if she knew his mind, she said, "Nick, about what happened at the Mill House . . ."

"You mean with Trevor?"

"No. After that."

"After?"

"The bit right before my parents arrived."

"Oh. That."

"I don't want you to think—I mean—I'm not generally inclined to—um—"

"Look, Lainey, you don't have to say anything. I wouldn't normally have—well—you know—"

"Yes, exactly."

"Our emotions are heightened by everything that's happened," he reasoned. "We're feeling everything on a greater scale right now."

"Do you really think so?"

"Don't you?"

"I suppose so. Right before you came out to the car I was very sad and then very annoyed and—well—"

"Confused."

"Right."

"In emotional turmoil."

"Right."

"I understand. So am I."

"Are you?"

"Yes. For example, I just learned that Kathy and I have broken up."

"Oh. That's too bad," she said without any sympathy, followed by a per-plexed silence. "You just *learned* it? Didn't you have a say in the matter?"

"I thought I did, but Kathy decided otherwise."

She slid off of the counter and closed the magazine. "Well, if it's any consolation, I think you're one of the good guys."

"Thank you."

She turned to face him. "I have a question, though."

"Go ahead."

"I think I'm still in emotional turmoil. Will you please kiss me again?"

"If you insist." He pulled her close, kissing her playfully at first and then more seriously. It became a long, passionate kiss.

She moved her lips from his mouth to his cheek, then whispered in his ear, "Let's go upstairs."

Sure, he thought. *Why not?* he thought. *Who wouldn't?* he thought. There was nothing he wanted more in the entire world.

She took his hand and they started across the kitchen.

He stopped in his tracks. "No, wait."

"What's wrong?"

"I can't."

"You *can't*?"

He blushed. "I won't."

She looked at him, rejected. "Did I get something wrong? I thought ..."

"No, you're not wrong. But I can't, er, won't, or whatever." She looked wounded, so he stammered on. "It's not you, Lainey. *Believe me*, it's not you. It's just that, I don't think ..." He struggled with the words. He'd never had to explain it before, certainly not in this kind of cir-cumstance. "I believe that making love belongs in marriage. That's what makes it love."

She looked at him with disbelief.

"It's a commitment I've made," he said. "As a matter of obedience, actually. And as a matter of respect."

"Obedience and respect to whom?"

"Obedience to God. Respect to women."

"Because you're becoming a priest?"

"Because I'm a Christian."

She looked at him as if he'd announced he'd grown a third ear in the middle of his forehead. "Well."

LAINEY LAY IN HER BED IN THE DARK, A LIGHT FROM OUTSIDE SPRAYING the shadows of tree branches across her ceiling. They shifted and changed as a new weather front blew in.

She thought about Nicholas and the strength of his character. The moment could have been terribly awkward—even insulting—but he was so gracious and sure of his mind. *Out of respect for women,* he'd said. *Out of obedience to God.* Had she ever known anyone who practiced his faith even when it was inconvenient? None came to mind. Most of the professing Christians she knew were either smugly sanctimonious or the traditional Church of England type, attending church on Sunday, but never letting that get in the way of doing whatever they wanted for the rest of the week. That wasn't to say they weren't good people, much like her parents, but Nicholas was a fish of a different color. Or was that a different kettle of fish?

Whatever he was, it impressed her.

Ever since their first e-mails, he had responded to her with kindness and compassion. He seemed determined to help her grandmother, even when it risked his relationship with his family.

His family. What happened with Nicholas's telephone conversation? No grandfather, but he'd certainly exchanged words with his parents. She'd heard that much when she took him his tea. She'd also heard him say her name. What must they think of her for interfering with Nicholas's relationship with Kathy?

She rolled onto her side, burying her head into the down pillow. She needed to sleep. They were going to London tomorrow. A visit to Chiswick and, hopefully, Julie Peters. Then there was the meeting with Penelope Young. Perhaps she'd have something helpful to say about Dr. Sheaf. Perhaps they could find Dr. Sheaf himself and get some insight about how he'd helped Elaine back in 1954. *Then* Lainey might have some solid information to give her grandmother's doctors.

Closing her eyes, she thought of Nicholas again and wondered where in the world all this would take them.

CHAPTER FIFTEEN

TUESDAY, THE 20TH OF JULY

FOR REASONS HE COULDN'T DISCERN, NICHOLAS SEEMED TO SUFFER FROM jet lag the minute he woke up. Unlike yesterday, he felt thick-headed and tired, wanting only to stay in bed and sleep. But that wasn't an option. Lainey was driving them to London.

Serena had fixed them all a light breakfast of poached eggs and toast. She and Lainey chattered like sisters and Nicholas caught only that Serena had had dinner with Father Gilbert the night before. There was much giggling from Lainey and a blush from Serena and Nicholas drank his tea as if he hadn't noticed any of it.

"He's not married, you know," Lainey said as she sat down next to Nicholas.

"Father Gilbert?"

"Right. His wife died of cancer or something like that, before he became a priest."

Nicholas sipped his tea. "I really have to hear his story."

"You will." She leaned closer to Nicholas and said softly, "Do you think he's taken a vow of chastity?"

Nicholas glanced quickly at Serena, who was on the other side of the kitchen buttering the toast. "I have no idea," he responded. "But I would hope that, as an unmarried man of God, he would be chaste."

Lainey looked at Serena and giggled. "Oh, he'll be *chased*, all right."

"Stop it, you two," Serena said with a mock sternness as she delivered a rack of toast. "You're like a couple of children."

"I talked to Mrs. Peters this morning," Lainey said. "We're going to have lunch with her."

"Did you tell her what we learned from Trevor?"

"I'll save that for when we see her."

The phone rang and Serena picked up the receiver next to the refrigerator. After the "hellos" she said a friendly "good morning" and then beckoned Lainey. "Your mother," she said.

"I'll take it in the office." Lainey left while Serena informed Mrs. Bishop that Lainey would pick up momentarily. She listened, then put the phone down when she heard Lainey's voice.

Nicholas chomped into his toast. "Serena, Lainey tells me you're in AA."

"If you mean Alcoholics Anonymous, that's correct."

"Is there another?"

"In this country it's the Automobile Association, but I assumed you weren't asking about that."

"No," he chuckled. "How long have you been sober?"

"Do you want the round figure or shall I give you the exact number of hours, days, weeks, months, and years?"

"Do you know that?"

"Yes."

"I won't torture you. A round figure."

"Eight years."

She brought him his coffee and he thanked her. She sat down opposite and seemed to relish her own cup of tea.

"How did it happen—your getting sober, I mean."

She tapped her long fingernails against the side of the mug. "I suppose AA was the catalyst, but God was the source of my help."

"The 'greater power' that AA talks about?"

"Well, I'm not so vague as that. He's more than just a greater power."

"Are you a Christian?" he asked.

"Yes."

"May I ask a favor?"

"Of course."

"Will you pray for Lainey? I honestly think that what's happening to her grandmother is as much about Lainey's faith as it is Elaine's recovery."

"I pray for Lainey all the time."

IT WAS A LITTLE AFTER NINE BY THE TIME LAINEY AND NICHOLAS HEADED for London. They were expected at Julie Peters's at noon, which meant they might have an hour and a half to look around Chiswick, if traffic was merciful. It was. Lainey took the A4 into the heart of Chiswick. "Two hundred years ago this was considered country," she said as they worked their way through the suburban streets and homes. It was hard to imagine.

She turned onto a broad avenue. "This is Staveley Road," she said. It was lined with cherry trees, its claim to fame. The houses and town-houses—or "terraced houses," as Lainey called them—became hard to distinguish and may have gone back to the early twentieth century. She slowed the car down in front of a long row of newer homes, probably only ten or fifteen years old, Nicholas guessed from the design. A sign indicated that this section of homes was called Fitzroy Crescent. She stopped the car along the curb.

Nicholas looked, but couldn't see why she had stopped.

"Your grandfather and his parents lived in a house where those new homes now sit," Lainey explained. "This is where that first V2 rocket fell and killed your great-grandfather."

"Julie Peters told you?"

"Yes."

"What about my great-grandmother?"

"Mrs. Peters thinks she was killed during the Blitz of 1940, shortly after it started. Sometime in September, I think. It was on this road, too. She was trying to help some friends get out of their burning house. I'm not sure if it collapsed on her or if another bomb hit it while she was there."

Nicholas looked up and down the quiet suburban street. It was impossible to picture the bombs and fire and death visited upon this place.

They drove from there toward the River Thames. She pulled into Church Street and parked in front of the Old Burlington. It had been a pub from the fifteenth century until sometime in the early part of the twentieth century, when it changed owners and businesses. It still had Tudor beams, leaded windows, and a short slanting doorway. Across from that was St. Nicholas, the original parish church for Chiswick. The Norman tower dated back to the 1400s, but renovations in the late 1800s had given it a classic English Gothic style. Nicholas wanted to go in and have a look around, but Lainey said there wasn't time. Instead, she took his hand and pulled him away toward the riverfront. Green lawn and willows stretched out to the Thames, which now looked like liquid steel under the clouding sky.

"This is the Chiswick Mall," Lainey said, pronouncing *mall* to rhyme with *Hal*. She wasn't referring to the river but to a stretch of road that ran parallel to it. A wide assortment of Georgian and Regency houses faced the road, some with brick walls and iron fences. Only the very wealthy need apply.

They walked along the houses as bikers and joggers went past. An occasional plane roared overhead on its way to Heathrow Airport. "Just like Old Town Alexandria," he observed.

She took his hand. His estimation of the place went up by one hundred percent.

JULIE PETERS WAS DELIGHTED TO SEE THEM WHEN SHE OPENED THE DOOR. She was dressed in a white silk blouse and floral skirt and her white hair was styled in short curls.

"You look lovely," Lainey said and kissed her on the cheek.

"Thank you, dear," she said, then reached up and took Nicholas's face in her delicate hands and pulled him close for a look. "Yes, I see a hint of your grandfather. Just a hint, though. You have a gentler face."

"My brother, Jeff, looks more like my grandfather than I do," Nicholas said, and felt a sense of ease at this woman's genial knowledge of his family.

"I'll wager he's the one who'll take over the family business. A man with a face like that is bound to be the head of *something*." She laughed lightly and Nicholas noticed the blending of her accent—part American and part British.

"You're right," he said. "He's already the boss."

"Don't underestimate this one just because he has a gentle face," Lainey teased, hooking a thumb at Nicholas. "He's got the resolve to be a corporate executive."

"Then I'm glad he's studying to become a priest," Julie said. "We need men with resolve to become priests. Now, come in. The kettle's on and I've just finished laying out the sandwiches."

"You promised not to go to any trouble for us," Lainey complained.

"No trouble at all," she countered. "They're from Marks and Sparks."

"A department store," Lainey translated for Nicholas.

Mrs. Peters suddenly raised a wrinkled finger, as if suddenly remembering something. "While I lay the table you should go upstairs."

"Upstairs?" Lainey asked.

"Go all the way up to the loft. That's where Adam lived when he was with us. Your grandmother visited him there a few times, as well. It's a bit musty and cluttered, but you'll get the idea. The tea will be ready by the time you come back down."

Nicholas followed Lainey up the stairs to the first floor. The hall led in two directions, one to three closed doors, the other doubled back to the front of the house and what appeared to be an upstairs front room. The door was half closed and all Nicholas could see was the side of an upright piano and an easy chair. They went that way, to the next set of stairs, and continued upward.

The loft was cluttered with boxes and junk, just as Mrs. Peters had promised, but there was an old bed along one wall, an antique dresser under the eaves, and a matching wardrobe on the inside retaining wall. A small bookcase held musty hardbacks and tattered paperbacks of Agatha Christie, Graham Greene, and other popular British authors from four decades ago. There was also a large text about the history of printing in London, and several magazine-style pamphlets about the activities of a printers' union. Presumably, they'd been left behind by his grandfather and Mr. and Mrs. Peters never bothered to get rid of them.

Nicholas tried to imagine his grandfather living in the room. It was so austere. Had he had any photos of Elaine? Had he destroyed them in the tidal wave of his anger after he'd left the Mill House?

The windows looked out over the rooftops of Chiswick. Nicholas drifted over to take in the view. Lainey joined him. The treetops floated like green clouds among the housetops, gables, and chimney pots. Nicholas reached over and took Lainey's hand in his.

He thought of their respective grandparents also standing in this room, maybe enjoying a similar view, maybe holding hands.

"I can't get it out of my head," Lainey said quietly.

"What?"

"How different their lives might have been if Gerard hadn't interfered. I'm having a hard time with all the *what might have beens.*"

"But if their lives had gone on as they thought, then we wouldn't be here now," Nicholas observed.

"It boggles the mind."

"That's why we have to keep our heads firmly on the *what is,* and let God redeem the *what might have beens.*"

"Can he do that?" Lainey asked. "Do you really think he can redeem this mess, even after fifty years?"

Nicholas brushed a finger through her hair and thought, *Isn't he doing that already?* He kissed her.

She looked up at him. "I'm scared, Nicholas."

"Of what?"

She turned to look out of the window again, saying no more.

He kept his eyes on her, following the curves of her profile from the top of her head and down to her chin. "Lainey, I don't want to be hasty, but . . ." He paused. The words weren't there. "What I mean is that I was half serious when I said that this kind of emotional turmoil heightens feelings. For me to be here in England, with all of its enchantments . . ."

She faced him with a bemused expression.

"Ask anyone," he continued. "I overanalyze. I'm not inclined to say things casually. Well, not the important things. Like 'I love you.'"

"So, hypothetically, if I were to ever hear you say those words, then I should believe you. Is that what you're telling me?" she asked.

"Well, yes."

"That's helpful information, Nick. Thanks." She crossed the room to the door.

He watched her go and the impulse welled up inside of him, making him take a step and then stop again. Just as she reached the doorway, he said, "What I mean is that I think we have something remarkable happening between us."

She stopped where she was. She didn't turn around, but kept her back to him.

"You don't have to respond," he said quickly, embarrassed. "But I thought you should know."

She turned, but didn't look at him. She said, "I think we do, too, Nicholas." Now she looked at him fully, her dark eyes filled with impossible questions. "That's what scares me."

Mrs. Peters called from the ground floor. "Are the two of you going stay up there all day? I'm well past my sell-by date, you know."

NOT KNOWING WHAT THEY LIKED, MRS. PETERS OVERDID IT WITH HER selection of sandwiches. There was smoked salmon, bacon, egg salad, tuna, and cucumber. Nicholas knew they couldn't eat them all.

"Don't worry," she said when she saw his expression. "There's a meeting at the church tonight. I'll take leftovers there." Her attention went to Lainey. "Now, you said you have news. So do I. But you go first."

Lainey told Mrs. Peters about their conversations with Adam in America and Trevor at the Mill House.

Mrs. Peters listened attentively and interjected the occasional "Oh dear." When Lainey finished, Mrs. Peters hung her head, shaking it slowly. "That may be the saddest account I've ever heard in my life."

"Now you can understand why Adam reacted as he did, and why my grandmother was so distraught," Lainey said.

"Yes," she said, nodding slowly. "I would like to visit her. I want to personally invite her to the special memorial service for my John."

"That would be very kind."

"Nonsense. It will be good to see her again. You let me know when she's up to it." Mrs. Peters leveled her gaze at Nicholas. "Lainey told me you have some thoughts about your grandfather's spiritual condition."

Nicholas looked at Lainey. She smiled sheepishly.

"I only mentioned what you had told me about him," Lainey explained.

Nicholas felt defensive. "I've gone by what I've seen in my grandfather in all the years I've known him," he said to Mrs. Peters. "There's nothing Christian about him, as witnessed by his refusal to help Elaine now."

"That's not an unreasonable conclusion," Mrs. Peters said. "But before you pass judgment, let me tell you about the Billy Graham Crusade."

"I know he was here in 1954 and that—"

She interrupted him. "No, no. If you hope to be a good priest, then you have to put the whole thing in context."

Nicholas backed off. "Yes, ma'am. I'm sorry."

"It was Billy Graham's first crusade here. And we were personally involved."

"We?" Nicholas asked.

"John had joined the multichurch committee to sponsor it—make arrangements—that sort of thing." She turned to Lainey. "Your grandmother helped in Southaven. She coordinated the televised broadcasts of the crusade that fed into the churches in that area."

"I had no idea," Lainey said, wondering why Mrs. Peters hadn't mentioned it during their last visit. "That explains the notations in her diary. B.G.C."

"It was an amazing time," Mrs. Peters said. "Here was this American Baptist dressed in silk suits, with movie-star good looks and wavy blond hair, holding the Bible in one hand and pounding the pulpit with the other, telling people to accept Jesus."

"Not very English," Nicholas observed. "I'm surprised they let him in."

"They almost didn't," she said. "The leaders in the Church of England tried to keep him out on the grounds that his 'hot gospel circus' wasn't appropriate to the mood or sensibilities of the nation. The newspapers in Britain complained about his crass commercialism and the mass-market appeal of his gospel. The columnists blasted the presumption that he was needed in England. Right before the crusade was to begin, a Labor member of Parliament announced that he would block the admittance of Graham to England on the grounds that the evangelist was interfering with British politics."

"How in the world could he interfere in your politics?" Nicholas asked.

"Apparently Graham's organization had produced a brochure that referred to the evils of socialism. As die-hard socialists, the Labor Party considered it a direct attack. It turns out that it was a typo. The brochure meant to say 'the evils of secularism.' But it was too late. Wembley Arena wouldn't let Graham conduct his crusade there. So he wound up at the Harringay Arena, which was far less prestigious. But Graham surprised everyone. He wasn't a foam-at-the-mouth evangelist, as some tried to characterize him. He was polite, intelligent, and well-spoken. All the negative publicity in the press backfired and people came out to see this young preacher for themselves. He preached for three months at Harringay, and to thousands in Trafalgar Square, and the same again in Hyde Park to a crowd of fifty thousand. He met all of our leaders and even the queen. It was amazing."

Nicholas didn't understand how this connected to his grandfather. He opened his mouth to say so, but Mrs. Peters preempted him.

"Adam wanted nothing to do with Graham. He had been working so very hard to make money and impress Elaine's father. He was desperate to win her. So desperate that he couldn't be bothered with church or the crusade. But I got to him and persuaded him to go on the third or fourth night, I don't remember which. I went with him. The sermon that night compared the rich young ruler from Luke 18:18–30 with the rich man in Luke 12:16–21. Do you know the stories?"

Nicholas nodded.

Lainey shook her head. "I don't remember them, I'm sorry."

"The rich young ruler in the first story had asked Jesus what he must do to have eternal life. The rich man in the second story had earned much wealth and at his moment of greatest success was taken by God to his death. The common denominator, according to Graham, was the call to give up the treasures of this earth for the greater and eternal treasures in heaven."

"I do remember," Lainey said.

"This had an enormous impact on Adam. He wanted Elaine so badly that he'd forgotten about God. So when Billy Graham said that there was hope, but only the hope that comes by following Jesus, Adam responded. He went forward as everyone sang 'Just As I Am.' Adam told me later that he knelt and pledged his life to Christ. He meant it. The change in him was amazing."

Genuinely surprised, Nicholas tried to make this Adam line up with the Adam he'd always known. "I'm sorry, Mrs. Peters, but if that experience meant anything to him then, it doesn't show now."

"Context, Nicholas," Mrs. Peters said, playing vicar's wife. "Context."

Nicholas thought about it, drew a blank, and gave up. "Blame my jet lag. I don't understand."

She sighed, a teacher with a thick-headed student. "I believe that Adam truly thought that a commitment to Christ would fix everything with Elaine and her father. He expected everything to change. But it didn't."

IF MRS. PETERS WAS RIGHT, THEN NICHOLAS'S GRANDFATHER HAD thought he'd negotiated some kind of deal with God that night at the crusade. When it all went wrong, he'd decided the deal was off and dispensed with God completely. "That would explain a lot," Nicholas said.

"You see? Things are not always what they seem," Mrs. Peters said. "To help people, you have to look beyond the surface."

"My grandfather doesn't want my help," Nicholas said.

"But you haven't told him all the things you've told me," she pointed out.

"No. But that's only because we can't find him. As of last night he had gone fishing somewhere."

"I have something for you to see." With noticeable delight, she pulled a white envelope from one of the compartments in her handbag. "This was put through my letterbox this morning. *Not* delivered with the regular post." She handed the envelope to Nicholas.

He took it and looked at the front. Mrs. *Julie Peters*, it said. Nicholas recognized the handwriting immediately and looked at Mrs. Peters. "My grandfather?"

She smiled and nodded.

Lainey moved in close as Nicholas held up the envelope. "But it isn't postmarked. There're no stamps."

"You said it was put through the letter slot *apart* from the post?" Lainey asked.

Mrs. Peters had a satisfied look on her face; she was pleased with her surprise. "That's right."

Lainey leaned even closer to look as Nicholas took the notepaper out of the envelope. Inside was a handwritten note, also from Adam Powell. It said: *I'm pleased to accept your invitation to the Special Service for Father John. I'll be in touch soon for details. Yours sincerely, Adam Powell.*

Nicholas's jet-lagged brain couldn't cope. "He's coming to the service?"

"Apparently so."

"But how did he know about it?" Lainey asked. "You couldn't have posted it to him that quickly."

"I e-mailed him," she said. "I may be old, but I'm not completely out of touch with the modern world. After you were last here, Lainey, I got on the Internet, found a number for Powell Publishing, phoned his assistant, and got his e-mail. I also warned her that she better not give me the runaround, nor delay getting my message through to him. I guess she took me seriously."

Nicholas turned the letter over and over, as if touching it might answer the dozen questions crowding his mind. "So how did this note get to you?"

Mrs. Peters said, "Early this morning I heard a black cab pull up to the front of the house. I know them by the sounds of their engines and those awful squeaky brakes they have. I was in the kitchen, making some tea, when the note slipped through the door. Curious, I thought. I went to retrieve it, saw who it was from, and opened the door just in time to see a man get into the back of the cab. He didn't see me and it pulled away before I could get down the steps. I'm not as agile as I was. But the man was your grandfather. I know it was."

Nicholas and Lainey looked at one another.

"He's *here—now?*" Nicholas asked, his mouth dropping open, his brain addled.

"It would seem so."

"But *where?*"

"I don't know," the old woman shrugged, relishing this little mystery. "More tea?"

CHAPTER
SIXTEEN

Perhaps you should ring your family again," Lainey said when they were back in the car. She handed him her cell phone. "They have to know where he is."

Nicholas shook his head, his mind buzzing from this unexpected twist. "I honestly don't think they do or they would have said. Fishing indeed!"

The cell phone rang in Lainey's outstretched hand. They both looked at it suspiciously, as if Adam Powell might be on the other end. Lainey looked at the screen. "Serena," she said. "Oh, I hope nothing's happened to Gran." She flipped the phone open. "Hello?"

Nicholas sat back, watching Lainey anxiously. All he could get was her side of the conversation, which consisted mostly of "Really?" and "When?" and "This is *very strange*" and "Hang on." She then thrust the phone at Nicholas. "It's for you."

"What?" He took the phone from her and put it to his ear. "Hello?"

Serena's voice came through on a crackling line. "A letter came for you by special courier, not five minutes ago."

"Who is the letter from?"

"Adam Powell," she replied.

"Will you open it, please?"

"I think I can figure out how to do that." He could hear the tearing cardboard. "Oh. It's from the Ritz. Their logo is on the back."

"The Ritz? As in *Puttin' on the Ritz?*"

"I suppose so."

"It's on Piccadilly," Lainey said. "Next to the Green Park tube station."

Serena opened the envelope itself. "The note inside says, 'Nicholas. I am at the Ritz. Call me immediately. Adam Powell." Serena harrumphed. "A touchy-feely sort of person, isn't he?"

"That's my grandfather," Nicholas said.

Lainey gestured for the phone.

"I'm handing you back to Lainey. Thanks for calling." Nicholas gave her the phone and tried to think while she asked about her grandmother. Nothing had changed, so she thanked Serena and hung up.

"What do we do now?" Lainey asked. "We can call directory assistance for the Ritz's phone number."

"I'd rather not call. Is it far from here?"

Lainey glanced at her watch. "I couldn't drive you. It's in the opposite direction from Richmond—Penelope Young's house—and if I don't leave soon I'm going to be late. She's not someone that you want to keep waiting."

"I could take a cab, couldn't I?"

"You could," she said and started the car. "I'll drive you to Chiswick High Street. I'm sure we'll find a cab there."

"How will we reconnect?"

"Write down my mobile phone number. We'll figure out how and where to meet up later."

With a roar of noise, the car pulled away from Julie Peters's house and headed back to Chiswick.

THE RITZ WAS ON THE NORTHEAST CORNER OF GREEN PARK, SERVING AS the starting point for the long parade of shops and offices that stretched onward to Piccadilly Circus. It was an ostentatious building in an ornate Louis the Sixteenth style, evoking Paris rather than London. The cab driver dropped Nicholas off directly in front. Nicholas paid him and dashed under the old-fashioned lights announcing the name of the hotel, through the revolving door, and into the lavish lobby of deep red-and-gold carpet and gold-framed mirrors. The words *glamorous, elegant, flamboyant,* and *grandiose* all came to Nicholas's mind. Cream-colored curtains hung over high archways and French doors (what else?), wall sconces blazed over statues of lithe maidens in repose. A large gold clock, consistent with the French style, hung above the reception desk. A concierge, a stiff-backed man with oiled hair, stood behind a dark wood desk and lifted an eyebrow at Nicholas as he approached.

"What may I do for you, sir?"

"I need the room number for Adam Powell, please."

The concierge pointed to the white phone at the end of the counter. "The operator will connect you to the room."

"I'd rather go straight up, if you don't mind."

"For the privacy and security of our guests—"

Nicholas didn't let him go through his recitation. "Okay, never mind." He picked up the phone and the hotel operator cheerfully said she'd connect him to Mr. Powell's room.

It rang four times before Adam Powell picked up. "Hello?" His voice was low and thick with sleep.

"Grandad?"

"Jeff?"

"Nicholas."

"Oh. Right. Sorry. I made the mistake of lying down. Must've fallen asleep. Where am I?"

"The Ritz."

"That's right. And where are you?"

"In the lobby."

"Oh. Then you'd better come up."

He gave Nicholas the room number.

On the third floor, Nicholas made his way past one brown door after another until he came to his grandfather's room number. He knocked loudly, in case his grandfather had fallen asleep again.

"Come in," Adam Powell called out.

The door was slightly ajar so Nicholas took a deep, steadying breath and walked in.

The room maintained the Louis the Sixteenth theme. Yellows, golds, and blues with the simple lines and rich detail of the neoclassical style. The furniture had the characteristic square shapes with ornate scrollwork along the tops and borders and around the cabinet doors. The chairs had fluted legs and shield-shaped backs. There was a fireplace on one wall with a dark marble mantel. Two large closets framed the short hall leading to the bathroom where he could see his grandfather moving around.

"This is your room?" he exclaimed. "It's bigger than my apartment. Pretty impressive."

"If you like gaudy French." His grandfather emerged from the bathroom wiping his hands on a towel. He was wearing dark cotton trousers and a white button-down shirt, open at the collar.

Nicholas considered shaking his grandfather's hand, at least a formal hello if not a familial one. The old man stood his ground and simply gazed at him. "Nicholas."

"So, what are you doing here, Grandad? I thought you went fishing."

"I may go up to Scotland," he said. "The bigger question is: what are *you* doing here?"

"I came to do what you wouldn't—to help Elaine Arthur."

He balled up the towel and threw it back into the bathroom. "Save me the guilt inducement," he said sternly. "You're Anglican, not Catholic. And it won't work anyway."

Nicholas sat down on one of the chairs and rubbed his hands over the ridges and grooves on the armrest. He wanted it to look like casual interest. In fact, he wanted to keep his hands busy so his grandfather wouldn't see them shaking. "Not very comfortable, are they?"

"They're meant to be looked at, not sat upon."

"So why are *you* here?" Nicholas asked.

"When I heard that you had impulsively and stupidly come here, I realized that I may have underestimated your complex."

"What complex is that?"

"Your messianic complex," he said. "Your desire to save everyone."

"Is that what I'm doing?"

"It's that, or you're hoping to hop in the sack with that granddaughter."

"Don't be vulgar, Grandad."

"I'm being realistic. You've fallen in love with the girl, haven't you?"

Nicholas didn't answer.

Adam grunted. "I've seen men throw their lives away for passion—for women they thought could bring them something. To fill a hole in their hearts, to satisfy a yearning. In the end it leads to nothing but waste."

"Are we talking about me, or you?"

"You seem determined to throw everything away."

"I took a last-minute trip to England. How is that throwing every-thing away?"

"You're embarrassing yourself. You broke up with Kathy—a suitable woman if ever there was one."

"That's for me to decide. Not you, or anyone else in the family."

"That's where you're wrong. As your family we're here to protect you, to keep you from doing the kind of stupid thing you're doing now. That's why I've come."

"To invite me to go fishing with you in Scotland?"

"To knock some sense into your head."

"My mom and dad don't know you're here. Why didn't you tell them?"

"Because this is between us."

"Oh, really? When was there ever anything between us?"

"When you decided to intrude into my past." He pursed his lips and looked at Nicholas with exaggerated impatience. "Your problem, Nicholas, is that you don't know how to let go. Maturity is when you accept life for what it is and get on with it."

"I disagree. I think life should be more than that. It *is* more than that."

"According to whom?"

"God."

"Oh, yes," he said derisively. "A life of service to God. The abundant life. Rewards in heaven."

"I've been told you believed that once."

Adam gave him a sardonic smile. "The difference between you and me is that I believe in God as he really is."

"And who is he really?"

"He's a sly fox. An old merchant in the marketplace, who likes to haggle and make deals. Just read your Bible. He wants everything he can get at the cheapest price. Well, I know how to play that game. And I bested him. I broke free and became a success to spite him."

Nicholas was speechless. His hands wrapped tight around the arm-rest. "Broke free? You mean by leaving Elaine and going to America?"

His expression was as good as an acknowledgment.

Nicholas leaned forward. "Is that what you did at the Billy Graham Crusade? Did you haggle with the *old merchant* and make a deal with him? Is that how you committed your life to God that night?"

"As I've told you repeatedly, that's none of your business," Adam said sharply.

"I'm sorry, sir, but fair is fair. You can't psychoanalyze me without getting some in return. Especially when there are a few things you don't know."

His grandfather looked skeptically at him. "And you've come to enlighten me, I assume."

"We found out what really happened the day you went to the Mill House to propose to Elaine."

"Oh? Elaine told you?"

"Trevor Mann."

"Trevor?" he asked. "He's still alive?"

"Yes. And he told us everything."

Adam feigned boredom as he turned a desk chair around and sat down. "Not that it matters much, but I'll indulge your obvious keenness to tell me."

"You were duped, Grandad. Set up and suckered."

Adam flinched, then set his expression. "I'm listening."

Nicholas recounted the story to Adam exactly as he'd heard it from Trevor. As he began to talk, he secretly relished getting the one up on his grandfather, knowing something the old man couldn't know, waiting for his reaction. This was the Ghost of Christmas Past showing Scrooge the hard truth about where he'd gone off the rails.

By the end his voice was strong and cocky. He locked his eyes on his grandfather's as he concluded with, "And that's what Trevor told us."

Adam Powell silently stood up and paced in one direction, then the other. His expression was rigid, his jawbones working. "That's quite a story," he finally said.

"We thought so. I tried to call you, to tell you right away, but Dad said you'd gone fishing."

"All right," he said. "You've been dying to tell me—and now you have. Satisfied?"

"Not at all."

"We're finished with this game," he said quickly, angrily. "I want you to go get your things and come back here. This afternoon. Tonight. We're going home first thing tomorrow."

"What?" Nicholas was caught off guard—not the reaction he expected—and it took a moment to find his voice. "No, Grandad."

"Yes. This business has gone on long enough. Get your things and let's go. You have a life to return to. I won't watch you waste it."

Nicholas stood up. "Grandad, didn't you hear anything I said? You and Elaine were tricked. You've eaten yourself up with bitterness over something that wasn't her doing! And even if it doesn't matter to you now, it seems to matter to her."

"And you think this great truth has some magic powers of healing?" He was pacing again, pointing wildly at Nicholas. "Are you a complete idiot? It was this truth—this truth that you seem to think so important—that threw her into her depression. Obviously Gerard told her before he died. So I ask you again: *What difference does it make?* We can't go back in time, Nicholas. We can't change a single choice either of us made then. It's over and done with."

"But it isn't. Elaine Arthur is in pain and I have to believe that this truth will somehow help us to get her out. God will use it to get her out. God may use *you* to help her, now that you know."

"Then you *are* a complete idiot."

"This is your chance, Grandad. To look beyond your own suffering, to reach out to her—"

"My suffering? You're delusional. I'm not suffering."

"You're so bottled up you don't even see it anymore," he said, his voice growing to a shout. "What did you say to me in your office the other day, before you shredded those letters? That to succeed in life I had to learn to value nothing. Was that it? Otherwise, someone else will always have the upper hand. That's what you learned from your experience with Elaine, wasn't it? Value nothing—like love and faith. It was all one and the same, wasn't it? You haggled with God about Elaine and when you didn't get her, you decided to value nothing. Ever. Is that how you think you bested God? Is that how you achieved your great success? *That's* complete idiocy, Grandad. It's pathetic."

Adam glared at Nicholas, then crossed the room in only a couple of quick steps. Before Nicholas knew what was happening, he felt the sharp burning sting of a slap across the face. The openhanded blow from his grandfather threw Nicholas's head to one side and the shock of it took his breath away. He caught hold of the chair before he could fall.

With a trembling voice Adam said in a pale rage, "Go get your things. We're going home."

The tears filled Nicholas's eyes, mostly from the pain. His own voice shook when he spoke, but he mustered as much firmness as he could. "I said *no,* Grandad. Run away again if you want to, but I'm not." Without waiting for a reply—or another slap—he sidestepped his grandfather and went to the door, swinging it so wide that it slammed against the opposite wall. He marched down the hall to the elevator.

Back on Piccadilly he rounded the first corner he came to and slumped against the side of the building. He touched the side of his face. It was numb and swelling. Now he truly felt like crying, but gritted his teeth and fought the urge.

He heard thunder and an ocean of water fell on him.

FROM THE FRONT ROOM OF PENELOPE YOUNG'S HOUSE, LAINEY COULD SEE the rain starting to fall on the large green that stretched out to meet the A4 as it cut through Richmond.

"If this information is for another book, I want to negotiate a credit and a royalty," Penelope said as she entered carrying a small silver tray of tea. She placed the tray on a small antique table—just one of many antiquities in the room, cluttering nearly every inch of floor and wall space. Lainey tried to discern if there was a particular theme or style to the décor, but couldn't figure out what it was. It was as if Penelope and her husband simply bought whatever struck their fancy and brought it home.

Lainey looked up at the middle-aged woman as she took the cup of tea. "It's not for another book. It's personal."

"How personal?"

"My grandmother."

"She was a patient of Dr. Sheaf's?" Penelope sat down on the edge of a Victorian love seat, her saucer and cup of tea balanced on her knees. Though Penelope was considered lively and social, she always seemed rather dowdy to Lainey in that academic way so many intellectuals aspire to.

Lainey gently cleared her throat. "My grandmother had an emotional breakdown, of sorts, back in 1954 and she went to Dr. Sheaf for help."

"You're sure she went to Sheaf?"

"Yes. Is there something wrong?"

Penelope sat her coffee cup down on the saucer again. Her tone was instructional, as if she were tutoring a muddled student. "Lainey, Dr. Anthony Sheaf was a general practitioner, and an average one at that. He wouldn't have been any better at diagnosing or helping your grandmother's emotional well-being than any other doctor in the country."

Lainey didn't know what to say. "Then I got it confused. I thought he was some sort of specialist."

"I suppose you could call him that," Penelope said. "He specialized in abortions."

Abortions, thought Lainey, the meaning of the word not fully penetrating her consciousness. It was like saying *infidelity* when one meant adultery, or *deceased* when a person was dead.

"It was illegal, of course. But some of the rather liberal-minded Harley Street doctors helped their wealthier patients when an unwanted baby came along."

Abortion? She shook her head, a flat denial. "There must be some sort of mistake."

"Maybe so. But I can't think of any other reason she'd go to see Dr. Sheaf. He was listed as a general practitioner, but he performed abortions on the side. It was a well-known secret, if you understand my meaning."

"No."

A light laugh to disarm a silly child. "My dear girl, I can show you the documents I found, his personal records. They're all there. He had a little phrase that he put next to the patient's name. It was his code for the procedure. 'Discomfort from abnormal growth of tissue,' was the diagnosis, then 'removed benign tumor' was the treatment."

"*No,*" Lainey said.

"He was later disgraced for his part in the Profumo Scandal of 1963, the one that brought down the MacMillan government. You learned about it in school, I'm sure. Christine Keeler? Dr. Stephen Ward? It's believed that Dr. Sheaf was the man in the mask who served at Ward's dinner parties. Committed suicide shortly thereafter. Are you listening to me?"

Lainey wasn't. It was as if a shrill whistle was blowing throughout her mind. "My grandmother was pregnant?" she asked stupidly, refusing to believe it.

"I can assure you that your grandmother would have had no other reason to see Dr. Sheaf," Penelope insisted. "If you want to hire me to go back through the files, I'll be happy to do it. Give me your grandmother's name and the approximate date she went to Sheaf. Oh, dear. You've gone pale. Are you all right?"

She was pregnant, Lainey thought, the reality now coming like a scream, louder and more potent than the shrill whistle of denial. *She was pregnant.*

Yes, of course. She was pregnant with Adam Powell's child. It all made sense now.

Guilt. Regret. Recrimination.

It suddenly came clear with a precise sharpness, and the pain followed like a razor's cut.

"Lainey?" Penelope said, now concerned, reaching for her.

But Lainey was on her feet, struggling to keep the tea from spilling. "Oh my God," she was saying, the cup and saucer rattling as she clumsily put them on the table. "*Oh my God.*"

"Lainey, please sit down. Let me get you something."

It was too late. Her heart pounded in her ears. She had to go, to get out of there. The room was too crowded. It was closing in, making it hard to breathe. She needed air. "I'm sorry," she gasped and fled the house.

NICHOLAS WALKED IN THE RAIN, NOT SURE WHERE HE WAS GOING OR WHAT to do next. He reached the hyperactive lights and advertising displays of Piccadilly Circus, London's answer to Times Square. He was drenched by the downpour, seemingly endless, but he didn't care. The wash of water took his mind off of the dull ache on the side of his face. The crowds jostled him like a small boat on a restless sea. He was nearly impaled by umbrellas, and buses and cabs did their best to keep him from crossing the roads.

He seethed about his grandfather. The slap replayed again and again in his mind. He'd never been struck in the face before—not by anyone, ever—and he felt a deep sense of betrayal that it had happened by his grandfather's hand.

He had to call Lainey. He wanted out of the rain, out of London. Spotting a Burger King, he ducked in and saw a sign indicating that bathrooms and a telephone were one floor down. He took the stairs to another dining room where a group of teenage girls were hanging out. He spotted the phone, then suddenly ducked into the bathroom for a look in the mirror. A drowned cat, he thought when he saw his reflection. The side of his face was red and a little swollen, but not noticeable to anyone who wasn't looking closely. It still felt tender to the touch.

Returning to the pay phone, he fumbled for some change and dropped a pound coin into the slot. He dialed Lainey's cell phone and waited while the line hissed and clicked. The distinctive British double-ring began—once, twice, three times before Lainey picked up.

"Hello," she said, her voice flat.

"Lainey, hi. Where are you?"

"In the car."

"Driving?"

"No. Sitting." She said nothing else.

Nicholas asked, "Are you all right?"

"No."

"What's wrong?"

"I can't talk about it now."

"Did you learn something from Penelope Young?" She didn't answer. "Lainey?"

"Where are you?"

"Piccadilly Circus. How do you want to meet up?"

"Do you think you can navigate the Tube?"

"The Tube?"

"It's the, uh—" She stammered impatiently. "Oh, what do you Americans call it? The trains underground."

"The subway?"

"That's right." Then she seemed to change her mind. "Forget that. Take a taxi to Victoria Station."

"Victoria? All right. You'll meet me there?"

"No. Take the train to Polegate. It's on the Hastings line."

"A *train?*"

"There'll be taxis at the Polegate station. One of them can take you back to Arthur House."

"But what about you?"

"I don't know."

"Lainey—"

"Please, Nick. Just do as I say." She hung up.

Nick listened for a moment, then put the receiver down, feeling as if he'd just been slapped again.

THE RAIN SLID DOWN THE WINDOWS. THE SCENE OUTSIDE THE CAR TURNED into melted lights and running colors. Lainey sat perfectly still, staring, as the drops drummed on the roof.

Now she knew the truth. Her grandmother's condition wasn't only about the understandable sadness of a life she didn't get to have, it was about a life she'd given away.

Lainey wanted to cry, but the tears would not come. Instead, she let out a sob like a dry heave. She pressed her hand to her mouth and bit at her knuckle, wanting the pain there to help her to feel *something.*

She started the car, put it in gear, and drove. The windscreen wipers pushed the rain aside for intermittent views of shimmering red lights, the spray of water from spinning tires, and white lights coming from the opposite direction. She didn't know where she was going, but she knew she had to move. She merged into the traffic leading out of London.

NICHOLAS FOLLOWED LAINEY'S INSTRUCTIONS AND LEFT LONDON OUT OF Victoria Station on a southbound train. He was relieved as they moved from the black and gray of the wet city, crossed the Thames, and headed gently into the outlying suburbs and then the scattered towns. The rocking rattle and clackety clack of the train helped to calm him down. He looked out of the rain-lashed window at dark skies and sodden fields. The weight of the storm's darkness pressed down on him.

He wondered about Lainey. The phone call had been disconcerting, and he couldn't figure out what had happened to make her abandon him. Was she going to work late with Penelope Young? Had they found something significant about Dr. Sheaf and Elaine Holmes? Nicholas's mind spun as quickly as the wheels under the train. But, unlike the train, his thoughts were going nowhere.

He thought about the slap across his face and tensed up again.

Far away, the clouds had broken and a shaft of late afternoon sun bathed a small village in yellow light. It was a picture-postcard effect— one that Nicholas had always suspected was somehow contrived by a photographer's trick. This was the real thing. The village, with its red brick houses, white-walled cottages, uneven slate gray roofs, and square church tower thrust up like a mast, looked like a large ship drifting on a sea of green.

If scenery could be a breath of fresh air to the eyes, then this was. And, as was often the case when Nicholas was caught up by beauty, he felt the spark he'd told Lainey about.

Dear Father, he prayed, *what are you up to? Help me to see the light you're shining into this darkness.*

Light was certainly hard to see at this point. The confrontation with his grandfather, the potential wreck he might be making of his family relationships, not forgetting the loss of a girlfriend he was expected to marry ... where was the light in any of that?

There was Lainey to think of, too. Where would their relationship lead? Where *could* it lead? He was studying to become a minister; it was his calling. As far as he could tell, she didn't share his faith. So how could she share in his calling? It was insane to pursue a future with her.

He groaned, pressing his hands against his temples. He didn't know what his motivations were anymore. Maybe this wasn't about his grandfather at all. Maybe it was about meeting a beautiful girl and escaping his family. Maybe it was about the adventure of doing something different for once.

Even if my motivation is all wrong, help me to be the light you shine into this darkness, he found himself praying. It was too late to undo anything. He had to see this story through to its end. *Oh, God, redeem my wrong choices.*

IT TOOK LAINEY OVER TWO HOURS TO GET TO ARTHUR HOUSE, TIME SHE spent venting her mixed-up emotions. She was angry at the rain, angry at the traffic, angry at the world.

Emotionally drained, she entered the empty house. Serena was gone, probably at the hospital. Instinctively she walked to her grandmother's room. The effort of suppressing her tears for the drive down had exhausted her. Now grief came upon her in a convulsion. She dropped onto her grandmother's bed and wept. For Elaine and her lost baby.

When her tears and energy were spent, she rolled over and lay quietly. The questions came quietly, slipping into the room like unwanted guests. Did Gerard know? Had Elaine confided in him—in James Arthur? Whose idea had it been to go to Dr. Sheaf? Perhaps Elaine's father's, knowing so well the social stigma of a pregnancy out of wedlock; a pregnancy with that working-class boy from London.

The letters to Adam Powell—the ones he'd destroyed—had they carried the news of what was growing inside her? Lainey could picture her grandmother as a young woman, sitting at her writing desk, filled with a sense of abandonment and despair, writing those letters to Adam, perhaps begging him to come back.

Was there ever a moment of hope during those long days of that summer? Did she wait by the letterbox or the phone? Did the sound of a car in the drive, or a knock on the door, make her heart race, believing he had come back?

Lainey could imagine the anger and sense of betrayal her grandmother must have felt toward Adam. Lainey felt it now—loathing even
Nick as if he, too, had some part in what had happened. It was irrational,
but she couldn't help it. That was why she didn't want to see him. If he
was with her now, she would say something they'd both regret.

There was no doubt in Lainey's mind now that Gerard's confession
to her grandmother before he died was like ripping the scab off of the
old wound and then giving her a new one at the same time. Who
wouldn't withdraw from the enormity of that kind of pain? Lainey certainly would. She would have relived the isolation and loneliness, the
embarrassment, the awful indignity. And then there was the abortion
itself. God only knew the crudeness of the procedure in those days, not
to mention the psychological damage it must have done to her. She was
a churchgoing woman. She'd had some sort of Christian beliefs and con-
victions. To learn she was pregnant was scandalous enough, to decide to
get rid of the baby was beyond imagination. She must have been devas-
tated from the guilt and sorrow, the grief and shame. The worst of all
human emotions must have lined up like a malevolent parade and bludg-
eoned her heart with all their strength. How had she coped? How did
she—how does anyone—ever recover from that?

She thought of her grandmother lying in the hospital bed, a self-
imposed exile into an impenetrable darkness. In that darkness there was
no seeing beyond the moment or the emotions of pain and loss. Her
carefully maintained life had fragmented into a million pieces, like the
exploded stained glass windows in the old chapel. No question now that
that was why, in her initial delirium, she had returned there. What was
she trying to do? Reassemble her life or restore some sense of order or
reclaim the lost days of her innocence. And last night she had wanted
to return to her own bedroom. To make her confession.

Would God hear it, or was he also pointing an accusing finger at her?

Lainey sat up and wiped her eyes. Her head throbbed. The room was
enshrouded in muted shadows. She looked at the closet door, now
closed, and remembered that her grandmother hadn't said she wanted to
make her confession; she'd wanted to go to her closet *for* her confession.
What did that mean?

Lainey slid off the bed and opened the closet door. She found the
light switch on the wall just to the left. It was a spacious walk-in closet
with double racks for clothes, one up, one below, on two walls. Every

inch was taken with dresses, blouses, and skirts. Shoes littered the floor. There were shelves with boxes of all sizes and shapes on the opposite wall.

What kind of confession was her grandmother thinking about?

Lainey stood in the center of the closet and slowly spun around. She hoped that something would catch her eye, give her a clue into her grandmother's mind.

Clothes, shoes, and boxes.

Boxes. Hadn't her grandmother said something about boxes?

What did she have in them?

One by one, Lainey pulled the boxes from the shelves, peeked inside, and put them back. Some had hats, others had old photographs of family members or keepsakes that her grandmother must not have wanted displayed anymore. There was certainly nothing to suggest why her grandmother had tried to leave the hospital.

When she was about to give up and turn off the light, she spied a separate file box on the floor, almost completely concealed by a rack of formal dresses. She pulled it out and took the lid off.

"Oh," Lainey cried out softly.

The box was full of letters. All from *A. Powell, The Vicarage, Chiswick, London.*

There were also bound diaries. Not appointment books, but chronicles filled with page after page of Elaine Holmes's handwriting.

Her confession.

THE TRAIN REACHED THE POLEGATE STATION ALMOST NINETY MINUTES after it left Victoria. It was twenty minutes to seven when Nicholas caught the cab driver's eye, got in the car, and asked to be taken to Arthur House. He wondered if Lainey would be there.

As the cab navigated through Stonebridge, Nicholas saw the spire of St. Mark's and asked the driver to stop in front of the entrance. He felt so confused and conflicted. Some time praying in the church might help. If nothing else, it would give his face a little more time to heal before Lainey saw it.

Father Gilbert was locking the door to the church when Nicholas approached. He turned and said with a startled smile, "Hello, Nicholas. What brings you here?"

"Oh, I thought I might—well, never mind. You're closing up."

"Do you want to come inside?"

"I don't want to bother you."

"It's no bother. Come in, if you want." Before Nicholas could protest, Father Gilbert had the door unlocked again and pushed it open. "Did you come to pray by yourself, or did you want to talk?"

"You want to go home." A feeble answer.

"Nonsense," he said. They walked through the dark church to the priest's office and Father Gilbert paused at the small table near his secretary's desk to put on the kettle. "What happened to your face?"

Nicholas touched it lightly. It ached. "I had a meeting with my grandfather."

"He's here?"

"In London."

"And he hit you—intentionally?"

"Yes."

"What happened, if you don't mind telling me?"

Nicholas explained as briefly as he could. Reliving the moment wasn't something he wanted to do, and the anger welled up in him again. When he finished, the kettle had come to a boil and Father Gilbert made two cups of tea without comment. They went into the office and sat down.

"Well," Father Gilbert said.

"I hate him," Nicholas said, his voice trembling, then giving way to a sob. "I *hate* him." Nicholas had never said so before. It made him weep.

Father Gilbert waited quietly until Nicholas could get himself under control. He handed him some tissues from the box on the desk.

"I'm sorry," Nicholas said.

"Don't apologize," he said gently. "This is important."

"I've never admitted it before." His voice shook again and he struggled to keep his composure. "My feelings for my grandfather have always been neatly wrapped up. I've always tried to look at him with detachment and objectivity or, worse . . . as a superior Christian."

Father Gilbert nodded.

"But he *slapped* me, Father, and . . ." The tears came again. "It's all garbage. No matter how I've wrapped it up, the truth is that I *hate* the man."

"Quite an epiphany, isn't it?"

"Everyone tried to tell me that my grandfather was an issue, but I refused to believe it. I thought I've been on some kind of godly mission."

Father Gilbert considered him for a moment, then said. "Perhaps you are. And perhaps this moment is part of the mission. But you have to get it all out, Nicholas. All the poison. What do you hate about your grandfather?"

"Are you kidding? Where do I start?"

"Somewhere. Anywhere."

Nicholas sputtered at first, then came a great torrent. "I hate the way he bullies people, the way he manipulates them, his smug self-justification for what he's done to my family. He looks at my father and is *proud* that he's made him in his own image. He thinks he's done a good job! But what he's done is turn my father into a spineless version of himself. My poor dad doesn't dare think a single thought of his own."

"What else?"

What else? Nicholas's brain went into overload and he continued the list: his grandfather's preoccupation with wealth, with power, with getting the upper hand. The list went on and on, down to the tiniest details of mere gestures and mannerisms, and Nicholas heard himself spew out everything he could think of until there didn't seem to be anything left. In the empty space, he now felt a terrible guilt creep in. "This is awful. I'm studying to be a *priest*. These feelings are all wrong."

"You think priests don't have problems with their families? Don't get me started on *my* father," Father Gilbert said.

"But what am I supposed to do now?" Nicholas asked.

"You mean with Lainey and her grandmother? You can still help them. As for your grandfather . . . what do you think you should do?"

"All my Christian beliefs tell me I should forgive him. Try to understand him. Accept him for who he is."

Father Gilbert smiled. "That's a nicely articulated textbook answer. Thank you."

"Then what am I supposed to do?"

"Under normal circumstances, I'd say to stay clear of him for a while—at least until you've had time to pray, work through your feelings, and allow God to heal you. But these aren't normal circumstances. You're in the thick of it now."

Nicholas lowered his head and felt like a failure. "I've blown it."

"No. But now that you know how you truly feel, you have to be careful. Strive to understand your grandfather, yes, but don't kid yourself about why you're doing it. You'll be angry and resentful and the temptation to use your understanding to hurt him will be great. Truth can be a terribly blunt and painful weapon."

Nicholas shook his head, feeling worse about himself. All this time he'd been wanting to use the truth of his grandfather's past to bludgeon the old man—and had tried to do that very thing at the Ritz!

"And don't succumb to the myth that you can change him. Only God can do that."

Nicholas looked at Father Gilbert, aware that others had said the very same thing. "I know."

"This doesn't take you out of play, Nicholas. You can work with God to create an *environment* for change. But that's all. What happens from there is between your grandfather and God. And only then will redemption take place."

FATHER GILBERT GAVE NICHOLAS A LIFT TO ARTHUR HOUSE. AS THEY pulled up the drive, Nicholas was relieved to see Lainey's car sitting in front. He was puzzled, too, since it raised the question about why she didn't want him to ride back from London with her.

"Do you want me to come in?" Father Gilbert asked.

Nicholas thought for a moment and then declined. "I don't know what happened in London, so maybe it's better if I see her first."

"Call me if there's anything I can do."

"You've done plenty, Father," Nicholas said. "Thank you."

Inside, the house was still. He checked the kitchen—it was empty—and then went to the staircase and listened for any sound of Lainey or Serena upstairs. There was a loud thump from down the hall. Nicholas followed the sound, peering into the office, and then on to Elaine's bedroom. For a second, he wondered if Elaine had come home and maybe that was why Lainey wanted to come alone, so she could leave London more quickly than if she had to meet up with him.

Peeking into the room, the bed was made and nothing looked disturbed. He was about to turn to leave when he noticed the closet door ajar and a light coming from inside. He found Lainey sitting cross-legged on the floor with a box, books and papers on the floor around her. She reminded him of a child, sitting among her toys and coloring books. His heart warmed.

He put his hand on the door and it moved slightly with a groan. Startled, Lainey looked up at him. Her eyes were red-rimmed from crying.

"Nick," she gasped.

"Hi. Are you all right?"

She wiped at her face self-consciously. "What time is it?"

"Almost nine."

"Oh dear, I've lost all track of time," she said. "Nick, I'm sorry about London. I couldn't see you. Not after—"

"Not after what?"

"Penelope Young." Lainey tilted her head, catching sight of Nicholas's face. "What happened to your cheek? It looks red—bruised."

"My grandfather didn't like the story I told him."

"He *hit* you?"

"Yeah. Funny, huh?"

"Not at all." Her gaze fell to the collection around her. "I don't like your grandfather much, you know."

"I'm struggling with that myself." He knelt down next to her. "What are you doing?"

She waved a hand over the journals. "My grandmother's confession."

"What?"

"Journals," she said, then gestured to stacks of papers and envelopes. "And all the letters from your grandfather."

He picked up a couple of the pages and found a younger version of his grandfather's handwriting all over them. "You've been reading them?"

"No, not the letters," she said quickly. "But I've been reading my grandmother's diaries. From the time. That summer."

Struggling to put the pieces together, he asked: "Is this connected to Penelope Young?"

"In a way, but not really."

"I'm confused."

Her lip quivered. "I don't know if I can explain."

"Is it that bad?"

"Worse than bad. We've been chasing after the wrong thing. We thought everything was hinged on that day at the Mill House. But that was only part of it. My grandmother—" She couldn't speak.

Nicholas waited, wanting to touch her but instinctively knowing better. "Take your time."

Abruptly, as if it was the only way, she said, "My grandmother was pregnant."

The third slap of the day. No, a full-fledged punch. He dropped from kneeling and back onto the floor. "By my grandfather?"

"*Of course* by your grandfather. He was the only one!" she snapped. "She found out the Friday, the day before he was going to ask her to marry him. She was going to tell him at the Mill House. But then . . ."

"He didn't know," Nicholas said softly, his mind numb.

"She wrote to him. All those letters in that box you found. She was trying to tell him." She gestured to the journals again. "It's all in here."

"God have mercy," Nicholas said. Those unread letters, now shredded. *Like their lives*, he thought.

"She hoped . . . ," Lainey said, her voice breaking again, then finding strength. "She wanted him to come back. But he didn't reply. So she had to tell her parents. They were furious. Her father began to pressure her to . . . to have an abortion."

The truth dawned on him. "Dr. Sheaf."

She nodded, wiping the tears away. "Her father told Gerard. Gerard knew about Dr. Sheaf because . . . because one of his other girlfriends had made use of his services."

"Gerard arranged the abortion?"

"Yes. And Trevor drove her to London."

"Trevor!"

Lainey sobbed again. "Her own parents didn't go. Not even Gerard. Trevor took her. Alone."

Nicholas remembered Trevor's change at the table, his relief when he realized what they were talking about. He was thinking of this.

"How terrible. How lonely," she said.

Nicholas could feel his heart throbbing in his chest, his throat, his head. The side of his face ached again. He reached for her. "Lainey—"

She recoiled. "No, please."

He fought back the feeling of rejection. *This isn't about me or my feelings*, he reminded himself.

"I'm sorry," she said quickly. "I've been reading these journals and it's as if I'm there. I'm *her*. She wanted your grandfather to come and rescue her and he didn't, the *no good* . . ." The expletives came, even milder than Nicholas was inclined to use. "She didn't understand—how could she? She didn't know what had happened at the Mill House. She didn't know! So out of desperation, she gave in to the pressure. She killed her baby."

"She *said* that?" he asked, struck by the harshness of the words.

"Over and over. After it was done. *I killed my baby.*" She clutched one of the journals to her chest. "She grieved, Nick. It wasn't simply a breakdown she had during that time, she was *grieving.*"

She's grieving now, Nicholas thought.

"Think how she felt," Lainey said, imploring. "When Gerard confessed a few weeks ago about the trick they'd played on your grandfather—so that she suddenly understood *why* your grandfather had rejected her—and their baby—it was more than she could bear. The stupidity of it, the waste . . . It broke her." Her voice choked again and more tears fell.

My grandfather didn't know, Nicholas thought. *He still doesn't.* The enormity of it rolled over him like a wave. It sent him spiraling. He drew his knees up, encasing them in his arms, and put his face down. His eyes burned and he wept. For Elaine Holmes. For Adam Powell. For the lost years. For the pain that had brought them to where they were today.

"Nick," Lainey said, her hand on his arm.

He couldn't look at her. He felt out of control and thought he might put his head back and wail like a baby. So he kept his head down and fought to master his own grief.

Lainey's hand moved up his arm, gently pulling. Then another was on his shoulder and she drew him close, burying her head against him, and she was crying again and so he wrapped his arms around her in a tight embrace and they fell into one another, weeping there together as one on the floor of the closet.

"What are we supposed to do?" Lainey asked Nicholas.

They were in the kitchen now, the kettle roaring its boiling water at them. A pot of tea, the English antidote to all ills and crises, was on its way. The box from the closet, which Lainey had carefully packed up again, was on the counter.

Before Nick could answer her question, the phone rang.

Lainey picked up the receiver. "Arthur House." She paused, listening. "Oh, hello, Jeff. Yes. Hold on, he's right here." She handed the phone to him.

"Hello?"

"Hi. Do you want to tell me what's going on over there?" Jeff asked.

"What do you mean?"

"I made the mistake of answering the phone when Grandad called a little while ago. He's downright apoplectic. I've never heard him like this. He says you're wrecking your life, that you're throwing it away on Lainey, and he's going to *drag* you back to America if he has to."

Nicholas chuckled. "Let him try."

"Laugh if you want," Jeff said seriously. "But I think he means it."

"I think so, too."

"What in the world is going on? We didn't even know Grandad was *in* England."

"Neither did I."

"So, what are you doing?"

"I'm doing what I said I was going to do."

"But what did you do to Grandad? What did you say to him to make him so mad?"

"I told him the truth."

"Well, you better watch out. I got the impression that he's coming for you."

"He's coming to Stonebridge?"

"Head for the hills, brother." Then, in a quick change of tone, low and conspiratorial, Jeff asked, "He says you're in love with Lainey. Is that true?"

"He was just guessing. But yes, it's true." He looked over at Lainey as she poured the tea into their mugs. *It's true.*

"You work fast. Is she in love with you?"

Nicholas was still watching Lainey as she turned and caught him. An inquisitive look. A slight smile. "I think so," he answered.

"Even though she knows you're going to become a priest, right?"

"Right."

"Is she a Christian?"

"I don't think so."

"You better convert her fast."

"Right," he sighed.

"I'll say a quick prayer for you."

"Not quick, Jeff. I need the full-blown, widescreen, Dolby Digital director's cut with popcorn, soda, and an intermission in the middle."

"I can do that."

"Thanks."

Nicholas hung up the phone. Lainey looked at him expectantly.

"More trouble at home?" she asked as she offered him the mug of tea.

"No," he said. "Trouble right here in River City. My grandfather is coming to get me. He thinks he's going to make me go back to America with him."

"Is he?"

"Only in a coffin."

"That's a relief," she said. "About you not going, I mean. Not the coffin."

"I understood." He drank some of his tea and they looked at each other across the kitchen. She raised the mug to her own lips when he said, "Lainey, I love you."

She nearly sprayed herself with tea. Recovering, she asked, "Has anyone ever talked to you about *timing*?"

"I mean it. I love you."

"So you've said." She put the mug down on the counter, leaning against it, folding her arms. "Since we've dispensed with the usual romantic trappings for this conversation, then I suppose you should know that I love you, too. I'm not enthralled with men as a species right now, but I love *you*. So there. It's out."

"We don't have to dispense with all of the trappings," he said and crossed the kitchen. He pulled her close and kissed her.

Looking up at him, she lightly touched the side of his face where he'd been struck by his grandfather. "Are you going to tell me what happened?"

"Not now," he said. "First we have to deal with your original question. What are we going to do?"

"And the answer is?"

"If my grandfather is coming to Stonebridge, then I want to be here to talk to him." He hooked a thumb at the box on the counter. "He needs to know about that."

"And what will I be doing?"

"You're going to see your grandmother."

She looked anxious. "I am?"

"You must tell her what you know."

Her look of anxiety turned to fear. "Me?"

"Yes, you. Who better? From the beginning you've been motivated by your love for her. And you said yourself that reading her journals was like being there, as if you were her. You felt for her, Lainey. You empathize with her like no one else." As he spoke, he was struck by the thought that Lainey was going to have to go into the darkness and bring her grandmother back out. Like Jesus.

"But I'll say the wrong thing. I'll upset her, like I did before."

"God'll give you the words," he said, and meant it.

"No. He gives people like *you* the words, not me."

"You watch."

"I can't, Nicholas."

"You can," Nicholas said gently. "You can talk to her—speak into her life, her heart. Right now she believes she's completely alone, that no one knows or could possibly understand how she feels. She can't even see God right now. But she can see you. You know the horrible truth, which means you can join her where she is and help bring her out. Tell her she's not alone. You can do that."

She pulled him tight and lay her head against his shoulder. "I wish I had your faith."

"I'll have the faith for both of us for now. Yours will come later." He said it as a prayer. "Now, let's work out our strategy."

NICHOLAS WAVED TO LAINEY FROM THE DOORWAY AS SHE DROVE OFF. HIS heart ached for her. He wanted to go with her, but everything in his being—his instincts—told him it was best to stay. Everything that had happened over the past few weeks pointed to this. His grandfather would come.

He paced around the house, aware only of the eyes of the many portraits gazing on him like a cloud of witnesses. His hands were clasped in front of him like a monk, and he prayed. He kept waiting for a car to pull up, a knock at the door.

The phone rang, a shrill shout throughout the house. Nicholas was nearest to the office and stepped in, not sure whether to answer. He doubted his grandfather would call. Or would he?

Nicholas picked up the receiver. "Arthur House."

"Nicholas?" his grandfather said.

"Grandad."

"I'm glad you picked up. Playing the house-servant now?"

Nicholas didn't want to succumb to the taunt. "What do you want, Grandad?"

"I'm in Stonebridge. We have to talk."

"You know where I am," Nicholas said.

"I won't come there."

"Then let's meet at the Mill House."

"No," he said firmly. "Somewhere else."

"Then forget about it," Nicholas said.

"Now listen to me—," Adam started angrily, then stopped himself. He said with forced calmness. "I could call your bluff, you know. I could go back to London."

"You could," Nicholas said. "But then you'd miss out on some late-breaking news."

"*More* news? Oh, well, you're just a plethora of information these days."

"Grandad, let's drop the banter. What I told you yesterday was only part of the story. We learned something else that you really need to know."

"Like what?"

"Not on the phone."

Adam didn't say anything for a moment. Was he thinking it over? "I'll make you a deal," he finally said. "I'll meet you *if* you agree to bring your things. You say what you have to say and then I'm taking you home."

"I'll bring what I have to bring," Nicholas said. "But I don't understand why you care what I do. Why's it so important to you whether I stay or go?"

"Because, like it or not, you're a Powell." Nicholas could almost hear the sardonic smile on the other end of the phone.

"The Mill House in half an hour," Nicholas said and hung up.

IF SERENA HADN'T BEEN AT THE HOSPITAL, THE EVENING NURSE WOULDN'T have let Lainey in. Visiting hours ended at eight o'clock *sharp*, the starched-white woman said, and it was now well past nine. Serena, who'd been given carte blanche permission by the doctor to stay at Elaine's bedside, interceded with the nurse and Lainey was allowed in.

It was a mixed blessing for Lainey. She'd spent the drive to the hospital wishing she could get out of talking to her grandmother. She'd wanted to help her and had to believe that this would. But she kept remembering her little gamble when she'd mentioned Adam Powell's name and how upset Elaine had been.

This was hard. So very hard. And she found herself wanting to believe that Nicholas was right—God would give her the words.

"You *better* have enough faith for both of us," she'd threatened Nicholas last thing before she got in her car.

"What are you doing here?" Serena asked in the hallway, her voice taking on that half whisper people used in hospitals.

"I could ask you the same thing," Lainey countered.

"I wanted to see her," Serena said. "I like the quiet of the hospital." Then she added with just a twinge of self-consciousness. "It's a good place to pray."

Lainey understood. They'd never really talked about Serena's faith, though Lainey knew that it ran deep. "I've come to talk to my grandmother."

"Talk to her?" Serena asked. "She's off the sedatives, but she's still not responding to anyone."

"I know." Lainey took Serena's hand and walked her over to the pair of chairs sitting against the wall. They sat down. Lainey found herself fighting back the tears again as she told Serena what she'd learned about Dr. Sheaf and what she'd found in the box.

Serena went pale at the news, making her face ghostlike against her black hair. Her eyes welled up, but no tears fell. "I see," was all she said.

It was enough. In those two words, Lainey saw the connection between Serena's life—the many mistakes she'd made and the family she'd lost—and the compassion Elaine had shown to her. They were kindred spirits in so many ways, but Serena had no idea why until now.

Lainey took a deep breath and stood. "You'll pray?" she asked, feeling helpless and weak-kneed.

Serena nodded. Then she added, "I'll call her doctor. He should know."

For a moment, Lainey thought she was off the hook. *The doctor.* He could talk to her grandmother. Certainly he was better qualified to do it.

Serena seemed to sense her hesitancy and said, "You're the one to do it."

"But I'm afraid," she said. "I need help."

"Help will be there when you need it," Serena replied.

It was the kind of statement that reminded her that people like Serena and Nicholas lived in another world, with a vocabulary she didn't really understand. But even if she was alone, she had to talk to her grandmother.

Lainey walked into the room. The light on the small bedside table was off, putting Elaine and her white blankets into a half shadow. It was ethereal—reminding her of the first time she'd walked into her grandmother's bedroom after she'd learned of the breakdown. She had thought about angels then. She thought about them now.

Oh, God, she prayed. *You're real to so many people I love—and who love me. Help me.*

Lainey went to the chair on the side of the bed. Her grandmother appeared to be asleep, her eyes were closed, and her hands lying limp over the blanket. A peaceful repose, Lainey thought. No sign of the inner turmoil, the emotions and memories that now weighed her down and threatened to drop her like a large bucket into the bottom of a very deep and very dark well.

"Gran," Lainey said softly as she sat down. No response. "There's something I have to tell you, Gran. I know what happened—" She wanted to add *at the Mill House and with Dr. Sheaf,* but the words were not there. Instead, she dropped her head onto the bed and began to cry.

Control, she told herself. *Get control. You don't want to upset her with your blubbering.*

Something touched her hair, a feather-light touch. Then it bore down and caressed her hair. Lainey looked up. Her grandmother was watching her, stroking her as she had over so many years, all the way back to Lainey's earliest memories of her childhood.

Their eyes met, locked on one another, and Lainey had the same feeling that she'd had that day in the bedroom. Her grandmother was talking to her, pleading with her. *Help me,* her eyes said. *Help me.*

Lainey felt an enraging impotency. *I want to help,* she thought. *I understand how you felt. I could feel your loneliness, your shame, your loss, your guilt, and your pain.* "I know," was all she really said out loud and it wasn't enough. She put her head down again, new tears coming, and prayed out her own despair, *God, where are the words you promised? Where are your angels? Give me something now, anything. Help me.*

There was nothing. Nicholas's faith wasn't enough after all. She had to have her own. She saw the stained glass images in St. Mark's Church in Stonebridge—of Jesus with his disciples, of Jesus with his arms outstretched on the altar, the phrase *In This Place, I Will Give Peace.* She had yearned to believe it then, sitting with Father Gilbert in the church. She yearned to believe it now.

I want to believe, she prayed. *Help me to believe.*

The hand remained on her head, stroking, soothing. And then another hand, larger and heavier was on her shoulder. She looked up. Father Gilbert was there, smiling gently. His expression told her that he knew, that he'd spoken to Serena in the hall.

She wanted to cry out, to leap into his arms. She slowly stood up.

"No, don't," he said.

"Sit down, Father," she pleaded. "You're meant to sit here." She stepped aside and let him have the chair.

Elaine's hand lay where it had dropped from Lainey's head. Father Gilbert now took it up into his own. He looked Elaine in the eyes and said in a voice full of compassion. "You've been keeping secrets from me, Elaine. All this time we've met together and you didn't tell me what this is really about."

A tear slid down Elaine's cheek. To Lainey's surprise, her grandmother nodded.

"So now we know the truth," Father Gilbert said, the softness of his voice unwavering. "A truth God has known all along." He paused, allowing the words to work the air like a massage. "You've attended church since you were a child, Elaine. Every Sunday you have said the words in the liturgy, speaking of the grace and forgiveness of God, even of our unworthiness to receive them. But he offers them anyway. Sometimes we say the words, but don't fully appreciate their meaning. Elaine, now it's time to claim them as your own. They're not some vague concepts for other people. They're *yours*. He offers them to you, knowing full well how you feel."

Again, the silence. The room—the entire hospital—seemed to have emptied itself of its usual noises and activity, just for this moment. Elaine's tears fell with greater strength, but she didn't utter a sound.

Father Gilbert continued, "King David, in his deepest moment of grief-stricken repentance, said, 'Against you and you alone have I sinned, O Lord.' Whatever we have done to others, even to ourselves, we do them to God first. Which is what makes his forgiveness so important. So important that Jesus died to secure it for us—for you. In the darkest of places, he offers it. He's there with you now, Elaine. Forgiveness is yours. Do you hear me? He forgives you. Accept his forgiveness, and forgive yourself."

Elaine clasped Father Gilbert's hand tightly and used his strength to sit up in her bed. The picture stayed in Lainey's mind that it was like one of the stained glass windows with the crippled man clasping the hand of Jesus and rising to his feet. Was this no less a miracle? Then her grandmother reached, not for Father Gilbert, but for Lainey herself with arms outstretched like a child's. How a man of Father Gilbert's size could disappear into the shadows was more than Lainey could know, but he was out of the way as Lainey leaned in for her grandmother's embrace, the trembling hands pulling her closer and closer.

"Yes," Elaine whispered in her ear.

No other words were needed. The angels had come.

ADAM POWELL WAS SEATED AT A TABLE IN THE BAR AREA OF THE MILL House. Nicholas wondered if it was purposeful; was the old man stubbornly refusing to go into the dining room again? He carried the box from Elaine's closet and sat it on the table.

Adam looked at it with a jaded eye and asked, "You couldn't afford a normal suitcase?"

Nicholas didn't respond, but sat down.

"Would you like something to drink?" his grandfather asked.

"Nothing, thanks."

Adam shrugged with a *suit yourself* expression and drank from the glass in front of him. "I'm sorry for what happened earlier," he said in a formal tone, fulfilling a sense of obligation. "It was inexcusable and I deeply regret it."

"All right," Nicholas said, he leaned forward, folding his hands on the table.

"But I stand by what I told you," he said. "It's time to put an end to this nonsense and get back to our lives. You have a duty to your family and to your future. You won't fulfill it here. Let's go home."

"I'm not ready for that yet," Nicholas said.

"Oh, come on, Nicholas," he said irritably. "This is ridiculous. I know we haven't been close. But maybe we can rectify that now that I'm not running the publishing house anymore. We won't know unless we go home and give it a try."

An interesting offer. Did he mean it? "I'd like to get to know you better, Grandad. I think I've been unfair and judgmental about you. I've also made the mistake of thinking that I can somehow change or redeem you. I can't. So I'm sorry and hope you'll forgive me."

Adam leaned back, surprised.

"In the meantime," Nicholas continued, "I don't see how any of us can move forward without getting everything out in the open."

He tipped his head toward the box. "That must be your cue for your big news. In the box, I assume?"

"In the box."

"Do I have to guess what it is?"

"No. They're your letters to Elaine, written between 1941 and 1954."

Eyebrows raised, he said, "So she kept them."

"Yes."

"How sentimental of her."

Nicholas ignored the comment.

Adam tapped the side of the box. "Elaine has given you permission to show these to me?"

"Lainey has, if necessary."

"You expect me to read through everything now?"

"I brought them as backup. A little *proof*, since you're not inclined to take things in good faith."

"Proof of what?"

"Of what happened."

Adam groaned. "You're banging on about that again. All right, Nicholas, I believe you. I believe that Gerard and Trevor were scoundrels who interfered in our lives."

"I told you there was more," Nicholas said, now wishing he'd ordered something to drink. His mouth was going dry.

"Then get on with it, will you? You're milking this thing beyond endurance."

"I'm sorry, I didn't want to blurt it out." He suddenly felt self-conscious about where they were. What made him think he could deliver the news to his grandfather in a crowded restaurant, of all places? "Can we go outside?"

"No, we're not going outside," his grandfather insisted. "Just tell me what you have to say and be done with it."

Nicholas gazed at his grandfather, suddenly amused by all the bluff and bluster. "You make it very hard to be sensitive and diplomatic, you know."

Adam leaned forward. "I don't want sensitivity and diplomacy. I want you to speak so we can get out of here."

"Fine," Nicholas said, then did the very thing he didn't want to do. He said bluntly, "Elaine was pregnant."

Adam was visibly stunned. His eyes widened and his mouth opened, then closed.

Nicholas went on in a steady tone. "She was going to tell you on that Saturday, the day you came to propose. When you didn't answer her calls or her letters, she fell into deep despair and gave in to her father's wishes to have an abortion."

Adam's eyes snapped back to Nicholas. "An abortion," he said, the word sounding as if it had been squeezed from the back of his throat.

"She married James Arthur because her father wanted it, and because she felt that no one else could ever possibly love her."

The color had drained from Adam's face and Nicholas suddenly feared that the old man might have a stroke or a heart attack right there. Adam picked up the glass, but put it down again because the ice inside was rattling so much.

"I don't believe it," Adam said, his voice a low rasp.

"As I said," Nicholas said and finished the sentence by tapping the box. "I'm leaving this with you—as a loan—so you can read for yourself the hell Elaine went through that summer and, I guess, her entire life. I'll give you an hour to look it over." He got up to leave, then said quietly. "You weren't the only one who suffered, Grandad."

NICHOLAS TOOK A WALK. IN CONTRAST TO THE FEELINGS OF POWER HE'D felt at the hotel, he now felt weak. His heart ached for the old man and what the contents of the box would reveal to him. He wouldn't have wished it on his worst enemy. Or maybe he had, but now realized that his grandfather wasn't his worst enemy at all.

He looked up at a clear night sky—the clouds had moved on—and he felt a sense of release. His grandfather would respond to the box however he would; it was out of Nicholas's hands.

As if it had ever been in them. Nicholas had done nothing. It had been God who was at work all along, from the very beginning. There was no such thing as coincidence. The timing of Gerard's revelation to Elaine and the discovery of the box by Nicholas was entirely providential, no more or less than the dance the constellations made above him every night, every season, every epoch.

Glancing at his watch, he wondered if Father Gilbert had made it to the hospital. It was a last-minute idea and he'd disrupted Father Gilbert's evening when he called, but the good Father hadn't seemed bothered. In fact, he'd acted as if he'd been expecting the call.

Nicholas strolled to the edge of the parking lot and noticed a lit path heading in the direction of town. He thought a stroll on such a nice evening would be restorative. He wondered if his grandfather and Elaine had thought the same thing and taken a similar walk down this lane.

Dodging the many puddles left by the earlier rain, he found himself jumping around them like a little boy. He didn't feel that light in his spirit, but he felt as if a wild, manic run through deep puddles was exactly what he needed. And so he did, starting at a jog and then running faster and faster, his feet hitting the water and gravel like explosions. He was a sprinter in a race, pushing forward harder and harder until his side ached and he thought his heart would burst. Boy, was he out of shape.

Breathless, he turned around and walked back toward the Mill House.

Had it been an hour? It had. He went inside and looked for his grandfather. Not at the bar, not in the restaurant. Flagging the maître d' he asked, "Where is Mr. Powell? The man I was with earlier?"

"Oh, yes," the maître d' said as if remembering. "He left."

"Left!"

"But he gave me this and asked me to make sure you got it." The maître d' reached behind a small podium and produced Elaine's box.

"Was that all he said? Nothing else?"

"Nothing else."

IT WAS THE NURSE WHO THREW THEM OUT OF THE WARD. NINE O'CLOCK was one thing, but now it was approaching midnight and the nurse had had enough of rule-breaking. Lainey didn't mind, though, since her grandmother had fallen asleep and she was wrung out.

After her grandmother's singular "yes," little else was said. Father Gilbert read aloud from his Bible and Prayer Book comforting psalms and prayers, which Elaine seemed to appreciate. Then they sat silently, Lainey holding her grandmother's hand.

The difference was in the silence, Lainey thought. Unlike the empty and cold silence they'd experienced with her grandmother before, this silence was warm, full, and companionable. On the way out of the hospital, Serena called it a "spiritual silence," and explained that she meant it was a silence that seemed full of the Spirit.

There seemed to Lainey no other way to explain it.

In the car park, Serena went to her car. Father Gilbert lingered with Lainey and she suspected there was something he wanted to say.

She preempted him by saying, "Thank you, Father Gilbert. You were an answered prayer."

He smiled. "Actually, I answered the phone."

She looked at him curiously.

"Nicholas," he said, and it was all the explanation needed.

Suddenly she couldn't wait to get home to him.

"Lainey," Father Gilbert said, his hand on her shoulder again. "I hope you realize that this experience wasn't only about your grandmother. It's about you, too. While you've been searching for her, God was searching for you."

She blushed a little, thinking how awkward words were when it came to the most important moments in one's life, and said, "I think he found me."

NICHOLAS HAD FALLEN ASLEEP IN WHAT HE, AS AN AMERICAN, WOULD HAVE called the "family room." It was no less beautiful or opulent than any other room in the house, but this one had a television and furniture that looked less formal. He had chosen a large easy chair and marveled at the programming on the four channels (there was a fifth, but it was nothing but snow) from which he could choose. They were as vacuous as the two hundred channels he could watch as an American. Turning the TV off, he put his glasses on to read for a little while. Within a paragraph, he'd fallen asleep.

He was awakened by a gentle kiss on his forehead. Then his cheek. Without opening his eyes, he said, "Serena, please. What if Lainey comes in?"

Lainey laughed and slid onto his lap, burrowing into his neck.

"How's your grandmother?" he asked.

"A miracle."

"Oh?"

In an impressively calm voice, she explained to him what had happened.

"Thank God," he whispered when she finished.

"Exactly," she said. "And your grandfather?"

"I don't know. I told him, then left him with the box. When I went back later, he was gone."

"With the box?"

"No, I put that back in your grandmother's closet."

"Where do you think he went?"

"Back to London? Fishing in Scotland? I don't know." Nicholas was annoyed and disappointed. "I had really hoped that when all was said and done, he'd be affected by what he saw. I didn't think he'd run away."

"Didn't he run away once before?" she asked simply.

"I suppose he did."

"It's very late," she said.

He *hmmed* his acknowledgment.

"Are you tired?"

"Not really. Why?"

"I want you to explain something to me."

"If it's anything to do with nuclear fusion, forget about it. I can explain anything but that."

"I want to know how to be a Christian."

He couldn't see her face, but her tone told him that this was the moment he'd been praying for.

So he told her while holding her on his lap, her head on his shoulder and her body curled up like a small child's.

CHAPTER
SEVENTEEN

Wednesday, the 21st of July and Afterward

Adam had disappeared. He'd checked out of the Ritz and Nicholas assumed he'd gone back to Maryland. But a phone conversation with Jeff a day later proved that theory wrong. Their father had had a brief conversation with Adam and, as far as he understood, Adam was off fishing and wouldn't be in touch for a few weeks.

Elaine's recovery was slow, but steady, as she made her way out of the dark places she'd been for so many weeks. Father Gilbert helped, as did her professional counselor. Dr. Gilthorpe checked in daily. It wasn't easy for Elaine. Nicholas thought of the many men and women who'd been touched by Jesus—their miracles recorded in Scripture—but no one told the day-by-day stories of their healed lives and how they had to cope with life thereafter.

With each day, however, Nicholas began to see in Elaine the strength of character that everyone had talked about. "She's returning to herself," Father Gilbert noted one afternoon, "but now the scars show a bit more."

Julie Peters made the journey from London to Southaven to visit Elaine in the hospital. As promised, she invited her to the memorial service for Father John Peters at St. Luke's on August 15. Elaine said she would be pleased and honored to come, if the doctors would allow. It was a sweet reunion, but not nostalgic. The two seemed to avoid, by some unspoken pact, a lot of chitchat about the past. Instead they discussed their gardens and how much London had changed over the years.

The doctors were not a hindrance. Within a week they were impressed enough to allow Elaine to return to Arthur House. She could travel to London as long as she behaved herself in the meantime and took the medications they'd given her.

In spite of the rather dubious start to their acquaintance, Nicholas got along well with Lainey's parents and found that he and Lainey's father had a mutual love for quirky card games.

No one spoke of Adam to Elaine. They all feared that for her to know that he had been so nearby might somehow set her back again. They didn't dare take the chance.

LIFE AROUND ARTHUR HOUSE TOOK ON AN ALMOST HOLIDAY-LIKE FEEL. Lainey resigned her position at the publisher, but they insisted that she continue to work freelance and she agreed. That gave her time to take Nicholas around the countryside, driving him to places in the south like Winchester, Southampton, Salisbury, Bristol, Bath, and up to Oxford and Windsor. The north would come later, they decided.

More than any sightseeing in what he considered a beautiful and majestic country, Nicholas relished the domesticity of his life as one of the family, and that led him to an important decision.

On a Sunday afternoon, after they'd all been to St. Mark's for the service in the morning, Nicholas stole Lainey away for a walk. He'd worked out the route ahead of time and tried to behave as if this was nothing more than a casual stroll. When they arrived at the outskirts of the Boswell place, Lainey became suspicious. He took her hand as they stepped through the break in the wall.

Both of them were surprised. Many of the trees surrounding the old chapel had been knocked down, and the ground around it had been stripped and leveled by construction equipment. The chapel itself still stood, but a sign indicated that it was marked for demolition.

"This doesn't bode well at all," Nicholas said, disappointed. "I really have to work on my timing."

"Bode well for what? What timing?"

"Sit down," he said.

The large log was still in its place—the last thing that was, apart from the chapel—so she sat down. Nicholas dropped to one knee next to her. "Lainey—"

"Yes, please," she said before he could say another word.

"Yes, please, *what?*" he asked.

"Yes, please, I'd love to marry you. Nothing I want more."

He presented a ring, picked up from a jeweler on High Street, which he put on her finger. Then he blew out his cheeks. "We *really* need to work on our timing."

She laughed, hugging and kissing him.

He sat down next to her, brushing at his knee. "Well, that was easy."

"Oh," she suddenly said, "the stained glass pieces are gone."

Nicholas looked around the ground. "You're right. Do you think they covered it over with the dirt?"

"I don't know and I don't want to dig to find out," she said. "But we mustn't tell my grandmother. She'll be very disappointed."

As they stood up to leave, Nicholas noticed something sparkle in the distance. He was certain it was the sunlight glancing off of glass. A pair of binoculars. No doubt Trevor had been watching from afar.

Nicholas's family took the news of his engagement with mixed responses.

Jeff feigned a complete lack of surprise and said he'd known all along that it would happen. The question, though, was how to tell Kathy. Nicholas said he'd call her. Jeff said no, that wouldn't be appropriate, and then volunteered to break the news to her himself.

"*You* want to tell her?" Nicholas asked. "Wouldn't that be worse than a call? I can't ask you to be a messenger boy."

Jeff disagreed. "I've been talking to her since you left."

"Oh, really?"

"We've had a meal or two together. I thought she might want a shoulder to cry on."

"Has she been crying?" That seemed so unlike Kathy.

"Well, no. She hasn't. I think she knew when you left that it was over. It was a loss, but she hasn't been withering from grief, if you know what I mean."

Nicholas did. Kathy was a rose of iron. "Well, if you really think it's the best thing to do."

"Trust me."

Nicholas's mother was concerned about how quickly everything had happened, then excited, and then worried about where the wedding would take place and how in the world would she help coordinate it if it was all the way over there in England.

His father was politely cordial, but reminded him that, as a student at the seminary, he would need the bishop's blessing before he could get married. "Kathy's a tough act to follow. The bishop may not approve."

Nicholas didn't admit that that was the least of his concerns, since he wasn't even sure he would return to Virginia to get his degree. Apart from Lainey, he'd also fallen in love with England itself and now began to explore finishing his degree somewhere there, if possible. He also investigated the job market for American priests living in England. Father Gilbert indicated that there might be a place for him as a curate at St. Mark's.

"How tidy," Lainey had said after Nicholas told her of the possibility. "Does everything work out this well for Christians?"

"In spite of the evidence," he replied, "no."

In his heart, he wasn't thinking of Christians in general, but of his grandfather.

On the morning of August 15, Nicholas drove with Lainey to London for the special service at St. Luke's in Chiswick, with the intention of dropping by her flat afterward. Serena drove Elaine in the larger family car. Elaine had nervously dressed for the occasion, choosing and re-choosing which dress to wear.

Nicholas worried that she might be thinking that Adam Powell was going to show up. Nicholas was certain he wouldn't. Wherever the old man had run to, Nicholas couldn't see him surprising them with a visit.

St. Luke's was yet another English Gothic church, tucked away down a side street of Chiswick. It had been hit in the Blitz in 1941, so more than half of it had been rebuilt. Father John had spearheaded that enterprise when he became vicar in 1943, against many who thought the church should be torn down and the parish incorporated back into a church in Bedford Park. Father John worked a miracle by overcoming the personal and financial obstacles and bringing the church back to its former glory.

The gathering filled a quarter of the church and consisted mostly of people on pensions. Nicholas guessed a median age of seventy, maybe more. These were parishioners, past and present, who had known and respected Father John.

Julie Peters was dressed in white and looked proudly radiant. She invited Elaine to join her on the front pew as a special guest and beamed as she talked from the front about her husband and his accomplishments. In the middle of the service, she invited others to speak up about Father John. Elaine took the invitation and, with a quivering voice, praised the man for his Christian love and charity. She recalled his tireless efforts to bring Billy Graham to England in early 1954, working hard against those who had tried to thwart the effort. Many there commented that their Christian lives began as a result of the Graham crusade. One elderly couple mentioned that they'd met and married as a result of one of Graham's altar calls.

Then came a clear and distinctive voice—one with a corrupted British and American accent—speaking about Father John's generosity to those in trouble. Nicholas swung around to look.

"He never held back a single farthing from anyone in need," Adam Powell said from a back pew. "He was kind, especially to me, and took me in after I'd lost both my parents in the war." He then blew a kiss to Julie, with a mischievous smile. "I'll say the same about you, Julie, when they do a service like this for you."

The crowd laughed and Julie wagged a finger at him from the front. "Don't disappoint me," she said.

He waved and sat down.

Nicholas had bruised ribs from Lainey's repeated nudges.

"I *know*," he whispered to her. He sneaked a look at Elaine, but her face betrayed no reaction. She had a fixed smile in place.

The service turned more serious as a formal Anglican liturgy was used for the unveiling of the plaque. It was gold, with a silhouette of Father John, and the words "For Service unto God in this House of Worship, 1943 to 1988."

After the service, Father Lowell, the current vicar, invited everyone into the reception hall for refreshments. Nicholas immediately turned to seek out his grandfather, but he was gone.

"Does he think he's the Lone Ranger?" Nicholas complained to Lainey.

"Put yourself in his position," she replied. "You dropped a bombshell on him that night and maybe he needed time to think it through." She'd clearly softened to the old man over the past couple of weeks.

The refreshments consisted of punch and those little sausage things wrapped in bread. "The international church food," Nicholas said.

People mingled but most, because of their advanced ages, sat in the folding chairs that lined the walls. Nicholas waited near Julie Peters until a break came in her bright conversation with guests, then asked, "Did you know my grandfather was going to come?"

"He knew not to disappoint me," she said.

"How long have you known?"

"He rang me this morning."

"From where? Where is he staying?"

"He didn't say."

"So you don't know where he is now?"

"Well, yes, actually."

"Where?"

"Coming through the door."

Nicholas almost spilled his punch as he spun around. Adam Powell walked in and then stopped, surveying the room. Nicholas's first impression was that he looked older somehow, the lines in his face deepened, his suit rumpled. Yet he crossed the room with his back stiff, exuding pride and dignity. He came straight to Julie and kissed her on the cheek.

"Thank you for coming," Julie said.

"I told you I wouldn't miss it," he said. Then he turned to Nicholas and put out his hand. "Nicholas."

"Grandad." Nicholas shook his hand, the grip firm. "You've been fishing, I hear."

"And so have you," he replied, then looked over at Lainey, who had only just seen him from her seat next to Elaine. "Congratulations on your engagement," he said politely. "I have a gift for you."

"It's not a stuffed trout, is it?"

"Mounted *haggis*, which is more than you deserve," the old man said, then moved away toward Lainey—or was it Elaine? Nicholas followed a few steps behind.

Lainey was on her feet, intercepting him with an outstretched hand. "Mr. Powell."

"You may call me Adam or Grandad, considering the news. But not Mr. Powell," he said. He took her hand, but kissed her cordially on the cheek. "I hope you know what you're getting yourself into," he said.

"I think so."

"And you're still going to do it?" It was a brief punch line before he said, "Excuse me," and stepped around her, continuing on his path to Elaine.

Nicholas may have imagined it, but he'd swear later that a hush fell on the crowd and all eyes turned to that moment when Adam reached Elaine. By the time he was at her chair, she had stood. She, too, seemed stiff with her own pride and dignity. Serena joined Nicholas and Lainey as they watched from where they stood.

"Get the medication ready," Serena whispered. Lainey took Nicholas's hand and squeezed it tightly.

Adam and Elaine stood face-to-face. "Hello, Mrs. Arthur," said Adam.

"Hello, Adam." She put out her hand, which he shook briefly, and then she kissed his cheek. "It's been a long time."

"It has," he said. "How are you?"

"I'm well, thank you."

And so they had a very polite conversation that, for Nicholas, was maddeningly mundane. But his better sense told him that he should've expected nothing else. Both were well-practiced in social protocol and how to diffuse potentially embarrassing situations. They certainly weren't going to make a scene or exhibit any emotional displays there.

After a moment Julie joined them, and then the three walked back over to the nave to look at the plaque for Father John.

It was all perfectly amicable.

"You can let go now." Nicholas held up his hand, now beet red from being squeezed by Lainey.

THE RECEPTION WAS WINDING DOWN AND SERENA WAS MAKING OVERTURES out getting Elaine back to Stonebridge. Lainey told Nicholas that they ldn't bother with her flat, she'd also like to go back to Stonebridge. lear to him that she was concerned about her grandmother. As

Adam Powell had been chatting with some other parishioners. As they parted, Nicholas approached him and asked, "How long are you staying in England? May we have a meal together?"

"I'll call you tomorrow," he replied. "Are you staying at Arthur House?"

"Yes."

"I'll contact you there."

Lainey, Serena, and Elaine now came close and Adam turned to Elaine, taking her hand again. "I have something for you, Elaine. I hope you don't mind, but I've sent it on—to Arthur House."

"Oh," she said. "Well, thank you in advance. I can't wait to see what it is."

He bid them all a good afternoon, gave Julie another kiss, and was gone.

"Very Stewart Granger, isn't he?" Serena said.

"Yes, he is," Elaine said, hardly above a sigh.

WHEN THEY RETURNED, THERE WAS A NOTICE ON THE DOOR OF ARTHUR House indicating that a delivery company had attempted to drop off a package. Since it was before six, Serena was able to call to find out if it could be picked up. They were in luck. The driver was still in the area and would make the delivery shortly.

It turned out to be a large rectangular crate from Adam Powell, at least five feet high and three feet wide, which both the driver and Nicholas struggled to bring inside.

"What on earth—?" Elaine asked.

"It's a door from Scotland," Nicholas suggested. "Or his fishing boat."

"Let's not jabber on about it," Lainey said. "Open the thing!"

Opening it was no easy task, as the crate was made of wood and carefully bolted together to protect the contents. After fifteen minutes of unscrewing, Nicholas finally had what he construed to be the front of it undone and ready to pull off.

"Do we need a drum roll?" he asked.

Elaine fanned herself with her hand. "Oh dear, my heart is racing. What ever has he done?"

Nicholas pulled the front panel of wood away and they stood staring at a stained glass window. But it didn't depict a specific image. Instead it was alive with colors, made up of hundreds, if not thousands, of pieces of stained glass.

"The glass from the old chapel," Lainey gasped.

Elaine was speechless, her hand over her mouth. Tears gathered at her eyes.

Attached by a sliver of tape to the top of the leaded frame was an envelope. Lainey pulled it off. Nicholas recognized his grandfather's handwriting. *Elaine*, it said.

She handed Elaine the envelope.

"Where are my glasses?" Elaine asked as she sat down in the nearest chair.

Serena retrieved them from somewhere and brought them to her.

Elaine opened the envelope and pulled out a small slip of notepaper. She read it, then gasped, "Oh!" and burst into tears. She thrust the note back into Lainey's hands and said, "I'm sorry" as she raced down the hall to her room.

Nicholas and Serena moved in close to Lainey, who held up the note.

"The pieces can never be put back as they were," the note said, "but they can be put together in a new and beautiful way. If you can find it in your heart, please join me for dinner Saturday night at 7 at the Mill House. Adam."

ADAM PHONED NICHOLAS THE NEXT MORNING AND ASKED TO MEET AT A pub called The Rose in the nearby village of Hitchings. Lainey dropped him off five minutes before their scheduled meeting of noon. She kissed him before he got out—a *good luck* kiss more than anything.

"Don't let him eat you for lunch," she said.

"I'd taste like chicken," Nicholas replied as he closed the door. "He hates chicken."

The so-called pub was actually an old thatched cottage that had been restored as a restaurant. It had a patio area that looked out over a rolling green field with a stone fence and, further on, a small river cutting rough like a tiny scar. It was a gloriously hot day, so Nicholas opted to ᗡ the patio at one of the metal tables.

"his was a real dive in my day," Adam said as he sat down with two You couldn't pay people to come here. But they've done it up

"Very nice." Nicholas adjusted to see his grandfather more clearly. He definitely looked older somehow. "Thank you for going to the service yesterday," Nicholas said.

"As if I had a choice," Adam said without guile.

Nicholas leaned forward, folding his hands on the table. "So . . . what are you doing? By sending that gift yesterday."

"You didn't like the window?" he asked. "Was it inappropriate?"

"I *loved* the window. We all did. It was thoughtful and definitely appropriate and . . . well, that's not the point, is it?"

"What is the point?"

"What do you think you're doing by sending the window and inviting Elaine to dinner?"

"I don't understand your question," Adam said, feigning perplexity.

"What are your intentions, Grandad? And no banter, please. This isn't about us. It's about Elaine. She's still very fragile. Her recovery isn't easy. You *cannot* toy with her."

Adam dropped the act and gazed at him earnestly. "Is that what you think I'm doing? Toying with her?"

"I'm afraid for her."

Adam sighed, and it came from somewhere deep and sad. "I know you don't think so, but I have a deep affection for you, Nicholas. You get on my nerves, but I respect you. So I will make a few concessions."

"What kind of concessions?" Oh no. The deal-making was already starting.

"I will concede that you've been right about a handful of things. And though I don't care for your methods, I acknowledge the legitimacy of your motives."

He's talking in contract-speak, Nicholas thought. He blinked. "I have no idea what you just said."

Adam frowned, thought about it and rephrased his statement. "While I think you went about things the wrong way, I think you did them for right reasons. For that alone, I'm going to say two things that I will say to no one else."

"Okay." Nicholas waited.

With a thoughtful expression, Adam turned his face toward the sun and closed his eyes. "First, you exposed the stupidity of my stubbornness . . . And, second, you exposed the absurdity of my relationship with God."

"You've practiced this, haven't you?" Nicholas asked.

He shrugged. "I'm a publisher. If I ad-lib, I won't say it right." He looked at Nicholas. "Nicholas, you effectively shocked me with the box that you brought to the Mill House. I admit that I held the letters, I picked up the journals—but I didn't read them. Those were private thoughts that are none of my business. If Elaine herself invites me to read them, then that's another matter."

Nicholas began to protest. "But—"

Adam held up a hand. "But the *truth* you spoke was mine to see. The truth conveyed the—what did you call it, a tragedy?—the tragedy of what happened. My heart broke, *is* broken, to realize how I abandoned Elaine and our child. *I* was the one who got her pregnant and I pressured her to have the abortion, by my abandonment if nothing else. I am responsible. That responsibility will stay with me forever. So will the loss."

Nicholas sat quietly for a moment.

"This hasn't come easily," Adam said, his voice now distant. "I've spent the past couple of weeks thinking it over. I didn't go fishing, as you've guessed. I used that time to collect the stained glass pieces and assemble them into the window you saw. Trevor helped."

"Trevor!"

"He found me picking up the pieces at the old chapel and when I explained what I intended to do, he insisted on helping. He turned out to be fairly knowledgeable about making the window."

"I have a hard time believing that you didn't slug him."

"I felt sorry for him."

"So you were here in Stonebridge the whole time?"

"And London. I've been revisiting my past. Allowing the memories to come, the ones I've been stuffing away for fifty years." He paused, an awkward glance. "And I've been talking to God."

"Talking or negotiating?"

"I've been allowing *him* to talk to *me*, through my past, through the places I once knew and loved." He squinted against the sun and looked out at the field. "This area hasn't changed much. Many of the pathways Elaine and I once enjoyed are still there. I found an old shelter that— well, never mind." He turned to face Nicholas again. "My concession, ⸣, is that God is at work. It's not a done deal, as they say, but he's at   That may be a disappointment to you, since I'm sure you wanted   ⸢t of cataclysmic change to happen to me. But that's as much as   ⸢or now."

"Thank you." And that was the essence of the briefing. Nicholas knew he would never have a conversation like this with his grandfather again. Considering what it must have taken for the old man to sidestep his pride and confess as he had, this was a once-in-a-lifetime event. But Nicholas had one more question. "So what will you say to Elaine at dinner?"

"The only thing I *can* say."

Nicholas waited to hear what that might be.

"I will ask her to forgive me."

EPILOGUE

Elaine Arthur stood in front of the mirror attached to the closet door in her room. She pressed her hands over the gray skirt, adjusted the white blouse, and fiddled for the tenth time with the pearl brooch at the center of her collar. Lainey and Serena had helped fix her hair and it looked very nice, if she was permitted to say so herself.

It was silly to feel the way she was feeling now; nervous and giddy, like a girl getting ready for a first date. Her body had changed, but she could still see the young girl she'd once been.

She harbored no expectations about her dinner with Adam. She had no idea what he might say, or what he wanted. But if there remained still a small piece of the heart of the man she once knew, she could guess what would happen.

Forgiveness. Accepting it is no easy thing, far harder than she had ever imagined. No wonder people the world over manufactured penance and good works for themselves in order to feel forgiven. To believe that God offered it as a matter of grace was, understandably, very difficult. Yet she had accepted it. Not once, but again and again as the guilt and the shame still came to her, wrapped in splashes of darkness, like drops of black ink on a snow-white page. Or like splashes of mud on pale white skin.

She nodded at her reflected self. As she has been forgiven, so she must forgive—and then be forgiven by him.

She believed she could. With time. With grace.

Glancing at the clock on the mantel, she realized she was in danger of being late. She couldn't have that. Punctuality was important. Lainey and Nicholas were going to drive her there, then go off to Southaven to see a movie. It was all so cozy. So familiar. She loved to watch the two of them together. They were like children, in a way. But weren't we all when it came to love?

She selfishly hoped that they wouldn't move to America after the wedding. She wanted them to remain in England, even Stonebridge, where she could see them. In them, she saw a life she'd missed. In them, she saw God's redemption.

Ah, but her life had not been so bad. It had been good, in fact. James had been a caring, doting husband. They had dear children. There was redemption there, too, only she was too blinded by other possibilities to see it. Now she could.

The grandfather clock down the hall struck the three-quarter hour. She had to go.

Leaving her room, she glanced back briefly as if someone had whispered her name. Funny how the curtains, when they billowed, looked like angel's wings. She walked out.

It was a Saturday. She was going to the Mill House where Adam Powell was waiting for her.

ACKNOWLEDGMENTS

To Elizabeth, who gave me her dream of the Mill House and should have written it herself. I think she would have done a much better job. She almost did write it, with her guidance and ongoing input into this manuscript.

To Tommy and Ellie, who sacrificed their time and seemed to forgive me when I said, "I can't now, I have to go to work." Though, in ten or fifteen years, their therapists may get an entirely different report from them.

To my mother, Nancy Davis, and stepfather, Jack, who also read and responded to the first draft.

To Catherine Duerr, who came all the way from Switzerland to correct my English.

Thanks to Father Don Armstrong and Father Theron Walker, for their insights and recollections about seminary life. To John Duffield Sr., my father-in-law, who filled in many of the gaps about life in England after World War II. To the long-suffering servers at the Egg & I and the café staff at the Barnes & Noble in Colorado Springs. To Kay Bailey at Virginia Theological Seminary in Alexandria, Virginia, for her helpful conversation. To Philip Glassborow for the guided tour of Chiswick. To Ian Peirce for his recollections of Sussex in wartime. To Cindy Martinussen for her thoughts and encouragement. To Dave Lambert, for being the best danged editor in Christendom. To Autumn Miller for making final sense of it all.

Thanks to Jim Daly, Susie Rieple, Yvette Maher, and John Bethany for the line *She stumbled into the situation not knowing that he'd ordered the same thing. "Let me finish my thought, I've never managed to do that,"* which was contributed to the novel on Friday, April 25, 2003. Don't ask.

REFERENCES

With GRATITUDE TO THE MANY AUTHORS AND PUBLISHERS ...

General

Clegg, Gillian. *Chiswick Past*. Historical Publications.

Opie, Robert. *Remember When*. Mitchell Beazley.

Ziegler, Philip. *Britain Then & Now*. Weidenfelt & Nicolson.

Yesterday's Britain. Reader's Digest Books.

The Blitz

Brown, Mike. *Put That Light Out!: Britain's Civil Defence Services at War, 1939–1945*. Sutton.

Collier, Richard. *1940: The World in Flames*. Hamish Hamilton.

Creaton, Heather. *Sources for the History of London: 1939–1945*. British Records Association.

Harrison, Tom. *Living Through the Blitz*. Schocken Books.

Longmate, Norman. *How We Lived Then*. Arrow.

Minns, Raynes. *Bombers & Mash*. Virago.

Ramsey, Winston, ed. *The Blitz Then & Now, Vol. 2*. After The Battle.

Opie, Robert. *The Wartime Scrapbook: 1939–1945*. New Cavendish Books.

Ziegler, Philip. *London at War*. Knopf.

The British People at War. Odhams Press, Ltd.

The Home Front: The Best of Good Housekeeping, 1939–1945. Leopard.

Sussex

Angell, Stewart. *The Secret Sussex Resistance*. Middleton Press.

Baker, Michael H. C. *Sussex Scenes*. Hale.

Burgess, Pat, and Andy Saunders. *The Battle Over Sussex: 1940*. Middleton Press.

Gilbert, Richard. *Everyman's Sussex*. Robert Scott.

Russell, Barry K., and Alan Gillet. *Around Hailsham*. Budding Books.

White, John Talbot. *The Countryman's Guide to the South-East*. Routledge & Kenan Paul.

Sussex Photographic Memories. Frith Book Co.

Post-War Britain

Lewis, Peter. *The 1950s*. Book Club Associates.

Opie, Robert. *The 1950s Scrapbook*. New Cavendish Books.